DESIRE'S AWAKENING

He dropped his hands on her shoulders, cupping them, his long fingers splayed. His thumbs rubbed the slender collar bones before sliding off into the hollow beneath them.

She shivered.

"Cold?"

"I don't feel cold." She struggled to control her voice. "I feel frightened."

"I think that's only natural, Madam Wife."

She shrugged off his hands and stepped back against the door. "If you're going to make me your wife, at least have the decency to learn my name."

He opened his mouth. Hesitated. "Norma?"

"Noelle. Like Christmas."

"Ah, then. You were a gift," he murmured, pulling her close. "I understand your fear and admire your courage. Only a fool has no fear of the unknown."

His grip tightened. The hard body pressed against her softness felt impossibly harder. He leaned above her, slanting his head. His mouth lowered gently and fitted itself against her own.

"Let me taste you, Madam Wife."

His husky words sent shivers through her . . .

DISCOVER DEANA JAMES!

DEANA JAMES

SEEK ONLY PASSION

ZEBRA BOOKS
KENSINGTON PUBLISHING CORP.

For
Lela Unruh
Your friendship has sustained me through
the best and the worst.

ZEBRA BOOKS are published by

Kensington Publishing Corp.
475 Park Avenue South
New York, NY 10016

First Printing: August, 1993

Printed in the United States of America

One

"My queen, Whittcombstone."

A moment's hesitation only to try to overcome the suffocating pounding of his heart. A moment to drag breath into lungs deflated by the harsh sigh that despite his best effort he could not suppress. "Yes."

"I believe you are out of funds."

A rueful twist of his lips. "I believe you are right, sir."

The conversation from the rest of the room filled the intervening silence. Then the Duke coughed delicately and cleared his throat. "Would you perhaps like to wager something else?"

"No." The Third Earl of Whitby glanced at his adversary's thin, pale mouth. It lifted at the corners in what might have been a smile. Unable to meet the eyes, he stared again at the cards.

No. He had not made a mistake. The Queen of Spades—the Wicked Woman—lay at the top of the flush that comprised the winning hand. Her frowning face edged in black and gold wavered. Pain

5

sliced through his head, pain as fresh as the instant the sabre tore him apart.

Robin blinked hastily.

Regain control, he counselled himself. He lifted his hand toward his temple then lowered it. Useless to try to press the pain away. Mind over matter was the only way. Only a moment more and he would be able to breathe normally.

Then his long fingers swept up his cards that contained nothing but a pitiful pair of sevens. Willing himself to calm, he evened the edges and turned the cards facedown on the green baize surface. There his fingertips rested with nothing more to do.

The man opposite him coughed and cleared his throat again.

Slouching sideways in his chair, Robin crossed one long leg over the other, and draped his elbow over the back of his chair. Thus arranged, a very model of boredom, he lifted his head.

Across the green baize expanse, across the scattering of cards and chips sat Averill, the Ice King — so-called by his detractors, of which there were legion. His skin was translucent white revealing the blued veins running beneath it. His thinning hair, his pointed beard, his eyebrows and eyelashes, all were palest gold. More stunning, the irises of his eyes were the color of deep ice, clear with only a hint of blue. From out of these, the pupils were black wells. Now as the eyelids narrowed, they expanded to take in more light with mesmerizing effect.

"So." The Duke's voice was deep with a rasping quality. "You are finished playing for the night."

By the light of the chandelier suspended over the table, Robin's right eye glittered in his dark-skinned face. In a movement that had become habitual over the past year, he turned his head slightly. Thereby he presented the black patch over his left eye. It acted as a protective shield to conceal the emotions that whirled in his mind and set his belly afire.

"Oh, right, Duke, finished. At least finished for the night." His voice faltered, but he forced a careless defiance into it.

The Queen of Spades had finished him. Her unhappy face had made him a pauper. Not even a pauper, but a debtor. For his debts were many and widespread. He slid his fingers from the backs of the cards to the stem of his wine glass. Little but purple dregs remained, but he tossed them down, swallowing bitterly.

A muscle twitched involuntarily in the scarred cheek beneath the patch. As if a string had been plucked, its vibration set up a trembling in his hands. His heart thrummed against his ribs. The muscles across his concave belly began to quake. If he had been asked to rise at that moment, he would have staggered and fallen.

Marshalling his inner forces again, he clenched his scarred fist and willed his body under control.

Meanwhile, Averill consulted a tiny pad of paper at his right. "I make that something in the neighborhood of between ten and twelve thousand guineas, Whittcombstone."

"I beg your pardon." Robin blinked again, straightening his spine. His good eye skipped incredulously from the small pot in the center of the table to the few stacks of chips neatly arranged beside the paper.

He pressed two fingers against his hollow temple. Since his return from the continent, months of debauchery had taken their toll. His normally spare body had been reduced to a skeletal thinness, but his mind had remained crystal clear. Until now. "I make the amount in the low hundreds."

Averill might have been said to smile. "Certainly the table stakes were very low tonight."

Pain lanced down the temple and into the socket where Robin's left eye had been. Its force almost made him cry out. He lifted his other hand and snapped his fingers imperatively.

The waiter stepped forward. "More wine, milord."

"Yes."

The pain in his head eased only when he drank an ample quantity of alcohol. Wine seemed preferable to the hideous addictions of opium and morphine.

"May I offer you a brandy?" Averill's voice sounded hollow as it rang in his head.

The waiter paused.

The pain was so intense that Whittcombstone could not think. He shook his head slightly, his eyes vague. *What was the question?*

"Brandy," confirmed the Duke.

Two glasses arrived in good time. Robin raised his and drank deep. Averill merely swirled his, warming it in his hand. His pale eyes continued to study the wreck across the table.

What he saw was a man at the end of his tether. Black hair, badly in need of a barber's attention. A

8

stock, tied haphazardly, without the services of a valet. A coat badly wrinkled at the elbows and water spotted on the lapels. The Duke let his gaze drift to the cuff where a thread dangled. Whittcombstone himself was contained in that cuff—frayed, tired, hopeless.

The reflexive tickling in Averill's throat threatened to produce a spasm of coughing. He drank quickly, letting the brandy soothe the spot.

Whittcombstone gulped down the rest of the fiery drink and set the glass down. His eye rolled, then focused on the Duke. He sucked in a harsh breath. "Shall I summon the script board and write you the usual?"

He scarcely recognized his own voice, so unaccountably husky had it become. He half-raised his hand to summon the footman whose task it was to bring that most necessary end to a night's gambling.

The Duke shook his pale head. His expression chilled imperceptibly and his voice contained a sneer. "I have too much paper of yours already, Turk."

Robin stiffened at the name. His irascible personality combined with his unusual dark skin and hair in the midst of predominantly blonde Englishmen had won him the sobriquet. However, until tonight no one had called him that to his face. His hand clenched around the brandy glass. He half-lifted it before he remembered it was empty. He looked around for the waiter.

Averill pushed back his chair. "I think I have drunk quite enough tonight—as have you."

A dark red color instantly flushed Robin's gaunt cheeks. He too pushed back his chair. "To the devil with you, Duke."

Averill's smile never wavered. "Don't add foolishness to your sins, Turk. I suggest we leave the table together and make this settlement at my residence. So much more private, you understand."

Both the waiter who had brought the brandy and the footman with the script board hovered close at hand. Drawn up stiff and imposing beside the door was the burlier lackey, who patrolled the floor to handle gentlemen who became disgruntled after too much deep play.

Averill spoke again, his voice still soft but grating, like a file tearing across silk. "If you behave badly here, Whittcombstone, you will lose what remains of your consequence and you will still owe me everything." He paused, then added significantly. "And I will collect."

Robin looked around in confusion. Behind his shoulders another footman moved his chair also. He felt a spurt of resentment at being hustled about like a child, but his feelings quickly subsided. He could not gamble any longer. He had no more money. His substance, if such it could have been called, was gone to Hell. He might as well follow it to the devil with Averill.

Outside Brooks, St. James Street traffic was still moving, despite the late hour. A minute or two elapsed before the Duke's carriage could be brought round. For himself Robin's horse arrived immediately.

The Duke scanned the black mare appreciatively.

Her heavily muscled hindquarters and length of limb were topped off by a small shapely head with a dish face.

"Arabian blood in the line," he commented. "Appropriate for a Turk."

Despite his absolute misery, Robin swung into the saddle with a flourish intended to be defiant. Instantly, he regretted the action. The pain increased in intensity, making him grit his teeth. His vision swirled. He swayed and locked his legs. The mare started, then sidled nervously as Robin hauled her back. Her iron hooves struck sparks from the paving stones.

"Waste of good horseflesh," Averill called. "You'll ruin her mouth if you continue to handle her like that."

"Damn you!"

At that moment the Duke's carriage rumbled up forcing Robin to rein the animal back out of the way. She whinnied as she wheeled in a tight circle. While the tiger was turning down the step, Averill smiled at the restless black. "If you find you are too drunk to ride, Whittcombstone, you may tie your mount—"

"I will follow, damn you. I will need a clear head to murder you if you continue this baiting."

Averill's smile for the first time looked genuine. Without another word he climbed into the carriage.

The night air clawed at Robin's body through the thin wool of his coat and breeches. To the pain in his head was added the pain of damaged muscles and ligaments, laced with scar tissue, now thoroughly chilled and suffering from exposure. His only cloak, an exceedingly shabby survivor of the European campaign, still hung on a peg in his rooms. Before they had traveled a mile through the fogbound streets, his teeth had begun to chatter.

The initial effect of the alcohol rapidly deserted him. His body began to ache. The only thing hot about him was the gaze he directed at the well-sprung carriage ahead. He could picture the Duke sitting at ease on velvet squabs. The Ice King's legs were undoubtedly wrapped in a fur rug. Perhaps even now he took a nip from a silver flask stored in the pocket on the door.

Robin clenched his jaw until his teeth ached while his fingers turned numb around the reins. He had no one to blame for his suffering but himself and his abominable pride. Indeed, tonight he knew himself to be his own worst enemy.

The carriage picked up speed as traffic began to thin. The street became a lane. Robin spurred his mount alongside the driver's box. "How much farther is this bloody residence?"

The coachman looked down at the shivering man with annoyed hauteur. "Quite a distance, m'lord. We're taking His Grace to Graytharpe."

"And how far is that?"

"A couple of hours yet, sir."

"A couple of hours!" Robin allowed his horse to fall back. He would never make it. He would arrive with a case of pneumonia. He would freeze in the saddle. Why was he going on this fool's errand? He did not owe the man ten thousand guineas.

On the other hand he might as well ride. If he died, then his troubles were over. He had nothing to return to. Except a couple of grim lonely rooms. He switched the reins to his right hand and thrust his left under his armpit. This was no worse than the Pyrenees after all. And certainly he was not bleeding.

An erect and proper butler showed them to a panelled room dominated by a large mahogany desk. The Duke immediately seated himself behind it in a brown leather chair. Robin made straight for the fire.

"Brandy, milord?"

A silver clock on a side table chimed four times, but Averill did not even take note of the time. "And a hot supper. Some coffee, immediately."

The butler bowed. "At once, milord."

A footman lighted a branch of candles near the door and then another behind the Duke's left shoulder. Robin side-stepped stiffly as another man added more coals to the heart of the fire.

Averill skimmed over the papers on his desk, then raised his eyes. "Sit, Turk." He indicated a leather chair across from him. "Sit down."

Robin wished he could say, "To the devil with you," and leave. Unable to do either of those things, he wished he could refuse to sit, but the long ride through the icy night had so exhausted him that if he did not sit soon he would fall. In a tiny rebellion he took a chair adjacent to the fireplace, rather than the one the Duke indicated. The footman rose from the hearth and bowed himself out.

Robin barely suppressed a groan as he sank onto the warm upholstery. He stretched out his long legs until the bootheels rested on the stone, less than a foot from the blaze.

Averill watched him, pale eyes calculating as they slid over the scuffed leather and worn heels. He chuckled.

Whittcombstone turned his head wearily. He did not speak.

"Turk, you're an idiot." The Duke extracted a key from his waistcoat pocket, unlocked a drawer in his desk, and drew forth a brown packet.

"I must be to have come all this distance." Robin leaned forward, holding out his hands to the blaze, flexing his fingers.

"Crippled, debt-ridden, drunken—" Averill pulled the ties and flipped back the flap of the envelope. "—quarrelsome, stupid—"

"Please don't spare my feelings, Duke." Robin spat the mocking words from between his teeth. "A reading of my character is just the thing to—"

"—human wreckage. A disgrace to—"

"—make me feel quite the thing." Robin rose, his fists clenched. "If that is all you have to say, Averill—"

"Sit down!"

A footman opened the door for the butler, who entered carrying a silver tray with a crystal brandy decanter and glasses. Neither servitor gave any sign that he had heard the vicious tone in his employer's voice nor seen the man in black take a step toward the Duke with fists clenched. Stately and serene, the butler set the decanter on a round table near the door, poured brandy into two crystal snifters, and brought them first to Robin and then to his employer.

"Sit down, I said," Averill repeated.

Robin accepted the brandy and let it run down his throat in a burning gush. Then he retreated to put his shoulders against the mantel. The fire blazed behind him and warmed him. "Why did you bring me here, Duke?"

Averill set the glass to the side untouched. He pulled back the envelope flap and drew forth a number of soiled papers. His lip curled as he dropped them onto the desk and dusted his hands together. "Filthy things."

The brandy was burning in Robin's stomach. He pressed his fingers into the center of his forehead. "I could easily have written you a note at the club. You did not have to bring me here."

His eyes glowing wells in his pale face, the Duke leveled a sardonic stare at the drooping figure. "I don't want any more notes of yours, Turk. I have too many already." He indicated the papers. "Do you recognize these?"

Robin stared at the pile.

Averill lifted the first by its upper corner holding it between his thumb and index finger. His other three fingers splayed out straight away from the rumpled paper. "Toby Calcingham," he read aloud. "Fourteen guineas." He allowed it to flutter to the desk and picked up the next. "Rex Sandford. Two hundred. And I believe the estimable Mr. Sandford had another paper of yours for two hundred fifty."

15

"I would have paid him."

"He did not seem to think so. Even still he is your friend. He seemed reluctant to sell these to me, thinking I meant to do you some harm by them." Averill raised his colorless eyebrows.

"Rex —"

Averill covered his mouth with his fist to stifle a cough. With the other hand he reached for the brandy. For several minutes he continued to sip as he picked the slips of paper up, one at a time, and read them. "Morris Abraham, Tailor. Don't know his work myself. Not much competition for Weston."

Robin finally rested his head in his hand.

The Duke looked up. "I looked for you a long time before I finally located you. I made it my business to discover that you were in Dun Street all over London with no hopes of paying. You owed quite a sum."

Whittcombstone raised his head. Despite the fire that limned his spare figure, he felt frozen to his very bones. "Why?"

The Duke continued to turn the papers over. "Why? You don't have any idea? You really don't know?"

"Not the faintest notion."

The Duke tapped his own temple. He frowned. "How much do you remember?"

Robin flushed. "Enough."

The Duke regarded him steadily. "I beg to differ. I believe you do not remember nearly enough." Then he shrugged. "However, I have a good reason. Believe me, I've plotted and planned. No, I didn't se-

16

lect you at random, Turk. And now, for the sum of much less than ten thousand guineas, I own you body and soul. I can order you to do anything and you will do it. Or I will have you deported or jailed for the rest of your miserable life."

"You can't want me to murder someone," Robin murmured. "I think you could have hired a murderer for much less."

"Interesting how often you speak of murder."

The door opened again. The butler stepped aside to allow a teacart to be brought through. Immediately, the aroma of beef and burgundy wine assailed Robin. His lean stomach growled despite the brandy, and his mouth watered.

"A simple *bourguignon,* milord." The butler apologized as he lifted the lid from the silver chafing pan. "Cook can prepare a more elaborate meal if more is required."

The Duke lifted a pale eyebrow in his guest's direction. Robin swallowed heavily.

"This will be acceptable."

"Very good." The butler bowed and signaled to the footman who brought a small table from beside the door and spread a white cloth over it.

The two men waited in silence while the meal was set.

The butler bowed. "Shall I serve now?"

Averill nodded. When both plates were filled and the wine poured, he spoke. "That will be all. I'll ring when we've finished."

When the door closed, Averill indicated the meal with a languid hand. "By all means eat, Turk. Fall to. Imagine it's rations in the field, or something that you've brought home to your rooms to keep body and soul together."

Robin stared at the steaming dish, then shook his head. He slumped back against the mantel. "Let's finish this, Duke."

Averill took another sip of the brandy and set the glass down. "Very well. I have made it my business, at some expense, I might add, to acquire your notes. In some few cases I had to pay full value for them. In most however, tradesmen were convinced to release them for a quarter or half their amounts. Others . . ."

Favoring his left side, Robin lowered himself into the chair. His face remained turned toward the flames.

The Duke smothered another cough. "Your reputation for honest dealing was not quite dead. That reputation bothered me for a while. But I decided that even the devil must have some qualities that appear at least on the surface to be good. After all, if you had had a dishonest reputation in addition to your shocking bad luck, you could have found no game at all. Ergo, you were honest not because of inner convictions but because circumstances forced you to be. Am I right?"

Robin inclined his head. "Of a surety."

"Your gambling acquaintances, indeed, demanded every penny. They maintained that you were merely having a run of bad luck and you would pay." The Duke turned more papers over one by one. "Of course, we know that you could never have paid any of them back, don't we?"

"Do we?"

"They call you Turk. Behind your back, that is. I wager I'm the first one to call you Turk to your face, am I not?"

Feeling himself in a nightmare, the dark man nodded his head faintly.

"It's because of your reputation for bad temper and hard drinking. It's infamous. You're also a dangerous brawler. According to the story, you were given your name when you beat a couple of rowdies bloody one night."

"They were vicious toughs—"

Averill raised his hand. "You smashed one man's kneecap, Turk."

Robin opened his mouth to speak. His throat was dry. "They were trying to rob me."

His adversary snorted. "You hit him again when he was trying to crawl away screaming."

"I lost my temper."

Averill smiled. "Exactly." He motioned toward the food again. "Eat. I wouldn't want you to be out of temper."

A grim fatalism swept Robin. He crossed to the table and sat down. Determined to acquit himself well in what might be his last meal for a long time, he lifted knife and fork and cut a precise cube from a tender piece of beef. Without a waste of motion he carried it to his mouth.

Averill watched him like a hawk, then sighed. "I had rather pictured you shoveling the food in with your hands, but I suppose that was too much to hope for."

Robin did not raise his head. The beef was tender and delicious. It put heart into him and counteracted the dizziness invoked by the alcohol. He was surprised at how hungry he was. With swift, efficient motions, he ate everything that was on his plate. Then, with a defiant gesture, he lifted the glass of burgundy and drank it off.

A sharp laugh burst from the man behind the desk. He raised his brandy glass to return the salute. Unfortunately, this time the drink did not slip easily down his throat. He choked, then coughed, deeply.

Robin stared.

The spasm continued. The white face of the Ice King reddened.

Finally, the convulsions ceased. Averill leaned back in his chair, taking careful shallow breaths. "A family weakness," he explained in a dry whisper. "Strange shape to the throat. My mother had it."

Robin waited. The room was warm now. He allowed his head to rest against the chair back. He could almost go to sleep. If he were to drift off, would he awaken to find this misadventure had been a nightmare?

Averill's next statement seemed a *non sequitur.* "I have no son."

Robin blinked and straightened.

"We are a very old family, Whittcombstone. Norman conquest. Agincourt. Bosworth Field. When I die, the name and family estates are entailed to a very distant male relative, should he survive me. Unfortunately, the name will die. But the blood, however diluted—"

He clenched his fist about the notes. His listener stared at him puzzled. The Duke's icy cynicism had deserted him. Rage seethed beneath the cold, white surface and leaped in the ice-blue eyes.

"I have no son," he repeated. The cost of uttering these words was great. His voice gave way to another cough. He took a cautious sip of brandy.

Wearily, Whittcombstone waited. He could do no less. He had an uneasy feeling that the Duke was mad, and that his madness was of the coldly analytical kind, the kind that destroyed all it touched.

"The Duchess, you will remember, died several years ago." Averill watched him closely.

"My sympathies," Robin murmured.

"You didn't know?" Averill seemed somewhat taken aback.

"Your Duchess? No, I didn't." He was genuinely puzzled.

"No. I suppose you didn't. Ah, how quickly one forgets. Still, I have considered marriage again, but the thought of living with another woman — " He ground his teeth. "I shall have to consider it deeply." He rose and walked to the window, away from the fire, away from the warmth and the light. He drew aside the drapery and stared out into night. The north wind gusted against the window. The Ice King pressed his hand flat against the pane.

Watching him, Robin shivered. Without waiting for an invitation, he leaned forward to pour himself another glass of burgundy.

Seemingly restored by the cold, the Duke turned back to the room. Hands behind him he stalked slowly to within a yard of his guest to stare down at him. Like a man scrutinizing an expensive purchase, he ran his colorless eyes from the soles of the

21

scuffed boots to the top of the black head.

At last, he nodded. "Perfect. Perfect." His voice was hoarse from the coughing. "You're perfect. Maimed. Drunken. Vicious. Black as a crow. Wastrel, Spendthrift." He grunted. "You should be able to ruin even the finest animal."

The words cut deep. Robin pushed back the chair so fast that it overturned. Shoulders hunched, black eye glittering, he came toe to toe with the Duke. One dark fist fastened in the perfectly tied neckcloth and hauled the older man up on tiptoe. "What did you bring me here for?" he grated. "Whatever it is, say it and be done without the insults. Or I swear, at the next one, I'll tear your head off."

The Duke made no effort to defend himself. Indeed, he smiled that oddly genuine smile Robin had seen only once before. "Of course, Milord Whitby. Immediately."

Still seething, Robin gave the man a shake, before letting go abruptly.

The Duke sprawled over the top of the desk. From there he propped himself up on his elbows, then threw back his head and laughed as if he richly enjoyed a joke he was about to play. "Wonderful! Wonderful! The civilized veneer does run thin with you."

With a growl Robin reached for him again, but the Duke raised his hand. "Enough. Enough. I'll say no more. You will be perfect for my purposes. A workman should never despise his tools."

After straightening his clothing, Robin crossed his arms over his chest.

22

The Ice King rose and reseated himself at his desk where he gathered up all the slips of paper and stuffed them back into the envelope. "Please don't let your gratitude play a part in any of this," he remarked with heavy irony. "The fact that I have saved you from The Fleet, which I understand is a most unpleasant place, should not enter your mind. Concentrate on how you have been wronged, insulted, inconvenienced."

Robin Whittcombstone waited.

"I have no son." The words—*non sequiturs* again—fell like lead between them. The man's body seemed to clench inward as if to reacting to a blow.

Disgusted, Robin dropped into the chair in front of the fireplace. Weary unto death, he closed his eyes. His words came softly. "I think you've lost your mind."

"Excellent. You insult me. Me—your better, your savior, your peer. Good. Good. I like the idea. Defiant. Rebellious. Irreverent." The Duke reached for his brandy.

"Damn you." Robin's head rolled on the back of the chair. "What do you want of me?"

The Duke smiled as he raised his glass to his lips. "A great task. A sacrifice of your own welfare, a subjugating of your emotions. Oh, you will be asked to give your body for the purpose."

"What? Damn you!"

"I want you to marry my daughter."

Two

Lady Noelle Amalie Jacinthe Rivers, only child of the Duke of Averill, drew rein and waited for the rider who galloped toward her.

Holmesfield, the Duke's factor, slowed his horse, then walked the last few yards until his mount was almost nose to nose with her own. "Milady, His Grace requires your presence immediately."

"*His Grace*. My, but we're formal, Archie, and at such an early hour."

He sighed deeply. "Milady . . ."

"Tell me, Archie, do you actually take off your clothes and lie down in a bed or do you prop yourself in a corner at attention?"

One corner of the agent's mouth curled. "You'd best come with me, Lady Noelle. If you know what's good for you."

"Oh, I know what's good for me." She reined the chestnut mare in a circle.

"Lady Noelle—"

"Tell *His Grace* that I'll be in as soon as I finish

24

my ride." At the touch of her spurred heel, the mare sprang forward.

"Lady Noelle!"

"Tell him, Archie!"

Holmesfield scowled and shook his head as he watched girl and horse disappear into the trees.

At ten she presented herself in the Duke's study.

The Ice King's colorless eyes took in the leather gloves and coachman's coat over her riding habit. Her hat was tied down with a woolen scarf over her ears. "You've been riding."

"No. I wore this outfit to practice with the dancing master."

Averill's chair scraped back noisily as he sprang to his feet. "Get up to your room," he snarled. "Make yourself presentable."

She held her ground. "I thought you wanted me immediately. Archie took great pains to inform me—"

From where he sat at a small desk in the alcove, Holmesfield shot her an accusing look.

"Get yourself up and take off that rig!" Averill thundered.

She smiled sweetly as she tugged at the knotted scarf beneath her chin. "Your wish is my command. A velvet gown. My mother's diamonds. I can be ready by mid-afternoon. Of course, I—"

He rounded the desk and swooped down on her. Catching her by the shoulders, he shook her savagely. The loosened scarf fell to the floor, her hat tumbled off, and with it the skein of hair tucked under it. Mahogany brown with glints of red—thick, heavy, curling like firesnakes.

As if he feared the heat, the Duke jerked his hands away. "Stay here if you want. I don't care what you do."

"Then I'll stay—" Her voice wavered, but she cleared her throat heavily. "—and please myself."

He backed away from her. "Just like your mother."

"Exactly."

He smothered a cough, then fumbled behind the desk. His hand sought and found a document. He swept it up and thrust it at her. "I've done it."

She shuddered. Her hands doubled into fists.

"Did you think I wouldn't?" A malicious grin lifted the corners of his mouth. "Did you really think I wouldn't?"

"I—I knew you would."

His breathing sounded harsh and raspy. Suddenly, he began to cough, hacking, convulsive. Bright color stained his pale cheeks, beads of perspiration dotted his brow. He spun around and collapsed on the desk, supporting himself on both elbows, coughing in great heaving spasms.

She watched him in silence, her face drained of its natural color until she was white as a lily.

Finally, the coughing ceased. He slapped the paper down on the desk and croaked, "Sign it!"

She shook her head.

Hunched over the desk, leaning on his elbows, he looked over his shoulder. "Sign it!"

"Not until I read it."

"You don't need to read it. It's only the wedding license."

"Then I won't sign it until I see the contract." She folded her arms. Her nostrils flared. "I intend to know the worst."

He raised himself. The red color faded rapidly from his face. "Oh, you will. You will."

"I won't sign it—"

He caught her wrist. "Sign it. Whether you know or not, I will have my way in this. Your signature is not required."

She twisted futilely trying to free herself. "But you want it. You could sign for me, but that would be a written document naming me—"

"Silence! I won't have that word from your lips. Not ever again. From my lips or yours."

"Daught—"

He slapped her. Hard. Slapped the hated word from her mouth before she could finish it.

In the alcove Holmesfield broke the nib of his pen on the ledger sheet.

Noelle neither winced, nor cried out. Dark eyes, brown without a hint of gold or green, stared at Averill unblinkingly.

He dropped his hand to his side, fingers twitching. "I've spent your mother's portion acquiring you a husband—as is only just."

A muscle flickered in her jaw.

His face might have been carved from alabaster. "The man I've selected for you owed quite a large number of debts. I did not want you to start your marriage with such encumbrances."

She glanced at Holmesfield. He seemed engrossed in sharpening another pen. "I want a solicitor—"

"One will do you no good. The terms of your mother's will allow me to spend your money for your benefit. I've acquired you a husband with it." He made no attempt to conceal the triumph in his voice.

"And effectually left me a pauper."

For form's sake only the translucent eyelids drooped over the pale eyes. "Your husband will provide—"

"How can he? If he was in debt before you—I mean *I*—paid his creditors, then he—we—must begin to live on credit again."

"Only if you live in London, which is so expensive."

She nodded, fully understanding that part of his plan. "Where will we live then? Some log cabin in America? I understand the savages have all sorts of interesting customs. I shall quite enjoy them."

He glanced down at the perfectly groomed nails on his right hand. "To my knowledge he has no holdings there. No, I believe you'll live somewhere in Devon actually. The south coast. I believe there is a house on the property, although in rather neglected condition."

"I can imagine."

"His land, now free thanks to you, may be turned to some advantage. He should be very grateful."

She smiled mirthlessly. "I'm sure he's overcome with thankfulness and thrilled at the prospect of marriage to a woman he's never seen. How did

28

he come to have all these debts? Or dare I ask?"

"That you may ask of him yourself. And soon. He is even now eagerly awaiting your appearance."

"I'm sure. However—"

The Duke caught her by the right hand and forced it to close around the pen. "Sign there beneath his signature and I'll take you to him."

She struggled briefly, trying again to twist her hand free. "Let me go."

Averill threw his arm around her shoulders. "Not until you sign."

The battle became more physical as she braced herself pulled back. Her force threw the Duke off balance. They staggered against a chair and jostled a table. Averill began to cough wildly.

Thoroughly alarmed, Holmesfield left his desk and came to the entrance to the alcove.

Exerting his greater strength, Averill tightened his right arm around her throat. "Be still!"

Abruptly, Noelle ceased to struggle.

Coughing in great spasms, choking for breath between them, tears streaming down his cheeks, the Duke dragged her to the desk again. There he forced her hand toward the inkwell, dipped the nib into it, and guided it back to the paper.

"Damn you!" she whispered.

He exchanged his arm for his hand gripping her neck, thumb clamped over her windpipe. "Will you sign?"

"Yes!" His grip eased and she shook his hand off. Trembling violently she made the motion herself scratching and jabbing at the paper. "Damn you!"

He stepped back and pulled out his handkerchief to wipe his perspiring face. "Such language. No lady would ever utter such," he sneered. "And now your bridegroom awaits."

She held the paper out of his reach. "Wait! Tell me how he acquired such debts? Gambling. Drinking."

The Duke smiled icy assent. "His entire existence was on credit."

"And you have acquired his paper."

"It was easy enough to do."

She nodded. "I'll take it."

He looked at her in surprise.

"I'll take it. After all it belongs to me now."

"You'll never collect," Averill sneered. "Everything a wife has belongs to her husband."

"Nevertheless, I'll have the paper now."

"No."

"Then you lose this." Defying him, she took the special license in both hands.

He made a grab for it but missed when she darted away. His expression venomous, he straightened. "Very well. Holmesfield."

The factor located and handed over the notes.

Noelle let go the license. The factor caught it as it wafted toward the floor. She weighed the thickness of the envelope in both hands, then looked at Averill. "I swear I will hate you till I die."

He smiled. "I have no doubt you will. My only comfort is that you will be miserable the entire time."

He took the document from the factor and crossed to the door. Holmesfield hurried to open it and the Duke bowed Noelle through. "We must hurry, my dear. Your bridegroom awaits."

Dark, dank, and unheated, the chapel was little more than a closet with a *prie-Dieu* for an altar. An ancient tree of candles trembled and smoked to one side. The cross hanging on the wall at the back appeared only as a wavering shadow. Noelle could see why the room had seldom if ever been used.

As the icy air chilled her body, Noelle raised her hand to her face. Tears. She was weeping. Surreptitiously, she brushed at one cheek but left the other to dry. Not for anything would she allow the Duke to see her cry.

A dark figure rose from the bench on the left. Shivering uncontrollably, she halted to stare intently as the man came forward.

A very tall man. His height would intimidate her if she did not keep constantly on guard. She pulled herself up very straight.

The Duke urged her forward by his grip on her elbow. "Ah, Robin. I may call you that now. You are to be my son-in-law. May I present your bride. Lady Noelle Rivers. There's more to her name, a couple more of those French things her mother stuck on, but . . ." He went on and on, an hysterical note in his voice. "Holmesfield, bring the light. Let these dear children see each other."

Neither of the "dear children" heard him. Instead, they stared into the dimness in mutual horror and disgust.

To Robin his bride-to-be looked like a bedlamite. As the factor lifted a lamp, the Earl took in her pale face, her dark hair wild about her shoulders, her coachman's coat, and mud-spattered boots. Her dark eyes surrounded by dark lashes glittered in the poor light. He thought she might be weeping.

The corner of his mouth pulled down in a sneer. No doubt he was a sight to make a woman weep. Of course, she was staring at his eyepatch.

Even prepared for the worst, Noelle could not suppress a horrified gasp. Her bridegroom looked like a pirate from a seventeenth century manuscript. Over his left eye was a black leather patch. Its leather string bisected his forehead. Contrasting vividly with it was a silvery white scar that started in his hairline, disappeared behind the black leather, then reappeared again below its bottom edge. It tore its way across his cheek and jaw where it disappeared in the folds of a carelessly knotted neckcloth.

Apart from that startling mark, the man's face was devil dark, almost brown-skinned. Coal black hair fell in a tangle over his forehead, except for a lock of white that sprouted at the top of the scar. Blue-black shadow covered his jaw.

Desperately she fastened on something that could be changed. The unshaven cheek freed her tongue. "God's bones, Averill. Couldn't you at least have prevailed upon the bridegroom to shave? His jaw looks like a briarpatch."

The jaw in question clenched. "My wedding finery is certainly the equal of your own."

She laughed mirthlessly. "Too bad we have not

invited guests. We would start a new fashion. Rags and patches."

Robin's hand rose toward his eye, then clenched into a fist. He took a step toward her.

Averill allowed a short bark of laughter. He patted her hand where it clenched over his forearm. "Children. Children. Please restrain yourselves. You have a lifetime before you to do your billing and cooing."

Noelle pulled her arm free and stared in wonder at the Ice King. "I never truly understood the depth of your hatred for me until this moment."

His eyes were chips of blue ice. "And now you do." He leaned forward to whisper loudly in her ear. "If I were you, my dear, I would put a bridle on that tongue. Your bridegroom will shortly have the power of life and death over you. He can make your life very, very unpleasant if he chooses."

"I'm sure you have chosen someone who will make my life very unpleasant at the outset," she scoffed.

Robin felt his own temper rising as they discussed him as if he were not there. "One minute more of this and I'll murder the both of you and take my chances with the law."

"Ah, the gentleman says he will murder us." Averill bowed mockingly and offered his arm to Noelle. "Come, my dear." He led her to the altar. "Come along, Whittcombstone. Holmesfield will be delighted to serve as your best man. We can't dally all day in these drafts. *Padre!*"

The factor urged Robin forward and motioned to him to stand on Noelle's left. The candlelight fell full on his ruined face.

An old man in a clerical collar rose from the bench on the right of the altar. His hands clasped around the Bible were grimy and swollen with chilblains.

"So much pomp and circumstance," Noelle observed. "Are you sure you can afford such a spectacle, Averill?"

"It is no more than you deserve," came the reply. "Begin."

The priest muttered a few words, cleared his throat, and looked around uncertainly.

Noelle looked to her bridegroom. "I believe he's asking if anyone knows of any reason why the marriage should not be performed."

Robin swayed slightly. His eyes blazed. "I can think of several, but let them go."

She could smell the brandy on his breath. "Too drunk to make any sense."

Whittcombstone's hard hand shot out to fasten on her wrist. "No, madam. Cold sober."

"Go on. Go on." Averill directed. "They want to be on their way."

The old man nodded. In a droning voice, he asked Noelle if she wished to marry.

She hesitated. A word and she would be committed forever. Given by one man who hated her, to — She looked at Robin. He was staring straight ahead, so she could not see the ruined side of his face.

Presented in profile, the good side was not much better. His skin was so dark, his lips so thin. Both his temple and his cheek were hollowed as if he had

34

been starved. The blue-black jaw was strong, however, and the cheekbones high.

The old priest asked the question again. Averill nudged her.

She nodded, wordlessly assenting.

Beside her, Robin made some response.

The old priest muttered a few more indistinct words. His trembling hand made a couple of vague passes in the icy air. Her wedding was over.

Until the vows were truly sworn to, Averill's hand had never relaxed its pressure on her elbow. Likewise, her hand felt numb below her husband's grip on her wrist.

His office done, the priest stepped back. Now all the parties relaxed. Suddenly, the Duke began to cough. He released his grip on Noelle's arm to try to smother the spasm.

Noelle jostled against her husband. His already crushing grip on her wrist tightened. Stiffly, they turned to face each other. He turned his head slightly to the right, presenting the dark patch rather than the good eye. He must have suffered terribly when this thing happened. Perhaps he was still in pain.

From somewhere behind her, her father found his voice. "Not even a kiss for your bride, Whittcombstone?"

"I hardly think that's neces—" Noelle began.

Robin's teeth flashed, startling in their contrasting whiteness. His thin lips parted in a travesty of a smile. "Why not?" he mocked. "Dear wife—" He raised her hand to press it against his chest in mimicry of a loving gesture. His other arm passed

35

around her slender body to pull it against him.

"This is a travesty."

His smile disappeared. His lips tightened. "Oh, but I insist. Dare I hope, dear wife, that I will be bestowing your first kiss."

She heard the Duke's dry chuckle at her shoulder. Angry, she pushed back against her husband's chest. One fist clenched and punched at him. "Let me go, you fool. Don't let Averill direct your life any more."

The protest would have won him, had he not taken her anger for repugnance. He stared at her curled mouth, her bright eyes, then dragged her against his frame. His head turned, his face angled over hers. The dark eye flashed. Then his mouth came down hard and punishing on her own.

She tried to close her mouth, but he thrust his tongue in between her lips, burrowing deeply, almost strangling her. When she tried to twist away, he clapped his hand to the back of her head and held her still while he punished her. He was aware of the shape of her, shivering, fighting, resisting to her utmost. Her hands crushed against his chest flexed and clawed at him. Unintelligible protests issued from her throat.

The kiss went on and on, a contest of wills observed by the priest, who closed his eyes, by Holmesfield, who looked away in embarrassment, and by Averill, whose grin widened.

Furiously angry and repulsed, Noelle managed to eel her right hand up between them. She clawed at the side of his face, catching her fingernails in the leather string that bound the eyepatch. Before she could pull it off, Robin released her. His hands flew to his face and he spun around, fumbling, adjusting it until it was back in place.

The chapel was silent except for Noelle's panting breaths.

Then Averill coughed and chuckled. "Perhaps the three of us should retire and leave you to it, sir."

"I think not." Robin turned back to face their stares. Fury had turned his face into a cold mask. "I think we can all go together. My wife and I can contain our passion till a more appropriate moment."

Noelle snatched her fingers away from her mouth. It was red and swollen where his whiskers had savaged it. "That will be when you shave," she said baldly. "And bathe."

Lips widening in a cold smile, he bowed mockingly. "A rough soldier, Madam Wife. But then I didn't know until this morning that it was to be my wedding day."

"And you both have quite a journey ahead of you." The Duke of Averill stepped forward and tapped his new son-in-law on the shoulder with false heartiness. "I'm sure my cook can manage a bite of breakfast to send you both on your way with full stomachs."

"I must have time to pack my things." Noelle stepped back. "And change out of my wedding finery."

"Just tell the housekeeper what you want. She can take care of the details." Averill made a dismissive gesture. "We'll willingly delay the feast for you. Come with me, Whittcombstone. I am anxious to sign over to you the quarterly allowance left by the girl's mother."

His words brought Noelle up short in the doorway. "That quarterly allowance is mine."

"Nonsense. Everything you have belongs to your husband."

Her eyes flew to Robin's face. "And you will take it, won't you?" she said bitterly. "And run through it every quarter."

He wanted to say that it was hers. That he would not touch it, but her contempt made him angry. "If I choose."

The Duke gave a bark of laughter and clapped his son-in-law on the back. "Excellent. Begin as you mean to go on. Hurry, girl. You don't want to leave anything of importance behind."

Noelle turned on her heel and left.

"Don't worry. She'll have everything she's entitled to. All her goods will be in the coach. I'm lending you a coach, my boy. For the honeymoon journey. I know you'll want to be on your way in the afternoon, so you can make good time before bedtime." He fairly radiated good will and triumph. "And my daughter shall have her mare, her mother's horse, but a good one. You'll appreciate that mare, let me tell you . . ."

The door to her room stood open. Two serving maids, in the presence of the housekeeper had nearly finished folding her garments and putting them into a large trunk.

"I'll need a portmanteau with my nightgown and robe and a change for tomorrow."

The housekeeper frowned. "I don't have any instructions—"

"I'm instructing you. Send someone for one immediately. No. No. Don't put that in on top of the silk—" She hurried to correct the maid's mistake. She threw over her shoulder. "A portmanteau, now."

The housekeeper nodded.

"I need another trunk too."

"Another trunk? Milady—"

"For the linens. Come this way." She led the girl down the hall to the gigantic mahogany and camphorwood press.

"But—"

Opening its double doors, she pulled out the folded sheets and covers, and loaded them into the girl's arms. "These were my mother's. They're mine now."

"Yes, ma'am."

Her thoughts whirling. "The plate. My mother's plate."

The housekeeper had returned with the portmanteau. She stared disapprovingly at the maid who scurried past into the bedroom. "His lordship didn't say anything about that."

"Of course he didn't," Noelle scoffed. "What man would think of things like that?"

"Well—"

"Another trunk please."

Holmesfield came slowly down the hall. "Milady—"

She dug her fists into her hips and barred the way into her room. "Archie, what do you want?"

"Don't make this difficult, Lady Noelle."

"Oh, too bad, Archie. Little Lady Noelle won't roll over and play dead for you."

He swallowed, but stood his ground. "His Grace has sent me for the Averill jewels."

"The Averill jewels!" She threw back her head and laughed. "There are no Averill jewels."

"I believe he gave your mother—"

"What he gave her was hers. She gave them to me. He doesn't have any right to any of them."

"The diamonds."

"So, he's going to call those the Averill jewels, is he?"

The factor nodded.

"Even though his own father bought them for him to give to his wife."

"I wouldn't know about that, milady."

"Well, I would." She moved aside for a footman to move in another trunk for the bedding.

Holmesfield followed the man into the room. "I must have them."

"Damn you! Damn you both!" She stalked to her wardrobe, opened the bottom of it and lifted out her mother's coffer. It was an antique box, bound in leather and studded with brass. Seating herself at the vanity table, she placed it carefully in front of her.

"That's the box. My instructions are to take that," Holmesfield said.

"Over my bleeding body."

He drew back at the language. "Milady."

She started to rise.

He held out his hands placatingly. "Please, milady, let's not make this more unpleasant than we have to. The Duke means to have it. He will only send someone less accommodating than I."

With a sigh she capitulated. Taking the key from her dressing table, she opened the box. Holmesfield edged closer, peering inside what he was sure was a treasure chest. He was disappointed. Each of her mother's pieces, from the most to the least precious, was stored in its own green velvet pouch. Her fingers sorted through, moved one and then another aside. At last she drew one out. "Here."

He took it carefully, weighed it in his hand. He nodded. "The—er—earbobs."

"No." She slammed the lid down and turned the lock. "He bought those later for her. Grandfather had nothing to do with them."

"Milady, you'll get me into trouble."

"You'll think trouble, if you try for more."

He shrugged and looked around him. An interested audience of servants had gathered to listen to every word that passed between them. "Perhaps I've got everything I should."

"I'm sure you have. Now would you please leave so I can change for the journey?"

In the mirror Noelle watched the door close behind the factor. Her hand caressed the top of the box, her lips twitched at the corners. Then she stiffened. Swinging around on the vanity stool, she fixed the other servants with her coldest stare.

It was enough to send them scurrying back to business. With her arm across the jewel box, she watched them clear every sign of her from the rooms.

* * *

Holmesfield passed the velvet pouch to the Duke, who tossed it negligently onto his desk. "What's taking her so long?"

The factor looked uneasy. "She's taking several trunks full of household items, milord. Linens and such, I believe."

Averill frowned, then shrugged. "I suppose they are of no consequence. Her mother brought them with her from France. Let her have them. Holmesfield, I have another task for you."

"Milord."

"Leave immediately for the Earl's ruin of a place."

"Whitby?"

"Yes. Whitby. Find a servant that can be bribed. I can't believe any one round dozen of them wouldn't be anxious to sell information."

"I doubt that he has a dozen servants, milord."

"What? Oh, well. Doubtless." Averill tipped back his head and laughed. "Find someone, Holmesfield, and hurry back."

No sooner had the door closed behind the last trunk than Noelle opened the leather-bound coffer. With her thumbs she pressed the brass studs on the outside edges of the lid. A click, a second click, and a tray dropped out of the humpbacked lid. A pair of green velvet pouches lay in it. She opened the smaller of the two.

Diamonds winked from settings of highly polished silver each with a silver hook. She held them up to her ears and stared at herself critically. After a moment, she made a wry face and put them away.

From the second pouch she emptied the necklace into her hand—the Ice King's treasure for a treasured wife. Diamonds set in silver, plated over gold. In defiance of every tradition, Averill had caused to be created the ultimate icy setting. A *parure* of diamonds had encircled her mother's neck. From it six more diamonds on delicate silver chains had dripped like icicles.

Noelle shivered as she held it up against the dark wool dress. She would probably never wear it, but it would go with her wherever she went.

She slipped it back into its pouch and replaced them both in the tray. Pressing on its bottom with both thumbs, she lifted it back into place in the lid.

Her jewel box tight against her side, under an enveloping traveling cloak, Noelle descended half an hour later to find her husband and her father drinking amicably together.

"Ah, the bride." The Duke raised his glass in a toast. "I'll have the meal served."

Ignoring him, she turned to Robin. "Do you want to eat?"

He shook his head wearily. "I'm not hungry."

"Nor am I. My trunks are packed. I'm ready to leave." Without another word she went into the entry hall.

Averill stared after her. No trace of tears around her eyes. Her color was high. Her back straight.

Robin shrugged and polished off the glass of wine. "If she's not hungry, I suppose we might as well."

43

Not looking at either man, she watched as the footmen brought down her trunks. Icy drafts blew in as the butler opened the door.

The door to the Duke's study opened and Robin Whittcombstone stepped out, closing it behind him. He leaned back against it for an instant, his eyes red-rimmed with drink and lack of sleep. With his right hand he stuffed several folded documents into the inner pocket of his coat.

"My dear wife." He hailed her with mocking gallantry.

As he approached, she could smell his breath. She swallowed. "Husband."

"The carriage awaits. It is many long cold miles to Whitby Manor." He made her a leg which she acknowledged with a slight inclination of her head.

He made a sweeping gesture toward the front door. "Then will you precede me, my lady?"

Noelle looked around her. From Italian marble floor to hand-carved ceiling, she stood in the entrance of the only home she had ever known. She wanted to scream and cry and beg for mercy. Instead, she tightened her grip on her jewel box and stepped out of the warmth into the gray afternoon.

Three

"Archie must have had a very devil of a time finding anything as uncomfortable as this." Lady Noelle Whittcombstone, the new Countess of Whitby, caught hold of the window strap as the ancient vehicle's springs failed.

She addressed the remark to the coach's musty interior, not necessarily to her husband, who sprawled beside her, his booted feet resting on the facing seat, his hat pulled over his eyes. Out of the corner of her eye, she watched the dark figure stir, heard him mutter something unintelligible, and rearrange his long frame.

The vehicle jounced across the ice-encrusted ruts at a crossroad. Its ancient springs tossed its riders to and fro. The third jolt cracked her head against the window post. She cursed fervently.

Her husband did not comment. For all she knew he might not have heard. Only his thin lips and chin covered with blue-black stubble were visible beneath his hat.

Noelle looked at him crossly. "How can you sleep? My teeth are being shaken out of my head."

From beneath the brim, his voice came deep and raspy. "As a matter of fact I'm not sleeping. I can't sleep because my traveling companion chatters constantly."

The coach slewed sideways as they went round a curve on the icy road. The violent movement tipped her against him. She groaned as she hauled on the strap and dragged herself back upright. "I want to stop soon."

"Why?"

Feeling a blush rise in her cheeks, she pulled aside the edge of the curtain and stared out on the snowy landscape. It was singularly devoid of trees or hedgerows. A breath of frigid air slid in through the opening. She shifted uncomfortably. "Because I'm hungry."

"You told your father you weren't." Lazily, he lifted his legs off the seat and sat up straight. Not bothering to cover a wide yawn, he arched his back and massaged his spine at the waist.

"That was three hours ago." She moved her head out of the way of his stretch. "I thought you weren't uncomfortable."

"Just because I don't complain for ten miles, doesn't mean I'm not uncomfortable."

She bit her lip, then shrugged. Her husband clearly had no sense of delicacy. She sighed. "I'm hungry, but I could go on for a long time without food. I have another more pressing problem right now."

"The coachman can stop by the side of the

road," he suggested blandly, his face expressionless.

She slapped the curtain back into place and threw him a look that would have scorched steel. "No, he cannot. He can stop at the next inn where we will engage the private parlor and dine. At the same time we can exchange these—" She pushed one of the bricks on the carriage floor with her toe—"for some that are not ice cold."

Robin drew a flask from beneath his cloak and offered it to her. She glanced at him quickly, then shook her head. He shrugged before he turned it up and drank deep. Then he opened the curtain and leaned out. "We'll stop for the day at the next inn."

"Very good, sir."

He pulled his head back in and replaced the curtain. "Anything for my new bride."

She wrapped her arms repressively across her chest and huddled into the corner. "Let's just forget this bride and groom business for the time being, shall we?"

He raised his right eyebrow. "Why, Madam Wife, would you deny me my conjugal rights?"

She shuddered. "Don't call me wife."

"But that's what you are. If not wife, then what shall I call you?"

She curled one leg up under her and pushed even farther away from him. "You really don't have to call me anything. We don't need to go through with this."

"Your father would be disappointed indeed if you didn't get full value for his money." His thin lips spread in a mirthless grin. "I stand ready to serve you." He made an obscene gesture, then closed his hand in a fist as he realized it was totally wasted on her.

She stared at him, her eyes wide and faintly puzzled.

He should have let the matter drop, but he put his hand on her thigh. "For the sum of ten thousand pounds, I'll be your husband and gladly. One of the very last remarks your father made to me was a rather crude instruction regarding my behavior toward you." His long fingers pushed the folds of her skirt down between her legs.

"Stop that!" She struck at his hand.

Quicker than thought he grabbed her wrist, his lips pulled back from his teeth. "You stop that!"

Her eyes widened. She jerked back, but his grip only tightened. Ha pulled her toward him. She hung tight to the strap, but she was pulled into his lap.

Even in the decaying light of afternoon, his face was fearsome. Dark-skinned, hideously scarred. A three day stubble of beard on his jaw made the healed wound that sliced through it a streak of vivid white skin.

"Lady, I'll be your husband, but I'll not be your whipping boy, nor your lackey." His teeth ground out the words and fairly spat them in her face. "Your father has married you to me for whatever obscene and perverse reasons he may have. I think he does so to punish you, but you won't punish me in turn. I'm not part of your war with him. Do you understand?"

Thoroughly frightened, but still game, she pushed at him. "I understand that the money that paid off your debts was my money!" she snarled. "I bought thousands of pounds of your notes with my money! You owe me at least consideration. And I say let go of me."

"Your money! In England girls of your age have no money. What your father cared to give you now belongs to me."

Before she could answer, the coachman turned from the roadbed. It jounced over icy ruts jolting them until their teeth clicked together.

Whittcombstone cursed vehemently. He released his wife's wrist and braced himself with a hand on the door. "Is that coachman blind? Your father must have searched high and low for someone so incompetent."

She pushed herself away and wrapped both hands around the strap, fairly swinging from it. She was trembling from head to foot, her stomach clenched and burning, her teeth chattering. Though she sent him a defiant glare, inside she wrestled with the very real horror that the coachman's miserable driving had focused her husband's anger elsewhere. Otherwise, he might have done her harm.

All its parts creaking, the vehicle swung in under the archway of a posting inn where it lurched to a halt. The sounds and odors of the innyard rose all around them.

An ostler, muddy to the hips, pulled the door open and folded the step down. Whittcombstone pulled his rangy body up off the seat and swung his long legs out through the door. Both booted feet hit the lower step at the same time. He paused there, one arm bracing himself against the top of the carriage. His nose wrinkled as he surveyed the morass in the innyard.

"Bring a forkful of straw, man," Robin ordered. "We'll sink to our knees in this muck."

"It's just a few steps," came the whining reply.

The Earl caught him up on his toes by the shirt front. The carriage swayed and creaked as the added weight tilted it. "Yes, indeed. Just the length of your body, I calculate. Flat on your face, we'd have no need of straw."

The ostler spluttered and coughed. "I'll get it. Right away, sir."

"Right away, it is." The Earl let go so fast that the unfortunate man staggered back.

Inside the carriage, Noelle shuddered. Her husband's body despite the scars on his face was not crippled. On the contrary, he was tough and agile. The ostler had discovered—to his sorrow—that Whittcombstone was lightning quick, strong, and used to being obeyed without question. She put one hand to her temple where a headache was beginning. What would happen to her if she did not obey him?

When the Earl stepped down onto the straw, the ostler extended his gloved hand into the coach. "Ma'am."

"Yes." She unwrapped her fingers from the strap and flexed them.

"Watch yer step, Ma'am. It's slick even though we've strewed fresh straw for ye to walk across."

She took his proffered hand to steady her descent. But the carriage step cracked and tilted outward. Her foot slipped and she pitched down the steps.

Before she could fall, Robin caught her around the waist and steadied her. Clapping her to his side, he carried her across the yard.

"You can put me down," she protested, her toes stabbing for the ground. "For heaven's sake, I can walk."

"When we get inside," was all he said.

The entire innyard stared and grinned at her humiliating position as she was carried in hanging like a bundle of wash under her husband's arm.

Noelle disposed of her most urgent physical problem and entered the private parlor where she sank wearily onto a padded bench. A small fire that smoked only a bit burned fitfully in the grate. She held out her palms to it. Her fingers began to tremble. She gulped as tears welled over and trickled down her cheeks. Exhaustion, both physical and nervous, swept over her in relentless waves.

Behind her the door opened. Instantly, she ducked her head and swiped at her cheeks.

Her husband strode directly to the fire. Stooping, he hung above it, letting it warm his body as well as his hands. Then without looking at her, he dropped down on the bench beside her and stripped off his gloves.

She cleared her throat and assumed a bright tone. "Now wasn't this a good idea?"

"Warmth and food are always good ideas," Robin agreed. Elbows on knees, he stretched out his bare hands to the fire.

She stared at those hands. The fingers were long and very slender; the nails, clean but not particularly well-groomed. Averill's hands — she remembered — were soft and fleshy.

Robin flexed his left hand, then rubbed the white scar at the base of the thumb with his right. He turned it over and held the palm to the fire. Not an extra ounce of flesh clung to that hand. It was all bone and muscle and tendon. Likewise, Averill's hand was white. Blue veins stood out of Whittcombstone's brown skin.

To her surprise, she saw the fingers begin to tremble. He turned his head and caught her staring. His fingers flexed into fists. He leaned back, a disapproving look on his face. "We should have gone farther. There's still light to travel."

"Oh, of course. Perhaps in another three or four miles, the traveling conditions could have worsened. With a bit of luck, the coach could have wrecked and we could have broken our necks."

His mouth tightened. "You have a sharp tongue."

"So I've been told by more than one. Sharp enough to speak the truth as I see it." She softened her tone. "You must be very tired. Your hands were shaking."

He laced the long fingers together between his legs. His cheekbones reddened as he stared into the fire.

"Mine were too," she admitted lightly. "And, of course, another five minutes of jolting and jouncing and we would have been awash."

His mouth might have quirked at the corner. She could not be sure.

A knock sounded. A servant entered with a decanter and two glasses. Silently, they waited while he set the tray down, bowed, and left.

After a moment's hesitation Robin rose. "Now let's see what this wretched establishment has to offer in the way of a restorative." He splashed cloudy brown liquid into each glass and raised one to his nose. His eyebrows shot up, but he nevertheless handed one glass to her. "Just toss it off," he advised when she looked at it suspiciously. "After you've had a boost, you can start wondering about what you're drinking."

He demonstrated the technique, tipping back his head, opening his lips, and flinging the stuff at the back of his throat.

She watched his adam's apple bob.

He lowered the empty glass and sucked in a raw breath through his open mouth. "It might be sherry."

She smiled faintly. Raising the glass in a mock toast, she copied his action. Instantly, she regretted her rash bravado.

She gagged and choked. Her eyes watered. The liquor tasted horrible — sour, with a fierce bite, and a nasty aftertaste. Her stomach heaved, though she managed to swallow again and keep the stuff down.

When she could speak, she stared accusingly at him. "That was the worst stuff I have ever put in my mouth. A husband's duty is to protect his wife. You should have taken the glass away from me immediately rather than looked on while I drank it."

"How could I?" He actually lifted the decanter and poured himself some more poison. "It's not the worst stuff I've ever put in my mouth. One night in Spain I remember — but that would take too long to tell." He extended the decanter to her. "More?"

"Heaven forfend." She put her hand over the top of her glass. When he lifted his second glassful, she frowned. "It's certainly not sherry. At least not like any I've ever tasted. I don't think you should drink any more of it either."

His eyebrow rose. "Do you presume to tell me how much to drink?"

"Not at all. Except that it can't be good for you. It could make you very sick."

In a defiant gesture, he tossed off his second glass and poured a third. "It suits me well enough. Nothing else works quite so well."

"For what?"

He gave her a long forbidding stare. She began to think he would not answer. At last, staring into the flames, he answered. "To drive away the megrims."

She watched as he brought the decanter to the bench and dropped down upon it again. She caught her skirts to move them aside.

He did not miss the motion. His mouth curled in anger and self-contempt. He knew how he must appear to her. His scars, his patch, his sunburnt skin. So fearsome that she could not even bear to touch him.

He lifted the foul "sherry" and toasted her. Damn her and her father to hell!

He set the decanter on the hearth and leaned toward her, thrusting his disfigurement into her face. His mouth twisted, leering. "Mustn't have any megrims now. Madam Wife, won't you join me in a toast to what will soon become our wedding night?"

She flinched.

His mouth twisted as he looked away.

Then grimly she smiled. "That's right. It is our wedding night. Certainly I'll drink with you if you want me to. You go ahead and drink that and then pour some more for us both."

He stared at her suspiciously as he drank the rest of the glass.

He must have gotten very drunk, because he could no longer feel the pain in his head. That was how Robin knew how drunk he was. His bride— Where was she? For that matter, where was he?

In bed. In a welter of sweaty covers. He rolled over. His stomach revolved. The room spun. He thrust his leg out and planted his foot firmly on the floor to still the rocking motion.

When his stomach had quieted, he opened his eyes, concentrating on a crack in the ceiling, visible by the glow from the fire. When it no longer wavered and dimmed, he carefully raised himself to a sitting position. Someone had partially undressed him. His shirt was open at the throat, his feet were bare as the cold seeping up his ankle told him. Coat and stock, shoes and hose were gone.

He had no valet. Perhaps the innkeeper—

His wife—

He fell back. *God.* He was so confused. The drink must have been more poisonous than he had suspected. She had been right. She had been drinking with him. Or had she? She—*Where was she?*

His right hand patted the bed beside him. Empty. He thought to call her name. *What the deuce was it? Nora? No. No—uh.*

He tried to speak, but his tongue was dry and his throat hurt. He must have been sleeping with his mouth open.

Damn! Cautiously, he looked around him. A wingback chair had been pulled up to the end of the bench in front of the fire. He assumed the figure that lay upon it was his wife. She lay under a blanket, her head and shoulders rested in the chair-seat hidden behind the padded arms.

While he was considering whether to roll over and go back to sleep, she stirred, tried to turn herself over, and almost fell off the narrow bench. With a muffled exclamation she dragged herself back and struggled to arrange her limbs.

"Come to bed," he called hoarsely.

The figure went very still.

"Come to bed. You'll be warmer."

No answer.

"I know you're awake. Don't make me come and get you."

Noelle raised herself until she could peer over the arm of the chair. Her face was in shadows, but he could see light reflecting in her eyes.

"You'll be more comfortable."

She hesitated. "No, I won't."

56

"The bed is really surprisingly good." He patted it lightly.

She placed a slender hand on the chair arm. "As good as the 'sherry?' "

"Considering my condition, I'd say it's inestimably better."

"Thank you, but I'm quite comfortable here. I'll just stay here for the rest of the night. That way I won't bother you. I've been tending the fire, you know. And anyway, it's almost time to get up. I know you'll want to make an early—"

"Come to bed." He interrupted the nervous babbling.

A silence. Then, "No."

"Did you tell me 'no?' "

She hesitated. He could hear her draw a breath. "I don't intend to sleep with you."

He was over the edge of the bed in an instant, the covers falling away. Three swift strides carried him to the fire.

Before his charge, she fell back, tumbled off the bench, landing hard on her backside on the hearth stones, crying out in pain. Her skirts as well as her blanket fell onto the glowing coals. Swooping down, he caught them and pulled them back before they could scorch.

Twisting like a cat, she tried to scramble away, but she had no place to scramble. The bench and chair pulled so close to the hearth for warmth, now blocked her escape. He hung above her, his single eye blazing, his teeth bared in a mocking smile. Placing his knee on the bench, he caught her arm and hoisted her to her feet. Their

57

faces were on the same level inches apart.

He bared his teeth in a snarl. "Come—to—bed!"

She swallowed, her eyes wide and frightened, her teeth clenched. "I-I'm warm here by the fire."

"You'll be warmer." He swept her up in his arms, swung her over the bench, and strode back to the bed.

"No. Let me go. Put me down." She doubled her fists and hit at him. Once upon a time her feeble blows could have done him no damage, but his body was different now. One fist struck him full on the black patch. Pain streaked through him.

With a curse he dropped her.

She fell half on the bed, half off, and rolled away while he clapped one hand to his head and fumbled for the bedpost with the other. Cursing steadily, he lowered himself to the mattress. Through a red haze of pain, he heard her voice.

He felt her hand on his shoulder. "I'm sorry. Oh, I'm sorry."

"Damn you!" he whispered. He heard her gasp, a rustling movement. Then when he opened his eye, his wife was back across the room, standing with her hands crossed in front of her. Her expression was anguished. "I'm sorry. I'm truly sorry. I didn't mean to hurt you."

He pressed his forehead into the palm. The wound had settled to a steady throb. She had effectively destroyed the numbness that the vile liquor had won for him. He lifted his head and cursed her.

Her face turned white at the flat viciousness of his words. She ran to the pitcher and poured water in the basin. Wringing out a cloth, she came to him. "W-will this help?"

"No!" He slapped the rag out of her hand and caught her by the wrist. When she screamed and struggled, he lunged up and caught her other wrist. Twisting them, behind her, he dragged her in against his length.

"Nothing will help until you and I, Madam Wife, come to an understanding this minute."

"Please—"

"When I tell you to come to bed, I mean for you to do that. Now you can come gently and sweetly. You can lie down beside me and sleep in warmth and comfort, instead of falling off the damned bench and catching your stupid little rear on fire. Or you can be brought to the bed as I intend to do in just a minute."

"No, please—"

"You are my wife, and you seem to believe that you can hit me and hurt me."

"No," she protested frantically. "I didn't mean to hurt you."

"This is the second time you have struck me. If you think I'll allow the moment to pass, you're sadly mistaken."

He gathered her tighter against him. Her breasts were crushed against his chest, her belly against his belly. Her face, white and anguished, was only inches below his own.

"Sadly mistaken," he repeated.

He kissed her, brutally, dropping his mouth down on her soft lips with punishing force. Then thrusting his tongue between her teeth and driving deep for the back of her mouth, he strangled her protests.

Her chest heaved as she struggled to drag air into her lungs. Pitiful mewing sounds reached his ears.

When he reckoned that she was aching for breath, he pulled his mouth away. "If I want to kiss you, I'll kiss you."

Tears trickled down her cheeks. Her mouth trembled.

"If I want to touch you, I'll touch you."

She did not divine his intent even when he grasped both slender wrists in one long hand. Only when the other hand closed over her breast and squeezed, did she cry out in shock.

"And if I want to do more, I'll do more."

He left her breast to thrust his hand between the buttons and down to the jointure of her thighs. When she opened her mouth, he kissed her again not quite so hard as before, but longer, taking his time, caressing her shocked body with his fingers, digging the heel of his hand into her belly.

Suddenly, all the resistance went out of her. Her knees buckled and her head fell back on her shoulders.

Tucking her under his arm, he carried her not to the bed but back to the chair. There he deposited her, with her legs straddling the bench. She was not unconscious he noted. Her eyes were slitted as her head rolled on her shoulders. He tapped her cheek. "Lesson's over. Tell me what you've learned."

She kept her eyes closed and her body limp.

"Then I'll tell you what you've learned." He bent over with his face closed to hers. "If I wanted to rip your clothes off—" Here he pulled her skirt and petticoats up and pushed his hand against her mound. "I could make you my wife in fact as well as in name. You couldn't do a thing to stop me. And you would be hurt."

He moved his hand sensuously against her. She groaned and pressed her thighs together. "Open your eyes."

Her nostrils dilated as she sucked in a trembling breath, then she raised her eyelids.

He grinned menacingly, baring white teeth in his dark-skinned face. "I was the only person truly hurt in this little skirmish, Madam Wife. You hit me—"

"I'm—" She gasped.

He moved his hand so his fingers slid between her legs and rotated slowly. "—and I'll undoubtedly spend the rest of the night unable to sleep."

She gave a wordless cry of protest, but he pressed harder. "I swear to you, I'll never be the only person hurt again. If you strike me, I'll strike back. And you'll get much worse than you can ever give. Do you believe that?"

She nodded.

"What's more I could stand a better chance of sleeping if I buried myself in your sweet body." He sank his fingers deeper into her. "Do you believe that?"

"Yes." Her voice quavered.

He took his hand away and straightened wearily. "Good. Now, I'm going to drink from that decanter until I've had enough to get back into that bed and sleep. You can do whatever it pleases you to do. If your skirt catches fire and you are consumed in flames, try to hold your screams to a minimum."

Trembling with reaction and seething with indignation did not make for a restful night, Noelle discovered. Moreover, her rear end ached from falling off the bench onto the hearth. Her mouth from nose to chin was scraped raw by her husband's beard stubble. She probably had bruises on her wrists and around her waist where he had held her and lugged her around like a load of laundry. And most awful was the burning, tingling between her legs.

She shuddered. Never mind that he had probably kept her skirt from catching fire. His command had caused her to fall in the first place. Acute frustration rode her hard. While he had not precisely hurt her, he had handled her against her will.

In effect he had punished her with his kisses and his handling. She shuddered again and clenched her fists. A lifetime of being treated like a child stretched before her.

Her husband groaned softly and turned over to face the wall. He had finally drunk enough to put him into a fitful sleep. Still as a statue, she listened while he tossed and groaned, muttered, and once cursed.

Eyes burning with resentment, she stared at the mound beneath the covers.

A sliver of daylight slipped between the shutters. Moving silently, she went to the window and positioned her eye so she could look out. The cold, gray day was like the one before. They would drive for ten or twelve hours and then seek rest in another uncomfortable inn. Unless they reached her husband's estates. She wondered how far they had to go to reach them—and what condition they were in. If her ten thousand pounds had been spent to get them out of debt, they probably were neither well kept nor profitable.

Suddenly, she was struck with resolve. She would run away.

She could not stay here. No matter where she ran to, it could not be worse than what she had been subjected to the first night of her marriage. She had her jewelry and some money. Not much, but a little to start her on her way in the opposite direction.

He probably would not follow her. Why should he, when he already had her money? If she could only think of someone who would take her in, even for a few hours. Unfortunately, everyone she knew lived on Averill's estate. None there could help her, even if they would. Her mother had been French, orphaned by the Terror. Both her governesses had gone into service to other families and she had never heard from them again.

In the bed her husband coughed and groaned.

She sighed. Her choices were grim. She could remain with Robin Whittcombstone, subject to his ruthless domination. Or she could seek employment that would allow her to live apart.

Mentally, she took stock of her prospects. She could read and write in three languages. She could calculate sums of money. She had been Averill's nominal hostess for several years, his servants answerable to her. She could write her own references.

Very little to bank on, but together they might get her a position as a companion to an elderly woman or a governess or — as a last resort — a housekeeper.

The morning light was strengthening.

Glancing at the figure on the bed, she smiled grimly. She prided herself on not being a fool. As of now, he was the worst thing ever to happen to her. In the end, he might be the least. If all else failed, she would reserve enough money to pay the fare to return to her husband.

The innyard was astir. Animals were being fed and groomed and harnessed. Food for breakfast was being prepared in the kitchen. The coaches of guests who planned to depart early were being brought round.

She paused uncertainly. Her mother's mare was in the stable. Dared she have the animal brought round? On her back she could ride for miles.

Regretfully she discarded the idea. The mare was old and unused to more than a short canter through the meadow. She would have to abandon the animal to an uncertain fate long before she reached her destination.

No, she had no choice. She would have to walk.

No one noticed her as she picked her way across the hard-frozen expanse of ruts and clods. With the hood of her traveling cloak pulled over her head, she passed through the gate and out onto the frozen road, all fresh and untrammeled beneath a covering of new-fallen snow.

Nervousness goaded her. She broke into a run away from the inn, away from her husband, Averill's cruel choice. Heart pounding, skirts flying, cloak flapping behind her, she rounded one corner and then another. The inn disappeared behind the trees.

Finally, out of breath, she staggered to a halt, her chest heaving, her breath fogging before her face. Her lungs were on fire from the icy air she had sucked into them. She dropped her portmanteau in the snow and bent over it. One hand was braced on her knees. The other hugged the brass studded jewel case to her chest. After a couple of minutes, she raised her head.

Free! She flung back her head and laughed in great sobbing bursts of sound. Free!

Her exultation was shortlived. She began to shiver with cold. Her run had left her covered with perspiration. The prevailing wind penetrated her clothing, chilling her to the bone. She pulled the cloak around her and tossed one end over her shoulder to ensure that it would stay closed around her.

Then fumbling in its folds, she lifted the portmanteau and began to walk steadily. She would walk until a coach came by. She would flag it down and pay the fare for London. While she rested during the ride, she would make her next plan.

Four

Two hours later, Noelle stood on the edge of the road in snow above her boottops. More light snow sifted down in fluffy flakes that settled from time to time on her brows and lashes. It settled on the shoulders of her cloak. It filled her hood where it lay on her shoulders, blown there by the prevailing wind. It crusted the wool scarf she had wound around her head for warmth. She shifted from one foot to the other wondering how long before her toes began to freeze.

The sky was nothing but a vault of gray clouds so thick she could not guess where the sun was. The prevailing wind blew down the road directly in her face as she walked. Tears had frozen on her eyelashes and cheeks. She could not feel the tip of her nose.

Where were the coaches that were supposed to run daily between London and the outlying shires? One should have come along before now if it expected to reach any destination at a decent hour.

Utterly miserable, she sneezed violently and set

down her portmanteau to shift her jewel box from one arm to the other. She flexed her fingers and looked at them ruefully. Her thin kid gloves were providing almost no protection. Both hands felt frozen from fingertips to wrist. When she tried to pick up the portmanteau, she had to look at her hand to watch her fingers wrap around the handle.

Suddenly, she was afraid. She was so very cold. If a coach did not come along soon, she might suffer from frostbite. She pressed her chapped lips together tightly. Frostbite was not the only danger. If one did not come along soon, she might freeze.

To death, her mind added sternly. *To death* . . .

In an effort to restore circulation, she set her burdens down and began swinging her arms about her body and slapping her hands against her thighs. So intent was she on her efforts that she was not aware of the dark figure galloping out of the whiteness. The newfallen snow muffled the steel-shod hooves until he was almost upon her. When she did hear them, she swung around eagerly.

"Oh, no-o-o—"

The horseman slowed his mount to a canter. In his right hand he carried a riding crop of braided leather. He lifted it as he approached.

At the expression on his face, she staggered back stumbling over her bag. Her mind screamed, *Run for your life!,* but common sense told her that she had no possibility of escape on foot from a man on horseback. He could easily ride her down. From the expression on his face, she could guess he would take great offense if he had to do so. Noelle wrapped her arms around her jewel box and waited. Her violent shivering was not entirely the result of the icy wind.

When Robin saw she was waiting for him, he slowed his mare to a measured walk and let the animal come on until its nose was within a foot of his small wife. The animal's white breath fanned her cheeks as it tossed its head impatiently.

She tilted her head to one side and managed a tight smile. "I've always believed in a morning constitutional."

He regarded her in silence for a moment. Then he leaned over to pat the mare's neck. "I agree. However, I prefer riding to walking."

"Then you may continue your ride and I will continue my walk."

"You're going in the wrong direction, Madam Wife."

Her raw throat made her voice raspy. "No. I think I am going in the right direction. I just hadn't planned on walking this far."

He turned his good eye toward her feet which she could not keep still. "I wonder how much farther you'd have gotten. The snow's getting heavier and you've left the main road."

"What?" She looked around her incredulously.

With a wave of his riding crop, he indicated the way they had come. "A half mile back, the road turned. You kept going straight."

"But—but—"

"It matters little, of course. The mail coach hadn't arrived when I left the inn, and most of the travelers have decided to remain another day. The roads are expected to become impassable. If there had been traffic, I might have lost your tracks."

She hugged her jewel box tighter. Not only her nose but her lips were growing numb. "I suppose I'm lucky then."

"Very lucky." The horse stamped and tossed its head. "Another hour and you'd be in serious trouble. This is the old road my coachman was advised to beware of. Your tracks followed it. But if the snow had been heavier, I might have lost them. You might have walked until you fell—" He stared at her snow-covered figure. "—and froze to death."

She wanted to weep. So much effort. So much discomfort. All for nothing. She lifted her chin. "I understand freezing's not such a bad death."

"Young men who died that way in the Pyrenees thought differently."

"Perhaps they had no one to run away from."

"The French army," he remarked dryly. He lifted the reins. "Shall I leave you, Madam Wife?"

She hesitated. Blinking the snow from her lashes, she looked up into her husband's face. Despite the polite conversation he was furiously angry. His unshaven black jaw was clenched so tightly that a muscle quivered involuntarily in his cheek. The single black eye glittered.

"Answer me," he said softly.

Defeated, she closed her eyes. "No, don't leave me."

"Please."

She was too tired to resist. "Please. I'll come with you."

His right hand released the braided leather whip. It dangled from his wrist.

She shuddered. "Evidently I gave the right answer."

"I should whip you soundly." He reined the mare to stand broadside to her. "Perhaps I will later." He freed his foot from the stirrup and leaned from the saddle. "Take my hand!"

Picking up her portmanteau, she held aloft the jewel box. "You'll have to hold this until I get up?"

Silently, he tucked it under his other arm. Then with terrifying strength and efficiency, he drew her up into his lap. Once there, she sought the box, but he shook his head. "I can carry this."

"Thank you." She wrapped her frozen arms around her portmanteau and tried to sit erect.

His hard arms encircled her, pressing her slim body back against his.

"I can balance," she protested. "I'm accounted a good horsewoman."

"You'll keep us both warm." He reined his horse around and spurred it with unusual force. It sprang forward. Snow spurted from beneath its hooves as it galloped back the way Noelle had come.

In the innyard, Robin halted the horse beside the coach. The team was already harnessed. The coachman stood glumly holding their heads.

"I thought you said it was too bad to travel."

"I said *others* thought it was too bad to travel."

"But not you."

His teeth flashed in what was not a grin. "Not I. We leave immediately. I believe there's a necessary house out behind the stable if you want to make use of it. I suggest you do. With the late start, we won't be stopping again."

She flushed in embarrassment. "I—I would prefer to use the privacy of our room."

"I've already given up the room, Madam Wife. Go take care of your business and come back. We've wasted the better part of the morning."

"Milord—" she protested.

But he let go of her waist. Before she knew what was happening, she was sliding down. Her frozen feet slammed into the ground. Excruciating pains shot all the way to her knees. To save herself from falling, she dropped the portmanteau and clutched her husband's booted calf.

The horse shied, dragging her backward off balance. Her hands slipped. She fell heavily, sprawling full length on her back in the filthy snow and mire of the innyard.

"Damnation!"

From his position atop the horse, Whittcombstone grinned at the oath as well as the expression on her face as she pulled her hands out of the muck.

She caught the look. Her overcharged feelings exploded. "Damn you. Damn you. Damn you!" Her voice began low, but it rose to a shout. "How dare you drop me like that and then grin about it!" She scrambled to her feet, no easy task in the slippery mess. At her first step, her boot slid crazily. "You—you brute!"

Her garments, now soiled as well as wet, flapped crazily. The mare rolled a white eye and sidled away

71

as Noelle struggled to reach them. Robin gave a short bark of laughter.

His laugh drove every speck of good humor from her. She had been under an inordinate strain for the last twenty-four hours. She had had little sleep and no breakfast. Her escape attempt had ended in failure. Now came the final humiliation. The thin shell of her temper cracked.

"Don't you laugh at me!" With clenched fists she flung herself after the horse and pummeled at her husband's hard-muscled thigh. "You, beast! Beast! Monster!"

"Stop that, Madam. Get hold of yourself!" Tightening the rein as his mount half rose and buck jumped, the Earl shook his foot free of the stirrup and straightened his leg. The movement had the effect of propelling his Countess backward. The backs of her knees struck her portmanteau.

Down she went a second time. This time when she tried to save herself, her cloak tripped her up and she tumbled sideways. Her arm, shoulder and one side of her face all made contact with the ground.

She heard a man's chuckle, another's snort. Pushing herself to a sitting position, she shot a look over her shoulder to chill steel. The snort changed to a cough.

"Oh, the poor thing," a feminine voice shrilled. "Gi' 'er a hand, Jake."

Embarrassed, humiliated, hating herself and the Earl, she reached out a gloved hand. Dark brown mud oozed between her fingers. She could feel it caked on her cheek. Face flaming, she snatched the hand back and pushed herself up to her knees.

The innyard had suddenly filled with onlookers. Avid curiosity and not a few leers lighted the faces of ostlers, innkeeper, chamber maids, the Earl's coachman, and various other individuals who had moved quickly to the doors and windows to peer out. Not often did they get the chance to see the quality off their high horses.

The Earl had dismounted and come round his horse's head. He shook his head, his mouth curving with laughter. Instead of coming to her aid, he extended his riding whip. "Catch hold."

Noelle's scream of rage practically beneath the mare's nose, brought the big black head up. White eye rolling, it whinnied and reared.

"Damn! Steady, girl!" The Earl grabbed for the bridle as his wife scrambled to her feet.

Slipping and sliding through the slimy mess, she launched herself at him, while he struggled to hold the alarmed horse. The force of her body, her pummeling fists striking him in cheek and neck, and the violent shying of the animal knocked Robin sideways. His feet slipped out from under him. A sharp tug on the bridle jerked him forward as the horse strained backward. Before he could catch himself, he had measured his length in the mud beneath the animal's hooves.

Noelle felt a thrill of triumph. He would learn that she gave as good as she got. No one was going to kick her down in the mud and get away free.

Even as the thought warmed her, she felt the unnatural stillness of the innyard. A woman rolling around in the mud while her husband laughed was

73

one thing. A black-coated Earl with an eyepatch and a nasty temper was quite another.

The coachman sprang forward to bring down the horse. He carefully avoided looking at either the lord or his lady as he caught the beast's cheek strap and muttered in its ear.

So angry he was rendered speechless, Robin placed his hands beneath his shoulders and pushed himself up. The mud squeezed up between every gloved finger. His only pair of gloves were ruined. A low rumbling came out of his throat.

Despite the sound, Noelle planted her fists on her hips. "Not nearly so funny when it happens to you, is it?"

One of the chambermaids squawked in disbelief. Several of the observers were seen to shake their heads. Those closest moved back.

The Earl literally sprang off the ground. "It was never funny, Madam Wife, except that you made it so with your clumsiness."

"I was never clumsy. You dropped me." She looked around her for help, but the coachman led the mare behind the carriage.

The crowd of onlookers hastily dispersed. One of the serving maids crossed herself piously as she darted back into the inn.

Robin caught his wife by her upper arms and lifted her until her face was scant inches from his. "Listen to me. For the third time in the first twenty-four hours of our marriage, you have caused me trouble. First, you strike me."

"I didn't mean to."

"Then, you freeze me half to death."

"You didn't have to come after me."

"And now you knock me into the mud."

"You laughed at me. I lost my temper." She gulped and swallowed hard. He looked mad enough to eat her alive. "I guess we do look funny—to each other."

"This is all you fault!" he roared. He shook her. "Isn't it? Isn't it?"

She twisted, trying to get free. She had never seen even her father so angry. "Yes. I suppose so. I'm—sorry."

"You're going to be."

She could feel the dampness from his gloves soaking through her sleeves. Both of them were filthy and wet. She managed a tremulous smile. "Perhaps we ought to go back into the inn. We could get dry and I could brush off our things."

He snarled wordlessly.

She might have been a doll, so easily did he swing her around and thrust her body against the open doorway of the carriage. The step caught her under the knees and her hips struck the edge. "Wait! Stop! What? Listen!"

The Earl's black-coated arm swept behind her legs and lifted. Furiously he tipped her up and stuffed her bodily in between the seats.

She let out an outraged shriek.

The ostler cowered behind the open door. The coachman peered round from the back where he had stayed to tie up the Earl's horse. Each man in turn received the full blast of Whittcombstone's volcanic eye.

"Get this rattletrap moving!"

"Yes, sir." The coachman dashed back around to the other side of coach to pull himself onto the box.

The Earl swung into the interior flinging himself onto the seat and swinging his feet above his wife's struggling body.

" 'Ope y've enjoyed yer stay." The ostler tugged at his forelock as he folded up the step.

"Shut the damned door!"

"Yessir."

The coach lurched out of the innyard.

Frantically, Noelle struggled and clawed to right herself. Her body was crumpled into a ball wedged between the seats. Her muddy skirts and petticoats flapped over her head, blinding and muffling her.

The Earl propped his booted feet onto the seat, crossed his arms over his chest, and glared down pitilessly at the welter of flailing arms and legs, muddy boots and petticoat ruffles, and quite a lot of white cotton pantalettes edged with Irish lace.

The coach swayed and jolted across the frozen ruts. From beneath the confusion came muffled grunts and unintelligible exclamations.

When Noelle tried to bring her legs down, they encountered the Earl's stretched across between the seats. She went silent and still. Then one hand fumbled and found a hold. She drew her knees up to her chest. Unfortunately, she was in the process of pushing her legs under her husband's when the coachman sprang the horses.

Noelle was tossed back again. Her head thudded against the door. The word that she uttered at that particular time was extremely foul.

Robin allowed his mouth to turn up at the corners in a faint smirk of satisfaction. Then he glanced down at himself. Too late he remembered the mud on his gloves. He pulled his hands out and stared at the palms. A filthy mess!

Lip curling, he stripped off the gloves while his eyes ran down the front of his body. His buckskins were muddy. The front of his coat, likewise. His boots were probably the only thing salvageable, and he would have to work long and hard at them.

His anger kindled again. He did not own many garments. Someone would have to be sent to his rooms in London to bring his things, for his stuff at Whitby was nearly five years old. What he wore, deplorable condition and all, he would probably have to make do with for several days. He scowled down at the struggling figure, just as she managed to pull herself to an upright position.

"Damnation!" Noelle pushed her muddy hair out of her eyes. Her filthy skirts were bunched around her waist. Her pantalettes reached down to the tops of her dirty boots. Trembling with reaction, she took stock of herself. Then she looked up at the Earl.

Wordlessly, they stared at each other. Then she reached over and pulled a lump of mud from the top of his boot.

His glare should have blistered her skin.

She cleared her throat. "We'll probably laugh about this someday."

"If we live that long," her husband replied with heavy sarcasm. "I've come to believe that sometime within the next fortnight, I will murder you and then be hanged at Tyburn for the crime."

She pushed herself up and eased herself onto the seat opposite him. She hated to ride backwards, but at that minute farther from him was better. The road leveled out and the horses settled down to a steady pace.

She cleared her throat. "I truly am sorry about last night. I didn't mean to hit you. I was just—er—just—"

"Trying to drive me away."

"Yes."

"But I had a right to be there," he countered coldly. "And you had made a bargain."

She was silent. Tentatively, she patted her toes around on the floor until she found a hot brick. Robin pulled his hat over his eyes again and shifted into a more comfortable position on the seat.

"If you had just let me go this morning," Noelle began again, "none of this ever would have happened. I would be on my way to London and—"

"And I would not be listening to this." He lifted his hat and scowled.

She ignored his angry expression. "The way I see this is that you brought what happened on yourself."

"I fail to see how," he remarked nastily, "but I'm sure you're going to explain."

She nodded. "The marriage was in the nature of a financial transaction. Averill paid your outstanding debts. With my money, I might add. In exchange you were to take care of me. But I have no wish to be taken care of." She smiled ingenuously. "So I absolve you of your responsibility."

He looked at her for almost a full minute. Beneath her eyes were dark circles of exhaustion. Her hair straggled down around her mud-daubed cheeks. Her cloak and skirts were stiff with filth. She might have been a waif prowling the alleys of London — or a beggar roaming the streets of Lisbon. He tossed her the laprobe from the seat beside him. "Settle down and go to sleep."

Stung by his lack of response to what she considered to be a handsome offer she tossed the robe aside. "Listen to me. There's no need to continue this charade any longer. Averill certainly won't want the money back. You can just let me off at the nearest posting station."

Burrowing his shoulder deeper into the corner of the coach, he uncrossed and recrossed his booted ankles.

Noelle flounced back. "I want you to stop this coach and let me out."

"Be quiet."

"Oh, heaven forfend that I should disturb your nap." She leaned forward and tapped on his ankle. "If you'll just think a minute, you'll see—"

His booted foot hit the floor with a thud. Her eyes grew wide as he set his mouth in a thin line. His hands worked at his throat, untied the carelessly knotted swath of linen, and pulled it from his neck.

Her hands fluttered toward her own neck. "What are you going to do?"

"What I should have done the instant this journey started."

"What — ? Stop!"

He caught her wrists and looped the cravat around one wrist and then the other.

"How dare you? Don't be ridiculous. Let me go!"

"Oh, how I wish I could." His sarcasm was so heavy that his voice was a growl. "But since I can't, I intend to make the best of it."

"You can't — "

A couple of quick twists and the cloth was knotted securely.

"This is the nineteenth century," she sputtered.

For answer he pulled the ends through the leather strap beside the window and tied them again around her wrists.

"You can't mean to keep me like this?" She was aghast.

"Someone has reared you very badly. You lack discipline. And you have a distressing habit of striking out at your betters."

She lifted her chin and delivered the haughtiest stare of which she was capable. "Let me go."

"You hit me and knocked me into the mud."

She opened her mouth to protest.

He held up one finger. "I excuse you for that. You were provoked. But you haven't kept your hands to yourself since you climbed onto that seat. Nor have you used your head instead of your mouth."

"Bully." She thrust the word in when he paused for breath. "Bully. Brute."

He held up a hand. "I'm not warning you again. Not another word! I'm exhausted. My head aches like fury. Thanks to you, I'll be forced to travel all day in wet, filthy clothing. I've learned from long experience that the only thing to do under these circumstances is sleep. And that is what I intend to do."

"Monster."

"If I hear one more word of protest from you for the remainder of the trip, I shall gag you. Do you hear me?"

She did not acknowledge either the threat or the question. Her face was scarlet with anger. She twisted her hands, madly pulling at the linen and jerking against the strap. The knots tightened from her efforts.

"If you don't stop that you'll cut off your circulation."

"Beast!"

"Quiet," he warned. Reaching into his pocket, he pulled out a flask, uncapped it, and took a long drink of brandy.

Unable to do more than cause herself problems, she sank back, exhausted by her efforts. Her chin set grimly. "I swear I'll turn you over to the proper authorities the first chance I get."

"No authorities will interfere between a husband and wife," he replied loftily. He swirled the flask in his hand, warming it before he took another swallow of brandy. "No wonder your father was so anxious to be rid of you."

"No more than I was to be rid of him."

He threw her a calculating look. "You'll pardon me if I find that sour grapes."

She leaned forward again as far as her hands would allow. "Just set me loose," she hissed. "Be rid of me. You, of all people, don't need to be burdened with responsibilities."

He capped the flask and dropped it back into his pocket. "You aren't going to be that much of a problem."

"What do you mean?"

He considered her a moment, then lifted his feet back onto the seat. "Nothing."

"What do you mean?" she demanded.

"One of the stipulations in the contract was that you are never to appear in London."

She slumped back. Her breath escaped her in a long sigh. "And, of course, you intend to abide by those stipulations."

"You certainly have given me no reason to do otherwise. I intend to deposit you at Whitby and go on about my business."

She subsided glumly for a minute. The coach rolled on. Robin could feel his muscles beginning to relax.

She started up again enthusiastically. "All right then. Don't you see you have a perfect out? You can easily let me go. You'll never have to account to him. My presence or absence from your life won't be remarked on." She leaned forward, tugging at the strap. "Oh, don't you see."

Angrily, her husband sat up on the seat across from her. His hard right hand gripped her chin while his left fumbled in the pocket of his coat. "I told you to keep quiet," he reminded her. "I said if I heard one more word of protest from you, I would gag you."

"No. No. I'll keep quiet."

"Why don't I believe that? Open up."

She clamped her lips together. "Nu-uh."

"Yes." He pinched her nose.

When she opened her mouth to breathe, he stuffed his pocket handkerchief between her jaws muffling a shriek of anger.

She pushed at it with her tongue, but he stuffed it back in with his fingers and held it with his thumb. Her eyes promised dire punishments, but he only laughed.

"Now. If you try to work that out of your mouth, I'll tie it in place and make you much more uncomfortable than you are at present. Do you believe me?"

He felt her make the effort to nod her head against his hand.

He took his thumb away. "I intend to sleep until we stop for lunch. While you are riding along in silence, I suggest you forget all this nonsense about running away somewhere and contemplate your future duties as my wife and chatelaine of all my possessions."

She made one more violent effort at the neckcloth and only succeeded in tightening it further. She thought about spitting out the gag except that she knew that her husband would do exactly what he promised. Behind it, however, she called him every terrible name she had ever heard and then started through the list again.

He raised his eyebrows at the sight of the pure rage in her eyes. Then with a grin he wrapped his arms more firmly across his chest and sank back into his corner.

Finally, she subsided. She was acutely uncomfortable, but her husband was paying no attention to her. At last she settled herself as best she could and closed her eyes. Seconds after she closed her eyes, she was asleep.

Robin raised the brim of his hat. Stealthily, he reached forward and tugged on the tip of the handkerchief until it came out from between her jaws. Noelle stirred, murmured something, and closed her lips. He loosened her hands from the strap.

Limp as a ragdoll, she slumped across the seat. He guided her head onto his thigh. With a sigh she folded her hands beneath her chin.

His hand dropped naturally to rest on her shoulder. He stared into the gloom of the carriage. She was a handful and foolishly fearless. He had commanded men like her. Either they died in battle or they emerged heroes.

He supposed that battle fury was the result of having been reared by a crazy man. She acted spoiled, used to having her own way. Yet clearly she was opposed to this marriage. Probably she had shown her temper once to often to Averill and he had determined to be rid of his true match in unpleasantness.

The road curved. North wind struck the side of the carriage and whistled around the door. Noelle shivered and drew up her knees.

Robin sighed and reached for the laprobe. He tossed it over her body and tucked the ends around them both. Then he settled back in his corner pulling his hat down over his eyes.

The ride was going to be long and unpleasant. He had never been more sober.

Five

Whitby Manor crouched dark and uninviting in the late afternoon. Torrents of ivy cascading from the walls made it look like a woolly black box between the gray sky and the white snow.

Robin had pulled aside the curtain. Noelle leaned closer to him and stared silently at what was only slightly larger than an ordinary country house. Robin scowled as he let the curtain fall. His wife turned her head to look up into his face. Their stares locked. A muscle twitched in his scarred cheek. "You may speak."

"You are too kind." She sat back, her smile saccharine sweet. "Your house is — er — impressive."

The eyebrow above the good eye lifted sardonically.

"That is to say old," she added. She paused delicately. "I would guess that so much ivy takes a long time to grow."

Deep in his throat the lord of the manor made a noise that might have been a chuckle — or it might have been a growl.

The vehicle lurched to a halt. Both its occupants sat perfectly still for several seconds letting the blessed stillness seep into their bones after the jolting ride.

"I'm going to instruct the coachman to drive this coach around to the back of the stables and burn it," Robin declared fervently.

"A wise decision."

The man under discussion swung down off the box and climbed the steps to rap smartly on the front door with the butt of his whip. The lathered horses stood with heads hanging, white fog breath puffing from their distended nostrils. Their driver waited a minute then rapped again.

"Is anyone home?" Noelle whispered.

Robin shrugged. "A caretaker and his wife should be around somewhere."

"Elderly?"

He hesitated, trying to remember. "Yes, I suppose so."

"Maybe they've died."

He shot her a look of annoyance. The coachman knocked again.

"Who's there?"

A voice so old that it quavered and cracked twice on each word that came from behind the door.

"The Earl of Whitby," the coachman called.

"The Earl's dead. Go 'way."

Noelle did not quite conceal the spurt of laughter behind her hand. Her husband's look turned vitriolic before he reached through the window to grasp the handle of the door. He pushed it open so violently that it banged back against the cab.

"He's probably talking about my father," he informed her.

"I'm sure." She nodded primly.

She winced as her husband kicked down the step and climbed out onto the slippery stones of the drive. Mounting to the door, he snatched the whip from the coachman and banged with all his strength on the panel. "I'm not dead, damn you! Blivens?!"

The coachman retreated down the steps to hold out his hand to Noelle, who found herself almost too stiff to negotiate her own descent.

"Blivens!!"

Rusted locks grated, the door creaked open reluctantly. A heavyset man with a bald pate held a lamp aloft. His rheumy eyes opened wide at the sight of the Earl. "Is — it — milord?"

Each word was spaced as if to utter it required the utmost difficulty. "Milord?" quavered into three syllables the last of which rose and cracked at the end.

"Yes, it's milord," Robin said rudely, pushing the door open wide.

"B-but — we heard you were dead. I'm almost sure — "

"You heard wrong." The Earl growled in his throat more at the darkness and dankness of the hall than at the incompetence of the servant. "Is there a room with a fire?"

"A fire? I — Not tonight, milord." The old man shook his head. "No, not tonight. No one's expected."

"Light one. Light several. In several rooms."

"Tonight, milord?"

"Yes, tonight. For God's sake."

He turned to catch sight of his wife climbing the steps on the arm of the coachman. He strode to meet her and help her into the hall. "Blivens, this is my wife, my new bride, I might add, Lady Noelle."

Blivens looked stunned. "B-bride? Then you're—er—not—dead, milord."

"No, Blivens. Not dead." Robin was cursing under his breath as he opened the door and led his wife into a dark room, its furniture draped in dustcovers.

"Milord." Blivens trailed after them, a note of protest in his voice. "That's the best parlor."

"So I recall." Robin dragged the canvas off a chair. "Bring us some brandy," he said over his shoulder.

"B-brandy?"

Robin took the lamp from the servant. "Brandy. Or whatever restorative you might have on hand."

The caretaker hesitated. "Well, I don't—er—know. P-port, mayhap, mi—er—lord."

"Then bring it immediately."

The old man wrung his hands. "Without the light, milord—"

Both lord and lady gaped at him. Robin's face was a study in irritation mounting to rage. Noelle hastily glanced around her. A branching candelabra stood behind another cover that probably protected a couch. Stubs of candles remained in the sockets. "You may take the lamp—er—Bevens."

"Blivens, milady."

"Yes, Blivens. You may take the lamp with you

as soon as you have lighted the candles." She pointed to them.

Blivens looked helplessly at the candelabra and then the flame behind the lamp chimney. "Lighted the candles?"

"For God's sake!" Robin set the lamp on the table with unnatural force. Muttering unintelligibly, he strode around the couch. Noelle was thankful she could not understand his words as he twisted one of the longer stubs from the socket and, after some fumbling, lighted the wick. That accomplished, he turned back to Blivens, who was rubbing his hands together and hunching his shoulders against the cold.

Robin thrust the lamp back into his hands. "Is there anyone you can send to light a fire in here?"

Blivens stared at the floor while he appeared to be thinking. "Er—there's naught here, milord, but myself and Mrs. Blivens."

"What about yourself?"

Blivens shook his head as if he had not heard the question. "My wife's a sore trial t' me. Mayhap she'd get upset."

"I'll upset her." Robin ducked until he put himself in Blivens range of vision. "She has to rouse herself to fix us some supper."

"I don't know about herself gettin' up."

Robin caught the old man by the shoulder and straightened him up. "Go and tell her to get up, Blivens."

The old man nodded. He scratched his head uncertainly. "I suppose I—er—could light the fire, milord."

Robin sighed. "After you bring the port."

The old head kept nodding. "After I bring the port."

"And rouse your wife to fix supper."

"Yes, sir."

When Blivens would have turned toward the door, Robin put his hand on the bent shoulder. The light from the smoky lampchimney cast fearsome shadows on his face. "Be back in two minutes, Blivens."

"Two minutes." The voice trembled and quavered more than ever. "Yes, sir."

Noelle dropped into the uncovered chair and pulled her feet up under her. Her teeth were chattering. Of her husband she begged, "C-could you make the fire?"

"I could," he growled sweeping the darkness with an eye of fire. "If there's anything dry enough in here to make the fire with." His nostrils inhaled the dank air redolent of mildew and decay.

She blew on her gloved hands. "I think you'd better. We could freeze to death before he gets back."

Cursing viciously, her husband pushed back the fire screen and knelt with a candle. Unfortunately, like the rest of room, the tinder was damp. Each time it appeared to catch, it died when the candle was taken away. "Damned thing!"

"Shall I take a candle and see if I can find the kitchen?"

"No." At that moment the fire caught. Robin pulled back sharply, coughing as the smoke did not rise into the chimney.

Noelle uncurled from the chair and hurried to

his side. "Open the damper."

Hastily, he thrust the poker into the back of the fireplace. His action brought down a shower of black soot which threatened to smother the new blaze and sent a cloud of fine cinders into his face. He rocked back on his heels wiping at his eye and coughing.

They watched as the fire appeared to go out, smoldered, then blazed up, the smoke curling outside the fireplace and up into the room.

Noelle took the poker from his hand and reached inside. In the first pass, she found the hook and opened the damper. Still coughing, Robin knelt down and placed kindling in a practiced semi-circle. In a minute they both held out their hands thankfully.

"We did it," Noelle murmured.

Robin rocked back on his heels and levered himself up. "Yes, we did it."

Neither looked at the other. Instead they stared intently into the fire they had built together.

Before they actually saw Blivens, they heard him wheezing down the hall, his feet dragging. The door across the hall opened. "Milord?" the puzzled voice wheezed. "Milord? Now where did he go?"

Noelle burst into helpless laughter. Standing with her back to the fire, her skirts raised behind her, she saw her husband's shoulders shake.

Robin stood beside her draped over the mantel, his forehead braced on his arm, taking in the warmth by the lungful. He spoke without moving. "It's time to retire him."

She giggled again. Exhaustion and the bone-deep cold had produced a sort of hysteria. Everything seemed quite funny. "You can't retire him. You're dead."

He nodded with mock solemnity. "Death looks better and better."

"Mi-lo-ord!"

"In here, Blivens!"

Noelle tottered against Robin. "We should have tied a rope to his belt, so he could find his way back."

At that moment Blivens entered. "Er—I couldn't find any port, milord. The cellar's—um—empty."

His quavering voice coupled with the wronged expression on his face sent Noelle off into whoops of laughter.

Robin lifted himself off the mantel and turned to stare at the caretaker and shake his head. "My father had a well-stocked cellar five years ago."

Blivens set a tray down on top of the dustcover on a small table. "Really, sir. Don't—er—recall. Times—ah—gone by, milord." He sniffled and wiped his nose on his sleeve. "But Mrs. Blivens brews a bit of ale."

Robin growled low in his throat, but Noelle put her hand on his arm. "The ale is appreciated for now, Blivens. Perhaps we can find the cellar tomorrow, Milord."

"That'd be nice, Milady," the old man said vaguely.

"I'll murder him and heave his body into that cellar," Robin rumbled.

Blivens's chin began to quaver as his voice broke and cracked. "M-m-milord—"

Noelle put her hand on her husband's arm. "You must see how tired Lord Whittcombstone is, Blivens. I believe we'll have the ale later. For now just lead us to the kitchen?"

He shrugged. "Yes, ma'am, but Mrs. Blivens's not got much to fix."

"If you'll lead us there, perhaps I can help her put together something for us."

"You, milady?"

She gave him her sweetest smile. "Yes."

Blivens looked more alarmed than when the Earl had threatened to murder him. "But—"

"If my wife wishes to go to the kitchen," Robin interrupted, "lead her there immediately."

A strange party trailed out into the hall, through the dining room where the table and chairs pushed up too it, made a huge island of grayish white in the darkness, thence into a butler's pantry, through a narrow hall, and down a short flight of stairs.

As Blivens shuffled along, Noelle muttered out of the side of her mouth, "Do you know the way back in case he falls over dead?"

"We'll be able to follow our own trail in the dust."

Chuckling softly, she glanced back at her husband. The sight of his face sent her off into whoops again. He looked capable of the murder he had threatened and at the same time he looked totally perplexed as to whom to lash out at.

Daring greatly, she reached back to catch his hand. "We'll laugh about this someday."

"Someday I'll burn this place to the ground with Blivens in it."

The caretaker paused at the door and looked unhappily over his shoulder. "It's not fittin' for you to come in here, milady," he warned. "Cookin' be mucky work."

"That's true, Blivens," she nodded in mock sobriety, "but starving be mucky hard."

The old man laid his shoulder to the door which creaked inward.

Blissful warmth swept into their faces. They stepped into a big room, clean, well-lighted by a blazing fire in a huge fireplace. A slatternly woman, her gray hair straggling down her raddled cheeks, pushed herself up from a rocking chair beside it. "What'd y' bring 'em 'ere fer?"

The Earl's quick temper ignited instantly. "He brought us here, Mrs. Blivens, because my wife determined to come down and oversee the preparation of some food."

"There ain't no food. Just what Mr. Blivens and me eats." She rolled a walleye at the Earl. "Besides, 'ow do we know y're who y' say y' are? We 'eard the Earl 'as dead."

"Damnation!" Robin thundered. "Madam—"

Noelle stepped forward. "What you eat will be just fine, Mrs. Blivens. I assure you that this gentleman is the Earl of Whitby. He was wounded fighting for his country and has only just recovered sufficiently to come home."

"Well—"

Blivens shuffled forward, hands trembling. "He do sound a lot like the old Earl used to, Mrs. Blivens. Ain't we got a bit of stew left?"

"And some of that bread." Noelle pointed to a

couple of small loaves on the board in the center of the table. She looked around. "Perhaps a drop of that wine —"

Blivens hastily moved in front of the cabinet. "That's — er — that's not fit. It's all gone vinegar."

The Earl pushed him aside. "We shall see." He reached for it. "French." He uncorked it and sniffed. His eyebrow rose and his eye pinned Blivens where he stood. "Very like a vintage that my father laid by."

Mrs. Blivens swung around to her husband. "We don't got anything t' spare fer strangers."

Robin took down three cups from the rack along one wall. He poured a liberal amount into each one. He handed one to Noelle and then another to the old man. "Take this to the coachman, Blivens, and tell him to join us here as soon as he gets the horses stabled."

"Where do I take it?"

Robin tottered to the table and sat down at it. "To the stables."

"The stables?"

"Now, listen —" Mrs. Blivens tried to protest one more time, but her husband bowed his head and shuffled away.

Noelle hooked the pot of bubbling stew off the fire. "This smells delicious, Mrs. Blivens," she commented. "You must serve it often once we are settled in."

The woman's face was red with frustration and anger.

"We need baths." Robin pushed his plate back.

Blivens did not move. Noelle raised her head at the blessed suggestion although she wondered how she would stay awake long enough to take one. The coachman with a nod of his head excused himself and retired to his bed in the tackroom.

Mrs. Blivens poked her husband in the ribs. He jumped and rubbed the spot. Then he looked at her with a frightened, aggrieved expression. "Tell 'em," she prompted. "Go ahead. Tell 'em."

"What?"

The caretaker's wife sucked in her breath so hard that her nostrils pinched together. "Th' fact is that there just be th' two 'v us, milord. We be old. An' Mr. Blivens 'ere, 'e can't do things like a young'un."

"If you cannot, then I'm sure I can find someone who can." The Earl rose from his seat, his eye blazing.

Unimpressed, the old woman faced the Earl with chin outthrust, hands on hips. "That's as may be, but not many'll work fer no pay."

"Mrs. Blivens," Noelle interrupted smoothly. "Perhaps if you would set those two largest kettles to boiling, we could make do."

At Noelle's suggestion, the woman hesitated, then shrugged. "Well, I don't mind doin' that, but Mr. Blivens can't carry 'em full."

"Mr. Blivens can go straight to—"

"Mr. Blivens," Noelle put her hand on the old man's shoulder where he drowsed on the bench beside the fire. "Will you take the Earl up to the bedrooms and let him tell you which ones to build fires in?"

The retainer looked up vaguely. Then he smiled

and nodded. "Yes 'm. I can do that."

"Good." She smiled sweetly at her husband, who smothered his anger.

Despite Mrs. Blivens's hostile air, Noelle was nodding before the fire when their husbands returned.

"We have found a barely habitable room," Robin announced.

"We built a fire," Blivens told his wife. "I helped. It be blazin' away."

"Th' water's boilin'." She held out two thick pads to Noelle. "If that be all, we'll take oursel's t' bed." Without waiting for an answer, she took Blivens's arm and led him out.

The Countess of Whitby pressed a hand to her forehead. Her voice was so low it was barely a whisper. "I'm sure we'll laugh about this some day."

"I prefer that we forget it altogether." Scowling heavily, the Earl took the pads from her, fitted them carefully around the handles, and lifted the kettles. "If you'll open the doors for me, Madam Wife, we'll retire for the night."

Noelle was almost too tired to realize that the Earl intended that they bathe and sleep in the same room. Almost! When she opened the connecting door, the second room was empty. It contained no furniture at all.

Staring into its dark frigid space, she could feel the exhaustion so intense that she could hardly stand. For nearly forty hours she had been without rest. She had ridden mile after mile in a jolting coach, slept only a little on a hard bench, walked miles in the snow and blowing wind. She had dealt with hours of violent emotions. She felt her husband's hands on her shoulders.

"Come back to the fire," he said gently.

Dumbly, she allowed him to lead her back to a chair in front of the fire.

He set her portmanteau down at her feet. "Can you wash yourself, Madam Wife?"

His voice was hoarse, but not ungentle.

She looked up at him and nodded faintly.

He stared into her eyes, reading there the same exhaustion and shock that he had seen in the face of young soldiers. He might have found her wandering a battlefield. Dried mud clung in streaks to her garments. Her hair hung in a snarl over her shoulder. Her face was streaked with soot. Only her hands were relatively clean where she had washed them before their meal.

He knelt and opened her bag, pawing through it to find her nightgown. At the sight of it, she roused. Her eyes widened. She reached for it, then her hands fell to her sides. She shook her head, her eyes closing.

"Madam Wife. Nora."

"Noelle," she whispered.

"Yes, Noelle. After I've gone to the trouble to carry this kettle of water up here, surely you will use it."

She shook her head. "I'm so tired."

He found a handkerchief in her suitcase and

dipped it into the water. It was still hot, but the trip through the drafty hall had cooled it considerably. "You'll feel better with some of that smoke and dirt washed off." He wrung the excess water from the handkerchief and tried to press it into her hand. "Here. Wipe your face."

He rose and moved behind the chair. There he stripped off his coat and shirt. Using his much abused stock, he washed himself briskly with the warm water. It felt wonderful to him. In Spain he had bathed in a canteen of cold water and thought himself lucky. Tonight, it felt good to stand in a warm room in his own house and wash the sweat and soil from his chest and arms.

Still, as he straightened from the kettle, he came up dizzy and trembling. Lack of sleep hit him even as it dulled the invidious pain from his wounds. He sighed. He might actually be able to sleep tonight without drinking himself into insensibility.

Rather than try the modesty of his wife, he sat on the bed to pull off his boots. By that time the water was barely warm. He put both feet into it with a sigh of pleasure. A little help to keep his feet warm before he thrust them into a cold damp bed.

"Madam Wife."

No answer.

"No — Noelle."

Still no answer.

He dried his feet with a sock and came round the chair. She had not moved. He shook his head tiredly. He had spent the entire day attending to his wife, rescuing her, disciplining her, building fires for her. The list to his mind was very long. Now he had to play lady's maid for her.

He removed the washcloth from her hand and washed the worst of the smoke from her face. "Now," he commanded, "stand up."

She did not move, but when he pulled her to her feet, she stood, with eyes closed, swaying as he unbuttoned her waist and stripped her down to her camisole and one petticoat. He pushed her back down and washed her neck and shoulders.

Wherever drops of water fell, they turned the white linen camisole into a semi-transparent veil. His hands brushed the tantalizing mounds of her breasts. He could see the circle of her areola and the darker center where her nipple peaked.

Suddenly, he felt a tightening in his loins. He glanced down at himself with some surprise and interest. At least he was not quite as dead as he had thought for a time. Of course, a tightening was a long way from a full erection. Pain and the alcohol to combat it had combined to render that impossible since Spain.

Nevertheless, he made a mental note to try and recall the feeling when he was not staggering with exhaustion. He sank back on his heels and reached for her boots. One came off easily, the other was tighter. He had to grasp her calf and exert a considerable degree of strength. Her body shifted in the chair.

He glanced up and found her staring at him beneath drooping lids. In her eyes were accusation and fear but, more than that, acceptance. When their gaze met, she breathed in sharply. Her breasts rose and fell. Her hands fluttered up to cover them.

"For heaven's sake, Madam Wife," he groaned. He set the boots beside the chair and pushed himself to his feet. "Judge my exhaustion by your own and acquit me of the sin of lust tonight."

She glanced toward the bed just a few steps away, its covers turned back on both sides.

"Yes, we will have to share a bed tonight, just as we did last night. And the result will be the same, I do assure you. I'm tired to the bone."

She managed a nod. "I am too."

"Then raise myself in your opinion. I'm not a rutting beast. A wedding night should be something of a rite, so I'm given to understand. And rites should be performed when the participants can concentrate on them. When they hold some meaning. Do you agree?"

"Yes."

"Then off to bed we go." He suited his words by taking her hands and guiding her to her feet. "I think both of us are clean enough for tonight, given the circumstances. Tomorrow we can take a longer time at our ablutions. Agreed?"

"Agreed," she mumbled.

"Then—" He turned her by the shoulders as if she were a child and pointed her in the direction of the bed. She took a couple of weaving, tottering steps.

The expression in her eyes was so like some of the young men of his troop, that he felt a stab at his heart. She was out on her feet.

He would pay for it, he was certain, but he stooped and lifted her high onto his chest.

She uttered a cry of surprise, her head rolled, her

fists doubled. He felt the pull of wounded tendons and muscles, but the pain was not as bad as he expected. In a couple of quick strides he deposited her on the bed and pulled the covers over her.

In the semi-darkness her eyes were wide. She clutched the top of the coverlet with her fists, drawing it up to her chin.

He returned to the hearth and added more wood to the fire. It would die down, but perhaps not before they had created enough warmth between them to escape the chill.

Then he came to his side of the bed. Her eyes followed him. He climbed in and pulled the covers up high. The sheets were clammy. They smelled unaired and musty. His injured muscles tautened.

With a sigh, he turned to his wife. He closed his arms around her and dragged her against him.

She was stiff as a rail, but her body was soft and above all warm.

"Warm me," he whispered, his open lips were against her cheek. "God, Madam Wife, I haven't been so cold and tired since Spain." He sighed deeply. "You feel good and warm. I should have had you in my blankets in Spain." His hand cupped her shoulder, clasping her smooth flesh as he warmed himself.

His hands were cold and his feet too. She shivered. He cupped his legs under her buttocks.

"Please," she whispered. "Don't. This can't be right. Don't."

He did not answer. Instead she became aware of his even breathing. He had fallen instantly to sleep.

She could not help but giggle. *Safe — or saved —*

for another night.

"God damn him to hell. This queer's the business for sure."

"Mayhap they won't stay. Th' 'ouse's a wreck."

The first speaker clenched his fist around the handle of the whip. "He'd better not. We've got a good thing started here for ourselves. He's no right to come and take it over."

"It's 'is from 'is father. Don't forget that."

"God rot him! We've worked for this place."

"If 'e wants to take it—"

He slashed viciously at the dried grasses. "He can try. But if he does, I'll make him bloody sorry."

Six

The bed dipped at his back.

Instantly, Robin opened his eyes. He opened them both as he always did unable to break the habit. And as always, he tasted the sharp, bitter aloes of disappointment as he had done every morning since the bandages had come off. Mouth tight, he closed both eyes, the good one and the bad, and listened.

The homely sounds of someone laying kindling against the grate reached his ears. He rolled over and raised his head.

His wife knelt in her petticoat and chemise. Her long brown hair was a snarl halfway down her back between her bare shoulders. Her feet clad in dark stockings were folded one on top of the other like a child's at prayer.

He cleared his throat. "I should be doing that."

He had not meant to startle her. Her whole body jerked. A piece of wood thudded onto the grate. Fine gray ash swirled up. She retrieved it and laid it straight. "I woke up first," she answered without looking back over her shoulder. "I decided not to wait for Mr. or Mrs. Blivens to come up and do it."

Uttering a mild oath, he punched up his pillow. "A decision well-made based on sound judgement. I daresay Blivens has probably forgotten all about us."

"And she won't remind him. Fortunately, there are some live coals down deep in the ashes. Ah, yes." A tiny flame licked between the sticks of kindling. She rose and dusted off her hands.

"Come back to bed."

She turned quickly. Her hands clasped her upper arms. "I—"

"Come on. Until the room gets warm." He sat up and motioned.

She shook her head as if considering his offer. "It's tempting, but I think I'd best put my clothes on and go find us some hot tea or maybe chocolate. If I got back in bed, I'd probably go back to sleep. You'd go back to sleep. We might never wake up. They'd find us months from now, starved to death."

He scowled blackly at her humor that successfully avoided contact with him. "Come back to bed until the room gets warm."

She thrust her arms into her blouse. "No. I don't think so. Thank you anyway, but I'm a very early riser, as you've no doubt noticed."

"You're blathering," he complained.

"I'm hungry. I didn't eat very much last night and almost nothing at lunch—" She stuffed her feet into her boots and pulled her skirt on over her head. The rest of her words were muffled in its folds. When she emerged, she snatched up her cloak and tossed it around her shoulders.

"Damn it, Madam Wife—"

She opened the door as she buttoned her skirt at the waist. "I'll be back soon."

He collapsed back on the pillows, disgusted. One hand rose to the patch, in place night and day. Of course, she would run from him. Anger lighted a fire in his veins. She was his wife. He might not be able to have love or any of the other trappings of a happy marriage, but she could at least treat him like a human being, rather than a monster.

With a sigh his hand left the patch to touch himself between his legs. For five years he had made no effort to take a woman. For five years he had been occupied with his own pain, his own struggle for survival. The sight of her this morning, kneeling to make the fire, the fine white skin, the dark hair, the slender well-shaped bones had stirred him.

He remembered undressing and bathing her last night. She was quite a presentable girl or would be if she were not defiant, frightened, muddy, snapping and snarling like a feisty dog. He had only seen her on her worst behavior yet he could not help admiring her. Faced with her prospects, most women would have wept ceaselessly.

Mentally, he commended her spirit. That same spirit, once she became more accustomed to him, would not stick at marital obligations.

The prospect warmed him. A day of rest. A good meal with a bottle of fine wine to allay her fears. Real baths under proper circumstances rather than a few trickles of fast-cooling water in a musty, dismal chamber. He would watch her today, fill his senses with her, tantalize himself—

Noelle observed that Blivens was willing enough when he could remember what he had been set to do. The old woman was openly hostile, using her husband's infirmity as an excuse not to work herself. Between them the Earl's black temper grew more and more explosive.

On the pretext of seeing to her mother's mare, she had left the house where her husband was attempting with little success to direct the servants. All around her the sun glistened off the snow's pristine beauty. The air was bracing without the fearsome wind and blowing sleet of yesterday. A blue tit and then another swooped across her path.

Her spirits lifted. She smiled as she followed their flight with her eyes. For just a minute, the air smelled like freedom. She was glad she had not escaped to London.

Inside the shedrow, the gray, so old her coat had turned almost white, stuck her head over the stall door and whickered softly.

"Silver Belle. How's milady feeling after such a long trip?"

Noelle stroked the velvet nose and arranged the forelock neatly.

The mare closed her eyes. Her ribs expanded in a horsy sigh.

"Accommodations not up to your usual standards, are they, lady?"

The mare snuffled at Noelle's pockets. She produced not one but two pieces of a rather withered carrot.

While the mare lipped them up and chewed, Noelle continued her low assurance. "Don't worry about a thing. I'll be here. And I promise you'll live out your days in comfort. No one will send you to the knackers to make room for a younger horse."

From the next stall the Earl's black stretched her neck for attention.

"Oh, you want some too." Leaving Silver Belle with a final pat, Noelle moved on. "You're a beauty," she crooned. "A real black beauty. What's your name? I hope I get to ride you some day."

In stalls across the way were the two coach horses. She patted their heavy shoulders and held carrots for them as well. The rest of the stalls — sixteen were empty although in good condition. In fact, they seemed in better condition than the house.

Puzzled, she strolled to the end. The condition of the box stall brought her up short. Fresh straw covered the ground and in the back a pile of fresh dung. A horse had been stabled in it quite recently. She walked to the back door of the stable and pushed it open.

Hoofprints of three horses bunched close together led away across the new fallen snow. A rider had mounted one and led the other two.

Thoughtful, she walked back down the shedrow, looking in each pair of stalls as she passed. Two more had straw spread. The rest were empty, their ground swept clean.

108

Back at the front, she patted the gray again. "Who was here when you got here, old girl?"

"May I help you, milady?" The coachman stepped out of the tackroom.

She turned. "Yes. Whose horses were stabled down at the other end?"

He walked down the shedrow, looked in the stalls, and shook his head. "I don't know, ma'am. It was dark and I couldn't do much more than make these comfortable and turn in."

"I understand."

He hesitated. "If you've no more need of me, my orders are to return to Averill immediately."

She caressed Silver Belle's nose. "What! You mean I'm not to have that priceless antique equipage as a honeymoon gift."

The coachman frowned. "Milady, I was told—"

"Ever the soul of consideration is the Duke. Since our backs were like to breaking during the ride, he's taking the thing back before it kills us."

" 'Twas a rough road, milady. All icy ruts and mud," he explained apologetically.

Clearly this man was not Archie Holmesfield. Her sarcasm was wasted. With a wave of her hand, she relented. "Take it and go. I've no more need of you. But you must check with my husband before you leave."

"Yes, ma'am." He tugged at his forelock and hurried out.

Eyes bleak, she watched him lope toward the house. The Duke was indeed washing his hands of her. Even his coachman must leave immediately.

Noelle tossed her head. Giving the mare a final

pat, she left the stable to explore the other buildings.

She returned to the house to be greeted by her husband's scowl. "Where've you been? I have to go now to hire a groom. I thought you might want to hire the housekeeper."

She blinked at him. She had not expected to be handed the responsibilities of the house so soon. "Can we afford so many servants?"

His scowl darkened. "We can't afford not to hire them."

He balled his fists on his hips. "If you are prepared to take on the cooking and cleaning, Madam Wife, I assure you that I can take care of the two horses in the stables."

She looked around at the neglected room. "I could scarcely do worse than the Blivenses."

He tried a softer tone. "I think we need not stick at one more apiece."

"If you wish." She lifted her chin. "Thank you, my lord, for allowing me to hire a housekeeper. And, of course, my quarterly allowance will pay for them."

His expression blackened. "Your tongue, Madam, will drive me to murder. I'll wait just five minutes while you change."

She was back down the stairs in four.

"No, yer bleedin' lordship. Ain't nobody in 'ere workin'."

Robin had chosen the Rose and Thistle, the only inn on the backroad just beyond Whitby, because it was unprepossessing. Its clientele at this time of the day should have been unemployed and glad of a chance to work. Instead, he had been greeted by belligerence.

"Jus' take y'r bloody arse right outta 'ere."

Robin estimated the size of the speaker, a good fifteen stone, with hands the size of hams. He calculated that a well-placed fist in the belly and another to the underside of the jaw would stretch him on the floor.

Alone, he would have welcomed the exercise. Unfortunately, he had brought his wife with him. A look in her direction surprised him.

Her eyes were on his face also, her breathing sharp, spots of color high in her cheeks. One hand had slid off into her lap. Her right hand remained on the table, seeming to rest to the right of her plate. But her fingers aligned themselves precisely beside her knife.

He could not quite conceal a twist at the corners of his mouth. Her appearance brought to mind a raw recruit on the eve of a skirmish. He stretched his hand across the table and laid it on her own.

He nodded to the man. "A simple 'no, thank you,' would have sufficed. I'm sure with unemployment rampant in England, I can find people to take into service."

"Not 'round 'ere," the lout insisted.

Robin rose. He was not up to the weight. Moreover, the brute towered over him by six inches, but the challenge suited him. He had been unable to

111

strike back for a long time. He solicitously pulled his wife's chair out from the table. "Will you wait at the door, Madam Wife?"

"Wait?" Noelle looked into his face. Tension strutted the muscles in his jaw and bunched little knots of skin alongside the scar. Yet his aura was ice cold.

The lout chuckled and looked about for approval from other occupants at the inn. To a man they had relaxed their guard.

Noelle walked quickly to the door, where she turned back in time to see the Earl pivot and drive his right fist into the big unprotected belly. With all the weight of Robin's shoulders behind it, it disappeared to the wrist in the huge mass of blubber.

The lout's breath came blasting out his open mouth. His eyes bugged. In a reflex action he clapped his hands over his injured middle.

Robin appeared to stoop. His right fist hooked up from the floor in a pile-driving blow that connected with the underside of his victim's jaw.

The lout's teeth champed together on his own tongue. His bellow of agony was only slightly muffled by the blood that flowed over his lips and chin. Unable to fight, he could only flee. Clapping his hands to his mouth, he set up a terrible howling. Tears spouted from his eyes. He collapsed backward on a bench that over-tipped with his weight and dropped him back onto the floor. He lay there writhing like a turtle on its back.

The Earl rubbed his hand that had delivered the terrible blow to the jaw as he addressed the room. "As it said, gentleman, a simple 'no' would have

112

sufficed."

A universal growl went up.

Robin backed to the door. Noelle opened it at the same time she thrust her whip at him. He took it and slashed the air in front of him. "Thank you, Madam Wife. How thoughtful you are."

"A woman's place, milord," she told him cheekily before she sprang down into the innyard. Their mares stood together, hitched to the same post. Noelle pulled their reins free.

"Mount up," he called to her, holding the doorway, his back to the yard.

She looked around her but found no mounting block. Setting her lower lip between her teeth, she caught the high horn of the side saddle and swung her leg for Silver Belle's croup. Her skirt tore and pulled her back.

He threw a glance over his shoulder and saw her predicament. "For God's sake—"

Thank the lord the mare stood like a statue. Summoning all her strength, Noelle tried again. Her ankle hooked over the top. The mount wasn't pretty. It wasn't dignified, but she was astride the mare's back.

Her husband leaped from the porch directly to the saddle. His spurs raked his horse's sides at the same time his hand descended on Silver Belle's rump. She whinnied in shock and lumbered away. Without stirrups, Noelle clamped her legs around her mare's barrel and hung on to the sidesaddle horns.

The Earl's fancy Arabian broke at a gallop and led the way out onto the lane. For almost a mile the

Arabian set the speed.

Silver Belle followed gamely. Finally wheezing, her sides heaving, her neck lathered, her head went down. Noelle reined her to a halt.

The Earl rode on several rods before he realized he rode alone. Scowling at the exhausted mare, he circled back.

Noelle raised an eyebrow. "If we're going to beat many hot retreats, I'll have to have a younger beast."

He cleared his throat, hesitated, cleared it again. "I intend to take very good care that you never have to beat another hasty retreat."

She grinned at him. "Actually, I thought that was exciting. You really knocked him off his pins."

"Where did you hear cant like that?" he asked suspiciously.

She shrugged. "I don't remember."

"Then try to forget the rest of it. I never had the faintest notion that I couldn't walk in and hire a round dozen if we needed so many."

Noelle regarded him, head cocked to one side. "Are you by any chance trying to make me an apology, milord?"

He studied the landscape ahead of them. "Never. I don't owe you any sort of apology. They do. Do you want to go back and get it?"

"I'll forgo that pleasure chiefly because I wouldn't be able to understand anything he said. He must have bitten his tongue nearly through."

Robin tried. He really tried to the keep his face straight. But a bark of laughter shot out of his mouth. He reined the mare around and headed her

114

toward home taking care to ride ahead to hide his laughter.

"Mrs. Blivens is nowhere to be found."

"I'm sure the house is just as we left it. I can't see her bustling around cleaning rooms, making beds—"

"—fixing a meal." Robin surveyed his wife. "Can you cook?"

She managed a half-smile. "A few things."

He groaned. "I can cook a 'few' things too, mostly roast game over a cookfire and a lentil stew. When the army got ahead of the cooks, we had to make do."

She stared at him, thinking he looked better than he had that morning. Despite the long ride and the fight, he looked quite cheerful. "I think I can do better than lentil stew. I'll see what's in the pantry and the stillroom."

He nodded.

She started past him, but he caught her arm. His face was closer than it had been since the nuptial kiss. "Would you have used that knife?"

"What knife?"

"The knife at the inn."

She tucked her head. "I probably couldn't have done any damage with it."

"But you were ready to pick it up and use it," he insisted.

She took a couple of steps backward. He was too close, his face too intense, his dark color too vivid. His nearness upset her. "Well, I couldn't let that

115

brute hurt — that is — we were outnumbered."

"They wouldn't have hurt you."

She grinned saucily. "Not without a hell of a mill, they wouldn't."

He crossed his arms in front of his chest. "Your tongue, Madam Wife—"

She tossed her head. "It's my best weapon."

He sighed. "You stopped at the door and waited for me."

"For form's sake only. Two looks stronger than one, even if one's only a woman. They weren't going to do anything by that time. You had punched out their fighter."

"You didn't believe that at the time. You passed me your whip."

"I expected you to defend me."

"I can't get a straight answer out of you, can I?"

"No more than I can from you." Obviously uncomfortable, she jerked Mrs. Blivens's apron from its peg. "Listen, if we're going to eat tonight, I've got to take stock of supplies, make a menu, and then cook and prepare the food."

He nodded. "I'll see to the horses." At the door he stopped. "I didn't know English women could be brave."

Bent over to inspect the vegetables in the bins, she did not acknowledge his comment. He shrugged and walked out.

Instantly, she raised her head and stared after him. He had not paid a compliment or offered thanks. He had all but scolded her for not behaving in a more womanly manner. Still she presumed that he approved of what she had done. In all probabil-

ity, like her father, he was trying to avoid acknowledging her competence.

Dinner proved to be less of a disaster than Noelle
had a right to expect. In the end she did make stew,
but Mrs. Blivens's cabinets revealed a receipt book
with instructions for making a quick bread. The
stew was savory and the bread was fresh and hot.

Without realizing that he did so, her husband
paid her the very first compliment of their marriage. "Are you going to eat that last piece?"

"You may have it."

"You can have it if you want it," he insisted as he
reached for it.

She smiled behind her cup.

He buttered it lavishly. When the last bite had
disappeared, he poured the last of the wine into his
cup and gazed around him with something very like
satisfaction. The silence grew between them. A log
snapped in the huge fireplace. They stared at each
other over the rims of their cups.

"You are my wife," he murmured.

His voice sent a frisson up her spine. Her skin
felt hot, then cold. Her knuckles showed white
around the cup.

He read her trepidation. A muscle in his jaw
flickered, then he smiled a grim little smile. "And
I'm your husband, such as I am. Not pretty,
Madam Wife, but I assure you I can play the man's
part for you."

He was not pretty, but she had not thought of the
patch and the scar for quite a long time. It was just

his face, the mirror of his emotions. Their bitterness drove her to retaliation. "Not if you drink yourself into a staggering fool."

He set the cup down so hard the wine sloshed. "I would never drink so much."

"You drink every night."

"You haven't known me every night."

They were arguing like children. She pushed back her chair and started for the door. "Every night I've known you, you've drunk."

He barred her way. "But I've never *been* drunk."

She faced him, trembling, her hands clammy.

He dropped his hands on her shoulders, cupping them, his long fingers splayed. His thumbs rubbed the slender collar bones before sliding off into the hollows beneath them.

She shivered.

"Cold?" His eye glittered in the firelight.

"I don't feel cold." She struggled to control her voice. "I feel frightened."

"I think that's only natural, Madam Wife."

She shrugged off his hands and stepped back against the door. "If you're going to make me your wife, at least have the decency to learn my name."

He opened his mouth. Hesitated. "Norma?"

"Noelle. Like Christmas."

"Noel. Christmas?"

"Noelle with two *l's* and a second *e*. I was born at yuletide."

"Ah, then. You were a gift," he murmured stepping close.

He was very tall. She had to tip her head back. His single black eye scanned her face, searching for the changes in color, the trembling of her mouth or chin, the faintest frownline between her eyes. When he saw none, he put his arms around and gathered her against his gaunt frame. "I understand your fear and admire your courage. Only a fool has no fear of the unknown."

Her mouth was dry. She sucked in her breath and licked her lower lip.

He started. His grip tightened. The hard body pressed against her softness felt impossibly harder. He leaned above her, slanting his head. His mouth lowered gently and fitted itself across her own.

His lips were dry and warm. His tongue lanced out between them and traced the slit between her lips. When she did not immediately open her mouth, he drew back.

"Don't kiss like a girl."

She frowned. "What did I do? How is a girl's kiss different from any other kiss?"

"Part your lips. Let me taste you, Madam Wife."

His husky words sent shivers through her. His fingers urged her up on tiptoe. Their mouths met again. The kiss went on and on. Warm and pleasant, then hotter. Disturbing. She felt her breasts prickle as their nipples tightened.

Between their bellies was a hard rod that grew with each passing moment.

At last he broke away with a rueful laugh. "You go to my head."

She stared at his face. His skin flushed with darker color. The name Turk flashed into her mind. She almost said it. Now was not the time. What she felt seemed to have driven all the sharp insulting things from her mind. He released her and stepped back.

She swayed, then recovered. "Milord—"

He took her arm. "To the bedchamber, Madam Wife. Perhaps at some later date, I might have you across a bench or over a tabletop, but the first time—" He smiled. "—the first time must be in the bedchamber."

"To beget the heir."

He frowned. "I suppose so."

"That's the purpose, isn't it?"

"It's only one of the purposes." All the way up the stairs, he kept her beside him. His hand slid tantalizingly down her spine, his palm cupped her buttock. His fingers slipped in between. When she gasped in embarrassment and tried to hitch her hips forward, he threw his arm around her shoulders.

"Gently," he murmured. His breath caressed her ear and raised the hairs on the back of her neck.

Their bedroom was quite warm. She looked up at him inquiringly.

"I laid a fire on my way back from the stables."

"You've been planning, milord." She tried to keep her voice even and unconcerned.

"Robin."

"Robin." She nodded. "Now what?"

"We begin as we mean to go on, Madam—er—Noelle. I believe it's customary on the wedding night for the bride's relatives or at least her maid to disrobe her while the groom waits downstairs. But since this is not a customary marriage, perhaps I could assist you?"

She sucked in her breath. Her eyes closed as he put his hands around her neck, then flew open as his palms touched her breasts.

Through the layers of clothing she could feel their heat and strength. Unconsciously she arched her neck. A dull throbbing had begun between her legs. "I—I don't know—"

He put his mouth to the pulsebeat beneath her ear. "How old are you?"

His nearness made her feel hot. "Almost twenty, mil—Robin."

He was nibbling on her earlobe. "Will you be afraid of anything I do to you?"

Her eyes flew open. "I don't know. What will you do?"

He took her face between his palms and kissed her, delicately nibbling at her upper lip. She kept her eyes open, seeing as well as feeling and tasting him. He drew back. "You may close your eyes if you like, Madam Wife."

"Noelle."

"Noelle."

"Why would I want to close my eyes? Am I supposed to?"

He kissed her again. "Some women do. They close their eyes the minute their husbands touch them and never open them again until their husbands leave."

"Is it so hideous?"

"Perhaps the sight of my body—"

She shook her head. "I want to see what's happening to me."

Her words set his blood to throbbing. She

wanted to watch him. The thought of her looking at him was almost unbearable. Suddenly, he was potently aroused in a way he had forgotten. Those clear brown eyes would find him hard as metal. He could have laughed with joy as tension sang in the muscles of his thighs. He felt as if he could ride forever, and at the same time as if he would explode the very instant he saw her.

And he desired to see her above all things. He could barely rasp out his question. "Then may I assist you in removing your clothing, Noelle?"

"If you like." She smiled a bit stiffly, her mouth lifting at the corners as if she had not smiled in a long time. She stared into the heart of the fire. "In fact, yes. I think you should. That seems only fair. If a husband wants a wife's clothes off, he should remove them. And turn about is fair play. I should remove yours."

He smiled. "Are you sure?"

She looked surprised. "Of course."

"I'm—not—like—you."

"I'm sure you're not." She put her hands on his shoulders. "But we begin as we mean to go on. And I don't intend to spend the rest of my married life with my eyes closed."

Her hands moved to the lapels of his coat and pushed them back.

"Noelle," he warned.

"Robin." She kissed him.

All unbidden, his hand found the buttons at the back of her skirt.

Seven

"You taste—good," she murmured against his mouth.

Her tongue caressed his and followed where it led, back into his own mouth, where it found the edges of his teeth and flirted delicately with them. Her hands caressed his naked ribs and met in the small of his back.

He groaned at the sweet pleasure and continued his exploration. His lips nibbled across her cheek to her earlobe. His body was on fire, his blood roared in his ears. He was trembling and sweating, desperate for her.

He pulled himself back, his body shaking.

Her eyes still open, but glazed. Her bruised lips parted, her breath coming fast. She blinked suddenly, a frown creased her forehead. She reached for him.

Her sensuality startled him. She was as eager, as flaming as he.

He swept her up in his arms and carried her to the bed. The cold sheets welcomed them, a tiny luxury for their sensitive skin. If only they could cool this desire for just a moment. He was sweating, his blood afire, his heart pounding. He recognized the feeling, welcomed it, and at the same time deplored it.

He was going to hurt her. Despite the commands of his mind, his body was out of control. He stared down into his wife's innocent, eager face. Like a young soldier searching for glory, she was searching for she-knew-not-what. And like the soldier, she was going to be hurt.

He set his teeth and lowered himself not on top of her, but beside her. He placed one hand on her breast and shaped the hard nipple.

She opened her eyes. "I feel—" She twisted restlessly, her mouth open, reaching for his, her hands trying to pull their bodies together. "I feel—"

"Yes."

"I don't know—I—" She moved her limbs. Her knee butted his thigh. One hand gave up trying to pull her toward him. It slipped over his ribs, pressed against his chest.

He groaned and shuddered. For five years no one had touched him like that. Even before, his unusual looks had warned off not a few, so his experiences had been selective. He had never had a sweetheart; his emotions had never been engaged.

How strange that a man's wife should be an entirely new experience for him. Her skin was so white in contrast to his darkness. As he watched fascinated, her fingers, so fragile, combed through the coarse black hair on his chest.

She followed his eyes, staring in wonder at his body. Her index finger traced the wide white scar.

124

She clenched her teeth against a shudder.

It was like a shard of ice to his heart. He lived the nightmare of every wounded soldier returning to see revulsion in the face of the woman he bedded. He twisted his head toward the ceiling, presenting the unmarked side of his face. His mouth tightened. "Not very pretty, I admit."

"Will you please stop saying that?"

"A hideous face, a scarred wreck —"

She put her hand over his mouth and reared up. She sounded like a cross mother scolding a pestering child. "I don't think about that."

The black eye narrowed in disbelief. "Madam Wife, how noble!"

"Noelle. My name is Noelle." Her fingers clasped his jaw, covering the scar there. "No, I don't think about your scars. What do scars have to do with anything?"

"They make me hideous."

"That's the Duke's idea. I refuse. I absolutely refuse to let Averill tell me what to think. Absolutely." She swooped down to plant a hard kiss on her husband's mouth. Her hand splayed out over his ribs, supporting her weight. She moved her hand and his own nipple hardened, his chest heaved.

He closed the terrible black eye to conceal his turbulent emotions. "You sound as if you mean that."

Her eyes shot to his face to find that it betrayed doubt for the first time. He looked very different. The hard lines of pain were recast in softer lines of desire and hope. He looked somehow vulnerable. At that moment, she realized she had the power to hurt him.

The thought made her shiver. Averill had always recognized weakness of that sort and taken advantage of it. She would not be like Averill.

She cast the feeling aside as she felt Robin's hand on her hip, the long fingers gently caressing, exploring the sensitive skin beneath her buttock. Heat followed where his fingers moved. A sweet pain and a strange weakness spread through her thighs. The fingers strayed, slid between her legs where she was embarrassingly wet.

She gasped. Her own hands stilled. She sucked in a deep breath expanding her chest, moving her breasts against him. "I'm sorry. I don't know why. I've never —" Despite the wonderful feelings, she tried to pull away.

"No." His voice rumbled out of his throat. "That's the way you're supposed to be. Thank God!"

He turned them over in a single motion that demonstrated the power and grace of his body. She was beneath him and he braced above her, kissing her on the mouth, his manhood pressing down.

"What are you doing?"

His lips nibbled at the corner of her mouth. "Open your thighs, Madam Wife. Open to me, Noelle."

"Yes."

He nudged her. Strong, tantalizing, his rod slid between her thighs, parting the hair, the folds of skin, delving the inner secrets of her body. "You're ready for me," he murmured. "See how easy. Feel it."

She did. She could still think to the extent that she recognized her body's readiness for him. If he were not offended by the wetness, then she would not be either. She opened her thighs a very little bit.

But not enough. He kissed her hard and pulled back on his heels. Eyes open, she looked full at his face. Dark, fearsome, angular, shocking, the black leather patch and with its strings bisecting his forehead and cheek. To others it might have been a face out of a nightmare, but to her, he looked like her husband—the man who was creating the most amazing sensations.

He dipped his hand between her legs, took the moisture onto his fingers, pushed one, then two into her. She twisted helplessly. He positioned himself. His hands closed over her shoulders. He leaned down and took her mouth.

His lunge hurt. Her scream tore into his mouth. She struck at his shoulder with her fists and bucked her hips, but he held on.

She writhed and twisted her hips, her fighting muscles clasping him more tightly as they sought to expel him. He lost control. He threw back his head and yelled. Then he was shuddering, shuddering, his muscles thrusting, burning, releasing into her. He felt as if everything in his life was draining from him, all the unhappiness, all the black memories and terrible emotions, all the pain.

With his last strength he slid off her onto the bed and closed his eyes.

"Did we beget the heir?"

Noelle sat facing her husband on the big rumpled bed. She glanced at him from beneath her eyelashes, faintly surprised when she should have been wildly embarrassed to be sitting cross-legged, facing her husband, who did the same. She pressed the plate of food more firmly down in her lap. The folds of their robes covered them decently. They ate like children at a picnic or soldiers in the field.

To answer her question, he halted the glass of port half way to his lips. "We might have."

"I hope so."

He took a fortifying drink. "Do you?"

"Well, of course. Don't you? That hurt as bad as anything I've ever felt. I don't want to have to go through it again if I don't have to."

He set the glass down with a sigh. "I'm sorry I hurt you."

She shot him a quick look. "I expected it to be painful."

"Oh, did you?" His eyebrow rose above his glittering black eye.

She moved the plate from her lap and straightened her legs, struggling with the edges of the robe to keep them together and preserve a modicum of decency. "I didn't come to this bed totally ignorant, Milord Robin. I knew what would happen. That is, I had asked questions. Others had told me. And I was right." She sounded well pleased with herself as she tasted the port, grimaced, and set it down. "Love is vastly overrated."

He frowned. "I'm afraid you were rather slighted, Noelle."

"I can't see how. It hurt like blueblazes. And you were groaning and yelling and sweating. And then all of a sudden, you collapsed."

"Actually, that isn't quite what happened," he began.

She smiled a self-satisfied smile. "At least I didn't pass out."

"Madam Wife—"

"I hope we begat the heir. We don't want to have to go through that very often."

He stared at her incredulously. From her point of view, she had drawn the proper conclusions. "Will you mind doing it again?"

She sighed. "Yes, I'm sure I'll mind. Won't you? But it's what's necessary. You have to have an heir. And I'll tell you straight out that to have my own baby was one of the reasons I agreed to get married."

She took another sip of port and shuddered again. (From the port or the thought of another session of lovemaking, he could not tell.) "Let's change the subject."

He smiled pleasantly. So she was willing to do it again. She was in for a surprise. He would have himself under complete control. He felt himself twitch and tighten.

God! He wanted her again. He could do it now, but she was looking quite pale around the mouth. The bleeding had alarmed her, even though he had told her that it was nothing serious. She was undoubtedly sore. Poor wife. He would give her time to heal. He folded a pillow behind his head and stretched out on top of the mussed sheets. Deliberately he crossed his ankles. "What do you want to talk about?"

She tore her eyes away from his long legs. "What are you going to do?"

"Right now?" He looked at her questioningly. "Probably drift off to sleep. I don't hurt anywhere, despite not having very much to drink."

"No. I don't mean right now. I mean here." She gestured with her hand. "Here. At Whitby."

The question stumped him. "I don't know."

She shook her head in exasperation. "What would you like to do?"

"I don't know." He stared at the ceiling, his glass of port balanced on his stomach. "I haven't thought about doing anything but staying alive in almost twenty years. And I didn't live here before that. I was sent off to school at age six, so I've only visited since then. My father was able to buy me a commission in time for them to ship me off to Spain."

"How old are you?" she asked suddenly.

"A great age. Thirty-nine."

"Is that all?" she scoffed.

He stared at her in amazement. "That's more than twice your age. I knew your mother."

"Age doesn't make any difference. Most girls marry men years older than they are. Men are allowed to 'sew wild oats' and have lovers and learn how to do things properly. Although I must say, I don't envy the girls they learn on. I'm rather glad you're thirty-nine. I'm used to dealing with Averill. He's only a few years older than you are. A man my own age would be a boy. I'm nineteen. Almost twenty."

He stared tight-lipped at the ceiling. "How can you talk the way you do? It's shocking."

She reached over and patted his bare knee. "Now don't stick your lower lip out."

He raised his head, his expression black.

She did not appear impressed. "That's what my

nurse used to say to me whenever I'd get ready to pitch a temper fit."

"Madam Wife."

"Let's talk about Whitby. What do you want to do here? What would you like to do?"

He was still shocked to the core at her attitude and angry with himself that he was shocked. He resented her patronizing tone. "I told you, I don't know!"

She was silent for a couple of minutes. He began to believe that his ferocious growl had finished the conversation.

She folded her arms across her chest. "I know what I'd like to do."

He shot her a warning glance. "What?"

"Raise horses." Her eyes were clear, her voice determined.

The black eyebrow winged upward. For the first time he looked at her as something more than a thing to be used. "A stable?"

"A stud. A horse farm—"

"I know what a stud is."

"Men will pay fine sums of money for good horses. Even for not so good ones. I've seen some of the hacks the Duke's guests ride into Averill on. Months away from the knackers, but Lord So-and-so's paid a hundred guineas for it."

He took another drink of his port and settled back a little more comfortably. "Were you thinking of a racing stable?"

"I suppose we could race eventually, but for now, I was thinking of fine horseflesh for riding and driving. Silver Belle is a prime example of a lady's mount. Her color is very fashionable. She's gentle, tractable, calm."

"She's also very old."

"If we could get only a couple of good colts from her, preferably fillies, her line would be perpetuated. She's gentle, well-mannered, affectionate. Her traits would be perfect for saddle horses."

"A very limited range I fear. She's too small for hunting."

"But your horse is bigger. If we had a horse colt and then bred Silver Belle's filly to your mare's — What's her name?"

"Kate." He said pointedly. "The Shrew. She's Arabian with a touch of Barb for size and staying power."

"Her name is bad for a lady's mount. Still the results might be something fine."

"You've said the word 'might.' Plus 'bred.' In order to breed the mares, may I remind you we have to have a stallion?"

"Well, that's true. But couldn't we take them somewhere to breed them to a really fine stud? Averill's Brandywine, for example, is a fine piece of horseflesh."

"Stud fees for good stallions are exorbitant."

She took a sip of her own liquor. "Do you have any money at all?"

Another sore point. He bridled instantly. "Madam Wife, that is none of your business."

She did not quite sneer at him. "I see. Well, then you'll have to borrow it."

He pushed his fingers through his lank hair and stared at her in astonished anger. "Like hell I will. You want me to run us into debt."

"You should be able to do it with little trouble. After all you've just paid everyone off. They'll be glad to advance you the money just until my quarter allowance is paid. Then you can pay it back. And we'll start all over again."

He sat up abruptly. "I will not have my wife telling me what I can do with my money."

She had been expecting the explosion. Every man including Averill resented any woman's suggestion, especially when it was a good one. With an unlady-like snort, she swung her feet over the other side of the bed. "Heaven forfend that a female should intrude upon a male's territory. Having ambitions and aspirations for a better life are strictly a male province."

"Men see the difficulties, whereas females tend to make decisions without practical bases," he replied haughtily.

She muttered something distinctly foul. Fortunately, he did not quite understand it. "Oh, indeed. I see that your decisions have been both infinitely wise and eminently practical. You were the one who had to marry me because you were in debt."

He sprang to his feet glaring at her. "Now just a damned minute—"

She rose hands on hips and faced him defiantly across the rumpled bed. "Why don't you listen to me for a damned minute. I've already looked at the stable building as well as the pens. It's all in very good condition, considering that it's been neglected for so long. We have two horses and a place suitable to stable them. We could borrow money for stud fees and have the first colts to sell in three years."

"You're just a female. You don't know anything about business. You think to keep afloat for three years."

"Why not? You stayed afloat for five."

Her contempt caught him on the raw. His temper flamed anew. This damned woman and her damned father had driven him to desperate straits in less than a week. He would be hanged if he would let them dictate the rest of his life. He snapped up his pants, whirled around, and sat down to draw them on. "This is preposterous. I want you never to mention this wild scheme again."

"No. Well, you can't always have what you want."

"This is a fool's dream." He strode round the bed and caught her by the wrist. "You will forget this nonsense."

"It isn't nonsense!" she cried. His pressure on her wrist tightened. It brought her back to a sense of herself. Her tone changed. "We can do it. You can be proud of it. It will give you something to do so you won't have to drink every night."

He flung her wrist back in her face. Hot blood flooded his dark skin. "We can do nothing of the kind. As soon as I've hired servants to take care of you and the house, I'm off for London."

She whirled away and strode to the fire. "Why thank you, but why delay yourself? You can leave me to the tender ministrations of the Blivenses. They will suit as well as any."

He followed her, caught her shoulder, and spun her to face him. His height and weight threatened her, in particular the muscled shoulders and the wide expanse of black-haired chest bisected by a terrible

134

white scar. His technique was well-honed. It was one that had overawed subordinates all over the Iberian Peninsula.

With a practiced eye he watched the play of emotions around her mouth, the fear in her eyes. He leveled his voice at her and shot the orders. "Shut your mouth, Madam Wife, or you will very much wish that you did."

She bumped over the hearthstone and staggered back against the wall.

"I won't hear any more about this." He placed both hands on either side of her head and hemmed her in. He could see the pulse beat in her throat.

She was no fool. "No, sir."

The corners of his mouth twitched. "Very good." He stepped back, letting his hands drop to his sides.

"Shall I salute too?"

He ignored her tone. "And when I speak, you will do exactly what I tell you to do." He tugged on his shirt and thrust his feet into his shoes. "After this I'm anxious to be on my way."

"Have a good journey."

"I'll take my mare and leave you yours." He picked up the decanter of port. The downstairs might be cold by now, but he needed something to cool his anger. Inside his head, a small voice kept whispering to him, begging him to cool his temper, counselling him to diplomacy.

"Good."

"Good." He slammed the door behind him hard enough to shake the house on its foundations.

He was only halfway down the stairs when he heard the bedroom door open.

"When you're half frozen, come back!" she yelled. "I shan't speak to you again!" Then the door thundered once more.

Fortunately for the Blivenses, the fire had been laid in the study. Still seething Robin lighted it, watched in some satisfaction as it blazed up. The chimney was unblocked this time and drew well. In a minute he had dragged the chaise in front of it.

But he did not drop onto the makeshift bed and dispose himself for sleep.

His anger was too raw. She had ruined everything with her blathering about ambitions and money. She wanted a baby and a stud farm. He could probably give her the baby, but the other—

His nineteen-year-old upstart wife with her impudent mouth had brought him up short. Eschewing the port, he pulled the cork from a bottle of brandy and dropped into the wingchair. Feet propped on the end of the chaise, he proceeded to drink.

First, his anger melted away. Then he no longer felt the discomfort of the chair. Then the scars on his face and body ceased to ache and draw. His last action was to curl his hand around the empty brandy bottle in his lap.

Robin did not arise until almost noon. The brandy had made him most unpleasantly ill, but he managed to stagger out the back and relieve himself in the snow behind a hedge. Pale but weak, he returned.

His wife stood in the hall watching him contemptuously. "You can go to your room, if you're able," she said coldly. "I have moved my things out of the room, so you may drink undisturbed."

"Good," he snarled.

"Good."

"Well, he did the deed." Mrs. Blivens held up the sheet.

Her husband looked vaguely in her direction. "What deed?"

"None of your concern. Just go on with your ratkillin'. Old fool." She said the last under her breath as she folded the material carefully and laid it under a pile of linens in the closet.

"They've had — er — an argument, I think," Blivens remarked to no one in particular. He uncorked a bottle of spirits and poured a healthy swig down his throat. He choked, coughed, and wheezed.

His wife came out of the closet and thumped him on the back.

Eyes still streaming, he stuffed the cork back in the bottle and fumbled it back into the rack.

"So they 'ave," Mrs. Blivens mused. " 'Imself'll be glad t' 'ear that. Wonder if 'e beat 'er. 'E'd want t' know that too."

Blivens looked at her puzzled. His brow wrinkled. "Who, m' dear?"

Robin rode ten miles in the opposite direction from the small hamlet where his few tenants traded.

In the adjoining shire, he chose from among several a man whom he judged might be a competent groom. Unemployment was rampant throughout the countryside, but men who could truly handle horses were always hard to find.

Oglethorpe claimed to have been a soldier. He wore a couple of tattered pieces of a uniform and stood straight when he was addressed. He assured Robin that he had been an ostler for a quartermaster and knew "horseflesh from mane to tail."

Robin interrupted the man's boasting with impatience. "Then you think you can manage to care for a lady's mount and do whatever else might be asked of you?"

The man looked deflated for a second. Then he nodded enthusiastically. "I can handle it, sir."

"You'll have your bed and board and a guinea a quarter."

"Yes, sir."

Robin rose and pulled on his gloves. "Report to Lady Whittcombstone."

"Yes, sir."

"Damn yer eyes, Fod. He's gone afield and hired a stableman. If you'd just laid low, I could have had that job."

"I lost m' temper. I can't stand them bleedin' lordships comin' back 'ere —" The lout fell to muttering.

"When he leaves, we could have kept right on with our business."

"Y' don't know 'e's gonna t' leave."

"They all do."

138

Fod spat on the ground. "When 'e leaves, maybe I could make t' new one leave."

" 'E's a big'un. Claims 'e wus a soljer." Another voice, slower, gentler, offered his worries.

"They all claim to be soldiers. More soldiers 'n England now than 'n Wellington's and Napoleon's armies all told."

"Mayhap somethin' else'll come along."

"Sure. Somethin' allus does."

"Well, you took your time in getting here," Robin snarled.

"I was in the stables," Noelle replied icily.

"Ah, yes. The vaunted breeding program. Do you find Oglethorpe satisfactory?"

As a matter-of-fact she found Oglethorpe most unsatisfactory. She did not tell her husband that she had dismissed Oglethorpe on the spot that morning when she had found him passed out in the tack room with a bottle between his legs.

When Oglethorpe had threatened to go to the Earl, she had dared him to do so. "The Earl can't abide a drinking man," she declared. "He's liable to take a horsewhip to any man in his employ who drinks on the job."

Oglethorpe had whined, but she waved the bottle at him.

He left.

Now, she smiled sweetly up into her husband's face. "Did you have something you wanted to say to me, or did you plan to insult me for an extra hour?"

"Much as that idea tempts me, I'm afraid I must

forgo it. I'm leaving for London."

"Good journey," she snapped.

"Sit down." He gestured toward the chair in front of his desk.

"I'll stand."

"Sit down."

She perched on its arm.

He grimaced, then pulled open the drawer at his left and held up a leather pouch for her identification. "I have placed a purse with a reasonable sum of money in the drawer."

"I didn't know you had any money."

"Believe me, Madam Wife, I had none. Your father's factor passed this to me as we left that establishment."

"So, it's my money."

"No, Madam Wife. It's *my* money. Petruchio's twenty thousand crowns for marrying the shrew."

She could think of nothing foul enough to say.

He dropped the purse back into the drawer as if it were contaminated. "From this you'll be able to pay for whatever household improvements you care to make as well as personal items." He stared pointedly at her clothing. "Although you probably won't need much."

She wore the coachman's coat he had first seen her wearing, as well as the hat tied down around her ears with the woolen muffler. She looked as though she had been mucking out the stables. "Probably not."

"You seem set on this foolish dream." He waited. His lips thinned when she did not respond. He had almost determined that if she asked for more, he would give it to her. In the week since their argument, he had located a stallion up country about twenty miles. The stud fee was negligible because of the horse's age, but if her mare's lines were as good as she declared, the colt might be good.

She managed to look bored, swinging her foot back and forth.

"In the matter of food, I've settled with the tradespeople, so all the debt in this area is clear. You start with a clean slate."

"How generous of you!"

"You don't need to pay them. They will wait until I return. The groom has been paid in advance."

She shifted uncomfortably and wondered how much Oglethorpe had received for one week's work — and all the liquor he could drink.

"The new lady's maid meets with your approval?"

"She's not a lady's maid, but she seems to be a clean willing girl."

"Good."

She nodded. "Oh, I'm most grateful, Husband. I have a groom, a maid, and, of course, dear Mr. and Mrs. Blivens."

He ignored the sarcasm, though it set his teeth on edge. "Then I believe everything is taken care of."

"If you believe it, then it must be so."

"Indeed. Now that I've put everything to rights, I can't allow myself to grow bored in the country. The season is in progress in London. I should have a splendid time."

"Splendid."

He closed the drawer with unnecessary force and locked it. Rising he came round the desk and held out the key. She extended her hand, palm upward.

He dropped it into it, without touching her flesh. Her fingers clenched around it.

He raised his dark eyebrow, cocking his head to one side, centering his black eye to appraise her. Suddenly, he was so angry he could feel his stomach tremble. "No tearful farewells, Madam Wife. No remonstrances to me to take care of myself. What am I to think? What will the staff think?" He leaned close. "You'd stand a better chance of being obeyed if they knew you had my voice."

"In that case—" Noelle rose and placed her arm through his. "—I'll accompany you to the door and bid you God speed."

"I rather thought you would."

Blivens held the door for them to pass out. The day was briskly cold and overcast, but the promise of more snow was slight. Noelle looked toward the skies then back at her husband. "You should have a good journey."

"Yes," he agreed with a stiff smile. Then he raised his voice, so even poor old Blivens could not mistake his message. "Madam Wife, I leave you in charge of the estate until the business I have in the city is concluded."

"I'll take care, milord," she replied unsmiling. "I'll try to the best of my humble ability to rise to the responsibility."

"See that you do."

"You'll take care of her, won't you, Blivens?"

The old man's eyes opened wide. He gazed around in confusion. "Oh! Yes sir. Yes sir."

The Earl grimaced. "Safe and snug, Madam Wife."

She nodded. "Yes, milord."

"Then I'll be on my way."

"Good."

The black mare's reins were looped through the hitching post ring. Robin looked around in annoyance for Oglethorpe. With a shrug he tested the saddlegirth, rocked the saddle on the broad back, then turned back to his waiting wife. The perversity which had become second nature to him tweaked at him. He caught her hand and drew her toward him. She had no choice but to come down the steps if she were to preserve the fiction that they were happily married.

The other arm went round her like an iron band. He pulled her against him, tilted back her head, and kissed her long and hard.

Blivens gasped. "Milord."

Noelle's scarf slipped and her hat fell off her head. Her cheeks were flaming and her mouth was thoroughly bruised when he let her go.

Black eye glittering in triumph, teeth bared in a grin, he pulled his own hat more firmly down on his head and swung into the saddle.

"Good."

Eight

Free. Free! *Free!* "Free."

Noelle fairly leaped up the steps into the dark hall. While the astounded Blivens gaped, she threw back her head and laughed. She whirled round and round, her face lifted to the beamed ceiling. Her skirts flew out around her. She pulled her scarf loose and flung it wide.

"Milady?" Blivens flinched as her hat shot by him and landed in a corner.

"Free, Blivens!" she caught his hand and attempted to dance with him, but the poor old man could only stare at her antics, an uncertain grin lighting his face.

"Yes, milady."

"Alone!" She let him go and ran a few steps, then slid down the length of the hall. "Alone." She stopped by wrapping her arm around the newel post, then brushed her toe back and forth over the floor. "This wood needs a good polishing. I can't get up enough speed."

"No, milady." He looked at her and at the floor helplessly. "I suppose so, milady."

"Oh, indubitably so, Blivens." She hugged the newel post giggling.

Her new maid stared at her with wide eyes, her hand pressed to her mouth.

Her expression set Noelle into another fit of giggles. She flung open the door to the parlor and dashed inside. "Light a fire in here, Blivens. I want to sit in here in the evenings. I want this room kept warm. This is going to be my room."

"This room?"

"That's right."

The caretaker *cum* butler looked around him nervously. The maid peered over his stooped shoulder. He cleared his throat. "I don't think this room has been used in my lifetime."

"Yes." She pounced on his sentence. "It has never been used. So I'm taking it for my own. It belongs to me."

She swished a canvas covering off a chair and swirled it around her before flinging it across the maid's arms. She caught hold of the edges of the draperies and flung them back. Dust billowed up. The maid retreated sneezing.

Through the grimy window Noelle caught sight of a rider's black silhouette climbing the second hill. Her husband was leaving her. She clutched the heavy material. Her back straightened. "Robin Whittcombstone," she chanted. "I hope you never, never, *never* come back."

She swung around. "Blivens! And you too—er—"

"Lily, ma'am." She dropped a curtsy.

"Lily. Blivens. I want this room clean and a fire laid. I am going riding. When I come back, I expect

145

to have a delightful breakfast on a tray in front of the fireplace. I expect the tea to be hot."

Blivens looked hopelessly confused, but Lily's mouth was quirking at the corners. They followed her out into the hall.

She retrieved her hat from the corner and tied it under her chin with her scarf. "Blivens." She put her hand on his shoulder and waited until he nervously looked her in the eye. "Clean the chamber. Lay a fire."

His eyes slid distractedly to her hand.

"Blivens." She tightened her fingers gently. His gaze flickered up at her. "Clean the chamber. Lay the fire."

"Yes, milady. 'Clean the chamber. Lay a fire.' "

"Good." She patted him on the shoulder.

"Lily."

"Yes, ma'am."

"Help him remember. And tell his wife that I want breakfast. If she doesn't want to fix the tray, then bring it to me yourself."

"Yes, ma'am." Lily curtsied again.

"And stop that bobbing. I'm not a Duchess."

"Yes, ma'am."

Leaving Lily and Blivens to stare, Noelle strode out of the room. They heard the front door close behind her.

Robin Whittcombstone paused in the door of White's. Clad in a new coat of black superfine, a black vest, and palest stirrup trousers, he felt the gaze of several players skim over him, then stop. Their eyes flashed back and widened in surprise. One man nudged another who turned to stare.

146

Robin smiled thinly. A waiter approached with a tray of chilled champagne. He helped himself to a glass and continued to gaze round the smoke-hazed room. Quickly, he found the man he sought. The silvery-white hair shone like a beacon.

He took another sip of the champagne and strolled to the nearest table. The play was deep as always. He felt his interest quicken. The temptation was there to gamble tonight without the terrible desperation that had created such havoc before his marriage. He had always accounted himself a good gambler.

He had promised himself that he would not gamble beyond his income for the quarter. And if he won—

Strolling leisurely, he made a circuit of the room, pausing to watch the impassioned playing, shaking his head at a couple of invitations to sit, speaking to no one. At last he came, as he had intended, to the table occupied by his father-in-law.

He paused directly behind Averill, who had not noticed him. The Ice King's cards were not promising. He coughed deeply and took a drink of brandy.

A silence fell at the table as the other players recognized Robin. The dealer dealt a card to top off Averill's hand. It was the wrong one. The Duke cursed softly and pushed the cards away from him.

The winner raked in his winnings.

"I—I must be going," stammered a pudgy young man across from the Duke. He pushed back his chair. "Will you take my place, Whittcombstone?"

The Ice King whirled round in his chair. He gaped angrily at his son-in-law. "What are you doing here?"

"Playing cards, if I may." Face impassive, he slipped into the vacated chair and placed his glass of champagne on his left. He passed a note to the banker who stacked chips in front of him.

The deck passed to Averill, who looked as if he might say more. Then he coughed and began to deal.

For several hours the men sat impassively, their faces reflecting nothing. Eyes hooded, they would glance only briefly at their cards. The majority of the time, they concentrated on the faces of their opponents. They sought the uncontrollables — a faint flush, a slight paling, tiny beads of sweat.

The smoke in the room thickened. It drifted in hazy swathes about their shoulders.

Averill coughed incessantly. His pale eyes grew red-rimmed. The contrast to the blue irises and the dead white skin was eerie. The other players watched him curiously. His anger was a palpable thing at the gaming table.

From time to time, men rose from the tables to leave the room for one reason or another. Waiters passed obsequiously among the players who indicated their wants with nods or gestures.

Flunkeys waited unobtrusively in the four corners. As the night wore on, they would step forward with more frequency as a game would require pen and paper. Robin finished his champagne. The others waited for him to order a more potent substance — brandy, perhaps, or even vicious absinthe.

Instead, he switched to a white burgundy and leaned back in his chair with an air of languid indifference. At every hand someone won, others lost, but at first the game remained about even. The cards did not seem to favor one player over another.

Then gradually a turn of fortune became apparent.

Whittcombstone began to win. His falcon eye hooded. His dark gaunt face, now shadowed by a blue-black stubble, became more and more severe as the pile of chips grew in front of him.

"Brandy for you, Whittcombstone?" Averill urged. Robin shook his head.

"No? Well, another for me at any rate."

While it was brought the two men appraised each other. "Quite a run of luck for you, Turk," Averill snarled, placing peculiar emphasis on the sobriquet. "A toast to your winnings."

"Thank you." Robin ignored the name. He lifted his own glass and sipped the still wine.

"Not your usual style."

"Not usual. No. However, I believe my luck may have changed after my brief hiatus in the country."

"Too brief. Too brief." Averill frowned and shook his head in an effort to clear it. "Why'd you leave?"

"The season's in full swing." Robin pushed back his chair. "Gentlemen, I bid you good morning. I think I may have caught the country hours. I'm fatigued."

A round of protests followed as he gathered up the contents of most of their pockets. Averill, in particular, glared after him as he cashed in his chips at the bank.

Outside on the curb, Robin stretched gingerly. The morning light hit his eye without causing him pain. His body still stiffened during long play but not so much as it had. His funds had enabled him to take better lodgings with a better bed. He ate better food.

When, he wondered, had the alcohol he drank come to be more the cause of his pain than the alleviator of it?

He turned at the sound of a familiar cough.

"Buy me supper?" Averill suggested. "Winner treats loser."

Robin suppressed his distaste. "I think it's too late for supper. I'm for breakfast myself."

"The very thing."

Seated across from the Duke, Robin studied the pale thin face. The man's skin showed every vein. The appearance was macabre when the eyes were bloodshot from the smoke and the nose swollen and red from the night's drinking.

The waiter brought coffee, hot and black.

Averill took a sip and set the cup down. "You've come up in the world, thanks to me," he observed.

Robin waited.

"You don't like me very much."

"No."

"And yet you owe your good fortune to me. You should be thanking me profusely."

Robin drank his own coffee. "You didn't choose me to visit good fortune upon. You chose me to visit ill fortune upon your daughter."

A moment's silence. "And did you?"

"Did I visit ill fortune upon her?"

"Yes."

"I think you'd have to ask her that. She seemed content enough when I left. She had a maid, a groom for her horse—"

"Yes. Yes. Spare me the list of your staff. I see I must speak plainly with you, Turk. You have no sense of delicacy whatsoever."

Anger surged through Robin. Why was he sitting across the table from this obnoxious man?

The waiter set covered plates before them. With a flourish he lifted the domes to reveal eggs, kippers, and kidneys. He set a rack of toast between them and bowed obsequiously.

The tantalizing odors sparked his appetite. He lifted his knife and fork.

Averill leaned forward. "Did she weep?"

Robin halted, silverware poised. "What?"

"Did she weep?" The Ice King's eyes glittered in the morning light slanting through the windows. "When you took her."

"I beg your pardon."

"When you put your crude, hard hands on her. Did she fight you?" He laughed—a mirthless bark. "I'll bet she did. She's a feisty baggage. Just like her mother before her."

"Sir!"

"Did she fight you? Did you knock the insolence out of her? Tell me."

Robin's appetite vanished. He laid down his knife and fork. "I'll do no such thing."

"I'll bet she did. Good. Good. What better person than the Black Turk to give her her come-uppance."

Robin pulled a pound note from his pocket. He tossed it onto the table between them. His napkin followed it. His chair scraped noisily as he pushed it back.

Averill looked taken aback. "What in hell's wrong with you, Turk?"

"I've decided to breakfast alone."

"Come back here."

Robin leaned across the table and grasped the man's cravat. He twisted his fist in it and pulled the Duke half out of his chair. "Never," he grated, his face inches from the angry countenance. "Never."

He slammed the older man back into the chair. The table rocked, oversetting the coffee cups, scattering the toast. Other diners whispered and stared. Several waiters and the manager converged on the table in alarm.

"Never," Robin repeated. He brushed past the servitors and slammed out.

"Would you be needing a stableman, ma'am?"

Noelle cocked her head to one side appraising the big man who had risen from the mounting block at her approach. "I might. Who told you I needed one?"

"Lily, ma'am. She's a good friend."

"She seems to be a willing worker."

He smiled. "She is that, ma'am. I'll swear to it."

"And she'll swear for you. How convenient!"

He nodded, unabashed. "That's how it works, ma'am. It's not how fine you are, but who knows you."

"And who you know," she added dryly. "What's your name and where have you worked before?"

He hesitated. Then threw his shoulders back. "Private Timothy Hardwicke. Portugal and Spain."

She raised an eyebrow. "The last groom claimed he took care of horses for the army. If he did, I'm surprised we won."

Hardwicke hesitated. "I didn't see that we did."

They measured each other recognizing each other's

cynicism. It was the beginning of understanding.

She walked past him into the shedrow. Silver Belle whinnied a greeting. Noelle patted the horse's cheek. "If you worked here, you'd work for me. Not the Earl."

"A man can lose his job fast like that."

"I believe I'm your best chance. The Earl has left for an extended stay in London. I've just dismissed the man he hired. If you don't do your job, I'll dismiss you."

"Then that's fine with me, ma'am."

"I can pay only a pittance. The Earl left very little money. But there's bed and board."

He nodded. "Whatever it is, it's better than nothing."

"I don't put a bridle on my tongue."

"I'll stand myself warned."

She held out her hand. He wiped his on his pantleg and shook. "So, Timothy —"

"Tim, ma'am."

"So Tim Hardwicke. Meet Silver Belle. I'll wait while you saddle her." She watched while he placed the saddle on the broad back. "Tell me, Tim. Who has the best stallion in the neighborhood?"

The Averill crest gleamed dully on the door of the carriage. Noelle shook her head in astonishment. Although the outrider had told her that His Grace, the Duke was only a few miles behind, she had not really believed him. The Ice King had washed his hands of her. He would never come here.

She looked around her in some embarrassment.

With the exception of the parlor and the bedroom she had chosen for her own, the house was still a shambles. For herself she did not care. Her husband had shown no interest in his home. He had certainly not left money for its improvement. Still, she disliked the idea that Averill would see her husband's poverty.

She shrugged away the thought. She had no interest in housekeeping. She had other things on which to spend the meagre contents of his purse.

The coach halted at the front stoop. The tiger in navy blue livery leaped from the box and opened the door. Averill, wrapped in a priceless cloak of gray astrakhan, alighted.

Noelle herself opened the front door in her mother's dress, some twenty years old, its black wool rusted. A band of black satin had been added two inches above the bottom of the skirt to conceal the worn line where the hem had been let out.

The Duke smiled. "The Countess of Whittcombstone, I see."

"Averill." She clenched her fists in the folds of her skirt. "Breaking your journey, are you?"

His ice blue eyes flicked over her. "Why, what a gracious hostess you are. Your husband must be pleased with his bargain."

"He's not here."

"I'm well aware of that fact." Without waiting for an invitation, he swept by her into the dimly lit hall. His smile broadened at the sight of the shabby furnishings, the dingy paneling, the grimy floor. "How romantic."

Noelle waited stonily.

Revolving slowly, his pale gaze flickering over

everything, he stripped off his gloves of Italian leather. "Well, aren't you going to offer me tea? Surely, you have tea."

Blivens shut the door and hurried to take the elegant cloak. "Oh, yes, sir. Right away, sir. Er—tea."

"And a dram of something warmer." Averill's voice followed the old man behind the stairs. Blivens did not hear. He continued on his way muttering to himself. The Ice King's chuckle ended in a delicate cough. He addressed his unwilling hostess. "Surely, you have something for me."

"Not really."

Averill's smile froze in place as he opened the door on his right. Dust covers remained on everything except the seats before the fire where Robin and she had sat the night of their arrival. "Charming," was his comment. "Certainly a wise precaution against deterioration."

She swung open the door to her own parlor. "Oh, come in and sit down, Averill. I believe my husband has some brandy. I'll fetch it."

He went directly to hold out his hands to the blaze on the hearth. Then with his back to it, he surveyed her hideaway. Books were stacked haphazardly beside a wingchair. A large table had been turned into a desk with inkstand and papers. More books were stacked on one corner. Curious, the Duke crossed to it and unashamedly examined them. He tilted one to the light to read it more closely.

"This is my house." Noelle announced from the door. "Those are my papers."

With a smile he released it to waft back down. It slid off onto the floor. "Sorry."

"What do you want, Averill?" She set a single glass of brandy down on the table.

"Why to satisfy myself that my matchmaking has borne fruit." He came around and perched on a corner of the table, one foot swinging indolently. His ice blue eyes appraised her figure. "Might I hope that you are with child?"

She started. "I beg your pardon."

"Enceinte. In an interesting condition. Up the stick," he finished crudely.

"I know what you mean."

"I'm delighted to hear that you are."

She cocked her head appraisingly. "I didn't say that I am. I said that I knew what you meant. You didn't have to explain."

"Of course, I didn't. You knew."

"I'm not a child."

He shook his head in exasperation. "But are you with child?"

"That is certainly between my husband and me."

"Damn you!" Hot color suffused his pale cheeks. He set the brandy glass down so hard that the glass cracked. The remainder of the liquid trickled out onto the desk. "How dare you give me such an answer!" He sprang to his feet.

Noelle started back.

He came toward her, hands doubled into fists. "You will tell me."

Blivens opened the door. "Tea, ma'am."

The Duke relaxed as the old man shuffled in behind an antique cart that creaked softly.

"I hope this'll be all right, ma'am. Mrs. Blivens didn't think it was the right time. Er—the right time for tea. She said I'd got it all wrong." His expression worried, he looked to Noelle for confirmation. "Did I?"

"You got it right," she told him with forced cheerfulness. "Bring it here, Blivens." She sat down in her accustomed place in front of the fire.

"Yes, ma'am." He positioned the cart beside her chair.

"And draw up a chair for the Duke."

"Yes, ma'am." He looked around uncertainly.

"That chair will do nicely." She pointed to one.

Noelle watched the muscle quiver in Averill's cheek as he waited impatiently for Blivens to accomplish his task. When the old man had finally finished and the door had closed, the Duke loomed over her.

"You and your husband must have consummated the marriage before he left for London? The real question is whether or not the mating has born fruit."

"I forget how you like your tea, Averill. With or without sugar?"

He swung away, pacing about the room, his eyes darting everywhere, as if seeking the answer. He turned back with a sly expression on his face. "Perhaps he found you so unattractive that he left without ever sampling the goods?"

Hands icy, Noelle set the cup and saucer down close to his chair. Then she poured for herself. A little tea splashed into the saucer, but she did not notice. Though her stomach burned and her heart pounded, she added sugar and lifted the cup to her lips.

"That's it, isn't it?" Averill tapped his finger thoughtfully against the side of his cheek. He shook his head as he surveyed her. "He took a dislike to you.

The face, the hair, the ugly dark French coloring. I would have thought he would have liked dark skin. Or perhaps you tore a patch off him with that tongue of yours?"

His pacing had brought him up to the window. He stared out at the black trees against the snow. "I would have thought the irascible Turk would have knocked the meanness out of you." He swung around. "Is he all show? A fool and a weakling as well as a gambling womanizer."

"He's the man you chose for me," she reminded him. "He certainly sounds as though he meets with your qualifications."

"You must summon him home."

She laughed mirthlessly. "Why would I want to do that?"

He hesitated. "All women want children."

"From a fool and a weakling. Heaven forfend."

"File that tongue!" Averill snarled.

Noelle set her cup down. Slipping from her chair, she all but ran across the room and flung open the door. "I think you'd better leave."

"Come back here."

"Blivens!"

"Yes, ma'am." The old man had stationed himself in the hall. He climbed to his feet, his smile cherubic.

"The Duke is leaving. Please fetch his cloak."

"Leave it." He overruled her. "I'm not leaving until I get the answers I want."

"You have the only one you're going to get from me."

"No. Tell me." He reached for her, but she eluded his grasp.

Dashing past the confused Blivens, she flung open the front door. The drive was full of the Duke's men. The coachy and the guard, the young tiger, two outriders, and—most importantly—Timothy Hardwicke.

"His Grace is ready to depart," she called hurrying down the steps to her groom. With him at her back, she faced Averill.

Had she not become somewhat accustomed to his rages, she would have shrunk back. The entourage did. All except Hardwicke. She felt him at her back. He had closed the distance between them and now stood at her shoulder.

"Your Grace." The coachy bowed. The coach rocked as he mounted to the box.

The tiger tugged open the door and folded down the step. "Ready, Your Grace."

Murder flaming in his eyes, Averill stood in the doorway. He opened his mouth to bark an order.

Every man on the drive tensed. Noelle pulled herself straighter. She had no recourse should he order them to bring her back in. All these men were in his employ. He could take over the house and stay as long as he wished.

Then Blivens came up behind him. "Wait, wait, milord," the old man called. "You don't want to forget your coat. It's so cold out." He draped it over the broad shoulders. "Let me just get your hat and gloves. Did you have a stick?"

The Duke had eyes only for Noelle. "The time will come, my girl, when you will bitterly regret not giving me the information I came for."

"Here y' are. Here y' are, sir." Blivens shuffled back

with his offerings.

To a man the assemblage gasped. The old butler had brought the correct gloves but had substituted the coachman's hat and scarf that Noelle wore for Averill's elegant beaver.

They all saw the Duke's expression grow apoplectic. His snarl was feral as he snatched the articles from Blivens and rudely tossed away the wretched hat.

Pulling on the gloves, he stomped down the steps. "Since I caught you unprepared, Countess, I'll stay at the local inn tonight, and continue my journey tomorrow."

"I think that would be wise." She stepped back out of his reach.

"I expect your husband to return to you almost immediately," he sneered. "I don't suppose you could be prevailed upon to summon him?"

"Never. I feel about him exactly as you would expect."

"Town will be exhausting for him. And dangerous. His health will definitely suffer."

"Perhaps you should tell him that yourself."

The Duke climbed into the coach. The outriders mounted and trotted their horses down the drive. Averill's last words reached only Noelle and Tim Hardwicke. "Very well, I shall, but you will be very, very sorry."

Nine

He had won!

Robin ran his hand inside the pocket of his coat. The wad of bills and notes felt surprisingly thick. Even though he had felt it twice on his way back to his digs, he could still not quite credit it.

When he had raked in the first pot of the evening, his mouth had twisted in self-mockery. He had won a bloody fortune.

Still, he knew better than to surrender to elation. This luck would not last. The next pot would be a loss.

And so it was! But he had not lost nearly so much as he had won. The hand had been poor from the beginning, a mixture of trash, three suits, a face card, nothing to draw to. He had folded.

But the next had been good. His opponents had little. They had folded early. The pot was small.

"It very much looks likes it's your night, Whittcombstone," Toby Calcingham had remarked as he flung his cards down in disgust.

The deal passed to him and he dealt himself a trey

of clubs. He looked at the card then at Toby. "Not a very impressive hand for 'my night.' "

Wonder of wonder, the trey of clubs had been the beginning of a straight. He had won so much money that Calcingham had dropped out with a salute. "You're not nearly so much fun to play with as you used to be."

Robin raised an eyebrow. "Why's that?"

Calcingham stared pointedly at the glass of watered wine. "Not dipping deep enough."

Robin had laughed. Another man had slipped into Calcingham's place and the play had continued.

Robin closed and locked his door behind him and lit the lamp. His head did not ache, nor did the muscles in his body ache anywhere. Perhaps his euphoria was quieting them.

He emptied his pockets on the table. For a long time he stared at his winnings. Then, his throat dry, he began to count. When he was finished, he stared at 24,287 pounds.

What irony! A month ago he had been bought body and soul for half as much. If he had but known, he could have spit in the Ice King's sneering face and never, never saddled himself with the devilish daughter. He shrugged. He had luck too late. Ever the story of his life.

He ran his hand through his hair, encountering the scar. His fingers traced it almost absently. The leather strap cut across his face, the skin puffed around it. He fumbled at the back of his neck and untied the strap. The patch fell away.

Cold air poured onto the socket where the eye had been. Tentatively, he touched the hole, felt the puckered, desecrated flesh. He had not looked at it in over a year. Never did he confront himself in the mirror.

When he returned home, he would have to drive his wife from his bedroom. It was damned uncomfortable to sleep with the patch on.

He divided the money into denominations and stacked it in order of worth. 24,287 pounds. What would he do with so much money?

He could gamble forever.

He trembled. That way was certain disaster. It had taken twelve hours to win it. It would take probably fewer than twelve hours to lose it. Before he had gambled to keep his head above water. Now he had an income. This was like a gift. What to do with it?

Tattersall's was not particularly crowded. The usual round of horses for racing had been trotted round with big money going to pay for them.

Then came the horse he was looking for. A tall mare, black, like Kate, with a lanky body and long legs. Her lines were good, but she was too tall for a lady's mount. He had noted her especially. She looked at him with mild eyes. A four year old. Because she was not a pretty animal, she went cheap.

Another older black with racing blood in her lines and two black two-year-olds followed. In all he bought four mares and a heavy shouldered black gelding, totally unexceptional for his own mount. When he had finished, he still had more than half of his money.

With longing, he looked at the stallions. But they were too rich for his blood and his pocketbook. With a bit of finagling, he could afford the stud fees for his ladies — and he remembered — for old Silver Belle.

He grinned. It was the beginning.

The real test of his wife and her proud declaration would be her reaction to his purchases. Would she see the potential of the black mare, of the others? He stroked the white race down the mare's forehead.

"She's a good 'un," the crippled handler told him. All the men who made their living working with horses eventually ended crippled in some way.

Robin stared at the limping gait. "So you think I made a wise purchase."

The man smiled. "Best of the lot today. She's got legs like iron." For proof he crouched and lifted the front hoof. "Just feel that. Feel that cannon bone. She'll never go down on you. No, nor any of her colts."

"You think she'll breed true."

"I'd stake my life on it. It's bred in the bone."

Beautiful to the horizon, the Downs of Somerset stretched before Noelle. They were sprinkled with tiny copses still white with snow. She had never ridden so far before, but the sun was bright and the day was un-usually warm. She lifted her face to it and inhaled deeply. Even in the dead of winter, a day like this should be enjoyed.

Suddenly, Silver Belle laid back her head and whickered.

Noelle turned in the saddle to stare at three men

trotting their horses along the winding road she had come. Hats pulled low and mufflers pulled high, they rode toward her.

She reined the mare to the verge and allowed her to pick her way slowly. Behind her, the hoofbeats quickened. One spoke. "There. Look there."

Something in the voice, the tone of command, the urgency made her spine prickle. She looked back over her shoulder in time to see the muffler slip from the face of the leader.

He was grinning, his teeth bared, his color high. Their eyes met. She recognized the man from the inn, the one who had attacked Robin.

"Get 'er!"

He spurred his horse. The other two followed. Still grinning, he reached out, his hand like a claw, stretching toward her.

She had no time to be afraid. With all her strength she brought the braided-leather crop down on the mare's rump. At the same time she reined the little horse off the road. Silver Belle whinnied in pain. She tucked her head and kicked out with her hind legs at the thing that had stung her.

One flying hoof caught the lout's horse in the chest. It reared and buck-jumped. The second rider jerked his mount into the shoulder of the third rider who was almost unseated in a confusion of flying hooves and twisting bodies. For a minute her three pursuers had all they could do to control their horses. It was the minute Noelle needed.

Over the next rise was a tiny hamlet. It would surely offer her refuge if only she could reach it.

Unfortunately, the mare's run lasted only a couple

of hundred yards uphill. Then despite the whip, she had no more speed to give. Her run dropped to a gallop.

Noelle tossed a look over her shoulder and saw them decreasing the distance with great strides. She leaned forward over her panting mount. "Run!" She shrieked. "Run. Damn you!"

One ear flicked back. The speed increased.

Noelle cast another frantic glance over her shoulder. Blood streaked the chest of the leader's horse. The rider's face was red with fury, his grin turned to a sneer.

Panicked, Noelle struck Silver Belle again. The old mare's sides heaved. Her breath came out in tortured grunts. Her gallop became a bone-jarring trot. She stumbled.

In desperation, Noelle hauled the mare's head around at the same time her right hand dived inside her cloak. With a curse worthy of the Earl, she pulled out her pistol.

At the sight two of the riders pulled their mounts, but the leader was furious. Ducking his head, he drove the spurs into his mount's sides. His mouth wide open, he gave tongue to a fearsome yell.

Noelle squeezed the trigger just as Silver Belle shied at the hideous noise. The mare's movement sent the shot wide. It also made her pursuer miss his hold. Reaching for her body, his clutching fingers fastened in her cloak.

As he swept on by, she grabbed for the saddlebow with her left hand. Fighting, fighting, she was wrenched off sideways. Her foot hit the ground. Fiery pain shot up her leg as her ankle buckled. She landed hard on her back. Her head cracked against a rock.

Archie Holmesfield stood in the door of the dining room. His eyes moved methodically from table to table. The sight made a bad taste in Robin's mouth. He laid down his knife and fork and lifted his glass of red wine.

Averill's factor found him in the act of drinking it. Relief evident, the man wended his way across the room and presented himself at Robin's table with a brief bow. "Milord, sorry to disturb you at your dinner."

"Then don't."

"A message of utmost urgency from His Grace."

Robin looked with some regret at the tender cut of beef. He had turned some of his winnings to his tailor and some to his own pleasure. A good meal well-served was a part of that indulgence. "Utmost urgency to him, indeed. But I very much doubt that it is of utmost urgency to me. Please wait outside."

The factor hesitated, looking somewhat nonplussed. At the next table another diner looked inquiringly in their direction. Not looking at the intruder, Robin cut a bite of meat precisely.

"Please, milord." Archie came closer. "It's about the Countess."

Robin put the meat in his mouth and chewed reflectively. It really was good — tender, moist, flavorful. Had money restored his sense of taste?

Another character entered the act in the person of the waiter, who appeared suddenly at Robin's shoulder. "Is this man annoying you, milord?"

Robin looked meaningfully at Archie, who threw discretion to the winds.

He leaned forward as far as he dared without falling on the table. "The Countess, milord, has disappeared."

"You bloody fool! She's dead." The voice of authority was sharp, accusatory.

"Nah," scoffed Fod. "She ain't dead. Lit on 'er foot, she did, 'an then fell."

"We wasn't supposed t' 'urt 'er." The third voice was almost weeping. " 'N' 'er a lady. Oh, y' bleedin' idiot. Tell 'im, Cap'n. We wasn't supposed t' 'urt 'er."

Noelle could hear the words, but she could not move. At least she did not dare try. Nerves all over her body were sending all consuming signals to her head which hurt too badly to identify them.

She could remember everything—and nothing. With a great effort of will, she tried to move. Her leg hurt from heel to knee, a pulsating agony, overwhelming her.

"Shut up, the both of you. Pick her up and let's get her stowed."

"Not me, Cap'n. Not on yer life. I ain't touchin' 'er. I ain't paid fer killin' a lady."

"I tell y', she ain't dead. Look."

Someone kicked her left foot, or merely nudged it. Whatever he did made no difference. The pain ripped through her. She screamed—a pitiful mewling cry. Her eyelids flickered before the blackness closed round her again.

* * *

"If my wife has chosen to leave me, she is free to do so."

Holmesfield shook his head. "I don't think that's the way of it, sir. That wasn't the impression I received from His Grace's message."

"What was Averill doing there in the first place? I didn't think he cared a tinker's dam about his daughter."

Holmesfield's color darkened. He looked out the window of the coach. "I don't know that you're correct about that, sir. After all, he's just arranged her marriage to an Earl."

"Don't be an ass. He arranged her marriage to me." Robin's voice sliced through the man's unctuous words. "More than twice her age, scarred, half-blind—"

Holmesfield interrupted. "The message was that she had disappeared. I would take that to infer that she had met with some mischance. Possibly she went riding and did not come back."

Robin stared at the man in the gloom of the carriage. "Is that what happened?"

"I don't know."

"I think you do."

"The Duke will want to tell you what happened." Holmesfield murmured forbiddingly. "I really don't know any more to tell you."

"You bloody brutes!" Noelle struggled and twisted with all her strength. The pain in her leg kept her from kicking, but her nails tore furrows through a wiry bush of whiskers.

169

"Bitch!"

Her captor dropped her onto the hard-packed floor of the stable. She screamed as her injured ankle came down first. Panting, gasping, weak with pain, she lay groaning unable to move.

"Hang on to her. Bleedin' hell, Fod, you're going to kill her."

"Th' bleedin' bitch scratched me, Cap'n."

"Then tie her hands," came the disgusted order.

Calling Noelle every foul name in his considerable vocabulary, Fod rolled her over onto her stomach. With a greasy handkerchief from his neck, he tied her wrists together.

"Bring her along."

"W'at I wants t' know is who died and made you m' boss?" Fod complained. Still cursing, he dragged Noelle up into his arms and bore her into what must have been a tack room. Light filtered in through spaces between the warped boards and holes where knots had fallen out. He set her on her feet in front of a low stool.

Instantly, she tottered back and sat down on it. Still falling, she almost went over backward, but the man called Cap'n caught her by the shoulders and steadied her. "Now just sit there right 'n' tight. You'll be home soon enough."

Noelle straightened her shoulders and tried unsuccessfully to shrug off his grasp. Despite the sickening pain, she forced herself to calm speech. "I am the daughter of the Duke of Averill. My husband is Robin Whittcombstone, Earl of Whitby. When my horse returns to the manor, there'll be a search. You'll be caught."

"Th' lady's makin' sense," a third voice protested. "I don't like this by 'alf."

"Y're being paid t' like it, Tuck," Fod sneered, "so quit yer bloody whinin'."

"What?" Despite her pain Noelle snapped alert.

"We'll swing fer this," Tuck continued to mourn. "Doin' stuff t' stay alive 's one thing, but coppin' a lady—We'll swing fer sure."

"No, we won't. This is a different deal."

Fod planted himself in front of Noelle. "An' 'ow's it different. I 'ate to say ol' Tuck's makin' sense, but y' know, we'll never get nothin' from gentry coves like them." He grinned down at her. "Best t' knock 'er in th' 'ead an' be done with it."

Noelle struggled to rise despite the hideous pain. "Did you say someone going to pay you? Did someone promise you money if you kidnapped me?"

"Shut y'r trap!"

"Was it the Duke?"

Fod gaped. The leader scowled furiously at his cohorts. "Now see what you've done."

"I ain't done nothin'. She don't know a damn thing. Just thinks she does."

"We oughta be movin'." Tuck edged toward the door. "What if they was t' come lookin' fer 'er."

"He's got th' right idea," Fod agreed. "Go ahead slip it t' 'er, and let's get outta 'ere."

"Get the stuff, Tuck."

"No. No." Noelle objected desperately. The pain was making her light-headed. If her captor had not had ahold of her, she would have fallen off the stool. "You have to return me. You'll never get any kind of money from my father. He doesn't deal with criminals, but if you return me safe and sound, he'll forget that I was ever gone. Otherwise, he'll come after you for revenge." Her voice trailed away in exhaustion. "He'll exterminate you, like rats."

The hands clenched for a moment as her words hit home.

"If you take me back and put me on my horse, I'll never say a word." She strove to make her tone reasonable. "You'll be free."

She could sense his hesitation. Then he shook his head. "And out a pile of blunt."

"He'll never pay."

The Cap'n's voice grated harshly. "You better pray that he pays. 'Cause if he don't, you're long gone."

"She's most likely right," Fod grumbled. "We ain't never gonna turn a profit outta this. It's queered from th' beginnin'."

"We'll wait. We'll come out of this."

"No." Noelle shook her head. "No. You won't. Let me go. My husband—"

" 'E's on his way."

"No, he's in London."

Fod suddenly cursed vilely. "Don't stand there arguin' with 'er. If y're gonna do it, do it. Slip 'er a tiger drencher an' stow 'er in a corner."

"What?" Noelle tried to rise. "What are you—"

"Now, don't get upset." The man behind her pulled her back onto the stool. "You're hurting. We've got a little drink that'll fix you right up. Bring it, Tuck."

"No." From a dim corner she heard the clink of glass against tin. She twisted around desperately facing the sound. "Don't you dare!"

The third man came toward her, a cup in his hand.

"No! You won't make me drink anything." Despite the pain, despite her captor's hands, she pushed herself off the stool.

"Here now. Settle back. Don't make a fuss. This ain't gonna hurt."

"No."

He caught her around the neck, one hand beneath her chin. "Now just take a drink nice and easy."

"Over my bleeding body." She rammed her elbow in his ribs and clawed at his wrist.

"Ow!"

"Best tell Tuck t' gimme that cup, Cap'n. Y're not gettin' anywhere."

"I'll do it, Fod. The last time you gave a bird a drink, she like to never woke."

Noelle moaned in terror.

Tuck passed the cup to the leader, who held it inches from her mouth. His breath was hot in her ear. "Now, open up. Just drink it right down like a cuppa, then you'll be out before you know it. We'll put you down nice and gentle on a pile of hay and cover you up. You won't hurt — "

Noelle twisted her head and sank her teeth into his thumb.

He howled and dropped the cup.

Fod laughed uproariously. "Sure, y' know 'ow t' do it, Cap'n."

Noelle managed to hobble a couple of steps, but Tuck caught her. "Please," she begged him. "Don't do this. It's wrong. You're in danger. You don't know my husband."

He shook his head stubbornly. His frightened eyes searched her white perspiring face.

"My husband," she gasped. "They call him Turk. He's absolutely ruthless. Cruel beyond belief. He's killed hundreds of men in battle. He's a crack shot with a pistol. He'll—"

Her flood of words ended in a cry as the "Cap'n" jerked her back into his arms and pried her mouth open with vicious strength. "Open up, yer bleedin' ladyship."

The lip of a bottle clinked against her teeth. A thick bitter dose rolled onto her tongue. Before she could spit, the heel of his hand drove up beneath her jaw, shutting her mouth.

She grunted with pain.

"Now you can't spit it out. You can't do nought but swaller it," he grunted in her ear. He pushed harder on her jaw, driving her head back, her face to the ceiling. Down her open throat the foul substance slid.

"She's done it," Fod observed. "I seen it go down."

Their bodies relaxed. The three stepped away from her. She swayed, then tottered. Her leg gave down under her, and she collapsed in a heap. Tears started from her eyes. "You bastards," she whispered. "Cowardly bastards. Three of you. Three of you. It took all three of you to bring me down and me with a hurt leg. Big, brave men. You'll pay for this. You'll never get away from him. He'll see you're drawn and quartered. He'll see you hang."

They looked at each other uneasily.

"He'll see you hang," she repeated. Her stomach roiled against the stuff. She tried to bring it up, but she could only gag at the taste.

The Cap'n dropped down on his haunches in front of her. "Nobody's going to hang," he said, not ungently. "Just tip on over there on that pile of hay. We'll cover you up. You'll drift off t' sleep just like a baby and when you wake—"

"I'll see you hang," she promised dizzily. Her mouth felt funny. In her ears was a soft buzzing sound. They were talking to her. How long had they been talking? Time had no meaning.

Someone pushed her shoulder. She felt prickles beneath her cheek, but as to moving to a more comfortable position, she had already left her body. The pain, the all-consuming pain was fading fast. She pulled her hand to her mouth, touched her lips. They were numb, or her fingers were numb, or both. She could not tell. They were still talking. The Cap'n was talking.

"Planning's no good," she whispered through stiff lips. "Robin 'll—He'll—"

She felt a covering settle lightly over her. With some difficulty she focused on the Cap'n. He was smiling now. One of his front teeth was missing. She had not noticed that before.

Her dazed eyes slid away, up the boards of the tackroom. *Odd how tall this room was. Very odd for a stable. Perhaps it was a barn.*

It seemed to be growing upward and upward. *How strange.* Dusty wisps of hay thrust down from the ceiling. Before her eyes they grew longer and longer. They writhed in snakelike imitation of life. *How could hay, long dried, long dead, be writhing?* She could feel the first ripplings of terror, even though she could not move a muscle.

A wind, a veritable storm, took the place of the buzzing in her ears. That must be the answer. A storm

175

of some great proportions must be building. She could hear the wind rushing, rushing.

"Don't think you'll keep me because of the storm," she muttered. "My husband's not afraid of storms. He'll be here. Soon. Soon."

She opened her eyes wide, fighting the drug. The Cap'n's face hung above her with his gap-toothed grin. The gap seemed to be widening, becoming a huge black hole. Her heart pounded in fear. She tried to gasp for breath, but her lungs would not move. She managed to redirect her gaze to her chest.

The Cap'n's hand rested on her breast. As she watched the fingers seemed to flex, though she felt nothing. He was touching her body. The insult flicked her on the raw. " 'Usba' 'll kill you."

The fingers flexed again, filthy black moons under every fingernail, grime creased in the knuckles. This time she distinctly saw them.

"Kill you," she promised.

Dimly, above the roar of the storm, she heard him laugh. She should scream. She would scream. Her mouth opened, but no sound came. No sound.

"Better give over, Cap'n," Tuck advised. "This ain't no ordinary bird. Y' could be in fer a pack o' trouble."

Regretfully, the Cap'n tucked the blanket up to her throat and rose. "I like them lively anyway."

"Regrettable that a decent woman cannot ride about her estate without harm coming to her," the Duke remarked.

Whittcombstone studied the features.

"Of course, she had no groom with her," Averill

continued. "I had no idea you were so under-staffed. I would certainly have provided — "

"Why do you think she has met with harm?"

The Duke raised his pale eyebrows. "When she did not return from her ride, one of your people came to the inn to inquire. I instantly ordered a search. Her horse, my dear fellow. Her horse was all we found."

"You were staying in the inn?"

"Naturally. I rather enjoy my creature comforts." He looked with cold disdain at the parlor that Noelle had claimed for her own.

"She might have abandoned the horse and taken a coach."

For the first time, Averill betrayed his irritation. "For God's sake, man, have you ice water in your veins. The horse's foreleg was broken. We had to put her down."

"The gray?" For the first time Robin felt the stirrings of concern. Whatever Noelle might have done to decamp, she would never have put Silver Belle in jeopardy. She had walked miles in ice and snow rather than take the old mare and then desert her. If her mother's horse were injured, then his wife must have been thrown. "Have the villagers back-tracked on the mare's trail?"

The Duke's smile was a serpent's smirk. "We waited for you. They are your people and this is your estate — such as it is. I did my duty by sending for you."

"You waited forty-eight hours to search for your own daughter?" Robin's voice roughened in anger.

The smirk faded slightly. He shrugged a bit uneasily. "She's your responsibility. How could I deprive the bridegroom of his chance to play hero to the bride?"

Robin's mouth tightened. "What game are you playing here?"

"I don't know what you mean."

The Turk's irascible temper burst into flame. With deadly economy of motion, he covered the space between them. His whipcord fingers fastened in the Duke's elegantly fashioned cravat. "Tell me!"

"Let go!" Averill raised his fist, but a fit of coughing struck him before he could land it.

Implacably Robin tightened his grip. "Tell me where she is!"

The coughing grew in intensity. The pale skin turned red, then purple.

"Milords! Milords!" Holmesfield caught at Robin's shoulder.

Robin jabbed his elbow into the factor's ribs, driving him back. "Tell me!"

"Yes—All—right—Leave—off—" The Duke managed between spasms.

Robin relaxed his grip.

Holmesfield, clutching his middle with one hand, managed to splash brandy into a glass with the other and bring it to his employer.

Averill grasped it greedily. He managed to sip a bit, coughed it out, sipped again, and finally managed to hold it. Wringing wet with perspiration, he slumped back against Noelle's desktable. "Bastard," he accused.

"Of course," came the reply. "Now tell me what the hell this is all about before I do murder."

Ten

Noises exploded into Noelle's consciousness in the form of thuds, each one intensifying the excruciating pounding in her head. She moaned and tried to clap her hands to her temples. Her fingers fumbled for the pulsing veins, but the vibrations continued until she thought her head would burst.

Nearer they came. She moaned again and tried to curse. Her mouth was so dry. Her swollen tongue fairly rasped across her lips. No moisture there. She remembered the drug. How long —?

She pressed her hands into the hay beneath her shoulders and tried to raise herself. Her head whirled so that she had to sink back and lie perfectly still to keep from vomiting.

Even though all she had to give up was the residue of the foul-tasting stuff her captors had poured down her throat, she would not, must not befoul the mouldy straw. Pride made her determined to keep this last vestige of control and not appear weak before her captors.

On three separate occasions as she lay miserable

and groaning, someone—the Cap'n perhaps—had come to lift her head. He had given her no water. Instead he had tipped the contents of a tin cup into her mouth and left.

Now, a hand touched her shoulder. At least she assumed it was a hand. She swallowed convulsively. "Hell," she whispered. "Oh, hell."

"Hell, is it, Madam Wife?" A voice close at hand reverberated in her ear.

Her husband. Where had *he* come from? She moaned. "Oh, don't talk—loudly."

"Sorry." Gently, he cupped her shoulders to turn her over.

She whimpered. Her stomach heaved. She whispered a warning. "Oh, let me be."

"What?" He sounded puzzled.

She managed to twist around before she vomited into the straw. She tried to brace herself, but her arms shuddered with weakness. Her husband still held her. He was beside her, pressed against her. The embarrassment was utterly mortifying. "Leave me alone," she gasped. "Go away."

"Don't be ridiculous." Putting one hand to support her waist and the other to support her forehead, he lifted her away from the mess and held her until she was through.

In a brief interval, he stroked her brow, pushing the tendrils of hair back from her temple. The tenderness of that touch let loose a wave of self-pity. She began to weep. Her brain told her to stop the nonsense. Her husband would have a great contempt for her.

"I'm sorry," she managed.

"Understandable," came the voice in her ear.

Exhausted, she leaned her cheek against the rough wool of his cloak and allowed herself the indulgence of being glad to see him. Then another spasm shook her and she pulled away. "Oh, God, I'm sorry."

He did not curse or release her. Instead he held her head again. "Good girl. Get rid of it all. It's poison."

The convulsions quickly turned to dry heaves and finally ceased entirely. He pulled out a handkerchief to wipe her face and mouth. She hung in his arms like a rag doll.

Then his hard-muscled arm passed under her knees. He gathered her limp body up against his chest. She put her arms around his neck and tucked her hot forehead under his ear.

In this manner he carried her into the light.

The brightness assailed her eyes, so long in the gloom and darkness. She wailed in pain.

"Drugged you, did they?"

"Yes." Her lips moved against the side of his throat.

"Bastards."

"Men from the inn," she whispered. Her voice had no timbre. "Water," she begged. "Please, some water. So thirsty."

Robin hugged her close. Poor old Blivens had had only a vague idea that anything was wrong, but Lily, the housemaid, declared her mistress had been gone three days. In that case she was undoubtedly dehydrated. He had seen soldiers in the field die for lack of water. Doubtless the extreme cold of the stable had acted to keep her from dehydration. Otherwise, she would have died as a result of her captor's thoughtlessness.

Rage blazed in the single eye he turned on Archie Holmesfield, who stood shifting from one foot to the other, a weak smile on his face. "So you just happened to have an idea where she might be. Received a note, did you?"

Holmesfield shrugged. "I didn't receive it, you understand. I was sent to fetch you." He tried to inspect the limp figure huddled in Robin's arms.

The Earl shouldered the factor aside to enter the carriage. The movement aroused the nausea again. Her head fell back.

Holmesfield paled at the sight. "She doesn't look so good, poor lady."

Icy air struck her face, reviving her to pain. Light broke through upon her eyes as her eyelids dropped open. She could see nothing but light. And she wailed again. Tearing her hands from her husband's neck, she tried to cover her eyes.

Robin's arms tightened and her sore ankle bumped against the side of the carriage.

This time she cursed.

"What is it?"

"Leg," she murmured.

He froze. "Is your leg broken?"

"Don't know. Ankle."

"Can you sit up on the seat?"

"Yes." She nodded when her effort to speak brought no sound.

"Holmesfield," Robin snarled over his shoulder. "Find her some water."

"Water?" Holmesfield looked around him distractedly. "I don't see—"

"This is a stable, you idiot. There's probably a well

or a trough out back."

"Oh—er—yes."

"Please," Noelle rasped.

Robin thrust her into a dark hole, and let her slump on her side. Her cheek came to rest on a velvet squab.

Robin climbed in and hovered over her. "Which ankle?"

"Left." He arranged the cushions and lifted her foot onto it.

She set her teeth against the pain that streaked up her leg. In the dimness their eyes met. "I—thank you for coming."

He looked away. "You are my wife."

"I—still—thank you."

Holmesfield appeared in the door with a tin dipper. "I found a trough milord. It had a skin of ice. But I don't know whether the water's safe to drink."

"At this point, I think she wouldn't be safe to ride all the way back to Whitby without water." Robin shifted himself until he supported her head and shoulders. He lifted her head and held the dipper for her.

Her thirst could not be borne another minute. She clutched at his wrist with both hands. The water dribbled down her chin as she drank greedily.

"Easy," he whispered. "Easy. There's plenty more where that came from."

He tipped it up, then handed it to Holmesfield. "More."

"But—"

"Please." Her voice was still a croak. She felt as if she could never get enough to drink. "It's so good."

The factor nodded.

"How?" she managed. "How did you know?"

"Your father sent for me."

"The Duke."

He picked his words carefully. Her face upturned to him was pitiful, hollow cheeked, her eyes sunken in her head. Her lips were seamed like an old woman's. She would not have lasted much longer. "When you didn't come home, I'm assuming someone at the house sent to the inn for him. He sent for me."

"The men who captured me—were from the inn. You remember. The ones who refused to work for us."

His expression was guarded. "We'll talk about this later when you're more the thing. Here's Holmesfield."

She drank again with more restraint. This time as the cold water slid down her throat, she began to shiver. "Thank you. I can last now," she whispered. "I just want to get home. I'm so cold."

The Duke's factor tossed the tin dipper to the frozen ground and moved to climb into the coach.

The fierce expression in Robin's eye stopped him. He backed down and closed the door. The coach swayed as he climbed up to the box. The driver sprang the horses.

When Noelle moaned with the pain of the noise, the vibration, her chills, Robin opened his cloak and gathered her up in his arms.

Despite the blessed warmth, she could not rest. Her mind struggled with the presence of the smarmy Archie Holmesfield and the remembered conversations of Fod, Jack, and the Cap'n. The Duke had had her taken, but for what purpose. Because she would not write a letter summoning Robin back to his estate. She must tell him.

"Wanted you back," she whispered.

"What?" He bent low.

"Wanted you back. He wanted you here with me."

"I gathered as much. But why?"

She could not answer. Why indeed? To get an heir. By her? Why was he so anxious that she have a child?

As the coach swayed and her husband rocked her in his arms, her mind whirled. She could not reason it out.

By the time they arrived at the house, she was in danger of vomiting the water she had drunk. So thoroughly had her body been poisoned that she could feel nothing but misery.

The only thing to cling to in the whirling world of pain, chill, and nausea was her husband, in whose arms she huddled like a child.

Robin carried her up the stoop. Blivens opened the front door, his quavering voice inquiring and complaining. "Oh, milord, did you find her? Oh, is she hurt? Why didn't she come home? We were wild with worry."

Robin's strong voice rumbled out of his chest. "She's going to be fine. She just needs care."

The door to Noelle's parlor opened. The Duke stood in it, his expression one of bored interest. "So glad to hear it."

"I'm sure you are."

Noelle roused herself. "Put me down," she whispered to Robin.

"Here? Now?" He sounded incredulous.

"Here and now."

Reluctantly, he let her legs slide from his arm to rest on the floor. He retained his arm around her waist, so she could rest her weight against him.

"Averill, you had me kidnapped. Why?"

The Ice King raised his white eyebrows. His gaze flicked over her and then to her husband's face. "She's obviously been through a great ordeal. She's confused. My dear Countess, I assure you I did nothing of the kind. You are obviously very ill."

"He did. I know it." She looked up at her husband to see how he was accepting this. Unfortunately, she looked up at the scarred side of his face. She could not see his eye. "But why?"

Averill gave a bored wave of his hand. "My dear woman, you are suffering from some form of dementia. That is the thanks I get for sending for your husband the minute I heard you were missing. And for lending him my carriage so he could fetch you after Holmesfield managed to extract information about the local undesirables."

"Why did you do it?" she repeated, her voice breaking with pain.

"The question is rather why *should* I do it," he countered. He sighed elaborately. "Take her to her bed, Turk. She'll feel better after a hot bath and a good night's sleep."

"Damn you!"

"A hot bath," he repeated. He drew a lace handkerchief from his sleeve and passed it under his nose. "She stinks."

"Come, Madam Wife." Robin stooped and lifted her again.

She moaned at the pressure on her injured leg. "Ask him," she begged, her voice weak. "Just ask him."

"Later." He nodded to Blivens. "Send the Countess's maid with a bath and some clear broth."

The old man nodded. "Bath and soup. Bath and soup."

"Please, milord," she begged as he strode down the hall. "Please believe me."

"Later."

"Silver Belle didn't come home?" Noelle's voice broke.

Robin's voice was gentle. "We found her down, with a broken leg."

"Oh, the poor thing. Oh, no." She put her hands to her cheeks. Robin was increasingly aware of how pale and pinched she looked — almost as white as the bed-clothes on which she lay. Even her fingers looked bloodless.

"I'm sorry. She must have fallen when you fell. The ground was torn up."

"And she couldn't get up?" The tears were pouring down her cheeks.

Robin cursed himself for not telling her a lie. Her grief was pitiful, tearing at her, ripping her over-strained nerves. "Don't think about it for now."

"Don't think about it. *Don't think about it!* My horse, My m-mother's horse. She lay on the ground for — How long have I been gone?"

He hesitated. "Three days."

Noelle covered her eyes with her hand. "Was she dead when you found her?"

"I didn't find her, Noelle. She was found quite soon after you disappeared. She was dead."

Her hand dropped. Her eyes pierced him. "She was still alive, wasn't she?"

He caught hold of both her hands. "Yes, she was. But you can't help her now. And you're not doing yourself any good. Weep about something you can do something about."

"I'm sure Averill's happy now. My mother's horse." She tried to jerk her hands away. "I didn't take her when I tried to run away to London. I was afraid I couldn't take care of her, and I didn't want to abandon her. If I'd taken her and gotten away—"

"You can't think like that." He shifted both her hands into one of his and caught her chin. Holding her firmly, but gently, he forced her to look into his face. "You can't think that because you were there and she was there, that you were at fault because she died."

The argument was a version of the one he had used with frightened, guilt-ridden young men, blaming themselves for the deaths of their friends and comrades.

"If I hadn't gone riding—"

"That was her purpose. That was what she was born and bred for. To carry a lady for a morning's outing. That was her job. She did it patiently and sweetly and so she will be missed. But whether or not you went that day had nothing to do with her death. She could just as easily have stepped in a hole or slipped and fallen on a patch of ice. Horses do things like that all the time."

She closed her eyes, but the tears still squeezed out. "I tried to get away."

"Good for you. Too bad you didn't make it."

Noelle relaxed back against the pillows. She plucked at the hem of the sheet. "I'd ridden her too far. She was too tired to escape."

"And too old." He remembered the mare. She must have been close to twenty.

"It'll make Averill happy. He wanted to get rid of all my mother's things. I couldn't save very much." She turned her eyes away. "A few dresses, some jewelry, and Silver Belle. And she died and I don't even have her colt." She began to shiver. Her teeth chattered until she clenched her jaw. "I'm so c-cold."

He left her side and stoked the fire. The room felt over-heated to him, but he was not in pain. Returning to the bedside, he found his wife's entire body seized by an ague.

Shock, dehydration, exposure. Depression of mind and spirit. Suddenly, he was afraid. He slipped his hand under the covers and felt her hip. The skin was cold, clammy. Her condition was dangerous.

He had meant to leave her to her solitary bed, not upsetting her with his presence. But countless layers of cover would not warm her. Nor would the copper pan of hot coals at her feet keep her until her own body could warm the bed.

The corner of his mouth lifted in a self-deprecating smile. His wife needed him. Quite a contrast to the last time they had been together.

He began to pull off his clothes.

She turned her head. Her eyes widened. A dim fire of rebellion flickered in their depths. "Going to enjoy your wife as long as you're home," she whispered.

"Might as well," he agreed without emphasis. "Why should I care that you've just endured a painful ordeal and that you're grieving? We brutish monsters just take what we want. Right?" He slipped beneath the covers and gathered her into his arms.

"Right."

He popped her smartly on her buttock. "Turn over."

"I'm not a rag doll." Protesting weakly, she lay stiff and sullen.

Sighing, he turned her onto her side with her back to him. Then he gathered her in against his chest, pressing her buttocks into his lap.

"You're embarrassing me."

"I enjoy embarrassing girls. It makes them warm." He slid his thighs up under hers. She fit him so perfectly that the soles of her little cold feet rested on his insteps. He put his arm across her. His hand rested on her knee.

At first, holding her was like holding a side of cold meat. He hugged her a little closer as he realized how close she had been to death. If Archie had not been able to persuade him to come, would her father have let her die?

He wondered. Wondered about the Ice King. What kind of man was he? Robin did not doubt that Noelle was correct when she accused Averill. What kind of father arranged such an ordeal for his daughter—his only child.

Perhaps the Duke had even supplied the nearly deadly drugs and instructed the kidnappers in their use. Then Holmesfield had been sent for him.

Why? What was the motive? Why the elaborate plot?

Anger heated Robin's blood. More than anything he hated the idea that he was being manipulated. Yet he could not escape the notion that from the moment Thomas Rivers, Duke of Averill had started collecting Robin's vowels, his very existence had been under the thumb. He ground his teeth.

His wife's body began to warm, her breathing evened. She slept in his arms. Somehow he was going to have to reach some sort of understanding with her and with her damned father. They would both learn that he would be master of his own life.

The bed was warm but lumpy. And noisy.

Noelle sighed and stirred, moving her cheek to find a softer spot. Suddenly, she became aware that the spot moved and thumped. Her eyes flew open. She could see the ruddy glow from the fire. She was lying on her husband's chest. His deep breathing and his powerful heart provided the motion and noise. The covers were pulled up over her shoulders and one of his arms was thrown loosely around her waist.

Likewise, her belly fitted into the hollow between his hipbones. One of her legs was lying between his, the top of her thigh pressed indecently against his—

She could feel a hot blush rising, spreading. She tried to lift herself, very carefully and roll off him, but he only tightened his grip and muttered irritably.

How could she extricate herself without waking him?

The springy black hair beneath her cheek tickled. She stirred again, trying to relieve the tantalizing feeling. Her breasts itched too, their nipples hardened. She breathed deeply, trying to dispel the tight feeling, but only succeeded in rasping the betraying nubs against his warm skin.

The terrible sensations created an insurmountable desire to move. She wriggled. And found herself in a greater pickle than before. She had rubbed her belly and the swelling lips between her thighs.

She clenched her hands which, unfortunately, were clasped round his shoulders.

"Should I pray for my virtue?" a deep voice rumbled beneath her ear.

She gasped and raised her head. "I woke up and here I was."

"So I see. Are you comfortable?"

"Not very. That is, I'm very warm, but I—I don't really know about the rest." She lifted her hands from his shoulders. By that movement she pressed her breasts more tightly against his chest. She muttered sharply and clasped him again.

"Trouble making up your mind, Madam Wife?"

She could swear she heard a trace of humor in his voice. "If you would remove your arm from my waist," she said primly, "I could slide off."

"Could you now?" Instead of removing one arm, he crisscrossed the other one over that. His hands slid down over her buttocks.

She could feel him as he hardened, rising between her thighs, pushing at her mound. The hot wet feeling began there too, to greet him. Except this time she was hotter. She longed to throw off the covers over her shoulders. Even her hair felt hot and heavy. "I think I'm warm enough now."

"I think you are too." His hard fingers cupped her bottom cheeks and pulled her up, hard. Her whole body slid up his through the hair, over the spare flesh on his long bones. His brutal action should have hurt. She should feel bruised.

Instead, she felt swollen and hotter than ever. "Please," she whispered.

"Please what?"

"Please—I don't know."

He rubbed her belly from side to side across his. His hard male organ rolled between her legs, making her itch more than ever. "Does this please you?"

"It shouldn't."

"But it does?"

She buried her flaming face in his neck.

"Does it?" he insisted.

"Yes. Oh, yes."

She lifted her head to receive his kiss. This time she opened her mouth. His tongue thrust deeply into her. It caressed her for a long time.

At last, he pulled away and stared down into her eyes. "Not a girl's kiss any longer."

She could only nod her head faintly. "Kiss me again."

With another chuckle he obliged.

She could feel the organ, probing her, as if it had a will of its own. It was at the opening where it had entered before.

"Are we going to beget the heir?"

He dropped his head back onto the pillow and sucked in a great lungful of breath. "Only incidentally."

"What does that mean?"

"It means that we are going to do this." His hands slid up her buttocks and fastened on her hips. Instead of pulling her upward, he pushed her down.

She cried out and arched her back. It eased her on down until she felt him deep within her. "It doesn't hurt," she exclaimed marveling. "Why doesn't it hurt?"

He laughed.

"What are you doing?"

His hands moved to her breasts and pushed her into a sitting position. She could still feel the rod inside her. Instinctively, she tightened her muscles around it.

"God."

"Oh, did I hurt you?"

"I may die, but not from pain." He set his teeth. His hands closed over her breasts and squeezed gently.

"Oh —"

"Feels good?"

"Oh, yes. Oh, yes. Oh, yes." With each exclamation, she responded to his upward thrusts with his hips.

"Do you like it?"

She threw her head back. Her hair swirled around her shoulders like a wild thing. She wanted to move herself. "It doesn't hurt."

"No."

Tentatively as if she touched a hot stove, her palms came to rest on the heavy muscles of his shoulders. She leaned forward supporting the weight of her upper body. Eyes on his face, she timidly lifted her hips and let them slide back down.

"Good God." He flung back his head. His eyes were closed, his throat arched.

She did it again and again.

"Don't — I — " His whole body spasmed beneath her. Spasmed and kept on spasming. Hot liquid jetted into her, ran down the sides of her sheath, a scalding river of it flowed out onto his belly.

She could not stop herself. Wild throbbing between her legs could not be denied. She pulled herself up higher than before and flung herself down on him. The pulsing nerves in the center of her body, exploded too.

Her scream of fulfillment was a mixture of all the pleasure and pain in the world.

Eleven

"Leaving so soon, Duke?"

"Milord. Er—good morning." Blivens fumbled and almost dropped Averill's fine curly-brim beaver. "Will you be wanting to go—um—out too?"

His Grace's back stiffened; but when he turned, his demeanor was as bland as cream. "My job is done," he said with an insouciant wave of his gloves. "I wouldn't want to interfere in the billing and cooing of newlyweds."

"I'm sure that is your intention," Robin agreed with vicious courtesy. "However, before you leave, I must insist that we speak privately on a couple of matters."

"Sorry. I can't spare the time. I've broken my journey far too long." Averill plucked his hat from Blivens's palsied hands.

The poor old man looked from one to the other uncertainly.

Robin opened the door to the parlor. "In here."

"And if I say 'no'?"

His son-in-law's black eye gleamed. "Then you'll be landed in on your ear."

The Ice King measured Whittcombstone. The Earl

196

topped six feet by a couple of inches. While his body was thin and angular, it was by no means frail. His shoulders were broad. More to the point was the air of menace that hung heavy around him. His weight was distributed evenly over the balls of his feet. The arm he swept wide to usher his reluctant guest into his parlor could drag that same guest in with efficient dispatch.

"Ah, well, if I must." Returning his hat to Blivens, Averill strolled past the Earl. He seated himself in a chair far from the fire and crossed one elegant leg over the other.

Robin closed the door behind them. A muscle flickered in his scarred jaw as he surveyed the Duke's pose. "Your daughter was almost dead when I found her. From cold and lack of water."

Averill's smile did not reach his icy eyes. "She should be most grateful. How fortunate that you arrived just in time to save her."

"I would say fortune had little to do with my saving her. Nor did fortune play a part when Holmesfield led me directly to the very inn where a man just happened to have overheard two men talking about kidnapping my wife."

"Do you think not?" The Duke pulled a solid silver snuffbox from his pocket and selected a tiny pinch. Crooking his fingers he delicately inserted it in his nostril and sniffed it up. He coughed once.

"Likewise, it's very strange that I received no ransom note."

"Perhaps they weren't intending to ransom her," the Duke remarked. "Perhaps they planned to sell her to a brothel keeper. One hears from time to time of girls disappearing. Whittcombstone, you saved her from a fate worse than death. She should be passionately grateful."

"Perhaps she will be—when she recovers from her ordeal."

Averill closed the snuffbox with an irritated snap. "The girl wasn't really hurt," he muttered. "You heard the hysterical way she spoke to me. I am well acquainted with your appetites. She should have been amenable."

Robin studied his father-in-law with a mixture of disgust and curiosity. "I asked nothing of her," he said truthfully. "I left her sleeping a sleep of total exhaustion. She couldn't eat at all last night. The drugs had done terrible things to her stomach."

The Duke made an unintelligible sound. He uncrossed and recrossed his legs.

Robin slammed his hand on the mantel. "Good God, man. Did you just abandon her to their hands? Surely you had the decency to check on her condition during the nearly seventy-two hours that she was drugged."

Averill pulled out his watch. "I don't know what you mean."

"Perhaps not, but hear me now." Robin turned his good eye to the Duke. Hands clasped behind him, legs astride, he delivered his warning. "I shall make it my business to apprehend the men who kidnapped her. And they will sign confessions naming whoever hired them."

"I certainly think that's wise." Averill nodded coldly. "Is that all you wished to say to me? The day—"

"I shall expect you to send the Countess a horse to replace the mare that broke her leg."

"Now that is surely none of my concern," Averill objected strongly. "That horse belonged to Noelle's mother and then to her. I had nothing to do with the bloody animal."

"That was the horse you saw fit to give her as part of her dowry. She prized that horse very highly. You must have bred the mare in all the years that she lived at Averill. Noelle shall have another mare, one of that horse's offspring. You will see to it."

"And if I don't."

"I shall publish the confessions of the kidnappers in the *Times*."

"Brave boasts about a paper that doesn't exist."

"But it will exist." Robin bared his teeth in a wolf's smile. "If I have to manufacture it myself."

Averill's mouth dropped open in amazement.

"Surprised? Don't be. You chose the Turk. You shouldn't expect him to behave like a gentleman."

"My solicitor will—"

"The mare you send will be sound of wind and limb and not above five years old. And she will be pregnant by that big stallion of yours Brandywine."

"This is robbery."

"And what you did was kidnapping."

"It was no such thing."

"It is a hanging offense. Even for a peer."

The Duke coughed deeply. Finally, when the spasm had passed, he looked curiously at his son-in-law. "Why are you so set on a pregnant mare?"

"My wife has the idea that she would like to start a stable—to raise horses to sell. I have a mind to give

199

her way. She'll have precious little to occupy her time. I have bought her some additional stock in London."

"With my money."

"True." Robin smiled blandly. "Yours and others." Then his face tightened. "She had planned to breed the old mare. She hoped to get two or even three good colts from her."

"Impossible," Averill scoffed. "She dropped her last colt three years ago."

Robin smiled. "Who can say? The kidnapping destroyed the chance, didn't it? Your only solution is to replace the mare. Do you agree?"

The Duke's face flushed with hot blood. But his voice was even icier. "May I leave now?"

"Do you agree?"

"Yes."

"Then I bid you good day." Robin unclasped his hands and strode to the door. "With only one more word. Lay hands on her again and you will be the one who is sorry."

"Where is the Countess?"

The maid Lily squeaked and jumped, clutching Noelle's pillow to her chest. "Oh, sir. She got up early and insisted on getting dressed."

"She was supposed to stay in bed for another two days."

"Yes, sir. But she said she'd feel better downstairs."

Robin found his wife in her parlor, listlessly leafing through a book. He studied her unhappy expression. "Since you refuse to stay in bed, come with me to the stable. I have something to show you."

She continued to turn the pages. "I don't think I want to go down there."

"Come anyway. I have something to show you."

She shook her head. "I really don't want to go for a while. I'll just think about Silver Belle and get hurt and mad. I'm considering writing a Gothic novel. With a supernatural villain defeated in the end by a desperate heroine. I think I could sell it with no trouble."

"You may know the right villain, but that's a poor sort of revenge." He hauled her to her feet. "Come with me. I insist. No sitting here feeling sorry for yourself. The mare's gone. Put her out of your mind."

"What! Let go! You have the sensitivity of a toad."

"I've been called much worse."

She was still objecting as they approached the stable. Timothy Hardwicke came out into the shedrow, his expression alarmed.

Robin halted scowling. "Who are you?"

"He's my man." Noelle shook free of her husband's grasp and stepped between him and the groom. "I hired him. The one you hired didn't know the front from the rear—when he was sober enough to care."

"Who are you?" Robin repeated.

The object of the discussion snapped to attention. "Timothy Hardwicke's the name, sir."

"And where were you when my wife was kidnapped?"

The man wilted before his eyes. "I shoulda gone with 'er," he mourned. "I swear—"

"You'd probably have been killed," Noelle interrupted. "At any rate you couldn't have done anything. There were three of them."

"Before God —" Tim began.

"You're discharged. Pack your kit and —"

"Stop this. Stop it this instant." Noelle tugged at her husband's arm. "Come with me." She dragged him away.

"He should have ridden with you."

"Not when I didn't want him. Listen to me, Husband. I hired that man to take care of my horses. I didn't hire him as a bodyguard. I didn't expect him to go ride with me."

"Because you didn't have a horse for him to ride," Robin pointed out.

"That's not a reason. I wouldn't have taken him anyway. I always rode alone at Averill."

"You'll take a groom from now on."

She looked away down the lane, blinking rapidly. "I don't suppose I'll be riding from now on."

He suddenly remembered why he had come. "You will. Come see."

As he led her into the stable, five heads appeared over the stall bars.

"Oh," was all Noelle said.

Robin, warming to his task, had a sober Timothy lead out the first black filly and then the other. Both were close coupled and sound. They stood together almost like sisters, the larger one nudged the other and whinnied softly.

Noelle pressed her hands against her cheeks. "Oh, they're beautiful."

"A little young yet for breeding." Robin patted a shiny black shoulder and tugged the forelock smooth.

"A touch of Arabian here." Hardwicke commented in support of the Earl.

"Arabian. Yes, indeed." The Earl nodded heartily. "Their papers say so. They're showy little things." He made no effort to conceal his pride. He led the larger mare forward and ran his hand over the raven black coat. As he did so, he realized she looked even better than she had the day he bought her.

Timothy turned the smaller mare broadside to the sun. He had curried and brushed them both until they gleamed. "Look at the dish face." He stroked the velvet muzzle. "You really picked beauties, milord."

"They'll make perfect lady's mounts," Robin agreed.

At the mention of lady's mount, Noelle's face fell. Her eyes sparkled with unshed tears.

Both men looked at her nervously. At Robin's signal the groom put the pair back in their stalls and led out the third mare.

The black came out of her stall in a rush and wheeled around, tossing her head. Her long black legs flashed as she pranced nervously. Still entranced with her, Robin took the halter and reached for her forelock. Her eyes rolled back. She snorted a warning. "Steady on, girl," he crooned. "Nothing to be afraid of."

Noelle's eyes lighted with interest. "Where did you get her?"

"From an Irishman. Where else? How do you like her?"

His wife ran her eyes over the lanky body. "She's the tallest mare I've ever seen. What are her lines?"

"To tell the truth, she doesn't have any papers."

"I see."

Robin turned his back on the mare and took his

wife by the elbow. "I was buying for confirmation. Look at the depth of chest. She looks like she could run forever."

But Noelle had turned her eyes to search his hard dark face. "Then she's—they're for breeding?"

He nodded. "For breeding."

A silence settled between them. The black mare, over her skittish behavior, bumped her nose against Robin's shoulder, demanding attention.

Suddenly, Noelle ducked her head. She pressed her fist hard against her mouth.

Still he could hear the dry sob. He caught her shoulders. "Here, none of that. I'll have to take you back to the house if you're going to cry."

Reading the intimacy of the situation, the groom made a discreet exit.

"It's what you wanted, isn't it?" Robin insisted.

"Yes, but I never expected it."

Uncomfortable with her emotion, still he kept his hand on Noelle's elbow. He turned back to the mare. "You still haven't seen the fourth."

"The fourth!"

"And a gelding. I bought him for myself."

"But Kate is your horse."

"We'll breed her too."

She looked up at him surprised to see that his customary impassivity had deserted him. He looked younger, enthusiastic. "Did you do this for me? Or for yourself?"

Turning away, he swept his hand over the mare's back and arranged her mane. "For you." He hesitated. "And for myself too. The two-year olds are unproven, but they have papers. The bigger one is Dark o' the Moon by Havenhurst. The smaller is Lady Bess. Her lines descend from Godolphin's stud."

"And this one?" Noelle stroked the black velvet nose. The mare closed her eyes in contentment and stood like a statue.

"Well, I believe she's going to be the premier mare in the stable." He amended that statement quickly. "After Kate the Shrew, of course."

"Of course."

"Since she's your horse, you should be the one to name her."

She smiled at him, a little hesitantly, then more broadly. "Really. I wouldn't know how to go about it. I've never named a horse before."

He managed to conceal his surprise. She was the daughter of a Duke, who kept a famous stud. She was obviously horsemad, but she had never been invited to name one. "It's remarkably easy to do."

She hesitated.

He shrugged. "How about Skyrocket?"

She flashed him an indignant look. "That's a name for a race horse, not a pleasure or military mount."

He tried again, beginning to enjoy himself. "Black Beauty?"

She looked at the lanky, rawboned frame. "People will think we're joking."

"Beauty is in the eye of the beholder."

She ran her hand down the long neck and over the withers. "Too long."

He looked again, catching the quirk at the corner of her mouth. "How about Kettle or Pot? They're both black."

She moved around the black hindquarters. They

were facing each other across the gleaming black back. "I think we'll call her something that will remind us of this occasion. A name that'll look good on papers as the dam of great horses. We'll call her Deliverance."

"Deliverance." He repeated the name. It sobered him. "Are you sure?"

"Quite sure." Her face was stark, dark circles under her eyes, a pinched look about the mouth. "I want to remember everything about what happened. You came for me. I'll never forget that. I'm sure you saved my life. I'll never forget Averill either."

"Sometimes it's better to put a battle behind you," he suggested. "Just forget it."

"That's only if the war is over," she said firmly.

Noelle's eyes flew open. A pale shaft of sunlight glimmered through a break in the draperies. Otherwise the room was dark and cold. So early had she awakened that Lily had not yet come with coals to light the fire.

Robin lay in the next room. Was he still asleep? She listened closely. Did she hear movement? Or were the sounds caused by her own fear. Was her heartbeat swifter? She shivered even though she was covered to her chin.

She rolled over in the bed and hugged her knees to her chest. Still the sounds persisted. The thudding of her heart, the rushing of her blood along her veins, the mounting vibration all along her nerves.

In her relationship with Averill, she had confronted unpleasantness. But it had always been thrust upon her. She had never sought it out. Certainly, she had never taken herself into danger. She wished fervently for some religious bent. A prayer right now would not go amiss.

But she had prayed before and nothing good had happened.

Today was the day Robin had set aside for this. She had agreed to it. But as the time drew closer, she became more and more afraid. She would be sick. When Lily came in, she would groan and cough and—

At that minute Lily knocked and opened the door. "I've brought your chocolate, milady."

Noelle closed her eyes tight, then opened them. "Good."

Breakfast consisted of strong coffee. She watched her husband down toast, eggs, and cereal, but shook her head when he urged her to try just a bite. One hand remained in her lap, pressed tight against the quivering muscles in her belly.

In grim-lipped silence she rode beside her husband unaware that he observed her closely. Familiar with young soldiers before a battle, he had recognized her efforts to rein in her nerves. He had spoken softly to her words which she did not hear. Her eyes were fixed, not on the road ahead but the far distance.

When the inn came into view, she paled visibly. She clenched her teeth so tight that a muscle corded beside her mouth. He purposefully reined his mount close so that his knee nudged the back of hers.

Startled, she had looked down then up at him. "Excuse me."

"My fault, Madam Wife. I fear I did it deliberately."

She smiled vaguely, though a frown line appeared in her forehead. "What are you saying?"

"You don't have to do this."

She flashed him a look of intense dislike. "You've waited a long time to discourage me."

"Noelle."

"I seem to remember that you steered me every step of the way to the stable this morning."

"You had your hand on my arm."

"You had your hand under my elbow," she snapped.

Furious, he reined his mount to a halt. "Is that how it looked to you?"

The black mare danced under her, turning in a circle. Noelle relaxed her grip on the reins. She shook her head. "Please, milord. Let's not say any more. You want this. I want this. I suppose somewhere Averill wants it too. It's not for discussion."

Robin would not budge. The groom pulled back out of hearing. "I say it is. I never—"

"I've made up my mind. You've waited too late to change it now. Learn to live with your decisions."

He almost fell out of the saddle. "You're crazy."

"I'd have to be to be doing this. But nevertheless we will do it."

Over their horses' heads they stared at each other. Teeth bared, they bristled and spat. Timothy Hardwicke gaped, then quickly swung his head away to study a particularly interesting arrangement of rocks.

Finally, Robin nodded curtly. "Very well."

He reined his horse around hers and trotted down the road.

"Very well," Noelle snapped as he rode by her. She yanked Deliverance's bridle. The horse half rose and turned in the air. Her rider clung tightly and brought her down. "Behave yourself. I don't have time for your foolishness."

In heavy silence the Earl and his Countess drew rein in front of the Rose and Thistle. The groom swung down and took the heads of their mounts.

"Hold the horses here," Robin ordered. "We want to be ready to run for it, in case we're badly outnumbered."

"You had to say that, didn't you?"

"A good tactician always prepares for a strategic retreat."

"Of course." Clutching her riding crop tightly, Noelle dismounted before either man could reach her. Face set in stone, she preceded her husband into the public house. Her face beneath her hat was white, though high color rode her cheeks. Swiftly, her eyes swept the room.

Bold as brass, Fod sat at his usual bench. He had risen from it to attack Robin. Now he froze in the act of lowering a tankard of ale. His eyes met hers then skittered off. His face, red with drink, turned positively puce.

When Robin came in behind her, Noelle pointed. "His name is Fod."

"Ah-ha." Her husband nodded. "Was he the one who dragged you off your horse?"

"Yes."

"And administered the drugs?"

"No. That was the one he called Cap'n."

"Do you see him anywhere?"

She let her eyes scan the other patrons. The normal talk of the Rose and Thistle had ceased. The half dozen or so patrons did one of two things. Either they turned and stared belligerently at the pair, or they hunched their shoulders and buried their faces in their tankards.

"I don't think so. I can't see everyone's face. No, wait."

Beside Fod, his back to the entrance, a man rose from the bench.

"I think that's Tuck."

"Let's see if you're correct." Robin raised his voice. "You there, Tuck!"

The man seemed to wilt. He slumped back onto his seat, exchanging a glance with Fod. Patrons of the public house rose from their benches and cleared a path for the tall, dark figure who strode to the table. Noelle followed closely at her husband's shoulder.

"Outside!" the Earl of Whitby barked.

Tuck nodded briefly. Slowly, he turned, coming face-to-face with the Countess. His face turned red as fire. "What y' want us fer?"

"To talk to you," Robin answered. "I think that should be fairly obvious, otherwise, we'd have brought the sheriff straightway."

Fod swung his head around. His eyes narrowed until they were mere slits in his face. "Y' didn't bring nob'dy."

"Outside," Robin repeated. "And don't think to try to get the better of me again." He swept aside his cloak, revealing a brace of pistols. "I came ready."

Fod gulped at the sight of the gleaming walnut grips, but his natural belligerence asserted itself. "I'm drinkin' a pint 'ere. S'pose I don't come."

Robin's riding crop lashed down across the hairy wrist. The pewter tankard went flying. The ale splashed in Fod's face and over his clothing.

"Y' friggin' b'stard!" He sprang to his feet but froze when he faced the business end of a horse pistol.

"It's cocked and loaded." Robin told him pleasantly. "It can leave quite a hole at this range. I've seen it. And I've done it."

Fod looked around for aid, but Tuck was already moving toward the door. With a curse he followed.

"Gentlemen." Robin addressed the room. "As you were."

With Tuck leading, the four filed out. Noelle turned at the door. "Drink up! Then be about your business. Whitby doesn't tolerate slackers."

Several pairs of ears turned red. A couple of men had paid their tab even as her skirts swished out the door.

"What y' want with us?" Tuck whined. We just does a bit of work, like a favor fer a friend, don't y' know?"

"What was the name of this friend?" Robin inquired.

Both men shuffled their feet uneasily.

"Who is the captain?" Noelle asked.

"Never 'eard uv 'im," Fod declared.

" 'E's a good man," Tuck stated.

Fod turned on his drinking partner, hands reaching

211

for his throat. "Shut yer bleedin' trap."

"Here now." Robin drove him back with the pistol. "Let him finish what he's sayin'."

" 'E's a good man," Tuck repeated doggedly. "Tryin' to pull us all together. Get us a job now an' agin. Nothin' t' do 'round 'ere."

"Except kidnap young gentlewomen and hold them for ransom," Robin inserted sarcastically. "Times are hard indeed."

Fod began to curse, but Robin's motion with the gun silenced him.

"We don't want to put you gentlemen in gaol, unless you force us to it," Robin said.

"W'at y' talkin' about?" Fod snarled. "Y' caught us fair and square. Never figured y'd bring yer missus in t' finger us."

"The Countess has a stake in this as well. And she doesn't take kindly to being manhandled." Robin threw her a wintry smile.

"W'at y' want then?"

"We want the name of the man who hired you."

"The Cap'n hired us," Tuck insisted.

"And who hired him?"

" 'E didn't tell us a name. A gentry cove, so 'e said."

"Did he pay you?"

"Huh?" Fod grunted. "Not much. And we did just w'at 'e tol' us. Nabbed the bird and 'eld 'er safe an' sound till y' come fer 'er. Didn't 'urt 'er a bit."

Robin exchanged a look with Noelle. "Take us to the Captain," she said. "We need to talk to him."

"He'll be madder'n hell," Tuck objected.

Robin thrust the pistol under Tuck's chin. His lips curled back from his teeth in a snarl. "Will he be madder than I am?"

The men exchanged glances. "Not likely."

"Then, let's be off." He turned to Noelle. "Madam Wife, you've done your part. Timothy can escort you home."

She looked at him affronted. "Over my bleedin' body."

Twelve

In the light of day, the Cap'n was dark as a Gypsy. Or a Turk. Looking at the two together, Noelle speculated that the men might have been from the same tribe.

But the resemblance was only skin deep. Where Robin was tall with long-bones and slender long-fingered hands, the Cap'n was stocky. His hands had square-palms and stubby fingers.

They had imprisoned her and handled her against her will. Who knew what they might have done while she lay unconscious? Noelle shuddered as the outlaw stepped down from his wagon to face the waiting riders.

"Cap'n," Fod began uneasily. "We brung 'im and 'is missus."

Robin spoke out of the side of his mouth. "Is he the third one?"

"Yes. He's the one who gave me the drug." Her voice quivered and she clenched her hands on the reins. Deliverance sidled and tugged at the bit.

"Relax," her husband said softly. "This is going to

be all right." Even as he spoke, his black eye traced the Cap'n's hand as it slid inside a pocket of his shabby greatcoat.

"Introduce me to your friends, Fod."

Fod climbed down, taking care to stay out from between the two men. "This be 'is lordship, th' Earl o' Whitby."

"And the Countess, whom you have already met," Robin added smoothly.

"Your ladyship." The Cap'n tugged his hat off and sketched a rude suggestion of a bow. "Glad to see you looking so fine."

"Thank you, Captain." Noelle assumed her grand-lady-of-the-manor posture. It steadied her. "I must confess, although I have met you before, the circumstances were rather difficult. I don't recall many of the details. Still, I would have been able to pick you out of a crowd."

He nodded sagely. "There's many that looks like me."

"But my wife's word would be sufficient for a magistrate's court." Robin swung down off his horse. He stood almost a head taller than the kidnapper. "You'd be transported, if you weren't hanged."

The Cap'n smirked. "I don't see a magistrate with y'."

"For a very good reason. I came to strike a deal."

"With gentry coves!" Fod spat at Robin's boot.

The Cap'n frowned. "Seems to be lots of lords wanting deals these days. Don't you have servants to do your dirty work?"

"Actually I have very few servants," Robin replied pleasantly. "In fact I tried the scowling Fod. I would

215

have taken his partner Tuck as well. Neither was interested in doing honest labor."

The Cap'n threw a suspicious glance at the men. Tuck dropped his head, but Fod growled and shifted. "Well, now maybe they didn't like what you wanted them to do. I might not neither."

"You won't know until you find out. I will tell you that it is honest labor."

The Cap'n grunted. "What might you have in mind?"

"Is there some place we might talk?"

The outlaw looked around with an air of unconcern. "What's wrong with right here?"

"The lady might catch a chill."

The Cap'n gave her an appraising stare. She smiled sweetly back. "Thank you, milord."

"Perhaps we could talk with more ease in that building down the road?" Robin urged. "My wife will probably appreciate the familiar surroundings."

Noelle looked around her in surprise. "Is it so close?"

"They had no intention of keeping you, Madam Wife. Merely holding you until I arrived. I intend to find out why."

"Not from me." The outlaw held out both hands. "It's not for me to understand the gentry's doings."

But Robin paid no attention. He swung back on his horse. "Mount up, gentlemen, and you too, Captain. We'll discuss this in a more hospitable environment."

Sick to her stomach, Noelle stepped inside the stableblock. It was cold, scarcely warmer than outside. It stank of mould and rotting wood and all the odors that rise from untended stalls. She began to shudder.

"Steady on," the Earl murmured, his hand warm around her elbow. To the groom, he said, "Hardwicke, you come in too."

Timothy stationed himself just inside the door, arms crossed over his chest.

Most of the stalls were empty. But in the dimness at the other end of the shedrow, she could hear horses moving.

"Tuck, bring a stool for the lady," the Cap'n ordered.

"No. Don't. I don't want it. Not that stool." She could have died of shame. Her voice sounded like the bleat of a frightened sheep. She took a deep breath and consciously deepened her voice. "I'll stand. Anything here wouldn't be clean enough to sit on."

The outlaw hesitated as if he might say something, then shrugged and looked at the Earl. "What did you want to say?"

Robin swung his crop against his boot. "First, let's set the record straight. I recognize the three of you as men who'll stoop to anything including kidnapping and drugging a helpless woman. You hurt her physically and frightened her half to death. Incidentally, the valuable mare she was riding broke her leg and had to be destroyed. You're destructive vermin whom I could shoot where you stand with no loss to the world."

" 'Ere now, y' bleedin' sod —"

"Shut up, Fod."

The burly man lapsed into grumbling.

"We didn't 'urt 'er." Tuck turned to Noelle. "We didn't 'urt y', milady. An' we wasn't gonna. 'E was 'spose t' come fer y'. An' 'e did."

Robin cut through the man's pleading. "I've no illusions about the three of you, so stop sniveling and begging." He pulled his coat aside to reveal a pair of pistols tucked in his belt.

"My groom—" He nodded toward Hardwicke, silent and watchful in the shadows. "—is similarly armed. You gentlemen are outgunned. The only reason you're not dead—one, two, three—is that I intend that this will never happen again."

The three waited sullenly. The Cap'n's eyes narrowed as he studied the Earl, trying to fathom his mind.

"First, I intend that my wife shall write down your confessions and you will make your marks. You, Captain, will name the man who hired you and how much he paid you."

The heavy shoulders rose and fell. "It won't do you any good. He was a gentleman. It's his word 'gainst mine. I lose."

"I don't intend to use these in a court of law. As I told you, if I wanted to have you taken up, I wouldn't have come myself. Nor would I have brought my wife."

"We didn't 'urt 'er none," Tuck mourned again.

"Fer Gawd's sake, quit yer sniveling!" Fod snarled.

The Cap'n gestured the pair to silence. "Is that all you want from us?"

"Not necessarily." Robin measured him closely. "How did you happen to be called 'Captain'?"

The man pulled himself to attention. "Sergeant was

218

m' rank, sir. Served in Spain and Portugal. Ended up at Waterloo. Then they didn't need me any more."

"And your companions?"

"I was with 'im." Tuck nodded fervently.

"What's it t' y'?" Fod wanted to know.

"Perhaps there might be honest work around here quite soon."

"When cows fly."

"Shut up, Fod!"

"I am still in need of help. My estates are long neglected. I have two choices. I can hire you as work develops, or I can shoot you and take the next three that come along. It's your choice."

"What'd we have to do?"

The British officer answered in his sternest voice. "Whatever I tell you to do. Or what the Countess tells you to do. Whatever the business of the estate is. When I'm in London, she will be in charge."

"Her!" Fod's contempt was vicious.

The Earl's hand moved toward his pistol. "Her word is mine."

"I can see that," the Cap'n rasped.

"I ain't workin' fer no female."

"Shut yer yap!" Tuck jabbed Fod in the ribs. The belligerent lout subsided, rubbing his midsection.

"Will you sign?" Robin asked.

The Cap'n looked at the other two. Tuck nodded eagerly. Fod scowled, but made no objection. "We'll sign."

In a matter of minutes, Timothy unfolded Robin's field table and camp stool. Noelle seated herself to take the statements.

The Captain described Archie Holmesfield, whose

219

name he did not know, as the man who had hired him and directed the entire enterprise. Noelle's writing became shaky as she heard that Holmesfield had furnished the laudanum and seen it administered.

"He was there?"

"Yes, ma'am." The Cap'n cast her a sympathetic look. "Waiting in one of the stalls. That's why we took you into the tack room."

She looked up at Robin. "Why? I don't understand."

Robin shrugged. "None of it makes sense. But at least with these papers, we'll see that it doesn't happen again."

"One of us was with you all the time, milady," the outlaw continued. "You weren't in a bit of danger."

"The man who paid you was working for someone else," Robin said. "You don't have any idea who hired him."

The Cap'n grinned. "Maybe I'm bait fer the nubbin' cheat, but I ain't a fool. I left Tuck here with her. He's a good chap, ma'am. Better than most."

Tuck actually blushed and shuffled his feet.

"Fod and me followed the beggar home that first night."

Robin waited.

"He took us right to the ol' Rose and Thistle. A quick question and I knew who I was working for. There was only one Duke in the place."

"Averill." Noelle's voice was like death. "But why? I'm no longer around him. Why this?"

"Perhaps you'll tell me later?"

She flushed but said no more.

"Averill's the name." The Cap'n nodded.

Noelle wrote the name on the document, sanded it, and turned the document around on the desktop. "Sign it."

Fod and Tuck laboriously made their marks, but the Cap'n wrote his name—Jeptha Walton.

When the paper was safely tucked away in the field table, Timothy carried it away to pack on the saddle.

The tension seemed to drain away.

"Madam Wife." The Earl offered his arm. He led her to the door of the stable.

The Cap'n watched them go, then pushed his hat back from his forehead. "Your pardon, milord, milady, but would you be interested in a fine piece of prime blood?"

Robin looked over his shoulder. His mouth curled. "Horse stealing to add to your sins?"

"Stealing? Us?"

"Never," Tuck put in anxiously.

Robin looked at Noelle's strained face. "Captain, my wife is very tired."

"She wouldn't have to ride a bit. He's right here. Come see for yourself. We traded him off a band of gypsies coming up from Devon."

"Some of your tribe?"

The Cap'n's face darkened. His eyes blazed. "I ain't a bleedin' gypsy."

"Sorry. If you're not a gypsy, how does it happen you trade with them?"

Noelle was suddenly conscious that a thread of humor underlay her husband's questions. She looked at him speculatively. Far from despising this man, Robin saw the Cap'n as less evil than she did.

She felt her stomach clench with fear. What sort of

221

man had she married? He extracted confessions to use for what was undoubtedly a nefarious purpose. He made deals with kidnappers. He bargained for what was most probably a stolen horse.

The lighter note in Robin's voice had reached the outlaw too. He appeared to relax. "Truth to tell, milord, I just couldn't let this horse get by me. Prime blood he is, and that's a fact. Just wait till you see him. You'll want him in a minute." The Cap'n led the way down the shedrow, his greatcoat swaying with his bandy-legged walk.

"Probably windbroken," Robin confided out of the side of his mouth. "Watch for dye around the muzzle. It's a gypsy trick."

"He's not windbroke," the Cap'n called over his shoulder. "He's about the best I've ever seen for trade. He's just fallen on hard times. And haven't we all?" He stopped in front of the end stall and swung around. His eyes went significantly to the black patch.

Noelle felt her husband's muscles tense, then relax swiftly. His voice assumed a bored tone. "Trot him out. We haven't got all day."

"Yes, milord. Right away." The outlaw touched his forehead, his gesture as far from subservience as he could possibly make it. He pushed aside the bar and entered the box stall.

A whicker, a snort came from its interior. Shod hooves thudded heavily denoting a big beast. The Cap'n cursed.

"Probably a draft horse," Robin asided for her ear only.

Then the outlaw led a magnificent animal out into

222

the shedrow. The horse was a black stallion without a white hair on him.

Noelle gasped as the exquisitely sculptured head rose. He was at least a hand taller than Averill's Brandywine. The nostrils flared as he caught their strange scent. A white ring showed around his eye as he pulled back.

After a moment of silent contemplation, Robin gestured with his whip. "Lead him out."

Smirking, the Cap'n led the way out into the sunshine, where they stared again. The horse was that most prized color—raven black. His hide had an additional sheen that reflected bluish highlights. His body was sculptured like a model of a horse—a bit too long, a bit too big, a bit too heavily muscled. At the sight of Deliverance and Dark o' the Moon, he snorted eagerly. The Arabian's ears flicked forward interestedly, while the black danced and switched her tail.

"Trot him around."

The Cap'n passed the rope to Tuck, who happily led the horse on a jog in a circle.

"Oh, he's crippled," Noelle mourned.

Indeed, the stallion moved on three legs, lifting his right hind leg clear of the ground, unable to bear weight on it.

"Hold his head."

Noelle watched her husband, the natural leader, give commands that none of the others thought to disobey.

The stallion's right side revealed a swelling scar low on the flank.

"Steady, boy. Steady on." Curiously, Robin approached the stallion. Talking softly, he ran his hand along the belly. The stallion tolerated the man until he touched the skin near the place. Then with a squeal of anger, the stallion side-stepped and reared, snapping viciously.

The Earl stepped back, as Tuck wrestled the horse down. "That's a bullet wound," he observed.

"How'd you know that?" the Cap'n wanted to know.

"I've seen too many of them. It's an old one, and unless I miss my guess, the bullet's still in there." Robin dusted his hands and looked around him impatiently. "Where'd you get him?"

"I told you. Gypsies."

"Then they probably shot his rider and stole him. Looks like you gentlemen are out of luck again. I can't buy a stolen horse."

The stallion whinnied again and snapped at Tuck's shoulder. His behavior angered the Cap'n, who jerked the beast's head around and pinched the nostrils hard. "Here now, you black son of Satan!"

Noelle shuddered. The sight of the Cap'n's hands on the horse's face made her cold. Unbidden came the memory of her struggles and the bruising pain that this man had visited upon her. Her heart was wrung with pity for the black.

"The Gypsies came through here with him. They was glad to trade him. They said with all their 'glamoring' they couldn't get him quieted down long enough to tend him. He's a wild one, for sure. Not fit for riding. But that don't make any difference with his bollocks."

He glanced hastily at Noelle, who blushed. "Begging your pardon, milady. He'd give you a prime stand at stud. And cheap."

The horse had quieted. The Cap'n slowly released the nostrils but kept his fist doubled under the stallion's chin knuckling the tender underside of the jaw. "Looks like one of them new A-rabs, don't he?"

"He's much too big for an Arab," Robin observed. "Are you ready to leave, Madam Wife?"

Noelle started. Her brows snapped together. She wanted the horse badly. He was the stallion Whitby needed. The crucial thing to give her dream a chance at reality. "Oh, please, milord."

"Noelle, let's go," he snapped.

Daring greatly, she rose on tiptoe and whispered in his ear. "I have some jewelry, milord. My mother's. I would—"

He whipped around, his volcanic voice blazing. "Madam Wife, you will hold your tongue."

"Well, now, if he's caught the lady's fancy, milord, you don't want to disappoint your new bride."

"You are a scoundrel, Cap'n."

"Me, sir. Naw."

Whittcombstone ran his black eye over the proud head, the light sweat glistened on the arched neck. The animal sidled nervously and pawed the ground, trying to relieve the pain in his jaw.

"Even if he don't tame down, you've still got his seed."

Robin looked at Noelle. Her expression was pleading. "Countess, ride out into the lane. Fod, you lout, help her mount."

High spots of color on her cheeks, Noelle rode out and halted facing back toward Whitby. She dared not look over her shoulder although the thought of the beautiful, wounded animal in the Cap'n's hard hands brought tears to her eyes. As she bent to pat her mare's neck, she resolved to have the horse somehow.

Minutes passed before hooves thudded behind her, and Robin pulled abreast. "Shall we gallop?" he called. Suiting his action to his word, he spurred the the gelding.

She spared a glance over her shoulder in time to see the three shaking hands and congratulating each other. Timothy Hardwicke was putting a leadline through the stallion's hackamore.

Flashing a delighted smile, she touched her heel to the mare's side. The long iron-hard legs stretched, the shod hooves tore into the road.

The tall black caught the gelding in a matter of seconds. She actually had to rein the mare to keep the two horses neck and neck.

The wind blew the pins from her hair and she had to catch her hat to keep from losing it. The ride had the effect of blowing away the pain and fear, as well as the last vestiges of the drug.

When the Earl signalled for a halt, her color was high, and she was smiling.

"Your groom will lead the stallion back to Whitby," Robin told her without preamble. "With you out of the way, we reached a fair price for the beast. Your ill-timed interruption almost succeeded in driving the price up."

"Oh. I didn't realize what you were doing."

"Fortunately, neither did they. You might trust me on occasion," he said dryly.

"I gather I'm not a very good horse-trader. Probably because I've no experience in haggling with thieves over stolen goods."

"You didn't mind buying the animal," he pointed out sarcastically.

"I wanted to rescue him. He was being brutalized."

"In all likelihood, he's been brutalized a long time. He may be an outlaw."

"Averill's Brandywine has savaged two grooms that I know of."

"There may be a very good reason why the gypsies had him. He may be permanently crippled."

"As the Cap'n would so quaintly put it, 'His bollocks are all right.' "

Robin eyed her severely. "A lady's vocabulary doesn't contain that word."

"No one who has known me has ever believed that I'm a lady."

"On that count, I concur."

He walked his horse toward home. She fell in beside him. "As a matter of fact, I had made up my mind to buy him the minute I saw him." He chuckled. "And the Cap'n knew I had. We were just testing each other."

She sighed. "I'm sorry I spoke."

"That mouth of yours will be the ruin of you."

The stallion threw back his head and screamed like a woman. Then his rear hooves shattered the boards of the stable. Teeth bared, eyes rolling, he lunged at the veterinarian. Only the cross-ties kept him from reaching the man. The horse doctor skillfully avoided the lancing hooves and rolled out from under the slats of the stall.

The black screamed again and reared, fighting the ropes attached to the headstall. They pulled him down. His hooves slammed into the floor of the stable.

The veterinarian rose, whitefaced, and brushed himself off. His hands were shaking. "I won't touch him, milord. He's too wild. If I could tie him down, perhaps. But he's too canny. And you don't have enough men in your stables to choke him down."

"You're an idiot," Robin informed him coldly. "Go then, but don't expect any commerce from this stable."

"That's as may be." The vet clapped his hat on his head. "But at least I'll be alive to enjoy the money I make elsewhere."

The man had not cleared the stableyard before Robin called to Noelle. "Fetch the surgeon's kit from my trunk."

"The surgeon's kit?"

"A square leatherbound box. Black. Brass handle. Brass lock." He ticked the characteristics off as if she were feeble-minded.

"In your trunk? Where?"

"Somewhere? Wherever it was stored when I came home from Spain. The attic probably."

"I'll find it."

He turned to Timothy. "I want every rope we have in this place. Hopefully a few are not rotten."

"Yes, sir."

"And set a pot of water to boiling."

Robin followed Noelle to the house, stripping off his greatcoat as he went. In his room he divested himself of his good clothing. He had donned his uniform trousers and was rolling up the sleeves of his collarless shirt likewise a remainder from his army days, when Noelle came into the room.

"Is this what you wanted?"

He nodded. "Exactly. In the attic?"

"Just inside the door."

He opened the drawer of his dressing table and took out his sidearm.

Her eyes flew wide. "What do you intend to do with that?"

"Defend myself if necessary. I don't intend to be killed or maimed." He thrust it into the waistband of his trousers. From her limp hands he took the kit and strode down the hall.

She shook herself out of her trance and hurried down the hall, trying to overtake his long legs.

At the door he paused. "You'd better stay inside."

She straightened her shoulders and shook her head briskly. "Don't be ridiculous. He's my stud. I need to oversee the entire procedure."

He laughed shortly. "You don't know what you're letting yourself in for. We may kill him in the process of getting him down. We may get hurt ourselves."

"I may be able to help."

He stopped in his tracks. "I won't be responsible for you."

His remark drew a laugh from her. "No one is responsible for me. I take care of myself."

He resumed walking. "And we have all seen what an amazing job you do of that."

"Thank you and be damned," she muttered.

Timothy met them with coils of rope draped over

his shoulders and hanging from his hands. "I think we've got some strength 'ere, sir."

Robin took the one the groom held out. "I'm depending on you, Hardwicke."

"Yes, sir."

"What can I do?" asked Noelle.

"Nothing."

"Horses like me. I'm good with them," Noelle insisted.

"This is a stallion. He'd like you all right—for breakfast, lunch, or dinner."

"I don't intend to leave. You can tell me what to do and I'll do it, and be a help to you. Or you can ignore me and I'll probably get in the way."

"Either way you'll hear language you shouldn't," he said.

"Heaven forfend. My delicate ears."

"I'll probably curse you."

"I wouldn't expect anything else. Most men do curse women."

He looked at her strangely. "If we survive this, Madam Wife, I want to have a long and honest conversation with you."

Her face was flushed with excitement. She shrugged. "If we survive, milord."

Thirteen

The stallion laid back his ears. His eye rolled showing the white ring. Still he came out of his stall willingly enough. Whittcombstone talked to him like a gypsy, saying nonsense words, complimenting him, carrying on a monologue about the weather as he led the way slowly down the shedrow.

As the big body cleared the stable door, the front hooves stepped into a wide loop.

"Now."

Timothy drew the rope tight, effectively hobbling the animal. At the same instant, Robin grasped the left ear and the headstall beneath the chin. With a violent twist, he threw himself backward and pulled the horse down on its left side.

The black's screams of anger and rage were terrible. He kicked furiously with his hindlegs. His big body spasmed so violently that both hindquarters and shoulders were off the ground at the same time.

Noelle stared open-mouthed, hands clenched against her cheeks.

The groom snubbed his rope around the hitching

post, keeping a steady pressure. The Earl scrambled to his feet and wrapped the one attached to the headstall around a fence post. He too applied pressure.

Still the black fought, his hind legs flailing wildly, tail switching, while he grunted and trumpeted pure rage. Noelle was sure that if the beast could have found his feet, they would all have been murdered.

"Watch his hindquarters!" Robin yelled as he threw his weight across the heavily muscled neck.

"Right y'are!"

"And his teeth." He scowled as Noelle shook herself out of her shock and dashed forward, oatsack outstretched to blindfold the struggling animal.

With the horse's head and neck pulled out straight by Robin's rope, she could bandage his eyes safely, even though the huge yellow teeth snapped inches from her hand.

With the blindfold in place, the stallion's cries ceased instantly. His ears flicked forward and back, picking out the sounds. His struggles decreased.

"Loop a rope around his hind legs if you can," Robin instructed. "The stiller he's lying, the better for him."

Timothy managed to cast a loop over one foot, but the other flailed as the horse realized what they were about and fought.

"That's good enough." The Earl stepped back, hands on hips to check his handiwork.

Noelle joined him, her face white. "Now?"

He glanced at her and grinned unpleasantly. "No, Madam Wife, not now. We'll let him lie there for a few minutes and think it over. The more exhausted he is and the more confused, the better. And he needs to

232

decide for himself that he can't get free."

"It seems a shame—"

"Madam—Noelle. The real shame is that he wasn't properly cared for when this happened. We may not be able to help him."

She looked at her husband with quiet assurance. "You'll take care of him. I know you will."

He gave a short bark of laughter. "Me! I don't know a damn thing about what I'm doing except what I've had to learn in the cavalry. You've got to have your horse. And horses stop bullets more often than men. You dig it out of your mount, just like you dig it out of your men."

She shuddered. "Sounds terrible."

He merely looked at her. "It doesn't sound half as terrible as it really is."

The horse lay still, breathing evenly, his ears twitching back and forth. She shivered as she realized that he was listening to everything they said. Of course, he could not understand. Still, he must be terribly frightened. She could feel tears prickling behind her eyes.

Robin knelt to open his kit. His wife peered over his shoulder. But when he moved aside a twelve inch saw to get to the gleaming knives, she clapped her hand to her mouth and spun around.

He looked over his shoulder. "I suggest you go into the house."

Timothy Hardwicke seconded him. "He's right, milady. 'Tisn't going to be pretty."

Robin passed the groom a pointed iron rod with a wooden handle. "Heat this."

"Right, sir."

"What can I do?" Noelle insisted stoutly.

"You can go in the house."

"Is this going to be any more pleasant for you than for me?"

"No."

"And are you going to enjoy it in some strange way that I can't?"

"Hardly."

"Then I'll stay. This is my horse—too."

"If you pass out, I'll step over your body and go on."

"And I'll do the same for you," she replied.

He snorted at her bravado. "Then listen. When we cut, he's going to feel it and he'll start fighting all over again. If I'm fast, we can get out of the way before he breaks free."

"Do you honestly think he could break free?" She stared at the thick ropes trying to calculate their strength.

"Of course, he could. He's stronger than the three of us put together. He's been hurting a long time. The pain's made him mean, maybe a killer. Ropes can't be depended upon to hold him."

Timothy returned in time to hear the Earl's discourse. "He's right, ma'am. One swipe of one of those big hooves would kill you where you stood. There's many a grown man struck down dead on the spot by a gentle horse. This one's a killer."

"I don't think he's a killer," she objected.

"You'll be just as dead if he kills you by accident."

She drew in a deep breath. "We're wasting time. The water's boiling. The iron's heating. The horse is still."

The Earl looked at the groom, who shrugged.

"What shall I do?"

Again the look, this time accompanied by a sneering smile. "Sit on his head."

The horse did not scream when the Earl drove the lancet into the center of the gray scar. But the whole black body vibrated. Noelle felt the quiver beneath her thighs. Instantly, sweat glistened on the black neck.

She cast one glance at the wound, saw the blood well out. It streamed down the black belly and dripped on the ground.

"Hand me the probe," the Earl barked.

Timothy complied.

"And tighten that leg, pull it back if you can." His words came out in quick gasps and grunts as he worked the knife deeper into the gristle. "I can't find anything."

Noelle turned her head away. Her stomach was still. At least she was not nauseated, but black spots were whirling in her vision. She lowered her head between her spread knees, trying to stave off unconsciousness.

"All right?" Her husband's sharp voice penetrated the roaring in her ears.

"Yes," she whispered.

"Leave if you must."

"If I pass out, I'll still stay."

"Good girl." He slid the probe into the hole.

The stallion whickered and snorted. White lather appeared on his neck and began to form in waves.

"Steady, boy." Noelle lifted her face over her knee

and whispered in the horse's ear. It flicked.

"I've found something," Robin panted. "It's deep in the muscle. God damn! and tight!" He began to curse. "Damn! I think it's stuck in the bone. Damn! Damn!"

She raised her head and stared at the intense dark face. The Turk might have been working himself into a fury. Or he might have been giving himself the resolute ruthlessness to inflict pain and shed blood.

The thought drove the weakness from her limbs. "Can I help?"

He did not answer. The lancet was withdrawn and a long slender pair of forceps disappeared into the bubbling wound.

The horse screamed like a woman and began to fight. Streams of lather dripped from his black hide. The free hind leg thrashed frantically. Timothy Hardwicke leaned his weight across the croup to hold the animal still.

Noelle leaned down to speak into the flattened ear. "Steady boy steady boy easy. It's going to be all right. It'll be over soon. Soon. Soon."

The ribs heaved in and out as if the stallion had run miles.

"God damn!" the Earl prayed. "Please God. Got it, I think." His face contorted. His hands were bloody halfway up his arms. Slowly, he began to withdraw the forceps, pulling the probe out with it. In a rush of blood the ends of the instruments cleared the wound.

The Earl's hands began to shake. The forceps opened and the ball splatted into the pool of blood soaking into the earth. "Now," he sighed. "Get the iron, Hardwicke."

"Yes, sir." The groom rolled off and hurried away.

Robin rested on his elbows, his hands loosely holding the instruments, blood dripped from their tips and from his fingers. He ducked his head to wipe his forehead against his shirt.

"Shall I get up now?" Noelle whispered.

He looked at her with a dull stare. "Better wait. We still have to hurt him one more time."

"One. Oh no." Noelle felt her stomach turn over. She closed her eyes and tried to think of flowers.

"Just once." His voice came from far away, over the roaring. "Quick. And then it'll be over."

Timothy returned with the iron that glowed red-hot. At his approaching footsteps, she opened her eyes. Her whole body clenched at the sight. She found she could not take her eyes off it.

Gingerly, the groom transferred it to Robin, who rose to his feet to stand over the horse's hindquarters. Noelle's eyes flew to the wound. Blood still flowed from it, although sluggishly. She swallowed.

Robin looked around at her. "Better look the other way."

"I can take it if you can."

"Then bedamned to you, Madam Wife!" He pressed the cautery to the wound and counted to five slowly. The stench of burning flesh and hair rose with a gust of steam and a sizzling sound. Beneath Noelle, the horse screamed again. The free leg kicked reflexively. Then the stallion lay still, its great barrel heaving.

Robin stepped back. The steaming iron dragged his arm down to his side. He started to wipe his forearm across his sweaty forehead, caught sight of the blood to his elbow, and wiped his face on his shoulder. "Let him free."

Timothy cautiously shook the loops free of the stallion's legs, then came around and untied the rope from his head.

"You can get up now." Robin held out his hand.

She gagged at the sight.

"Sorry," he murmured helplessly.

Why he's almost as shocked as I am, she thought. She caught hold of his shoulder and staggered to her feet. He led her away until she could throw her arm over the fence for support. "The blindfold."

Timothy pulled the towel free. The stallion did not move. His eyes remained closed. Foam covered his jaws and wet the ground beneath his head.

Noelle began to weep. "Have we killed him?"

Robin heaved a sigh. Moving like a man sixty-nine instead of thirty-nine, he paced to the rear of the horse. "High up, boy!"

The stallion lay still as a stone except for the heaving of his sides. Even his ears did not move.

"Maybe he's unconscious."

Robin bent and grabbed the swirling tail. "Up!" he called to the horse. "Come on, son. It's all over."

Still the horse did not move.

"Oh, don't hurt him anymore."

"Take hold of the halter, Hardwicke."

"Right, milord."

Still holding the tail, Robin kicked the horse hard in the rump. "High up! Up there!"

The stallion did not move a muscle.

"Up! Get up!" the groom called, tugging on the halter.

"He can't," Noelle mourned. Tears started from her eyes. "He's hurt too badly."

"Him. Not much. Up!" Robin put his shoulder against the horse's rump and heaved.

With a snort the black scrambled to his feet and stood swaying. "Good boy," Timothy crooned. He stroked the velvet muzzle.

The horse lifted his head, the ears laid back. Timothy stepped back hastily. The stallion blew a roller through his nose and then shook himself like a dog. Muddy lather and foam flew in all directions.

Robin gestured with his bloody hands. "That does it, Madam Wife. Lead him back in, Hardwicke, and rub him down."

As the groom turned the stallion, Noelle hurried forward. She laid a hand on the steaming neck. "Give him hot mash tonight, Timothy, and be sure to keep compresses on the wound."

"It needs to dry," Robin contradicted her. "Don't touch it."

She whirled. "But don't you think—"

Annoyance stiffened his features. "I did this. I know what—"

She put her hands on her hips. "But it might not be completely clean. It might need to draw. I think—"

"I'll take care of it," the groom assured them. "And I'll bring your case back to the house, sir."

"Good," Robin said.

"Good!" Noelle sucked in her breath. "Good! How can you say good?"

"Come, Madam Wife. Enough of your interfering." He gestured to Noelle then turned away and strode toward the house.

Angrily, she watched the groom lead the stallion back down the shedrow. With short jerky motions, she pulled Robin's coat from the fence and looped her skirt over her arm. Muttering under her breath, she hurried after him.

"I wasn't interfering." In the manor's kitchen Noelle pumped water over the Earl's hands and arms while he washed with a bar of lye soap.

He said nothing, but his jaw was set so hard not a muscle flickered in it.

She passed him a towel. Both of them ignored the Blivenses. The old man had cowered back at the sight of the blood and now stood wringing his hands and mumbling.

Mrs. Blivens looked like grim death as she flung a cloth over the butcher block in the opposite corner. "Nasty," she charged. "Nasty. Nasty."

When Robin had cleaned the worst off his hands, Noelle turned. "Mrs. Blivens, put water on to boil. The Earl and I both will want hot baths immediately. Blivens, will you call us when one is ready."

"I've got dinner to prepare," the woman protested.

"We'll forgive you if it's a little late. Boil the water first."

The woman pulled a large kettle down from a hook on the wall. It clanged against the stone floor. "I'm not the maid," she snarled. "I'm the cook."

The Countess whirled around, her brows drawing together in a terrible frown.

Mrs. Blivens cowered back. "Water takes a good while to boil," she countered weakly.

240

"Just do it." Noelle followed the Earl out of the kitchen.

Robin dropped into a chair in front of the fire and passed his hand over his forehead. The leather strap seemed to cut into his flesh. He started to work his index finger under it, but snatched it away as his wife followed him into the room.

Drawing a deep shuddery breath, he leaned his head back. His side ached from shoulder to hip. Scar tissue with no elasticity had threatened to burst when he had heaved and jerked the stallion around. Now he would pay for it. "Bring me some brandy," he murmured.

"I have it now."

He opened his eye. She was actually holding it out to him. He accepted it with a nod and drank, letting it flow down his throat.

Noelle stared at him. Color had drained from his face while he had washed his hands. Today had proved that he was infinitely more human than demon. The scars on his face and body were testaments to great suffering.

The clock on the mantel chimed the half hour. They had been in the stable nearly three hours. It seemed like forever and no time at all.

She knelt before him. "Shall I pull your boots off?"

He opened his eye a fraction. "Why are you offering?"

She took his ankle in her hand. "You bought the stallion."

"I bought him for myself. This is my stable." He lifted his leg so she would not have to bear its weight.

241

"But it was my ambition." She braced her feet and put her back into it. It came off more easily than she had expected.

"Don't be a fool," he murmured.

She lowered his foot to the floor and picked up the other. "Don't insult me. I'm not a fool. At least not very much of one."

"I own it," he said without opening his eyes. "It's not yours."

She pulled off the other boot, then straightened. "No more than your gambling debts, milord. Nor your debts against the estate."

"I see your point."

"Of course you do." She smiled as she picked up the boots to carry them to the wardrobe. As she passed, he caught her hand and pulled her down onto his lap. The arm containing the pony of brandy came round her. The liquid threatened to splash her skirt. "Let me go."

"No." His jaw was a hard line, bisected by the white seam. "For a female you think about too many things. I won the horses and I bought the stallion. I don't want to hear you say anything more."

She pushed against his shoulder. "Oh, heaven forfend, that I should tell the truth. If you want to lie to yourself, but indirectly, my money bought all the horses. You married well, milord. If you want to forget about it, that's your business."

Her color was high. Her eyes flashed. Her hip pressed hard against him. He stared up at her, his expression kindling. "I may murder you yet."

With that he pulled her down and kissed her viciously.

242

He tasted of brandy and smelled of horse and hardworked man. His skin was hot. The black shadow of his beard prickled her. His tongue drove deep into her mouth, taking everything, allowing her no escape, demanding abject surrender.

Her own response was instantaneous. As if her body had a will of its own, it lifted to him. Her breast hardened under his hand, the nipple aching. A soft inarticulate sound came from deep in her throat as the kiss went on and on. Moisture and heat blazed between her thighs.

Then he was pushing her away. "Come in!"

The door opened.

She had not heard the knock. Embarrassed, she staggered to her feet. One hand flailed out to steady herself against the fire place wall.

Blivens entered, his shoulders yoked. "I've brought the hot water, sir." He set it down. "The bath — er — the bath is here in the hall. I can't quite manage it."

Robin shoved his glass into his wife's unresisting hand and fetched the copper tub. When it was set in front of the fire and the water poured in, he set the yoke back on the old man's shoulders. "Two more buckets of water, Blivens."

"Two more, m-milord?"

"Just bring them around and set them outside the door. Then knock."

"Bring them to the door. Then knock. Yes, sir. Are you — that is — shouldn't I bring them in?"

"You don't have to trouble to do it. My wife will bring them in."

He threw Noelle a taunting look and caught her in the act of drinking his brandy. His smile broadened.

243

"Well—"

"Two more buckets of hot water, Blivens. As soon as possible."

"Yes, milord." He shuffled out.

Robin closed the door behind him. "Now, milady, you can finish undressing me."

She bolted the rest of the brandy. "I was trying to be a good wife. Because you had done so much, I wanted to repay. The stallion was so dangerous."

She backed away as he came to the copper tub.

"You can repay. I don't mind my wife repaying me for whatever she thinks I deserve."

"You're terrible."

"Is this news to you?" He held out his arms. "I'm waiting."

"I shan't feel anything again. I vow."

"Come here." His smile was everything that was sardonic.

She had to step close to untie the simple stock and pull it away. She could feel the heat from his body and see his pulse beat on the side of his brown throat. He was so dark.

The buttons took her no longer, though her fingers were trembling. She could feel the brandy working in her, its heat making her a little dizzy. She was hot outside and in.

Beneath his shirt, his skin was covered with black hair. It lay close against his skin and silky like the hair on his head. She pushed the shirt over his shoulders. It fell off his arms and hung at his waist.

She swallowed. Her hands itched to touch him. Even though her mind denied her desire, she could not help herself. Her fingers fluttered, and then came to rest with her palm on his chest. She bent her head to hide the flaming blush in her cheeks.

"I'm not undressed yet," he murmured, his voice unnaturally husky. He closed his hand around hers, squeezing her fingers almost painfully, guiding them to the buttons in the front of his pantaloons.

She made an incoherent sound. She dared not admit that she wanted to do this. Her body itched and twitched for him. She wanted him naked. Wanted him. But he had hurt her. Did she want him to hurt her again?

Pantaloons, small clothes, stockings were peeled off in a matter of seconds. She stared at his body, her mouth dry. She had never seen a naked man before, but she knew what he would do. The organ rising from the black curling hair at the top of his thighs, had hurt her terribly, but only once.

Now she was not afraid.

He stepped into the bath and eased down. A sigh of satisfaction rose from him as the heated water rose around his waist. "That's good."

She licked her dry lips. "I'll refill your brandy."

He held out the cloth. "Wash my back first."

Again the skin was dark and sprinkled with black hairs, although not so many as his chest. The muscles rippled under the skin, the black hair tufted under his arms. Beneath his ribs, he was narrow, with very little difference between his waist and hips.

She knelt and dipped the cloth in the water. Her fingers brushed the dark skin. It had a satiny sheen. Before her eyes she watched the skin prickle and turn pebbly. "Are you cold?"

"Lord, no. I'm on fire."

"But—"

"Just finish the job, Madam Wife, or you may not get your bath."

At that instant Blivens knocked.

He reached for the sponge. "Go get your water. I'll finish here."

She stood in the hall for a minute taking deep breaths of the cold air. Still she trembled. Her stomach muscles clenched and jumped. She pressed her hand against first one breast and then the other. Her nipples were hard and sensitive to her touch.

The water slopped as she carried it back into the room.

She heard the splash as he rose from the bath. She raised her eyes, to watch the silver rills of water sluicing off him.

Long bones, with heavy joints at knee and ankle, wrist and elbow. His belly was concave and for the moment the organ hung between his legs. At the sight of her it sprang to attention.

"Take off those clothes," he commanded stepping out onto a towel.

"I—" She could not think what she wanted to say.

Without bothering to dry off, he came toward her and took the buckets. She followed dumbly as he led the way back to the fire. Her fingers fumbled, but she was half unbuttoned before he could turn around.

His eye blazed at the sight of her white skin. He set the buckets down. "I can't wait," he whispered.

"Neither can I." Her hands clenched in her skirt. "I should be afraid. But I'm not—I suppose this is what happens. Something. I don't know—"

He pulled her against him. "Hush."

Then his hands caressed and stripped her. Blouse and camisole were off in seconds, the last hanging from the waistband at her skirt. His mouth ravaged hers, his hands pressed her buttocks.

She clasped his shoulders, lifted herself, to try to ease the ache in her breasts. Gasping, she pulled her mouth free. "Please."

He stooped and flung up her skirt. His hand dived through the split in her drawers, fingering her embarrassingly, finding her wet and hot. "Oh yes. Oh yes," he murmured. "I only hope I'm man enough for you."

One hard arm locked around her waist. Her feet swung free of the floor and he carried her to the bed, locked to him. His organ followed his hand through the opening. He had penetrated her as she fell backwards on the bed.

She cried out, but only in shocked surprised. Then he was scrambling up the bed with her, pushing her with the mighty thrusts of his body.

With each one she felt she would fly apart. Each one. All the nerves of her body were concentrated at the point where he entered her body. He rubbed against her as he pulled himself out to thrust in again.

The feeling of fullness, the ecstasy. No pain, but an ache, unresolved and nonspecific along all the nerves of her body.

He kissed her hard. His face, dark and terrible, with white teeth bared hung above her. "What—do—you—feel?"

She blinked and arched her neck to take in air. "I—don't—know."

"Let—it—happen—" He pulled farther out of her than before. "—now." He struck the very heart of her and she went falling over the edge, spinning, upward and downward in a hot space, where fire blazed along her veins and suns burned in her vision.

Fourteen

Robin lowered his wife into the bath. She leaned her elbows on her knees and rested her chin in her hands. Her mouth was curved in a foolish grin.

He grinned back. "Feeling better, are you?"

Embarrassed for the first time, she looked down at herself. Smothering an exclamation, she made a flustered attempt to straighten her body and draw her legs together.

"Don't." His fingers touched her cheek, slipped under her chin, lifted her face to his. "You have nothing to be ashamed of." Using the sponge, he squeezed streams of water over her inner thighs.

She sighed and then stirred helplessly as he dragged the sponge deliberately over the tingling area between her legs.

"Like that?" His voice was husky.

She saw that he was looking at her breasts, his breathing a little quick. The dark skin across his cheekbones flushed with hot color. She distinctly felt her nipples tighten. Her breath came out in a sigh. "I can't get used to the idea that we're naked. I think my body must look odd."

"Odd?" One black eyebrow rose quizzically as he lifted the sponge and squeezed it over her breast. His smile just missing a leer, he managed to squeeze the breast at the same time.

"You know. Sticking out in different directions."

He laughed. A short bark of laughter, but a real laugh nevertheless. "I will admit I do stick out in different directions. In fact, right now I'm sticking out in a very obvious direction."

She closed her eyes. The shudder that ran through her body set the water atremble. "You shouldn't be saying this to me."

"I don't know why not. We seem to be understanding each other—in more than one way. On the other hand, I've never said it to anyone before. In fact, I've never had this conversation before." He finished with the sponge. "Stand up."

Her eyes flew open. "Why?"

"You'll find out."

"Will you hand me a towel?" she asked suspiciously.

"Eventually. Up." He caught her hands and lifted her, then placed them on his shoulders. "Now."

The water was still trickling down her body when she discovered what he was going to do. "Oh! Oh, no. You shouldn't be doing that. Oh, no."

His long clever fingers parted the dripping curls, spread the nether lips wide. His callused thumb rubbed gently, then more insistently, over the tiny pearl of nerves.

She cried out, flinging back her head, arching her back in ecstasy. Her hips shot forward. Her fingernails dug into his shoulders.

"Am I hurting you?" His mouth was so close, she could feel the hot breath.

"N-No." She was swaying, shuddering uncontrollably. Her legs were quivering, the knees buckling.

250

He touched his tongue to the spot. Then his hot mouth closed over it, sucking hard.

"No!" She screamed the word to the ceiling. "No no no o hno."

His hands cupped her buttocks, holding her, keeping her upright, when her feet danced in the water, splashing them both.

He grazed her with his teeth. The bite sent her over the edge again, this time into a red haze of pleasure, that darkened into silence.

"Now, tell me why your father married you to me."

The water had cooled in the tub and the puddles around it had dried. Their lunch trays had been set aside.

She lay on her stomach, her eyes half-closed, her hand idly stirring the black hairs on his thigh. Instantly, her hand stilled. "I'd rather not."

He caressed the top of her head, smoothing her hair, brushing a tendril into place. "I know it's really none of my business. But perhaps you'd better tell me anyway. It might make it safer for you."

"I'm safe enough."

Robin's voice turned sarcastic. "If you can call safe being kidnapped and drugged. Such safety! Such force that a valuable animal was injured and had to be destroyed."

She did not answer.

"Suppose Holmesfield hadn't been able to find me. You might have died from lack of water. You met the men who held you prisoner. They were brutal and ignorant."

"They won't do it again."

251

"The countryside is overflowing with ex-soldiers who'll work for pennies and stick at nothing."

She rolled over on her back and pulled the sheet up around her chin. Her lips compressed.

Robin leaned over and kissed the corner of her mouth. "Tell me and I'll make love to you again."

She did not smile. "You may not want to."

He kissed her cheek and the tip of her nose. "Take a chance on a sure thing."

She concentrated on a spot on the ceiling. Her voice was flat. "My mother was a very beautiful woman. Little and dark. She was French, you know."

"If I didn't already know, I would have guessed it from your name."

"I didn't think you knew my name. You never use it."

He shrugged. "It's not as if there's anyone else around most of the time. Besides, Noelle, you don't use my name either."

She should have smiled. "Are you sure you want to hear this, Robin? Wouldn't you rather just make love now?"

"Go on."

"She was a French *émigrée*. I heard that she set London on its ear with her beauty, her charm, her wit. She was an Incomparable. She wore a red ribbon around her neck to remind everyone the guillotine was waiting for her in France."

He frowned. "Her name was Jacinthe."

"Yes. Jacinthe Chanfret. There were some other names and a title lost in the revolution, but that's all I remember." She closed her eyes, to hide the tears. "Isn't that terrible? I don't remember my own mother's name."

"Jacinthe Chanfret," he mused. "You know, I believe I remember her. Of course, we all knew her."

"Really. When?"

He ran his fingernail under the leather strap and moved it a fraction to the left. "Before you were born, infant. Twenty years ago."

"Really."

"Oh, yes. A whole group of us. We cut quite a dash. Let's see — Alistair, Clarence, Horace, myself. Our commissions were newly purchased. Our buttons were bright. We came to town to drink deep before sailing off to whip Bonaparte. We were going to be heroes. We were sure we'd be home in a year. Two at most."

"How long did it take?" she asked curiously. Perhaps if he began to talk about himself, he would forget about her.

"For me, fifteen years."

"Fifteen!"

"For me it was fifteen. For the rest, Ally, Horse, and Clare, it was quite a bit less."

"They came home."

"They died."

"How awful. Your friends."

He shrugged. "It was a long war. We lost Clare first. He went down with his ship. Ally and Horse were in the fore at Talavera. Brave lads. I managed to survive Portugal. I haven't thought about them in years." He sighed with regret. "Nor about little Jacinthe Chanfret. Now I know what happened to her."

"Yes, she married the Duke of Averill. The Ice King. I suppose he could afford to take a penniless *émigrée,* who was beautiful and gay. He didn't need

253

money."

"He needed warmth." Robin shook his head. "She was particularly charming to all of us. She believed that we were going to free her country and return her lands and title to her."

"She talked about that when I was little. I remember her telling me stories about the chateau on the tree-lined lane outside of Paris. She used to plan how she would dress me when I was presented to the villeins. It was her dream."

He bowed his head. "I wish we could have restored it to her."

"I do too."

He shrugged. "Long ago and far away. But the Duke was rich. She was beautiful. What happened?"

Her hands clenched in the sheet. "There really isn't much to tell. For ten years, I was happy. I thought about nothing except the pleasures of my life — when I bothered to think at all."

"Must have been idyllic."

"It was. And then everything changed."

He waited.

"I look very much like my mother. I'm dark like her, but taller. I must get my height from my father."

Robin frowned. "Are you saying — ?"

"Yes." She rolled over and presented him her back. Only the top of her head was visible above the sheet. "I'd rather not say anything more."

He drew on his robe and rose thoughtfully. He crossed the room to pour a glass of brandy and return with it to the bed. "Just so we'll be sure that we both understand the same things, perhaps you'd better tell me in plain English." He barely wet his lips with the amber liquid. "I've found that sometimes I don't know what I think I know. Attribute it to my advanced age, if you will."

She sighed and rolled back over to face him. Still she hid her body behind the covers. "When I was ten years old, the Duke of Averill called my mother and me into his presence. I had never seen him so angry before."

As she hesitated, Robin's eyebrow rose. "But you've seen him that angry since."

She nodded. "Constantly. He told her that he had proof incontrovertible. Those were his very words— proof incontrovertible—that she had foisted another man's b-bastard off on him."

Her husband sat silent sipping his drink. Suddenly, Noelle sat up in bed, clutching the sheet tightly to her breast. "Is that plain enough for you? I'm a bastard. I am not the heir of Averill. I'm not the Duke's daughter. I don't know who my father is—was—is."

"How did he suddenly discover this after ten years?" Robin wanted to know.

"I don't know. He raged on and on. His face was red as fire. He could hardly speak for coughing. You've heard him. You know how he does. I hardly ever cough."

"Can you remember what he said?"

She shook her head. "Things about how he knew he wasn't the first. He'd taken care of them. But he had been deceived." She looked at Robin. "I can understand some of what he was talking about now."

He nodded. "Many men find, on their wedding nights, that someone has been there before them. It bothers them."

"Averill is the devil for pride."

"What did your mother say?"

"What could she say? I stared at her in absolute horror. I was precocious for my age. Educated to be as proud as Averill." She choked slightly. Her voice wavered. "I really don't know which of the three of us was more upset."

"I can imagine."

"No. You can't. You can't know how she looked. Absolutely all the color drained from her face. It was like an admission of guilt. She looked from him to me. When she saw how I felt, she turned and walked out."

"Without a word."

"She never spoke to either of us again."

He looked amazed. "Didn't you try to find out her side of it? She was still your mother."

"She had destroyed my life. I wanted to kill her. I was sick with shame." She reached for her robe. Her hands were shaking. Her face was white. Beads of perspiration dotted her forehead. "You can't know what it is to believe that you are born into the finest family in England. That you are of the finest blood."

"Blood's blood," he contradicted her.

"No." She pulled on her robe, her body jerking. Threads popped. She rose from the bed and belted it around her with such force that the material made a ripping sound. "Blood is everything."

She began to pace the floor. "Suddenly, I was nothing. Suddenly, my father wasn't my father any more. The man whom I had worshipped like a god. The man who had taken me with him with such pride. Suddenly, he had nothing to do with me. He hated the sight of me. He packed my things that very day and sent me away to the least of his holdings."

"But he didn't renounce you," Robin pointed out.

"But don't you see? To do so would have shamed and embarrassed him. The only person prouder than the Ice King is God."

"When you'd had time to cool down, did you try to write a letter to your mother?"

"I never had a chance. She was dead within the year. I don't know what happened. She might have killed herself. He might have murdered her." She crossed to the window. The draperies had been closed. She jerked them open. The afternoon shadows were lengthening. "I don't know. I never asked. I don't want to know."

"But he didn't divorce her."

"Never. When she died, Archie staged an elaborate funeral for her. The Ice King looks so impressive in black. I was brought in from the country and dressed like a crow. So much black veiling I couldn't see a thing. He took my hand at the funeral. Then he flung it away from him when we entered the carriage. I couldn't cry." Her voice was shaking now.

Then she laughed, highpitched, cracking. She turned around. "So you see you really did get a terrible creature thrust upon you."

"But why?"

"Why you? To punish me, of course. He can no longer punish my mother. She's dead. So in his twisted way, he goes on punishing her through me."

He came to her, put his arm around her shoulders, and led her back to the fire. "There's something wrong here. Although you may not believe me, there are many much worse than I. I drink a bit too much, but

257

not three or four bottles a night. When I was wounded so badly that I couldn't be a soldier any longer, I had to do something to keep body and soul together. So I became a gambler. At first I was a good gambler."

"Not good enough, obviously."

"No, not good enough. But I've treated you decently."

Her lips curled in a sneer.

"Confess it. You haven't been hurt."

"Well, no."

"In fact. You've had your pleasures too." He refilled his half empty glass.

She ducked her head to conceal the heat rising in her cheeks.

He chuckled drily. "I'm not a fool. I saw this marriage and the infusion of your money as a chance to turn my life around."

"Averill expected that you'd continue to drink and gamble," she whispered. "He thought you'd make my life miserable."

"I left you immediately and went into town," Robin mused. "I thought that was part of the plan."

"Why don't you drink so much any more?" she asked.

"I can't say when it happened, but I suddenly realized that I no longer hurt so badly that I had to drink to ease the pain. I'm afraid I had grown so used to being in pain that I drank rather than take the chance that it might hurt."

"I'm glad."

"The best thing that ever happened to me was Averill's sending me off to the country." He stretched out on the bed with his glass of brandy on his stomach. "The Blivenses had, so to speak, drained the cellar. I was without it, even for that short time, and I realized I didn't have to have it. It was a revelation."

"I'm glad for you."

"Back in London I started winning again." He shrugged. "It was a classic irony worthy of those old Greek tragedies they used to make us read in school. When I no longer needed money, I began to win. I won so much money it seemed a shame to gamble it away. And then I had a thought. You wanted horses. So, why not buy horses?"

"So I have horses." She had begun to feel a bit calmer.

He waved a hand at her. "Speaking of drink. Why don't you have a little drink? Not too much now. A little will steady you. Too much will make you cry."

"I hardly ever cry," she protested, but she did as he bade.

"Come back to the bed and let's lie here contentedly and wait for dinner."

She stretched out beside him, setting her glass on her stomach as he did. "Why are you being so nice to me? I'm nothing but a bastard."

"My dear, at least one king of England and probably more, if the truth were known, was a bastard. So long as no one knows, you shouldn't give it another thought."

She stared into the flames. "It's the last thing I think about before I go to sleep and the first thing I remember when I wake up."

He smiled. "I have an idea. Let me think about it in the evening. We'll split the vigil. I'll carry part of it. I'm definitely stronger in the evening. And you can get a

259

good night's sleep."

She frowned. "Don't I wish I could do it? If only I could forget about it."

He patted her shoulder. "Forget about what?"

She laughed out loud and took a sip of brandy without grimacing.

He toasted her. "Except I still wonder. Why did he marry you to anyone at all? Why not marry again himself? Get a son and then renounce you."

"The Ice King hates women."

"But he didn't until—how long ago—ten years? And your mother died. Why didn't he marry then?"

"Shall I speak plainly again. Are you concerned that you can't figure out the answer? I'll tell you then. It's pride." She laughed bitterly. "My mother had a child by someone else, but never him, never in those ten years. Why did she never become pregnant again? She was fertile. My birth proved that. But he has no such proof."

"And he's too proud to let that be known," Robin said with a shake of his head.

"Exactly. He'll never, ever marry again." Noelle's eyes glittered with emotions too deep, too painful to give names too. "He's the last of his blood. And he hates me all the more because I'm not."

"The three older mares have come in season," Hardwicke informed Robin at the end of the week.

The Earl grinned mockingly. "And our stud."

"Pacing his stall like a tiger."

"Trot him out and let's see how the leg is healing."

"I've walked him. He won't put it on the ground."

"Then let's throw a saddle on him and see what happens."

"Saddle him?"

"We can do it together. Now's the time while he's still three-legged, or thinks he is. He was someone's saddle horse, I'll wager. His kind of looks appeals to a young dandy. Probably stolen goods."

Shaking his head, Timothy nevertheless led the black out of the stall and tied him down tight to the hitching post. The Earl stood at his head while Timothy lowered the saddle onto the broad back. The horse jumped and kicked, but the saddle stayed put. Cautiously, the groom reached under the belly for the girth.

The stallion kicked again, but half-heartedly. Clearly, he had been saddled before. He puffed his belly up, but Timothy punched him sternly. " 'Ere now. None o' that."

When the Earl offered the bridle, the horse took the bit willingly.

"It's like he's found his home," Timothy declared in an awed voice. "I'd never have believed it."

"We'll soon see his manners," Robin agreed.

The groom held the stallion's head while the Earl mounted. The animal stood like a statue for several seconds. Robin touched his heels to the black sides. The horse took a step, then another. His hind foot came down and he limped off it.

"Let go his head. I think he'll be all right."

No sooner were the words out than the horse dropped his head and sprang off all four feet like a great cat. The Earl clamped his legs and kept his seat.

"Gawd Almighty!" Hardwicke yelled. The fighting animal lifted the groom off the ground. Somehow he managed to hang on as the horse fought his way across the stableyard.

"Get away, Hardwicke!"

The groom threw himself backward out of reach.

Up, the stallion went on his hind legs, front hooves flailing. Ignore the pain in the injured leg though he might, the muscles weakened from long inactivity would not bear his weight. Down, he went with a squealing and grunting in anger.

The Earl stepped from the saddle, then mounted again as the black scrambled to his feet. Instead of letting the horse get his head down, Robin hauled back with all his strength, then brought his whip down on the rump with a cutting thwack.

With another squeal the horse sprang forward and tore down the lane.

The Earl leaned forward over the saddle, clinging like a burr. Mane slashed his face. Tree trunks whipped by. The wind rushed by his ears and his hat was lost in the road behind. Between his legs a storm of power was unleashed.

His teeth peeled back from his lips in a grin of triumph that was more grimace. Beneath him, all four hooves lanced the ground with equal vigor. The horse was running true. The bar gate rose before them.

No time to hesitate! Neck or nothing! The Earl lifted with hands and thighs and body. The big muscles bunched in the powerful hindquarters. The horse sailed over it and landed cleanly on the other side without breaking stride.

The Earl laughed with sheer joy at the power of the animal beneath him.

The breakneck pace continued for perhaps another

two hundred yards. Then again the months of inactivity took their toll. The stallion began to labor. He wanted to slow. But his rider swung the whip along his neck and kept him running.

In the army a runaway mount more often than not cost the life of its rider. Robin had sworn he would never own such an animal. Once and for all, the Earl resolved to teach the stallion that the penalty for running away was running until he could run no longer.

The big horse's breath was coming in grunts. Lather dripped from the neck and flanks. The ear flicked and the eyes rolled as Robin swung the whip along side the cheek.

At the end of a mile, Robin allowed his mount to slow to a gallop. Then to a lope, a canter, a walk, and finally to come to a stop. The proud head dropped. The sides heaved. The horse stood, breathing heavily, braced on all four trembling legs. Robin climbed down and came to the head.

"Good boy! You won't run away again, will you? But a good run worked off all that rage, didn't it? Now you're fine."

The stallion's ears flicked forward.

Robin smoothed the forelock and wiped lather from the cheek. "Now I'll take you back home, groom you and feed you and tomorrow I'll introduce you to a pair of lovely ladies."

"And can you assure me that he is sleeping with her?" Archie Holmesfield's expression betrayed none of the distaste he felt at having to ask the question.

His informant shrugged. "I ain't 'idin' under the bed, y' understand, but the bed in 'er ladyship's room's not been slept in. Not since 'e came back. They goes up early and they comes down late."

"Very good." The Duke's factor counted out coins and dropped them one at a time into the outstretched hand. He pressed his lips tightly together. He did not want to ask the next question.

Not for the first time, he wondered if he might not find other employment more to his liking. Oftentimes, the things he did for Averill left him devoid of both dignity and integrity. He sucked in his breath until his nostrils pinched.

"Now, my good woman. The next piece of intelligence is whether or not the Countess is increasing."

" 'Ow much y' gonna pay me fer that?"

"The same amount."

The woman laughed coarsely. "Silly thing, if y' ask me. That's one of them things that can't be 'id."

"I wish to know at the earliest possible time."

His informant squinted at the factor's purse. "Y' got some more coins there?"

Archie shook the object under scrutiny. "Yes."

"Well, I can tell y' right now. She is."

The man drew back in disbelief.

"Oh, she don't know she is. She's green as grass, that 'un. But I can count. She's been 'ere more'n two months now. I ain't seen a scrap o' cloth comin' down to the laundry. She'll be 'igh-bellied afore she knows what she's about."

"But are you sure?" Holmesfield shook his head incredulously, his face betraying his disgust at the plain-speaking.

"I told y' I'm sure. So give me m' pay."

"But couldn't she just — er — just —"

A nasty laugh interrupted him. "You're a green 'un yourself. Don't th' quality have babes th' same as th' rest of us?"

"I am a bachelor, madam."

"Well, let me give y' a lesson. Girls that don't have the flowers 'll be litterin' soon."

"Oh, for God's sake!" Archie fanned himself at the unaccustomed heat rising in his cheeks. "Have a little delicacy."

Again the laugh, full-bellied and raucous. "Pay me!"

"Here." The factor held out the purse. "Take it."

A grubby hand snatched it. "Thank y' kindly."

"But keep a watch for another month or two. You might be wrong."

"Do I get paid for keepin' a watch?"

"Yes."

"Then I'll do it. It's your boss's money."

"I suggest, Madam Wife, that you remain in the house for the morning."

"In the house? Why?" she asked curiously.

"Do I have to give an explanation for everything?" her husband demanded.

"Careful, Captain Whittcombstone. Your rank is showing."

Instantly, he knew he had gone about this all wrong, but he could not retreat. "You will be better served to obey me in this."

"Obey." She set her teeth on the word.

"I'm merely sparing your feelings."

"By making me angry. Very good."

He sighed. "All right. Suit yourself. But you may

prepare to be embarrassed. We are putting the stallion to the mares."

She sat up immediately and reached for her robe. "And I'm too delicate to see such things."

"Exactly."

She dashed across the room and began pulling clothes from the wardrobe. "Don't be ridiculous. The horses were my idea. I want to be a party to everything that concerns them. This is one of the most important parts by far."

He tried his most soothing tone. "Madam Wife. Noelle. Now don't be stubborn. This is not for a lady's eyes."

Her eyes flashed dangerously. "I'm not being stubborn!"

"Believe me. I wouldn't do it myself except that Hardwicke may need some help."

She stepped behind the dressing screen to pull on her clothes. "Fine. Good. You stay in the house and I'll help him."

That stubborn streak would try the patience of a saint. And he was no saint. "No. Damn it. You will stay here in the house."

"No."

"You'll just succeed in embarrassing yourself and everyone else and then you'll want to leave."

"I will not want to leave. I will want to see every facet of it."

"God give me the strength to keep from murdering you."

Fifteen

"She's hobbled."

Color drained from Noelle's flushed cheeks. She stopped in her tracks, her eyes fixed on the leather cuffs and thongs binding the mare's fetlocks.

Timothy shot the Earl a quick look before ducking beneath the stallion's neck. Away from the couple, he busied himself combing his fingers through the mane and speaking in soothing tones. The big horse stamped impatiently and half rose tossing his head and pulling against the restraining hands. He neighed shrilly and the mare answered.

Noelle faced her husband. She flung her arm in the direction of Deliverance. "Why?" she demanded. "What are you going to do to her?"

Robin hurried forward to take her arm and lead her away. His head dipped toward hers. "For the last time," he hissed. "Go back to the house."

His wife dug in her heels. "No! You said she was my horse. These are all my horses, aren't they? Well, I won't have any of them hurt."

His grasp tightened. "You don't know what you're talking about."

"If this is going to hurt her—"

"We're not going to hurt her. Quite the contrary."

"If this hurts so badly—"

He threw a harassed look at the groom, who was doing a good job of pretending not to overhear the conversation. The stallion snorted his impatience and stamped. "Listen to me." He shook her by the arm. "I don't have time to explain all of this to you. If you want to know every single detail, no matter how embarrassing, I promise to tell you tonight. But for right now, you have to trust me."

"But—"

"You were hurt, but you didn't die," he reminded her crudely.

She blushed to the roots of her hair and pressed a hand to her mouth, but her eyes never left his face, nor did they lose their accusing glare.

He shrugged. "Listen. Believe me when I say stallions have absolutely no sensibilities. Of course, you might say that I have no sensibilities either, but *they* have only one thing on their minds. It's their reason for being. If she were to fight him, he'd half-kill her. If she can't resist, he'll hurt her much less."

She stared into his face, facing the glare of that single obsidian eye. At last she pressed her lips together and nodded jerkily. Her eyes filled with tears, but she blinked them away.

"For God's sake," he burst out in exasperation. "This is the way it's done. I thought you wanted to raise horses."

She pressed a hand to her forehead, shading her

expression from him. Her voice was barely a sound. "I do."

"Then either go or stay. But quit that damn whimpering!"

Robin pivoted on his heel and marched into the pen. He positioned himself at the mare's head where she was snubbed to a hitching post. With one hand he patted her neck. With the other he straightened her forelock. "Now you be a good girl and this will be over soon."

The mare's ears flicked back. She rolled her eye nervously. Behind her the stallion whinnied.

"Trot him in, Hardwicke."

The black threw up his head as he entered. Nose pointed to the sky, neck craned, he caught the mare's scent. Noelle saw a shiver ripple under the shining black hide. His tail lifted. He dropped his head and plunged forward. Timothy prudently let the line run out. Robin backed across the pen and climbed the fence.

Deliverance whinnied and tried to get away, but the hobbles and the snubbing post assured her submission.

Snorting and grunting, the stud circled her. He snuffled and nudged, and nipped at her flanks until Noelle thought she personally would go insane. In empathy for her sister creature, she began to sweat. Her body clenched and heated.

The stallion tossed his black crest and rose on his hind legs. The mare whinnied again as he threw his foreleg over her neck. Her knees almost buckled from his weight, but she braced herself, tossed her head, and bit him.

The wound drew blood, but he paid no more attention to it than he might have a flea. Grunting, he backed off her neck and turned his attentions to her rump. The mare squealed and tried to kick backward. The hobbles tripped her. She staggered and almost went down again. He nipped her savagely drawing more blood.

Noelle pressed her fist to her mouth.

Then the stallion reared over the mare.

Noelle could watch no longer. She turned away and tottered into the stable. Behind her she heard the grunts from the stallion and the whinny of the mare.

Perhaps she only imagined fear and pain in the voice. Perhaps. But her imagination cut her to the quick. It signaled another female's subjugation, and she Noelle was the instigator. Her dreams of raising beautiful horses had been naive visions. Reality was terrible. Females used for and by males. By men.

She could feel the tears starting again. *Please don't let him come to find me!*

Farther into the stable, Dark o' the Moon whinnied urgently and kicked against the back of her stall. Still mopping tears, Noelle walked to the little black mare.

When Robin came up behind his wife, she was murmuring in comforting tones. The mare's ears were pricked forward, and she was resting her muzzle against Noelle's shoulder. His irritation cooled, but only slightly. She should not have come out here. Horse breeding was a man's job. Nevertheless, he gentled his voice. "All

270

done. You can relax."

Instead she stiffened. Her hand paused in its stroking. Then she stepped back and patted Dark o' the Moon's velvet muzzle. "Good girl."

"Kate's in season as well as the other older mare. This one probably is too, but she's too young to breed. We'll breed Kate tomorrow and the other the next day. Shall we go back to the house?"

"In season? Oh — er — yes, milord." Blushing furiously, Noelle caught up her skirt with one hand while she slipped her other through the arm he extended. Self-possession firmly in place, she matched steps with him along the path.

He did not comment on the smears on her flaming cheeks, but his voice was mockingly polite. "Did you find that edifying?"

"Very." She lifted her chin.

"Good. Shall I help Hardwicke the next two days, or do you prefer to do it?"

She flashed him an angry look.

"Perhaps I'd better do it. Then at the end of the week I'll be gone."

Her mouth dropped open. She looked up at him with a frown. "So soon?"

He raised one mocking eyebrow. "Why I'm surprised at you, Madam Wife. If I recall correctly, the last time I left, you were overjoyed. I have no doubt you turned handsprings down the hall before I cleared the gates."

She smiled with exaggerated sweetness. "Actually, I didn't turned handsprings. I've never been good at them. I merely danced around in a circle and poured myself a glass of celebratory sherry."

271

"A good choice. But as of now I detect no great elation on your part. Perhaps, my ears mislead me."

Her mouth framed a sarcastic retort, then she thought better of it. "This is your home, milord."

Blivens held the door open. They stepped into the bleak hallway. Robin looked around him grimly. "True, in name, it's mine. And what a palatial residence it is."

She looked around her. As his wife she should have perhaps assumed some authority in bringing his residence in order. Unfortunately, she disliked anything to do with housework. "It's not so bad," she informed him truthfully. "In fact it's quite snug and warm. It has a beautiful view of the rolling countryside."

"Don't patronize me," he warned. He helped her off with her coat, handing it and his own to the doddering butler.

"I'm not," she replied. "I swear. We could build this place into a jewel. With a fine stable of horses to sell and tenants to pay rents."

He stared at her eager face. Her youth struck him forcibly. The difference between twenty and thirty-nine seemed insurmountable. He shook his head. "Do what you want. After the army, I've had enough of horses to last me for the rest of my life. There's nothing else for me to do here. And nothing to keep me here. The stallion will service the other mares. You should wait at least eighteen months to breed the fillies."

"Very well." She realized that he was curtly dismissing the last few days exciting activities and their

272

constant companionship. He acted as if they had meant nothing to him. Odd, how he could hurt her feelings.

He nodded. "I rode the black yesterday. He seems completely healed. And he's a magnificent animal. Since his job is done here for a while, I've a mind to ride him to London." He grinned. "Cut a bit of a figure through Rotten Row. Show there's life in the old man yet."

"There is life in you, milord."

When she would have turned on her heel and left him, he caught her and ushered her into her parlor. From a drawer he produced a large book which he handed to her.

"What's this?"

"It's your new stud book. From now on, one of your first jobs, Madam Wife, is to keep the records."

"Oh!" Delighted, she clasped it to her chest. "Oh, thank you."

"I'm glad you're pleased. One of your first duties will be to name the other horses."

"Yes, sir."

"Your father—that is, the Duke—has promised to send a mare very soon to replace Silver Belle. Be sure to enter her in it also. And she's to be pregnant by Brandywine."

She blinked at his revelation. "You think of everything, milord. But how did you get him to agree to that?"

He grinned slyly. "Blackmail. After all I am the Turk. I stick at nothing. He wouldn't want his associates to know that he had kidnapped the woman he acknowledges as his daughter. And put her in peril of her life."

"No, it probably isn't done in his circle of friends."

"Exactly. I'll leave the gelding here for Hardwicke to ride, or you if you choose. The mares are now your responsibility." He looked at her like a governess with a difficult lesson. "They'll be a lot of work. You may find you don't like it."

She shook her head. "It's my choice."

"Yes. And you really want to make this succeed, don't you?"

"Yes. More than anything. It's been my dream and you've made it come true." She could swear he blushed.

Clearing his throat, he drew another purse from his pocket. It bulged and when he dropped it on the desk, it clinked. "Here's money."

"I still have most of what you left before," she protested.

"But I've won more." He laughed. "As I said, it's ironic. When I needed to win I couldn't. Now that I don't need to particularly, I can't seem to lose."

"Bankers never need money," she agreed with a genuine smile.

He nodded. "How true. Spend the whole of it if you want. Improve what you want. God knows, everything around here needs it. If you run out before I return, just send someone up to town for more."

"Whom do you recommend I send? The Cap'n or the lout?" She schooled her face to appear innocent.

274

He appeared to consider. "I don't think I'd make their first task to go for money. Lead them not into temptation."

"If you say so."

He laughed. "They'd probably get it and keep right on going. Hardwicke's your man. And he looks like a good one. He certainly knows his way around horses. If you think he can be trusted, send him."

"I think he can be trusted to return. He's paying particular attention to Lily, my maid. I think they may have planned their employment."

He nodded. "Speaking of the Cap'n and his band, they were supposed to come round for work. If they do, I promised, you'd hire them first."

She colored angrily. "Hire kidnappers! Oh, of course. And if a murderer comes along—"

"Times are hard," he interrupted. "In their own way they were kind to you."

"Obviously you've never had your arms twisted up behind your back."

"They didn't rape you," he reminded her.

She sucked in a deep breath. "Oh, very well. I'll remember to hire them. Anything for returning heroes."

"A man who fights for England ought to be given first chance to make a living in it."

"I'll remember that."

Silence fell between them. Noelle opened the stud book and smoothed back its pristine pages. "Did you want to tell me anything else?"

"I believe that's all." He consulted the clock on the wall. "I haven't had a ride today. There's still time before lunch. Will you ride with me?"

She shook her head. "I want to make the first entries in the stud book."

When he looked back at the door, she had already dipped her pen and begun to write.

When he had closed it, she put the pen down and stared after him. She did not want to admit to him that she would miss him.

His curt and impatient manner did not bother her. Indeed, she rather enjoyed their differences.

She acknowledged that he was patient enough with her desire to learn. He certainly had not taken her to task and told her she needed to clean his house and order his servants around. *Thank God for that!* She made a mental note to do at least a little something to make the house more comfortable by the time he returned.

Above all she felt a thrill of pride as she entered the mare's name and today's date. Her husband the Earl of Whitby was responsible for the very beginning of — she thought a minute — Black Horse Stud. From two horses, he had increased their number to seven in a matter of days — and all were black. A perfect name. She printed it at the top of the first page.

When Averill sent the mare to replace Silver Belle, she would probably be a gray or a chestnut like Brandywine, but they could be sold early on. The majority of horses would always be black.

She could not take in the rise in her fortunes, the reality of her dream. Her heart swelled when she thought of Robin spending his money for horses for her. She closed her eyes tightly. She had been without love and affection for a long time.

Even if Robin had treated her only casually, she would feel deep gratitude toward him.

As it was, she could very easily fall in love with him.

The next morning Noelle did not accompany her husband to the stables. Even had she decided to do so, she could not have found the strength. She awoke with a queasy stomach and an aching head. *Lie still a while. Ignore it,* she advised herself.

But lying flat on her back in bed did not help. The room spun and she kept having to swallow. What was wrong? She had had nothing to eat, food could not be upsetting her stomach, but she felt as if—

Suddenly, she could control herself no longer. She rolled out of bed and staggered to the basin.

"Oh, milady."

"Lily, I've caught something," she told her maid. Then she was very busy for several minutes.

Finally, she lifted her head. "I must've picked something up in the stables."

"Oh, I don't think so, milady." Lily was being quite disgustingly cheerful as she wiped Noelle's brow and mouth with a wet cloth. "I think you've caught something all right, but it's not anything y've caught in the stables."

Noelle gagged as another spasm struck her, but it was not so violent as the others. She straightened cautiously. "What do you mean?"

Lily grinned a little, as if the ignorance of some people tickled her. "Well, milady, since you ask me—I think you're increasing."

Noelle dropped into a chair and leaned back, taking controlled breaths through her nose. A frown marred her forehead. "Increasing what?"

The maid gave a snort of disgust. "Increasing. Oh, for heaven's sake, you know." She leaned forward to whisper. "Preggers."

Noelle's eyes flew open. "I'm going to have a baby!"

"Most likely. You've got all the signs."

Noelle dropped her head to stare at her belly. It was as flat as it had ever been.

"You're not *that* far along."

Alarm grew. "But I feel so sick."

"Yes'm. That's the way of it."

"Do you think something's wrong with the baby?"

"Oh, no. That's just the way you do. My mam's had six and was sick as a horse with everyone of us. Leastwise the first couple or three months."

"But it could be something else?" Noelle insisted desperately.

"Not likely. You haven't had the flowers since you've been here."

Noelle flushed bright red. Her stomach heaved again, but she quieted it by drawing long deep breaths.

"I didn't mean to say the wrong thing." The maid hastily turned her back and started to clean up.

"No, no, you didn't. I just—that is—I've never

heard anyone speak so frankly." In actuality, she had never in her entire twenty years heard a single word about a woman's pregnancy.

"I'm sorry, milady, but I don't know any other way to say it," Lily sounded as if she were about to cry.

"I don't know either." Noelle felt tears start in her eyes.

The maid closed the lid on the slopjar. "I'll just take this away," she said. "When I come back I'll burn some lavender in the fireplace. That'll take away the odor."

Instantly, Noelle felt ill again, but she managed to keep it down. "Thank you. I'll sit here a few minutes and get my breath back."

"I'll bring y' some hot tea, real weak. That'll make y' feel better."

"Thank you."

The door closed on a silent room. Noelle clutched her stomach, listening. Her fingers caressed, pressed deep, tried to feel, to imagine. She had scarcely seen a baby. Never been closer to one than—She had never even seen a baby's face. A baby had been a small bundle of cloth with a tiny fist waving free.

She grinned a little self-consciously and relaxed. She was an idiot, sitting holding her stomach and listening as if the baby would cry and she would feel it.

Would she be able to feel it before it was born? How long before it would be born? How big would it get? She had never even seen a woman who was "increasing." Perhaps Lily's mother could come and talk to her.

Before long Lily knocked and entered with a tea tray. "Now this'll make you feel more the thing, milady. And then we'll get you all bathed and dressed and you can go on about your business."

"Will I be sick again today?" Noelle asked, her eyes wide.

"Some few are, but mostly just in the mornin'. That's why it's called mornin' sickness." Lily passed her a cup of tea. "Now you just drink that slowly, just a sip at a time."

Noelle nodded trying to pretend knowledge. "Of course."

"And eat a bite of bread here. It's all that Mrs. Blivens had. Left over from last night, it is. But sometimes that's best. You don't want anything that's liable to upset you."

Noelle nibbled and sipped dutifully. She admitted that she felt a little better.

" 'Course you do. And the sickness won't stay around but the first few months."

"Of course not."

The maid looked at her quizzically. "My mam could always turn the house over after that. She said she never felt so good in her life as when she was carryin'."

"I hope I'll feel that way too."

" 'Course you will."

Finally dressed and feeling almost normal, Noelle donned coat, scarf, and gloves for a walk down the lane. Not for anything would she go near the stables. She needed time to be alone with her thoughts.

She would have to tell her husband. Her husband. She shivered at the thought. The irascible Turk was the father of her child. She wondered how he would react to the news. Would he be pleased? Averill had been pleased. Until he learned that she was not really his child at all.

The Turk could never question his heir. She had been a virgin without doubt when he had taken her to his bed. The blood and pain were the proof. She had known no other man.

The wind was getting colder. It blew a spray of sleet mixed with snow across her path. She shivered again. Of course, she might not really be with child. She had only Lily's word for it. She might have eaten something that upset her stomach. She might just be upset from everything that had happened.

Certainly enough had happened since her marriage to make her take to her bed. Her mind whirled. What should she do?

She clasped her arms about her waist. Tears stood in her eyes. Her husband must love her child. Even if he did not love her, he must love his son or daughter. She would wait until he returned to tell him. By that time she would be sure and she could think of ways to make it seem wonderful.

At the thud of hoofbeats coming up behind her, she spun around. Her husband, mounted on Kate, hailed her. "What are you doing out here?"

She raised her hand and waved. "Walking."

"I see that. I also see you're so cold the tears are freezing on your cheeks."

She scrubbed them away. "It's the wind."

"It has more than a promise of snow." He leaned

his forearm across Kate's withers. "Tell me. Why do you always pick an icy day like this to go walking?"

"I was thinking." She smiled helplessly. "I didn't notice how cold it was, or how far I'd come."

"If I give you a ride back to the house, will you promise not to attack me?" Smiling, he reached down a hand.

Returning his smile, she took it. "Only if you promise not to drop me in the mud."

"I think that can be arranged." He hauled her up in front of him and clicked his tongue to the mare.

She leaned back against his warm strength as he walked the horse back. His warm breath blew across her cheek. His arms encircled her. Her hip moved against his belly. For the minute, she felt safe and warm in his arms.

"So he's left her again."

"Yes, milord. The woman informs me that the Countess is assuredly pregnant." Archie kept his voice very flat to cover his embarrassment. "The Earl stayed long enough to breed three of the mares. The Countess now runs the farm and will receive the mare that we send."

"Splendid. He leaves his responsibilities at home and goes off to lead the life of a wastrel. Good. Good. It's what I hoped for." The Ice King leaned back in his chair, his smile as cold as death.

His employer sat so long that Archie Holmesfield thought he had been dismissed. He started to tiptoe away, but the Duke called him back. "She's alone then."

"With a few servants," the factor admitted. "Very few."

"Can any be bribed?"

"All."

"Good. Good. I haven't thought what best course to pursue there. Just leave her alone until the babe is firmly fixed."

"That may be wise, sir."

The Duke suddenly gave a harsh bark of laughter. "She thought she'd control him, did she? She's not the woman her mother was." His unpleasant laugh turned into a cough.

Holmesfield did not know what to say.

"For now. I think the one to focus our attention on is the Turk. He hasn't suffered nearly enough. No, not nearly. God! The French have the right idea. I could do with a convenient *lettre de cachet.*"

Holmesfield felt his skin prickle at the mention of the letter for instant imprisonment without trial. Before the Terror had swept them away, French nobility with the ear of the king had been able to request such documents to rid them of their enemies. From time to time a rumor had spread that an English lord had availed himself of the thing.

The Duke steepled his fingers. "Holmesfield, set a man to watch Whittcombstone day and night. Let me know the times of his comings and goings, his habits, where he dines, where he rides."

"Yes, sir."

"But choose the man well. He must be discreet." The Duke coughed. "I don't want to be associated with any of this too soon."

The factor pressed his lips tightly together. *The wages,* he kept reminding himself. The wages were better than he could make anywhere else in London. He inclined his head. "Yes, sir."

Long, Averill sat. Beneath his half-lowered lids, his eyes gleamed in the firelight. He sat so still that he might have been a statue, cold marble, rather than living flesh. Finally, he smiled. His pale lips curled back from his shiny white teeth. "Not a bad idea," he murmured. *"Lettre de cachet."*

The Ice King rose and crossed to the bookcase. He pulled the key from the gargoyle's mouth. Staring into the eyes of the stone demon, he swung the object by its chain. Swung it so hard both key and chain were a blur. Then with a cut-glass decanter of brandy in his free hand, he mounted the stairs to the first landing and the second and finally to the top of the house.

The stairway was quite warm, but when he opened the door at the top, a cold blast struck him in the face. He squinted. His breath made a fog in front of him, but he did not hesitate. Closing the door behind him, he strode unerringly to the draperies and pulled them aside.

Blue light threw patterns of panes on the bare floor. He turned and stalked to a single table and chair set in the center of the small room. He set the decanter carefully on the table, unstoppered it, and raised it in a toast. With a faint groan he sank into the chair and drank deeply.

His long-dead wife stared down at him. Her hair

was brown and softly curling about her face. Her eyes were brown also, as brown as her daughter's. He choked slightly and began to cough. Another stiff drink and he was able to clear his throat.

"So, Duchess, there you are," he croaked. "And how I wish you were here."

The face in the portrait was youthful, as youthful as Noelle's, but the smile was much sweeter. Tranquil repose could have been the name of the painting. One delicate hand held a rose, its thorns covered by a handkerchief dripping with Alençon lace.

The Duke coughed again. Coughed until the tears came to his eyes. One trickled down his cheek. "You may smile," he gasped. "But I have more to smile about. Much, much more. Your bastard's married, Jacinthe. And how I long to tell you to whom? Can you hear me in Hell, Jacinthe? Your repose isn't so tranquil there, is it? Do you grasp thorns? I hope you roll in them. I pray the demons roll you in them daily."

He took another drink. The light strengthened in the room. "You died so easily, my love. My whore. And left behind you the constant reminder of your perfidy."

He could feel his heart pounding, his blood heating. The anger that burned in him made him tremble. He coughed and coughed. His hands quivered as they clenched and unclenched. He could have torn the Duchess apart limb from limb had she stood before him in the flesh.

"Jacinthe!"

He drank again. The coughing eased marginally.

He curled his fingers around the arms of the chair and stared up at her. The light from the window slanted over her form and face. She seemed to smile at him alone.

"Jacinthe." The high color drained away and left him pale and drawn. "Jacinthe. I swear before God, I *will* drive you out of my mind."

Sixteen

> "*Oranges and lemons,*
> *Say the bells of St. Clements;*
>
> *You owe me five farthings,*
> *Say the bells of St. Martin's.*"

The clear boy sopranos drifted into the gamerooms of Boodle's. No one was surprised, since the fine old club had been designed like a lavish private residence. Well-to-do passersby outside the club could be counted on to drop money into the poor boxes. Even the gamblers, particularly the winners, might contribute a round sum in offering to Lady Luck if not necessarily to the Christ Child.

Only Robin raised his head and listened. For many years he had not thought about celebrating the Christmas season. Now, more and more in his thoughts were his home and, to his amazement, his wife. He shrugged stoically. His house was a chilly, uncomfortable cavern and his wife had been forced upon him. With a little extra force he spread his hand.

Other players at the table tossed down their cards in disgust. One groaned in mortification. "That takes the lot, Whittcombstone. Every last bit of it and on Christmas too. Shame on you, man."

Robin blinked vaguely, then raised one black eyebrow. The stout red face next to him looked quite chop-fallen. The Earl pushed a couple of stacks of chips across the green baize table. "Never let it be said that I took from a man on Christmas."

The other players politely occupied themselves with stacking and restacking their diminished resources.

"Nonsense." Pemberton pushed back his chair and hoisted himself to his feet. "Just funning. Have plenty more. Plenty more. Going home to sleep a bit. Get up. Go to the wife's parents for Christmas."

Robin called him as he turned from the table. "Take it, Charley."

Sheepishly, Pemberton looked around at the others. He cleared his throat. "Damned good man, sir. I say it, sir. 'Pon my soul. 'Preciate it." He swept up the chips. They clicked in his hand. "Buy a nice bit for the wife, so she'll have a present to open on Boxing Day."

"Good idea."

"That was a remarkably decent thing to do," a newcomer to the table commented when Pemberton was out of earshot.

Robin laid a finger in front of his lips. "Don't breathe a word of it. It'll ruin my reputation. People like Pemberton will be standing in line to lose to me."

"My lips are sealed." The speaker extended his hand across the table. "I don't believe we've met. Larne's the name."

Robin gripped it. "Whittcombstone. A pleasure to meet you, sir."

> *"Willie, bring your little drum,*
> *Robin, get your fife and come,*
> *One these instruments we'll play,*
> *Tu-re-lu-re-lu, pata-patapan."*

The game suddenly ceased to be interesting to him. He thought about his own wife. What if he were to get her a "nice bit."

Noelle. Her name was Christmas.

He looked at the stacks and stacks of chips in front of him. He had been playing for almost ten hours. Many were the times when he would have lost everything, but today his luck had never deserted him. Perhaps it had held because he had kept his wits. A little watered wine with a couple of plates of boiled chicken had sustained him while his opponents had drunk deep the more they lost. And now a new round were taking their places, their glasses filled at their elbows. Suddenly, it seemed all too futile.

> *"On these instruments we'll play,*
> *For to make Christmas gay."*

A group of carolers, their cheeks and noses red, strolled to a position at the curb just outside. Robin glanced out the window. Good God! Christmas was everywhere. A shiver ran through him. Once this had been an infernal day. He had cast it away forever on the slopes of the ice-coated Pyrenees where some of his young men had gone to sleep and never awakened.

That Christmas was too painful to remember.

"Lul-ly, lul-lay, thou little tiny child,
By by, lul-ly, lul-lay."

He signaled to the lackey to cash in his winnings.

"Not going to give us a chance to draw even?"

"I've played so long, I'm about to grow to the chair.
I'll leave it to you younger fellows." The Earl rose a bit
stiffly and strolled from the room.

He accepted his winnings and peeled off a ten
pound note from the pile. He placed it on the tired
waiter's tray.

Another went to the footman, who bowed low.
"Thank you, sir." He snapped his fingers for Robin's
greatcoat and held it for him to slide into. "It's been a
pleasure, sir. Good night and Happy Christmas."

"Good night."

The sky was overcast, heavy clouds, undoubtedly
snow-filled threatened to let loose their burdens at
any minute. Robin turned his collar up around his
ears.

"O sisters too, How may we do
For to preserve this day
This poor youngling, For whom we sing,
By by, lul-ly, lul-lay."

He pitched a handful of coins into the cap of the
nearest chorister, who thanked him in a piping voice.
Not even acknowledging his contribution, the others
sang on. Their voices blended as they rose and fell in
the electric winter air.

Robin hunched his shoulders against the cold and waited for the groom to bring his mount around. Perhaps he should go back in and purchase a bottle of brandy to take back to his rooms with him. The shops were all closed now.

Too late! A groom on a hack led the stud around. The horse pranced and grunted, exhibiting its usual bad temper. Robin scowled, admitting that he had made a mistake in riding the stallion instead of Kate. The black had been subjected to pain and mistreatment too long. It would never make a tractable saddle mount.

When a footman came to take the bridle, the horse bared its teeth and snapped at the man's arm.

Only the groom's firm grip on the lead kept the other man from being savaged. "Bloody damn killer," he muttered under his breath loudly enough for the Earl to hear. "The knacker'll be waitin' fer y'."

Robin stepped in front of the footman and took the horse's head himself. He ran his gloved hand down the black nose. The black quieted. The ears pricked forward. "He'll do for a while longer." Robin chided the groom. "He's not the first spirited animal you've handled."

"No, sir," the man agreed sullenly.

"I'll take his head now," the footman offered.

"No need." Robin swung up. He tossed a coin to the footman but overlooked the groom, who shot him a dirty look.

He cantered down the street.

"Hyaah!"

A dark figure sprang into the road wildly waving its arms and yelling. "Hyaah!"

The stallion neighed piercingly and reared, striking out with its front hooves. Relaxed and half-asleep, Robin fought for his seat in the saddle.

"Hyaah!"

Another figure leaped from out of nowhere and caught the tail of Robin's greatcoat. A violent tug brought the Earl sliding over the stallion's rump and crashing to the cobblestones.

"Hey there!" The first man grabbed for the bridle, but the stallion shied wheeled, and tore back into the darkness the way they had come.

Robin hit on his back. The breath whooshed from his lungs. Weakly, he hit out with his stick, but the footpad came at him from his left side with a cudgel. He never saw the blow that took him out like a light.

"Coo! Easy as coshin' a babe. Half blind's the ticket." The assailant caressed the club lovingly.

His partner knelt in the street and pulled Robin's purse from his pocket. " 'Eavy, 'eavy." He tossed it into the air, before thrusting it beneath his belt. " 'Is pockets were ripe."

"Now comes the 'ard part."

"Nah. Easy, easy. 'E'll be off our 'ands before 'e ever wakes up."

"W'at about the 'orse?"

"W'at about 'im? Somebody'll pick 'em up. We've got th' best part. Grab 'is legs."

Charley Pemberton blinked owlishly at the black horse cantering down the street. At that instant the stallion caught a trailing rein beneath his hoof. It pulled his head down and made him stumble. He slowed to a walk.

"I say—" Pemberton turned to the groom who had brought round the coach. "—that's Whittcombstone's horse. Catch it."

The groom bared his teeth. "That black devil. Not likely."

Pemberton himself stepped into the street. "Easy, boy, easy. Give me a hand here," he tossed over his shoulder to the footmen. When no one moved, his affable character deserted him. "Damn your eyes! I say catch that horse!"

The cursing made the black throw up his head. His eyes rolled wildly. But he was tired. He wheeled half-heartedly.

The footman whom Robin had tipped hurried out in front of the stud, arms outstretched. "Easy. Easy."

The horse shook his head, backing. The tack jingled. As one of the reins whipped through the cold air, the footman grabbed at it. The horse reared to plunge away.

"Romany Knight! Rom, old boy!"

The horse came down. Shivering, it stood. Its ears pricked forward. It whinnied.

"Romany Knight." Piers Larne approached slowly, his hand outstretched. "Boy, don't you know me?"

The long black neck stretched forward. The horse snorted and whinnied again. Piers put his hand out. "Here, boy."

Romany Knight dropped his nose into his lost master's palm.

" 'E surely knows 'e's your horse," the footman observed, as Larne smoothed the forelock and patted the sweaty neck.

Pemberton approached with caution, even though the black stood docilely enough. "But that's Whittcombstone's horse. How can he belong to you?"

"I — er — sold him," Larne replied. "Whittcombstone's you say. Where is he?"

" 'Orse came out of the dark alone," supplied the footman.

"Something's happened to Whittcombstone."

"Too drunk to ride," the head groom muttered.

"Not him." Pemberton shook his head. "He hadn't drunk anything at all. I played cards with him m'self. Sober as a judge."

"He was indeed," Larne agreed.

"And he's an ex-cavalryman," Pemberton continued. "He wouldn't have fallen out of the saddle." He remembered the coins in his pocket. "He's been set upon. Footpads, more than likely. Summon the watch!"

Robin's head threatened to split open. The blow had caught him over the left temple. The tender skin and bone of his scar made every second of consciousness pure torture. Gingerly, he raised his hand. His trembling fingers located a huge swelling.

He let the hand fall back to his side. At least his skull was not cracked. Experience had taught him that a blow to the head that did not instantly swell was a dangerous blow. A smooth or slightly depressed wound signified that the skull had been cracked. The swelling would be inward into the brain and the victim would probably die. He had a goose egg over his temple, but he welcomed it.

Cold seeped up from beneath him. He opened his eye cautiously. He did not lie where he had fallen. Instead of bumpy cobblestones, the surface was damp and squishy beneath his hand. No stars, no clouds. Only darkness. And odor—indescribably foul. His stomach rebelled against the terrible pain in his head and likewise the stench. He managed to roll over. The surface crackled faintly. He lay on mouldy straw. Where in bloody hell was he?

"Is this a governess cart?" Noelle called. She had noticed the hardwood shafts pointed upward toward the loft and had pulled the hay aside.

"Yes, ma'am." Hardwicke scratched his head at the sight of the square wickerwork basket that comprised the body. Uniformly gray with dust, it had probably been concealed under the piles of hay for years. "Looks like it once was."

"Pull it out."

At Noelle's command the groom manhandled the small vehicle down and out into the weak afternoon sunshine. "It's probably rotten," he complained.

"But maybe it isn't. It looks sound." She opened the back door and swiped a layer of dust from one of the seats that ran along either side. "Look! Dark green leather."

He went down on one knee to peer beneath. "Axle's rusted."

"This was an expensive one. I think it can be cleaned up. I'm sure one of the mare's can be harnessed to it."

"It's a children's cart," Timothy objected.

"It will do until I get a high-perch phaeton," she retorted sarcastically.

"You don't have any coach horses," he continued desperately.

He was beginning to irritate her. "A horse is a horse."

"If it's comfort you're after, milady, that little black mare Dark o' the Moon has a gait as easy as a rocking chair."

She wanted to scream at him, but she refused to discuss her increasing condition with a groom. "A horse is a fine thing for a pleasure gallop around the countryside, but there are times when I need to transport more than myself, Timothy. I need to visit the tenants. And the village. Purchases for the house can't be carried home on the back of a horse."

Timothy maintained a rider's concern for training. "Good mounts oughtn't to be hitched to rigs. They get confused. The signals are different."

Noelle ignored him. "Do we have the harness for it?"

His face was a study of gloom. "Mayhap back there in the tackroom."

"Then see to it." She plucked pieces of hay out of the wickerwork.

"Ma'am. Milady."

"Th' lady said she wants t' harness the horse t' the cart. Why don't you do what she wants?"

Hardwicke stiffened and spun around. Noelle too looked, her skin prickling.

The Cap'n, his muddy greatcoat sagging off his shoulders, lounged in the shedrow. An affable smile curved his mouth, but his eyes were not smiling. Indeed, they looked as if they would never smile again.

At sight of him, Noelle's stomach clenched. With an act of will, she forced herself to relax. She cleared her throat. "Exactly, Hardwicke. Why don't you do what I want?"

Old soldier that he was, Timothy was prepared to face the lady down, but not the steely eyes of the man in the shadows. He all but saluted before beating a retreat to the tackroom.

Noelle turned from the cart. She rubbed her soiled hands against the sides of her coat. "You must have truly been a captain. Is that what you want me to call you?"

"Captain will be fine. I was only a sergeant, but I gave m'self a bit of a promotion." Again the smile without humor. He inclined his head. "The Earl said you might have work for us, milady."

She shook her head. "I wish I did. Perhaps, later."

"Me and my men are willing to work with our hands," he told her. "I noticed your garden hasn't been turned."

She looked over her shoulder. She knew absolutely nothing about gardening nor how a garden should be tended, but she could imagine that some preparations should be made for spring. "No, it hasn't," she agreed. "If you're willing to do it, I can pay you a pittance above food and a place to sleep. The Earl's opening his house after a lengthy time away. He has left me some money, but I have to be frugal."

"Oh, we understand. Food and a bit of blunt will be fine." His eyes glowed with a peculiar light. "The inn's not so far away. I've been bedding down around there. And if something keeps us, we can always bed down in a stall."

"It's not much of a job," she persisted doubtfully.

"It's more than no job at all."

At that moment Hardwicke returned with the tack. With Noelle directing, the two men dusted off the cart and harnessed the mare to it.

He was all but naked. In darkness like the interior of a cave, he lay and shivered. He had drawn his knees up to his chest and wrapped his arms around them, but the huddling did precious little to conserve what little body heat he had left.

Robin groaned. Desperately, he tried to concentrate, to remember what had happened to him. Thieves. He had been dragged off his horse and robbed. Damn! So much for the joyous Christmas season. They had taken his purse and clothing and left him—where?

"Get yourself up," he muttered. His teeth chattered violently. "Lie here much longer and you'll die." He had seen it happen to others. If a man's body lost too much warmth, he would slip gradually into a sleep from which nothing could arouse him.

Robin pressed his forehead hard against his knees, seeking to draw a warm breath into his body. Why were the Pyrenees always in his thoughts? Perhaps he really was destined to freeze to death? Perhaps he had been supposed to die there with so many of his men? Perhaps somehow he had escaped?

"Idiot! You don't believe that nonsense. Get yourself up!" He flung his head back and rolled half over.

With a savage curse brought on by the shooting pain from the base of his skull, he pushed himself up on hands and knees.

" 'E's wakin' up," came a whining voice.

"Pity," a man growled. "Asleep 'e don't feel nothin'."

"Where the hell am I?"

"W'ere is 'e. 'E don't know." The whiner laughed a little, then coughed. Phlegm rattled in his throat.

"Don't tell 'im. Let 'im figure it out."

Robin pushed himself up and staggered a few steps. He stumbled over a leg.

"Bloody 'ell. Watch w'ere y're goin'."

He made a swipe with his hand and latched on to a greasy shag of hair. "Tell me where I am."

"Aa-ow! Leggo. Y' bloody fool." The whiner delivered a chopping blow to Robin's wrist and scuttled away across the cell. "Don't y' rec'nize Buck'nam peliss?"

Robin's eyes were beginning to become accustomed to the gloom. He made out one figure to the right of him, a man who had risen to his feet swaying, shoulders hunched. Another, the man he had caught briefly, crouched in a corner. He addressed the one standing. "Where am I?"

"Y' must 've been 'it wit' a sledge'ammer," the man growled. "Y're in wit' th' rest of us. Y're in Newgate, Dandy Dick!"

"We can't find any sign of him, milords," the watchmen reported.

Pemberton frowned. He needed to be on his way, but he could not forget that the money weighting his pockets was Whittcombstone's. He owed a debt. Still, he could not think what to do.

"Send to his lodgings," Larne suggested.

"Won't do no good," the surly groom opined. "He lives alone."

"Not even a valet!" Pemberton was plainly at an impasse.

"Swear to God. He's come into a bit just in the last few months. His pockets were to let afore that."

"That stumps me," Pemberton groaned. "If he's met with foul play—"

"Which I strongly suspect," Larne added.

"Don't know what to do now. Don't really know anything about the man."

"He's the Earl of Whitby," the footman supplied.

"The best thing seems to be to send a messenger to his seat," Larne suggested. "Does anyone of you know the countryside? Could someone ride to his home, if he has one?"

A footman raised his hand doubtfully. "I come from thereabouts, but it's a long way."

"Here." Pemberton counted out ten coins from the bag. The young man's eyes widened at the silver. "For your trouble. And if you bring back someone to institute a search, there's another five for you—" He looked at the darkness of the street, where objects were beginning to separate themselves in the earliest hints of gray dawning. "—after Christmas."

The footman buttoned his coat. "How do I get there?"

"Take his horse." Larne patted the stallion's neck again. "He tired, but he'll go all night for you. He always did for me."

"His horse?" The man grinned and stuffed the coins into his pocket. "Yes, sir." He swung into the saddle.

Pemberton shook hands with Larne. "We did the best we could. Hope the fellow's all right, but I have my doubts."

But Larne disagreed. "He was a soldier. He didn't strike me as a man who would die easily."

Blivens stared stupidly at the very bedraggled young man on the front stoop.

"I say, is someone here who knows the Earl of Whittcombstone? Is this where he lives?" The young man's voice was a froggy croak.

"Yes—that is—this is—the Earl—did you say?" Blevins turned helplessly and shuffled to Noelle's parlor. "Milady."

When she caught sight of the stallion, gray with road dust, and spattered with mud to the knees, Noelle felt a cold wave of shock. "That's my husband's horse."

The footman nodded wearily. "Yes, ma'am. If your husband be the Earl of Whitby?"

"The Earl of Whitby. Yes. He is. Whittcombstone is his name. Robin Whittcombstone." She went down the step to the horse's head. The black was in bad shape. "Blivens, fetch Hardwicke immediately."

"H-hardwicke, er—yes ma'am."

"And the Captain. From the stables, Blivens."

"The Captain," Blivens muttered. "Hardwicke and the Captain. Hardwicke and the Captain. From the stables." He shuffled away.

"What happened?" she asked the messenger.

"He was robbed, milady. Leastwise, that's what Lord Pemberton and Lord Larnaervon told me to tell you. And we can't find him."

"If you can't find him, how do you know he was robbed?"

"His horse came wandering back down the street after he'd been gone nearly an hour. We sent for the watch, but they didn't find him."

Suddenly, stiff and cold, Noelle looped the reins around the hitching post and mounted the steps. "Who sent for the watch?"

"Lord Pemberton and Lord Larnaervon. They were playing cards with him at Boodle's. That's where I work, milady."

"And you've ridden all the way here from London."

"Lord Pemberton paid me, milady."

Hardwicke came running up. "What's happened?"

"Take care of the stallion, Hardwicke," Noelle instructed. "Come in, fellow, and tell me everything."

She led him to the kitchen where Mrs. Blivens grudgingly set him down to a meal. While he ate, he told his brief story again. When he had finished, Noelle knew almost nothing else.

"When he finishes eating, Blivens, take him to a bedroom and let him sleep—while I decide what to do," she finished silently.

Alone in her study, she put her hands over her belly. A few weeks ago, she had not known Robin Whittcombstone existed. He had wed her and bed her and left her. Then he had returned to save her and bed her and leave her again. When he had left her the second time, she was carrying his child, though she had not told him.

302

Her money had cleared him of his debts. If that were all, she would owe him nothing, certainly nothing that would require her to hie off to London on Christmas Day to direct a search for him.

But it was not all. He had been good to her, in his own way. He had come immediately when she had been kidnapped and had undoubtedly saved her life. He was her husband and the father of her child.

If Robin had been robbed in London, perhaps he might be hurt, unable to make his way back. She would have to go to find him, if possible. But how to begin?

Should she apply to Averill for help? She very much imagined that she would be wasting her breath. He would think the whole thing vastly amusing. No, she would get nothing from the Duke.

Unprepared as she was and pregnant, she must find Robin herself. She must go to London and search as well as harry the authorities to help her. A cynical smile curved her mouth. Authorities were much more amenable to harrying if they were paid.

She seated herself at her desk and pulled open the drawer. The purse Robin had left was distressingly light. If he were injured, someone would deserve recompense for caring for him. If he had been kidnapped—She hunched her shoulders. A ransom would have to be paid.

Silently, she fetched her mother's jewel box. The pouches inside it were as light as the purse. She opened one containing a cameo brooch in a circlet of pearls. Its value was purely sentimental. Another contained a necklace of gold chains connecting enameled butterfly medallions. Again the value of the piece was next to nothing.

She heaved a sigh. Her thumbs pressed the secret springs. The tray dropped down. Without thinking about it, she thrust the two pouches in the pocket of her skirt and closed the box. For the first time, she left it out in plain sight.

Her next problem was whom to take with her. The Blivenses, Hardwicke, and Lily were all country people unfamiliar with the city. She herself had been reared on a country estate.

If she were to find Robin, she needed someone who knew his way around the world beyond the polite English drawing rooms, someone who knew the habits and haunts of thieves.

Her frown smoothed out. A tiny smile flickered about her mouth. She needed an escort. A thief to catch a thief.

She donned her coat. As she opened the front door, she almost bumped into the Captain.

Seventeen

"You can't go with us," the Cap'n pronounced un-equivocally.

The lout snorted. "If th' bird wants t' turn a trick or two, let 'er take 'er pleasure."

The Cap'n shot him a look calculated to blister paint.

Tuck's head jerked up. His face blushing brightly, he stammered, "Lor', ma'am. Nob'dy goes int' Seven Dials w'at don't 'ave t' go."

"But the more heads—"

"—the more to get themselves knocked about," the Cap'n finished.

"He's my husband."

"Yes, ma'am. And he'd have our heads if you were to get hurt. The thing for you to do is stay here. I can ask around, find out what happened. He rode up Margaret Street. I'll find out who's got the action there. Not so many streets in this town but that a lot of eyes cover every one of them. It's just a matter of getting to the person who saw what happened."

"And will he tell?"

The lout snorted again. "Fer a price, 'e'll sing loud an' clear."

"I haven't a lot."

"It don't take a lot."

She looked around the circle at their faces. How much had they been paid to kidnap her? She thought of her purse containing only the housekeeping pittance. She dared not tell them about the diamonds. She tried to keep any trace of suspicion out of her voice. "Do you need to take it with you?"

"Lord love you, no, ma'am. Carry money around with me in Seven Dials. I ain't ready to die just yet. There's them in there that'd slit my throat for a decent coat. Much less silver."

Impulsively, she reached out and took the Cap'n's rough square hands. "Then be careful. Do be careful. I'll visit Lord Pemberton and Lord Larnaervon and find out what they know about him. We'll meet back here at the Earl's rooms."

Heavy footsteps on the stairs brought her hurrying to the door. The Duke of Averill with Holmesfield in attendance climbed toward her. The sight made her long to shut the door and lock it in his face. Instead she gripped the handle tightly and waited. When Averill set foot on the landing, she trilled, "La, your Grace, you've arrived too early. The ball is much later this evening."

His eyes like a wintry gale blasted her where she stood. Using his size to intimidate, he shouldered his way into the apartment. A quick glance around the barely furnished room made his lip curl. "Your preparations leave much to be desired," he mocked.

"The decorators are late."

He revolved slowly, scanning the shabby interior. A faint satisfied smile played about his thin lips. "Depressing place." He turned to Holmesfield. "Wait outside."

The factor nodded shortly. When the door closed behind him, Noelle crossed her arms and regarded the Duke stonily. "Town must be boring in the extreme, Averill. Nothing better to do than come to a small apartment and insult me."

"I would have thought that Whittcombstone would have filed that edge off your tongue."

"He retreated to town rather than try."

"See, the conquering hero!" Averill jeered.

She answered Morell with Shakespeare. *"Great ordnance in the field, and heavens artillery thunder in the skies* but—like most men—not a woman's tongue."

He stared her up and down barely succeeding in not fastening on her belly. Did she already have a slight mound? She folded her arms across her chest and lifted her chin.

He shot his index finger into her face. "The agreement was that you were to stay in the country. You will return to Whitby immediately."

"I never agreed to that. Why don't you take your grievance to my husband?" As she asked the question, she watched the Duke closely.

"Your husband has disappeared."

"Honesty, Averill. I'm surprised. I expected you to pretend that you had no knowledge of it."

"Of course, I know about it. That's why I'm here. You're making a fool of yourself and embarrassing me. How dare you approach Lord Pemberton with your whining questions!"

"I did not whine. I wept. But only a few appropriate tears. I was most effective and he was most sympathetic."

"Bitch!"

She clenched fists. "What have you done with him?"

He blinked. Just once the blue-veined lids dropped over the pale eyes, but it was enough.

"Where is he?"

He spread his arms wide. "Why ask me? How would I know? Do you expect me to know what's going on in every brothel and hellfire club between here and the Thames. He's probably wandering around in some stew, so drunk his backteeth are awash—"

"Get out!"

"Why should you care? You should be glad." His voice rose, then broke as his cough began. "Remember how ugly, how scarred, how vicious. A gambler, a drunkard, a rake."

"Get out!"

He shuddered with the effort to bring himself under control. "When I have finished my business here."

She could feel nausea rising in her belly. Hot blood pounded in her temples. She raised her fists. "This is my husband's apartment. And mine. You are not welcome here. Get out!"

He stared at her. "Holmesfield will take you back to the country."

"He will not!"

He opened the door. "Holmesfield."

Instead of the factor, the Cap'n's square body filled the door. Averill fell back, gaping. Shabby hat, unshaven cheeks, muddy bedraggled coattails flopping around scuffed run-down boots, the man was the last person Averill had expected to see on Noelle's stairs. The Duke lost his breath in a bout of furious coughing.

With a show of great unconcern, the Cap'n pulled a knife from his belt. Crossing one booted foot over the other, he leaned against the door jamb and proceeded to clean his fingernails. "Got a problem, milady?"

Noelle had trouble repressing a fit of nervous giggles. "Why, yes, thank you, Captain. Only a minor one. The Duke was just leaving. Perhaps you might escort him down to his carriage."

"Be right glad to, y'r Grace." The outlaw bared his teeth in a travesty of a smile. "We met your man out in the hall. Funny thing about him. He looked just like a bloke we did business with a few weeks ago. Only it was some unfinished."

The Duke looked apoplectic. His cough died in his throat.

"Lucky for him he had enough money in his pockets to pay us. Still, Fod and Tuck was upset about the delay. They helped him down the stairs. He took a bit of tumble along toward the bottom, but they picked him up and dusted him off. He'll be right as rain in a couple of days."

"Poor Holmesfield. I hope you pay him well, Averill." Noelle held the door open wider. "Be careful of the stairs. I'm sure they are treacherous."

"I'll have the lot of you taken up," the Duke threatened.

"We won't be in town long," Noelle promised. "Just until we find my husband. Unless, of course, I find that you've harmed him."

"Me! Why would I harm the fellow? He'll turn up in a few months. Bad pennies always do. He's his own worst enemy. Drinking, gambling."

"Odd. Lord Pemberton said that he had drunk almost nothing the night he disappeared."

The Duke clamped his lips together. Shooting cold fire from his eyes, he pivoted and shoved the Cap'n aside. The man gave way easily, but the eyes that met Noelle's beyond the Duke's shoulder were murderous.

She shivered as she shut the door. The Cap'n, though he might grin, made her blood run cold. She dropped into the chair beside the simple Dutch stove that heated the room. She had felt nauseated that morning, but some biscuits and cold tea had settled her stomach. Both hands and belly were trembling now. Dueling with Averill took too much energy that she needed to spend elsewhere.

She pressed her hands against her abdomen and swallowed. Sounds of a scuffle drifted up to her. Probably the Cap'n was helping Averill down the stairs. She smiled. For all that he was dangerous, he was a good man to have on her side.

Her escorts returned shortly, trooping into the room, eyes shifting so as not to meet hers. The lout surreptitiously blew on his barked knuckles.

When they had arranged themselves in a semi-circle around her chair, she rose and smiled brightly. "Now,

310

that's accomplished. You gentlemen may take me to breakfast."

They gawked at her. The Cap'n grinned. "Yes, ma'am."

Tuck stumbled to help her on with her coat. She had to search for the second sleeve behind her, but his effort was obviously sincere. "When we finish," she continued, "we'll call on Larnaervon. Pemberton said he had Robin's horse."

"As I matter of fact, I recognized the animal." Larnaervon leaned his head back striving to recall the affair exactly. "I didn't know your husband, until I came to the table at Boodle's. I was only going to play a few hands. I've never been able to sit still long enough to play one of those all-day games." He cocked a reassuring glance at his beautiful wife, who smiled her affirmation.

"He had won a sizable amount off Pemberton, but then gave some of it back when Charley complained about having nothing to spend at Christmas. Good thing to do."

"That's like my husband." Noelle nodded, when in fact, she was surprised to find that he had been so generous. He must have been having a run of good luck.

"The watch hasn't been able to find a trace of him?" Larnaervon queried.

"Not a trace." She could feel the trembling beginning. What if he were lying drugged in some stable? What if he starved to death for water before she found him? The memories stung her eyes. She reached for her handkerchief.

"My dear, how terrible." Lady Larnaervon placed her slender white hand over Noelle's. "You must be beside yourself."

Noelle shook her head. Awash in emotions, she could not say she was precisely beside herself. Indeed she could not say for certain which emotion was dominant.

Of course, her pride drove her. He had come for her and found her when she was missing. She would find him. Averill would not triumph in this. Over and over, she kept thinking that Averill had a bigger plan than killing Robin. Aloud she said, "I've brought some men with me. They are of a sort that you wouldn't ordinarily associate with, if you take my meaning. But I think they stand a better chance of finding him."

The Larnaervons exchanged speaking glances.

"Perhaps Piers might help you too," his lady suggested.

"That's not necessary." Noelle replaced her handkerchief. Clearly, these lovely people knew nothing. Under more felicitous circumstances, they might have been her first friends. "Perhaps when Robin is b-back, you'll come to visit us at Whitby."

"But that's wonderful," the lady continued. "I'm sure we'll be delighted."

"I must go." She rose.

"Noelle—may I call you, Noelle? My name is Vivian. Piers has said that he would like to talk to your husband about the stallion."

"The stallion?"

"Yes." Piers rejoined the conversation. "I believe he was once mine. In fact I'm sure of it. His name is

312

Romany Knight. My father bred him as well as his own brother Romany Prince. We'd be interested to know how you came by him."

Noelle smiled. "That's a very long story for pleasant society. When I find my husband, he'll enjoy telling you all about it."

"We'll all enjoy it together." Vivian's smile was genuine. Her voice was unusual and unforgettable. Light and high, with a child's timbre, it was the most musical Noelle had ever heard.

"Shall I send the stallion round?" Piers offered.

Noelle considered. "Perhaps he'd be better in your keeping. We don't have time to put up with his tantrums. Would you mind?"

"Not at all."

"Now, I must leave you. My men have cooled their heels long enough. They need to be about and searching. Every hour is precious." Her voice quivered. "If he's hurt or sick, he needs help. He was wounded, you know, in Portugal. Quite badly." She clasped her reticule tightly. "I must go."

Piers stared at the three men who lounged beside the horses. Instantly, he recognized their stripe. "Lady Whitby?" he asked uncertainly.

She extended her hand as a man might. He gripped it. "My minions," she said softly, a suggestion of humor in her voice. "They are as loyal as money can buy."

The Cap'n offered his humorless grin and touched the brim of his hat. Fod scowled. Tuck hunched his shoulders and looked off down the street.

"But surely—"

"We'll take care of the lady, milord," the Cap'n

313

called. "Nobody'll lay a hand on her."

Piers nodded, his dark eyes measuring one and then the other. When he spoke, he spoke to Noelle. "I congratulate you on your choices. You look to have bought the best for what you want."

"Thank you."

He did not watch them ride away. Vivian met him at the door, a question in her expression.

"She's determined enough to find him if he's still alive, which I strongly doubt."

"I hope, for her sake, she succeeds. She's more than half in love with him."

The turnkey shook out the whip with malicious satisfaction. Twenty lashes was the punishment.

Measuring the distance with a practiced eye, he brought it whistling down across the prisoner's naked back. The man hardly jumped at all.

If he had had his way about it, the newest prisoner, the highwayman with a fierce look out of his one good eye, would have gotten fifty with the cat — well laid on. The bastard had raised a constant ruckus night and day since he'd been brought in.

Just when they thought he'd gotten tired of it, he'd attacked the helpers bringing the kettle of food into the common cell. At his instigation several others had joined in. They had overpowered the guards and made it all the way to the gate. In fact, most of them had escaped. Because this one had brought up the rear, driving them and commanding them, he'd been caught.

The turnkey swung the whip again. It coiled

around the man's waist like a black snake. He waited a few seconds before pulling the whip off. That way the skin swelled around it and it hurt coming out almost as much as laying on. He studied the dark red line that encircled his victim's middle. He wished he was using the cat. Now that was a punishment. This puny thing was hardly worth the trouble to swing it.

Robin sank his teeth into his lower lip. He had heard men telling tales about being whipped. Most of them said the same thing. Don't fight it. Plaster yourself to the post. Let the post take the force. He could hear turnkey's intake of breath, the whistle of the leather.

Oh, God!

He could not help himself. He bucked, arching his back, writhing at the burning agony that spread into a wide band.

How many? He had set himself to count. They had ordered twenty. He was a little surprised at that. So few. For what he had done! He would have thought—

Christ!

How many? How many more? His back was a sheet of flame. He could feel the hot blood trickling down. He was going to have some scars. No matter. He was already a mess. But they were all marks of honor. These were shame. He hated the—

"AAAh!!"

"Made y' sing that time," his tormentor chuckled. "There's plenty more where that came from."

Robin bit his lip until the blood came. Not again. Not again. Never another word.

The whip came down again immediately followed by the turnkey's bark of laughter. "That's the way. Surprised, me bucko! Knocked the piss and vinegar right outta y'."

Robin's groan this time was abject humiliation. The bastard had made him lose control. He could feel his urine running down his legs. At least, he thought hazily, nothing worse could happen. He would set his teeth and endure to the bitter end.

On the eighteenth stroke the tip of the lash curled round over his face and snapped against the scar of his temple. He slumped into merciful unconsciousness.

"We've found him, milady. He's in Newgate."

"Newgate? Newgate Gaol!"

"Yes, ma'am."

She stared at the Cap'n, as if he had not spoken English.

"Milady?" He asked uncertainly.

She let out her breath on a long sigh. "How can you be sure? He's not a criminal. How can he be in Newgate?"

"Oh, it's him all right. I got it from a fella who broke out."

"Broke out—of prison?" She could not take all this in. "He must be lying. People don't actually escape from prison."

"That's how I know he's telling the truth, ma'am. He's telling this tale about this big, tall gent with one eye. Said he yelled and banged for about a month about how he wasn't supposed to be in there. Kept tellin' them he was an Earl."

Noelle drove her fist to her mouth. "Oh, Captain."

"Yes, ma'am. Said nobody'd listen to him, so he rounds them all up and gets them to break out."

"Leading his troops." Noelle shook her head in amazement.

"With him leading them they made it through the gate. Some of them get away, but he don't. Seems he's covering their rear, keeping them all organized and moving. He's the one the guards catch."

"It couldn't be anyone else, Captain."

"No, ma'am." He shrugged one heavily muscled shoulder. "I don't think anybody else could manage it."

She hugged her arms across her body. "Shall I go to a judge, to a court, to the House of Lords?"

He considered a moment. "You want my advice, ma'am."

"I'm asking for it."

"Then take that high-toned voice of yours and that damn-your-eyes look."

She smiled and he grinned back.

"And that purse, of course, and go in and get him out. It'd be a whole deal faster." He made a cutting motion with his hand. "Slice right through the layers and get down to the bone."

She shivered and then hesitated. She had no choice but to trust this man. "I don't have very much in the purse, Captain. But I—er—have brought some jewelry with me."

He held up his hand. "Lord, ma'am. Don't tell me about it. And for God's sake don't mention it to any of the damn screws. They'll kill a man for tuppence.

317

What you have in the purse'll be enough."

She had only one more question. "Will you go with me?"

"Yes, ma'am. Me'n Tuck 'n' Fod'll stand by you." He grinned wolfishly. "It'll be kind of a change for us. Walking into the gaol on purpose."

"I must see him."

The warden was unctuous. The men didn't look like gentry, but the woman talked and dressed like a lady. "We don't allow anybody to see him. He's too dangerous. Mad, he is. Liable to kill someone."

"I absolutely have to see him." Noelle felt the edges of her temper fray. "I know people come in and out of this prison all the time, visiting friends and relatives."

"They visit the debtors. They're the ones that get company. Not the felons. They're too dangerous."

"But I think he may be my husband, Robin Whitt-combstone, Earl of Whitby."

At the mention of the title, the warden started. She named exactly who the fellow claimed to be. Money could be made here. He assumed a benign expression. "I would help you, my dear Countess, if I could."

Distractedly, she pressed her gloved hand to her cheek.

The Cap'n stepped closer. He leaned so near to her that his coat brushed against her back. His eyes gleamed at the warden. "Best let her see him. She's a dook's daughter."

The warden eyed her narrowly. He looked as if he might change his mind, then he shook his head. "Wish I could oblige you, ma'am, but those are the rules."

The Cap'n's lips moved close to her ear.

She nodded. Opening her reticule, she pulled out a coin. "I'm sure you have a poor box for people in need."

The warden's eyes lighted. His smile revealed snuff-brown teeth. "Why, yes, ma'am, we do."

"She's milady t' you, cowshard," Fod growled suddenly. He shifted his position until he was breathing on the warden's right shoulder.

The warden threw the man a startled look. "Er—yes, milady."

She extracted another coin and then another. They clinked together, the unmistakable sound of silver, as she hefted them.

Tuck moved up on the man's left. "Y'd better be sure th' poor get that."

The warden's interest in the silver had flagged as the menace of the men bore down upon him. Together they made a strange quartet. The lady wore a velvet riding habit, rumpled and muddy at the hem, but with the unmistakable sheen of silk. She looked pale as death.

Her companions balanced nervously on the balls of their feet, their shoulders hunched belligerently. They looked as if they belonged in the cells below instead of in his office, the warden decided. He'd wager they'd seen the inside of more than one in their time.

Noelle held out the coins in her fist. "For the poor box."

The warden slid a box across his desk. "Thank you, milady."

They clinked heavily, guineas everyone of them by

319

their weight.

He smiled. "I'll be your escort."

"Damme, I feel queer. I don't like this above 'alf," Fod groaned. "Cap'n, this gives me the shakes."

Noelle had the shakes herself and worse. The indescribably foul odor was making her stomach heave. She could feel the nausea rising. She pressed a perfumed handkerchief over her nose.

"They're gallows bait down here," the warden explained smugly. "No sense in wastin' money on them."

The flagstones were mucky with moisture and unimaginable filth. The lantern illuminated only a small segment of the passage at any time. Otherwise, it was in darkness. Suddenly, Noelle began to pray that he was not here.

As they passed one door, laughter burst out of the tiny window. At the same time, fingers stabbed between the bars of the grate. Noelle jumped and slipped, only saved from a fall by the Cap'n's arm. The laughter followed them along the way, joined by curses and groans. Somewhere she heard flesh striking flesh accompanied by whimpers and pleas.

At last, they halted before an ironbound door no different from the others.

"Are we in Hell, Cap'n?" she whispered in his ear.

"Close enough, ma'am."

The warden looked through his ring of keys until he came to one whose number matched the number on the door. "Now, I want you to stand back," he warned her. "The guard'll go in with a lantern. You can look through the door. If you recognize him, then I'll have him hauled out."

"Yes, sir." Noelle was thoroughly frightened. Robin could not be in this place. Icy cold, dark, terrible. If he were here, he had been imprisoned almost a month. She clenched her hands tightly.

The key rattled in the lock, the door swung inward. The guard armed with a club swung the lantern in through the opening. "Get back there!"

No answer. Nothing moved within.

He looked at the warden, who nodded. Club upraised he entered. The light spread to the corners of the cell. Noelle saw what looked like a heap of straw and rags and filthy limbs.

The guard saw it too. He advanced and poked it.

The heap did not stir.

"Get up! Up!" He pulled back his club.

"No!" Noelle shrieked. "No! Robin! Robin!" Only the Cap'n's hand kept her from dashing into the cell.

"Drag him around so we can see his face," the warden called.

"Not me. 'E might be foolin'. I r'member w'at 'e done."

"Robin," she pleaded. "If it is you, please—"

The figure lay inert.

She jerked her elbow free and lunged into the cell.

"Milady," the warden called. The guard stepped to the side, holding the lantern high. The Cap'n came behind her, his hand on his knife.

Noelle went down on one knee in the gray straw.

The man lay curled around himself. His legs shielded his belly. His face was tucked down behind his arms. She saw the leather string laced through the lank black hair. "Robin," she whispered. "Robin Whittcombstone."

He stirred and dropped his arm away from his face. At first she was not sure she was staring at her husband. A full growth of unkempt black beard covered his jaw. The one good eye had been blackened and a black bruise slanted across the cheek, nose, and temple.

"Robin?" she whispered uncertainly. Her eyes flew to the Cap'n, who shook his head.

Fod had followed close behind. He whistled through his teeth. "Damme, but they've sure worked 'im over."

"Robin." She put her hand on his shoulder.

At last he opened the single eye. It stared dazedly into the light.

"Robin."

"M-madam Wife?"

Eighteen

"Here now, you can't just walk out of here with him," the warden protested. "That man's my prisoner." Hands spread to bar the way, gesturing nervously, he moved into the center of the passageway.

The Cap'n urged the guard out of the cell, so Fod could get his arms under Robin's legs and shoulders. At his rough handling, the Earl stirred. His eye opened blearily. He groaned.

Noelle winced at the sound, then fastened her steeliest glare on the man. "On the contrary." Her voice fairly bristled with aristocratic authority. *"That* man's my husband. He's Robin Whittcombstone, the Earl of Whitby."

"But he's my prisoner."

"His being here is a mistake. Therefore, he is no prisoner. Furthermore, he is a war hero and the son-in-law of the Duke of Averill. You could very well lose your position here and find yourself in his place for wrongful imprisonment."

The warden's cheeks reddened. The guard backed away from her tirade.

Tuck took the lantern from the unresisting hand and held it high. His face contorted in a hideous scowl, Fod came into the light. "He's been whipped, milady."

"What! You whipped him. A peer of the realm."

The warden dropped his hands.

Fod brushed past them all and strode down the narrow passageway. Tuck had to skip to keep the lantern's light ahead of his friend's hurrying feet.

"Hold on there a minute. I can explain about that," the warden pleaded to Noelle. "He tried to escape. He was leading the others. How was I to know? I didn't imprison him. I've got the papers to prove—"

At the mention of papers, Noelle halted in her tracks. "Papers, have you. I would suggest you be very careful not to mislay them. In fact, I demand that a copy of them be sent round to the Earl's apartments by special messenger tomorrow."

"But, milady—"

"Tomorrow, sir." Noelle picked up her skirts and followed Fod.

The warden slumped back against the wall. The Cap'n grinned in the man's face as he brought up the tail of the procession.

They were descending the stairs into the yard when the warden caught up with them. His voice was shaking. "He was delivered to me as a highwayman. Dandy Dick, they called 'im. I was told he talked like a gentleman. How was I to know? I ask you, how was I to know?"

The Cap'n spun and planted himself to catch the man's cravat with a broad fist. "Who delivered him? Who told you he talked like a gentleman?"

The man's lips quivered. He tried to mop sweat from his forehead. "Well, er, I don't remember. Someone from magistrate's court, I assumed."

The Cap'n's lips pulled back from his teeth. " 'Ow much money did this 'ere magistrate give you?"

The warden clamped his mouth shut. He batted at the arm that held him. His eyes wavered and fell. "Let go of me. You can't lay your hands on a warden of the gaol."

"Scum!" The Cap'n shoved hard as he released the cloth. The man staggered back.

The group had made its way to the outer courtyard where the debtors were allowed to exercise and visit their families. Tuck set the lantern down and moved ahead to wrestle the guards for the last set of keys.

"B-but he had the proper papers," the warden squeaked. "What will I do? My count, don't you see? I can't be short."

Noelle pulled more money from her purse. "This is for your trouble. I am taking the Earl to his apartments where I remind you for the third time to send a copy of the arrest papers tomorrow. As soon as he can travel we'll go on to Whitby in Devonshire. If anyone protests, direct him to us there."

The gate swung open and Fod carried Robin through.

"But—"

Cap'n tossed a coin to the boy who had held their horses. "I'll take him up before me, ma'am." He vaulted into the saddle and reached down for the limp body.

Relieved of his burden, Fod whirled on the warden. Fastening his fist in the man's maligned neckcloth, he snarled, "Don't give us none o' y'r guff, cowshard. We knows y' fix the count ever' w'ich way. Go get a dead 'un from the stews an' throw 'im th' cell. Milady don't wanta see no damned protesters."

Their eyes were only a few inches apart. Fod's promised murder.

The warden gulped. "Yessir."

Robin appeared to regain consciousness as they stripped off his rags. "Get away from me, you damned scavengers!"

"Watch out, ma'am!"

The warning came too late. The Earl's flailing arm caught her across the side of the face and knocked her sprawling. His eye was wild, wide-open, staring into the middle distance. Then he arched his back as the pain of his efforts hit him. His face contorted.

"Grab him!" the Cap'n yelled.

" 'Ware, thieves! Get away!" Robin fell back on the bed even as he kicked out, driving both feet into Fod's chest.

The stocky man grinned as he absorbed the blow and caught Robin's ankles. "I got 'im. Wan' me t' flip 'im over?"

Noelle climbed to her feet massaging her jaw. "Yes."

"What the hell! Stop! Damn you!" Tuck rolled Robin's shoulders as the Cap'n caught the windmilling arms and hauled them above his head.

"God damn you all!" His voice was muffled in the pillow.

Bending over him, Noelle set the shears to the ragged shirt. "Robin, milord. We're trying to help you. Robin!"

He went suddenly still. His head lifted slightly. He blinked blearily. "Wha—?"

"Robin, you're safe. We're trying to help you."

He looked into the Cap'n's dark face. "Who're you?"

"Robin." Noelle put her hand on his brow at the same time that the tortured muscles in the back of his neck tired. She guided his head to the pillow and knelt to peer into his face. "Robin, you're safe."

He stared at her a full minute. Then he heaved a sigh and nodded faintly. "Madam Wife?"

"Noelle." She smiled. "We're getting ready to look at your back."

"I need a bath," he whispered. "Don't touch me."

"I don't mind."

"Need a bath," he insisted. "I'm filthy. I stink."

"We'll give it t' 'im, ma'am," Tuck volunteered from the corner. "You can wait in t'other room."

At the same time Fod eased his hands from around Robin's ankles. "Speak fer y'rself. I ain't bathin' no bloody Earl."

"Shut y'r mouth." Tuck shook his head in disgust. "Talkin' dirty in front of th' lady."

Robin pushed himself up on one elbow where he rested, breathing a bit hard. "I can bathe myself."

"Perhaps if you'll just get a tub and some hot water from the hallporter," Noelle suggested, "he can take care of himself."

"I'll fetch it," Tuck volunteered. Glad to be able to do something, he hurried out.

Fod's scowl deepened and he muttered under his breath as he followed.

Robin flexed his shoulders gingerly and eased to a sitting position. The Cap'n excused himself and Noelle poured a glass of brandy and brought it to her husband. He took a generous swallow and sighed. "How'd you find me?"

"The estimable Cap'n has many useful connections.

327

The prisoners whom you led in escaping were very forthcoming."

He nodded. "Some of them were pretty good lads."

"Do you have any idea how you happened to be taken up?"

He shook his head. "I thought I was attacked by thieves. I thought they wanted my horse and my winnings."

"If they wanted him, they didn't pursue him very far. He came wandering back to your club. That's how we knew you were missing. Lord Pemberton recognized him and sent word to me. The Earl of Larnaervon took the stallion into his care."

Robin digested this information slowly. "They helped me?"

"That's right. They were concerned. Can you remember what happened?"

He wrapped his hand around his neck to give his head extra support. Its weakened muscles were aching. A headache was forming. "I remember I fell, or the thieves dragged me off. They must have knocked me out. But how did I end up in Newgate? It must have been a mistake."

She turned away, afraid to meet his eyes. "You were put there on purpose. Papers were written. The warden is sending copies to you. He was told you were a highwayman named Dandy Dick and that you talked like an aristocrat. That's why nobody believed you when you protested."

Robin's dark eyebrow rose. "I wondered why he didn't pay any attention to me." He drained his glass and shuddered. "I wonder if the Duke of Averill was involved?"

"I don't know," she whispered. Without meeting his eyes, she brought the brandy bottle and refilled his glass.

"But you think so."

"Yes."

"But, why? Why imprison me?" He came to his feet where he hung swaying. "Why kidnap you to bring me home, then have me thrown in prison when I come back to town? The man's mad."

"I don't know," Noelle repeated. "I truly don't. He has a hatred of me. We have been at war for years. Perhaps he thinks to hurt me through you."

"You can't be hurt through me," Robin said slowly, his eye sought her face. "That's perfectly ridiculous. You don't love me."

She felt a tightening in her belly. She had to clench her fist to keep her hand from moving over it. "Of course not. How ridiculous! No more than you love me."

They stared at each other. Only inches separated them.

The thud of approaching footsteps and general grumbling from Fod put an end to the conversation. Noelle waited in the sitting room with Fod and Tuck while the Cap'n assisted Robin in his bath.

A short time passed before they emerged. Robin's face was excessively pale in comparison to the blackness of the new growth of beard. He made his way to the nearest chair and lowered himself onto it carefully and stiffly. He did not lean back. "I want to return to Whitby tomorrow."

Noelle shook her head in protest. "We can wait a few days. You need to get stronger."

"No!" His single word rang overloud. He clenched his jaw until the tendons strutted in his neck. "No. I don't want to take a chance. I don't think they'll follow me to Whitby."

His listeners stared at him. Noelle started to speak, then changed her mind. Tuck grinned. "Good idea. Get outta 'ere. It's all quiet an' clean in th' country."

Lord and Lady Larnaervon were visibly shocked at the sight of Robin Whittcombstone.

"Good God, man. You were actually in Newgate Gaol all this time. Why that's over a month?"

"Please be seated, milord," Lady Larnaervon begged. She beckoned him to a chair close to the fire. "I'll order tea."

Robin shook his head. The motion staggered him. The buzzing in his ears increased. "Thank you, but we really can't stay. I — er — I've been away from Whitby too long. Many things need my attention."

"But — "

"I understand you've been taking care of my horse, sir. Most good of you."

Noelle touched his arm. "Perhaps we should sit down for a few moments, milord. They'll have to bring the horse around."

Her voice dinned in his ear. He knew he was feverish and he knew she knew. If he sat down, he might have trouble getting up. And more than anything he wanted to leave London. Fear tore at him. Newgate and its horrors had almost broken him. "It shouldn't take so long," he protested.

"Please, Robin," Larnaervon's lady moved to his other side. "May I call you Robin? Tea can be brought

330

in a very few minutes. Your journey is going to be long and cold."

She came up on his blind side. He flinched and twisted his head around, then wished he had not done so when his wrenched muscles tightened painfully. "Milady," he said through clenched teeth, "we need to be on our way quickly." He felt a sharp pinch from Noelle. "But thank you just the same."

Larnaervon came at him face front, a slow smile lighting his handsome face. "Actually, we wish you'd sit down so we can get acquainted. I don't believe we've been officially introduced." He extended his hand. "Larne's my name. Piers to me friends. We might talk about the horse."

Robin accepted the hand reluctantly. He had made a mistake in coming here. He should have remained at his apartment and sent the Cap'n round. Now this dilettante dandy wanted to delay their departure. At this very minute the prison authorities might be issuing warrants for his re-arrest. He would be taken back — and whipped. The memory of the lash slamming into his back made him nauseated. He shook his head. "Thank you, but —"

"He thinks the stallion is one that was stolen from him," Noelle supplied.

"Stolen! From you?" His nerves were screaming. Did they think he had stolen it? He dropped Larne's hand.

"Actually, I lost him."

"Lost — a horse?" Noelle could not keep the amazement from her voice.

"I paid for him," Robin declared. "I have a bill of sale. And for your information, he was in bad shape.

Had a bullet in his hip and a hell of a nasty disposition."

The Larnaervon's exchanged glances. "Oh, I've no doubt you have the right to him," Piers said soothingly. "He's yours. I was just so flabbergasted when he came galloping, out of the fog that night. He and his brother were my favorite mounts. I'd like to buy him back."

"Piers," his lady advised. "Now's not the time and place. Robin and Noelle are anxious to be on their way."

"Perhaps you'd like to visit us?" Noelle invited. "The spring at Whitby is beautiful. The dales are extraordinary, or so I've heard. Isn't that so, Robin?"

His head was pounding and they were all talking. Another minute and he would leave the damned horse. He would not be imprisoned again. He muttered something.

A footman appeared. "The gentleman's horse, sir."

"Thank you. Please bring your wife and come to Whitby in the spring," he said curtly. With a nod he backed away from the women's hands and turned on his heel. Leaving Noelle to make polite explanations, he hurried out.

She looked helplessly after him, then across at her hostess.

Lady Larnaervon smiled and took her hand. "We understand. He's been through an ordeal. Be careful. Good journey."

"Thank you." Noelle smiled helplessly. "You're right. He's very upset. But you are welcome. Please come."

"A strange pair," Piers remarked as he watched the couple and their three scruffy retainers gallop away down the street.

Lady Larnaevon came up behind him and rested her cheek against his shoulder. "I think he was ill, Piers. His cheeks were flushed and his hand was hot."

"Still taking care of people, are you?" Her husband patted her hand where it curved round his arm.

"Every chance I get," she replied. "And unless I mistake the signs, his wife is increasing. I wonder if he knows."

Piers laughed. "Lord, Vivian, you should be in the foreign office. Castlereagh need only put you in a room with the French and you'll have perceived their deepest, darkest secrets."

She blushed. "I could be wrong."

He turned and took her in his arms. "You, my dearest love? Not you. Not where the human spirit is concerned."

Noelle sat straight up in bed. Staring into the frigid darkness, she tried to locate the voice.

The agonized screaming echoed through the house. She clutched the bedclothes to her chin, disoriented by the cold and the sudden awakening.

"God damn, you. I'm Whittcombstone. Whittcombstone! Captain, you bastards! I'm a Captain! Damn you!"

Next door. Robin was screaming and cursing.

She pulled her wrapper round her shoulders as she flung herself out of bed. Not stopping to find her slippers in the dark, she ran to the connecting door and tugged it open. The moonlight reflecting off the snow

333

gave enough light to see him, a dark figure writhing on the bed.

"Robin?"

He flailed both arms. "Get the hell away from me! I'm Whittcombstone! I'm a belted Earl, you friggin'—"

"Robin! Robin!" She slid to a halt and approached him gingerly. His arms were long and his strength enormous.

The figure on the bed stilled.

"Robin, wake up."

She was startled when he rasped, "Madam Wife," in a voice totally unlike his own.

"You were having a bad dream."

He coughed and tried to clear his throat. Stiffly, he sat up. Legs sprawled wide, arms draped over his drawn-up knees, he sighed heavily. "Sorry I disturbed you."

"Disturb doesn't describe it. You scared me half to death."

He chuckled. "Noisy, was I?"

She bent to scoop a pillow off the floor and toss it back on the bed behind his shoulders.

"Is there any water?"

"I'll get some."

"No, that's all right."

"It's here." She poured it, brought it to him, and waited while he drank.

When she took the glass from him, he caught her hand. "Stay with me."

A thrill went through her. His hand was warm and dry where the fingers curled around her chilled skin. "I'm liable to hurt you."

334

"No. The pain's about gone."

"I don't believe that. You're just trying to make up for screaming in your sleep. You're still feverish."

He tugged gently. "I'll keep you warm."

She could hear a smile in his voice. "Just for a minute," she told him with a show of reluctance. "If I stand here much longer, my feet will freeze to the floor."

He lay back on his side, one arm bent under his head. The moonlight streamed over him as she climbed onto the bed and began to straighten the covers. When she tried to tuck them about his shoulders, he objected. "I'm hot."

"But I'm not, so you have to have them."

"Whose bed is this?"

"You invited me. Now you're stuck with me. I won't stay long. When I leave, I promise to strip you down to your knees."

As she lay down on her back and pulled the covers up to her chin, she heard a quiet cough that might have been a chuckle. He put his arm across her waist and gathered her close. They lay in silence, but she could feel the tension in him, feel him staring into the darkness. At last she turned slightly and put her palm against his cheek. "Was it very bad?"

He sucked in his breath. "Yes. And I think it's going to be bad for a long time."

"Why? You're safe. You're home."

He lay still beside her, trying to find the words. "When a soldier goes through a battle, especially a bad one, it stays in his mind. He can't get it out. Sometimes for months and years, he dreams it. It's pretty bad."

"You think that will happen to you."

"It already has," he reminded her drily. "Besides, they might come after me."

"They won't come after the son-in-law of the Duke of Averill." She patted his shoulder. "I hope you appreciate how I've battered my pride for you. I wouldn't use the Duke's name to save my soul, but I'll use it to save yours."

"His name can put me back in there, perhaps."

"There are other people of importance in London. Larnaervon and Pemberton will stand for you. They're your friends. If it were known the Duke had put an innocent man in prison, society would shun him."

Her husband gave an impatient shake. "They wouldn't believe me. The Turk. Or if they did, it would be a ninety-day wonder, or less."

"Milord, please don't get excited."

His hand clenched into a fist. It lay hard and heavy as a rock on her midriff. "I won't go back."

She stroked the hard knuckles soothingly. "No one will send you back."

"I've been in battle. I've seen blood and mud and gunpowder all mixed together under the horses's hooves. I've seen men wounded and dying, heard their cries. Nothing — nothing was worse than the awful filth and degradation of that place. We were all alive like rats in a dark hole but worse than rats. At least rats can get out. Men stole from each other when there was nothing worth stealing."

"They were thieves."

"I stole. When I came to, I was naked. I stole rags of clothing to keep from freezing to death."

"Milord." She kissed his hand and cradled it against her cheek. "That's different."

"I don't think so. Some of them weren't so different from me when they had a bit of hope."

She pounced on the opportunity to change the subject. "We heard about the escape. That was very clever of you. That's how we figured out where you were. Tuck said everyone was talking about you. You brought up the rear and got caught. You were something of a hero."

He cursed himself mildly. "Something of a fool."

"Well, milord, why didn't you lead them out?"

He was silent for a long time. "You were calling me Robin for a while."

"Robin. Don't change the subject."

He sighed. "Too much training. A good captain always keeps the men moving as a unit."

"The army should never have mustered you out, Robin. The navy kept Wellington with one eye. Even when your whole purpose is to escape, you can't be less than a hero."

"I'm not a hero. Disavow yourself of that right now, Madam Wife."

"You were calling me Noelle before you left."

"Noelle, then."

"Does your back hurt terribly?"

"It's bearable. Noelle, I was coming home for Christmas."

She touched his cheek again. "We'll have many more. Go back to sleep. I'll keep watch."

He leaned toward her. His lips brushed her ear. "I could go to sleep much faster if you would move over here against me."

"I thought you were hot." She edged her body until it lay against the length of his.

"Might at well use the heat to keep you warm." He slid his leg over the tops of her thighs. His hairy inner thigh rasped across her skin. It stopped against the slight mound of her belly.

She tensed, sucking in her stomach as much as she could.

He did not appear to notice. His hand slid down to her breast, cupping it, weighing it. His lips nibbled her ear, her cheek, and then the corner of her mouth. He gasped and possessed her mouth, driving his tongue in between her teeth.

She fought against his kiss, twisting her face away. "Milord — Robin!"

"Don't. Don't stop me, Noelle. Please."

"But you'll hurt yourself."

He caught the hand she pushed against his shoulder and dragged it down. His shaft was hot and hard as oak, desperately throbbing. Beneath her hand it leaped uncontrollably.

"No." Behind clenched teeth, he growled the single word. His whole body was stiff.

She shuddered. Female called to male, plumbed primeval depths and left her weak. She stretched her neck, her breasts hardened. Their nipples began to throb.

He pushed up on the bed, his knee came down between her thighs. She opened them to him, sprawled shamelessly, heat rising from her. She shuddered again, as hot muscled skin butted against the soft secret places of her body.

She wanted him to ease the ache, to thrust into her, to drive it away. She drove her heels into the mattress and arched her hips, sliding herself up his hard thigh, leaving heat and moisture behind her.

He growled again unintelligibly. Against the moonlight he was a dark shadow, a silhouette of curved muscles and wildly tossed hair. He drew back.

She felt him — hard and hot — at her nether mouth. It opened for him, throbbed, sucked at him. With a cry he drove into her.

Her own cry mingled with his. Her legs clasped his hips, dragging him in tighter against her. He arched as if her heels had spurred him. Then he dropped onto her. His elbows came down on either side of her head. Bracing himself, he plunged again and again. His hot breath fanned her cheek. Heat surrounded her, kindled her own to a blaze.

She dug her fingernails into his shoulders and held on.

Impossibly, he was bigger. He stretched her, hurting her so that she groaned with the pain. But she wanted him to go on more than she wanted him to stop.

His chest expanded like a bellows. Skin slick with perspiration slid over her breasts, rasping the throbbing nipples. He drove into her filling her until she sobbed with pain. He drove so deep that he slammed against the spread lips of her mound. As if he had touched a trigger, she exploded, thrown into a starburst of ecstasy.

His own release thundered in her ear and jetted into her body. Release from the pain and the memory of pain. Culmination of desire. Affirmation of freedom.

Masculinity.

Pride.

"Happy Christmas, Noelle."

Nineteen

"Did I hurt you?"

He lay with his arm across his face, more than fever heat radiating from his body. With every breath he sucked into his lungs, his chest lifted high above the cavity of his belly.

"No." She was conscious that she lay open to the air. It chilled her limbs, her belly, her breasts. At that moment it felt good. Opening her eyes, she raised her head off the pillow. A cynical smile quirked her lips as she stared down the length of her pale body. Her legs sprawled rudely. The covers were tangled about her feet.

She brushed strands of hair from across her cheek and mouth. "You left me just as if you'd tossed me aside after you were through with me." She purposefully made her voice cross. "I've been played with and then discarded like a doll."

The heavy breathing stilled for a fraction, then he exhaled slowly.

Lazily, he turned over and braced himself up on one elbow. "I never played with dolls."

She sat up reaching for the covers. "It felt like you were in good practice."

His arm curled around her shoulders as she lay back down. He drew her against his side. "Are you sure you — er — enjoyed that?"

She snuggled against him. "Yes."

He stroked her waist and the curve of her hip. "I was fast and rough. I thought I simply wanted you to be beside me in the dark. I was glad you were there, then suddenly I had to have you," he sighed. "That's twice I've lost control with you. You would be within your rights to be angry with me, Madam Wife."

She pressed her mouth against his salt-rimmed shoulder. "You'd been in prison."

"It was more than that. I swear. I wouldn't use anyone like that. I don't know why I did it."

"It couldn't have been that I was beautiful and desirable and you have fallen under my spell." Her voice was seduction itself.

His breathing evened. He lay so quiet that she thought he might have gone to sleep. When he spoke he ducked his head, so his lips brushed her ear. "It might have been."

Her throat closed. She coughed so deeply she almost strangled. He had to pat her back to help her catch her breath.

"Oh, what a facer!" she gasped when she could speak. "I'll never believe that in a million years." When she had gotten control of herself, she rolled over on her side, facing away from him.

He edged his body after her and cupped her spoon-fashion. His arm found a resting place encircling her waist.

So they lay in perfect contentment until she said, "You don't have to wear that eyepatch to bed, you

341

know."

He cursed softly. "Do you hate it so much?"

"I don't hate it at all. I don't think about it. I don't even see it. I just think it must be uncomfortable for you."

He snorted his disbelief.

"I mean it. You don't have to hide behind anything in the privacy of your own bedroom. I'm your wife. You don't have to hide anything from me."

He stirred restively. His next words were so soft she could barely hear them. "The only trouble with the damned patch is it isn't big enough. It can't cover my whole face."

After a minute, she yawned and twitched herself around more comfortably. "Have it your own way. If you want to believe that I was groaning and hanging on to you because I couldn't stand the sight of you, who am I to tell you different?"

"A cat! A damnable cat! With nine lives and the devil's own luck!" The Duke bent over coughing.

Holmesfield had never seen His Grace so angry. Hands clasped behind him, he backed to the edge of the carpet. "I believe the Countess used your name when influencing the warden to release him."

"The devil she did! She'll rue that bit of trickery." Averill slumped in his chair. "Where are they now?"

"I went immediately to the Earl's apartments, but no one was there. Furthermore, the stables were empty. The ostler reported that no provisions had been made for renting the stalls for another month."

The Duke was silent for so long that Holmesfield stirred uncomfortably. The face resumed its normal paleness. The icy eyes narrowed. Long pale white fingers steepled beneath the pointed chin. "So he's gone to ground. Not a cat, but a fox. A fox fleeing to his ruined den, cowering there, waiting to be dug out." He laughed. "A fox and his vixen."

The factor felt the skin prickle on his forearms.

"I think it will soon be time to pay them another visit, Holmesfield."

Though his face remained impassive, the man would have given anything to ask why.

"In late spring, I think. Yes, in late spring. She'll be clumsy and ugly. And miserable." He gave another bark of laughter that ended in a cough. "Miserable. And how I long to add to that misery."

The Duke's mare had arrived in the late evening. Accompanied by Hardwicke, the tired groom presented her papers to the Earl and Countess.

"She's a real nice lady," he told them a little anxiously. "Nice manners. Good lines."

"And her age?" Robin passed the papers to Noelle to study.

"Five. I was there when she was foaled. She's been a beauty."

Noelle looked up. "Her name's Belgravia?"

"Yes'm. Her dam was the old horse you took with you, milady."

"Yes, I see." The eyes she turned to Robin shone with emotion. "She's a daughter of Silver Belle."

He smiled encouragingly although he had never paid much attention to the animal. "Perhaps we'd better have a look."

The four trooped down to the stable where Tuck had already mixed some hot mash and was holding a bucket for the new arrival to eat. She lifted her head and stared at them with liquid eyes.

The mare's gun-metal gray coat was just beginning to dapple. She would have to be nearly ten before her coat would whiten to the prized silvery sheen. Robin mentally made a black mark in his record against gray horses.

Noelle clasped her hands together. "Oh, she's beautiful."

"She is that, milady," Tuck agreed. "She be a friendly little lady too."

While his wife petted the mare's neck and crooned in her ear, Robin looked the horse over critically. Given the circumstances, he was not surprised at the quality of the animal the Duke had sent.

Smaller even than the old mare that had been killed, Belgravia was a singularly unprepossessing beast. If Brandywine bred true to his size, she might have trouble delivering. If she threw a small colt, the best thing to do would be to sell them both as soon as possible as ladies' or children's mounts. Likewise, he wanted no grays popping up in his Black Horse Stud.

He mentally shrugged. No, the mare was not the quality of Kate or Deliverance. Certainly she was not the quality of the stallion that Larnaervon claimed was his. He watched his wife talk lovingly to the horse and determined to say nothing.

"She's small," the groom was saying anxiously. "But she's a goer." He looked to the Earl. "Arabian blood, y' know."

Noelle looked over her shoulder at her husband.

"What do you think of her, milord?"

His lady, his groom, the Duke's groom, and the horse all looked at him. The mare pricked her ears forward. He cleared his throat. "Madam Wife, she is pleasing to you. That is all that really matters."

"Damning with faint praise," she muttered. "Come, sir. Tell me what you really think."

"She *is* small," he began reluctantly.

"Wait until you see how she moves," the groom interceded.

Robin shot him a quelling look.

Noelle put out her hand. "But I want—" She took a step toward him. Her knee buckled. A helpless, confused look flashed across her face before her eyes closed and she began to sink.

He caught her before she sprawled on the ground.

"I am with child."

Silence followed her announcement. She dropped her eyes from his incredulous face. The toe of her slipper poked out from beneath the skirt of her gown. She pulled it back out of sight.

"You're having a baby?!" His voice was hoarse, incredulous.

"Yes." Noelle shifted her eyes to the glowing bed of coals on the hearth. Orange flames licked out of them at intervals. Their appearance was random. *Where will the next one appear? From the center? From that red hot spot near the hearth?*

"Look at me!"

She shivered.

Robin banged his thigh getting around the corner

of his desk. In a couple of quick strides, he was beside her. His hand dropped to her shoulder.

Thrusting out her bottom lip, she looked up at him defiantly.

"You're having a baby?" he repeated, more softly. "A baby?"

"Yes. Is that a problem for you? It didn't seem to be when it was conceived."

He scanned her face, the dark eye penetrating seeking truth. At last he nodded and turned away. She watched him rest his elbow on the mantel. His other hand rose to his face. His normally swarthy color deepened, then paled. Suddenly, the heart of the fire was of great interest to him too. "I—I'm concerned for you, Mada—Noelle. When?"

"When will it be born?"

"Both. No. When was it conceived?"

"I suspect the very first night."

"The very first night." He felt so incredibly stupid. And afraid.

"I suppose it does happen on the first night."

"I suppose so."

"You suppose so? Of course, it does. You're the Earl of Whitby. Aren't you pleased? There's an even chance you'll have an heir."

He did not answer. His mind raced. What would his son or daughter think of him? Probably the child would scream at the very sight of its father. He traced the line of black leather that bisected his cheek.

"Robin?"

He straightened his shoulders. "Of course, I'm pleased." He turned. "But you've known for a long time. You've had time to get used to the idea."

346

She smiled a little apologetically. "That's true. I didn't tell you when you left because I wasn't sure. Lily had only just told me and she wasn't sure either."

He scarcely heard her blathering. Instead he wiped his hand across the lower half of his face. "When?"

"Probably in the hottest part of the summer."

"I see. Yes, it would be then." His voice trailed away. He felt so incredibly stupid. And helpless. He spread his mouth in a smile. "Noelle. Wife. Mother." He lifted her hand to his lips. In a gesture of uncharacteristic tenderness, he brushed her palm with his lips.

If he could be sincere, she could be too. "I want you to know that I've been pleased for a long time."

"That's good. A child should have a mother's love."

"And its father's." Despite her best aristocratic tone, he could detect a thread of anxiety in her voice.

"Of course. Believe me I will love it with all my heart."

Yet he could not keep the doubt and fear from his voice.

She looked at him uncertainly.

Winter lost its fight with spring as it did every year. Snowdrops and then daffodils appeared in protected copses. Not that Noelle saw the changes that year.

Hardwicke with Tuck's help had completed the restoration of the governess's cart. But her husband insisted that someone else drive her and help her out and back in again. The clumsy attentions of rough and ready former soldiers drove her crazy as did the loss of her freedom and independence. She had argued fiercely, but her husband had remained adamant. She was his wife and she was not going to take any chances.

The day she escaped and rode off alone, he came riding after her with the whole crew. Hot with embarrassment and anger, he had lifted her off her horse. Under the grinning eyes of Hardwicke, Fod, Tuck, and the Cap'n, she was placed in the governess's cart without her feet ever touching the ground.

"I will not be treated this way," she fumed. "I'm not sick. I'm never sick. I feel wonderful."

"Good," he enjoined. "And I want you to continue to feel wonderful. After you have the baby, you may do as you please. Now tell Tuck where you want to go."

"I wasn't galloping," she protested. "Surely a sedate walk wouldn't be dangerous? Why Kate has a gait like a rocking chair especially now that she's going to be a mother herself."

He signaled to Tuck, who grinned sheepishly. "Where to, milady?"

She was still angry. "Milord. Robin. I won't be treated like this."

"Would you prefer to come home right away?"

"No."

"Then we will bid you good day, Madam Wife. Just tell your driver where you want to go." So saying he wheeled his horse. The Cap'n grinned. Fod scowled. Hardwicke tipped his hat. They galloped away after him.

"Where to, milady?" Tuck repeated.

"Whitby," she grumbled. "And be sure you watch for rocks and ruts in the road."

"Yes, milady."

That night Noelle lay in bed her blood still coursing with outrage. The humiliating memory choked her. She punched the unoffending pillow. *How dare they! How dare he!*

Robin opened the door to her room.

She started up. "Get out of here! I don't want to see you tonight."

"Sssh!" He set the candle down on the chest and seated himself on the foot of the bed.

She rolled over and presented her back to him. "Go away."

"I'm sorry you're angry."

"It's easy to be sorry that *I'm* angry. I notice you don't say you're sorry that you did it."

"Well, no."

"Of course not. You had a wonderful time. Galloping down the lane, dragging the whole crew along with you including my own man. Making a fool of me. They were all laughing."

"They were laughing," he acknowledged, "but I don't think they were laughing at you."

"Well, they weren't laughing at you."

He waited a few minutes. She heard the rustle of cloth. "They could have been laughing because they were happy."

She half-turned over, then flounced back. "What do they have to be happy about?"

"They're all looking forward to the baby."

"That's easy too. They don't have to have it."

"No, but they want you to have it safely, just as I

349

do."

"I don't believe that. Why would they laugh?"

He shifted a little on the bed. Again cloth rustled. "I think—I think they were laughing with relief. I think they were happy to find you safe." His voice was as soft as she had ever heard. "I think it's because they've all come to love you."

She felt a chill up her spine. All the quick retorts and cynical posturings melted. Try as she might, she could not maintain her ire in the face of the word "love." It pierced her, settling in her heart and belly. If he were still laughing at her, she would die of the pain.

Slowly, hesitantly, she shifted in the bed and sat up.

His face was turned slightly away, so that his sighted eye looked full upon her. He had put his robe down off his shoulders and arms. It pooled around his lean waist. The candlelight glowed on his chest with its terrible white scars slicing through the dark skin.

"What are you saying?"

Slowly, he turned his full face toward her. He had removed the black patch! His face was bare, the white scar running from the hairline, through the ruin of his eye, down the cheek.

"Robin," she whispered.

"They all want you to have the baby. I want you to have the baby. You can't be hurt. You can't take the chance of being thrown." He ducked his head and fumbled with the bit of leather. The strings had tangled.

She closed her hand over his. "I'm very lucky."

"Lucky," he snorted.

"Another inch and you would have been dead."

He tried to throw her hand off. "Pardon me, Madam Wife, if I don't believe your platitudes. Pity I could have understood. I wouldn't have liked it, but I would have tolerated it. But to say that you're lucky—"

"Hush." She dared to put her hand over his mouth. "Don't say any more."

His mouth moved against her fingers. The dark eye blazed with anger. Quickly, she took her hand away and replaced it with her lips. Still silencing him, she let her body slide onto his lap. His arms closed round her, kissing her, holding her close.

They kissed for a long time, warming each other, kindling fires. At last, she pulled back. With her eyes wide open, she traced the path of the scar, down through the ruined eyebrow, into the hollow where the sightless eyeball withered behind scarred upper and lower lids, down across the cheekbone.

He shuddered at the touch and ground his teeth.

"Sssh. It's all right. It's nothing," she whispered.

"It's hideous." His whole entire body had gone rigid as stone.

"No." She ran her fingers lightly along the scarred jaw.

He jerked his head away. "You say that, but what do you think will happen when the child is born?"

She frowned. "I don't know what you mean."

He swallowed. "Will it scream at the sight of me?"

She rose up on her knees and put her arms around him. "Oh, Robin. Of course not. Is that what this is all about? You've worried about what the baby will think? Babies don't think anything. They don't know what to think. They'll think what we think."

351

"Not later. When it grows up."

"That's perfectly silly. Our child will only worry about why other men don't look like his father. If it's a boy, he'll be so proud that his father was a war hero that he'll be bragging about you. He'll brag to all his friends that his father has a patch like a pirate."

"And if it's a girl?"

"She'll love you to death."

He shook his head. He lifted the black leather patch again. His hand trembled.

"Listen to me. When I was little, I thought Averill was the most handsome man in the world. Then I met Susan Postlethwaite."

He began to tie the strings, but she jerked the thing out of his hand and threw it on the floor.

"Listen, I tell you! Susan Postlethwaite's father had a big fat belly. He could hardly move, he was so fat. His calves were as big around as my head. His face was red and his head beneath his old wig — which by the way had lice in it — was bald and red too. I saw it once, so I know."

"I don't see —"

"I thought he was ugly, but Susan loved him. She thought he was just fine. She even sniffed at the sight of my handsome father because he was so thin and pale." She put her hand on her husband's bare shoulder and bent to look into his face. "Don't you see? He was so good to her and so merry and friendly that she didn't care what he looked like. And I came to love him too because he was the same with all her friends."

He shivered. "I feel as if I've had a Sunday School lesson."

"Good. Everyone needs lessons now and again.

Come, now. Get under the covers. I'm chilled to the bone. Wallowing around on top of the bed in the middle of the night does that to you. You'll have to warm the sheets for me all over again."

He leaned to the side, scanning the floor to find his eyepatch in the darkness.

She pulled his face back around. "Leave it, for heaven's sake. It'll be there in the morning." She scrambled around until she was back on her side, with the covers pulled up over her shoulder. Then she lifted them invitingly. "Come on. Climb in."

With a sigh he snuffed the candle out. In the darkness he unknotted the belt of his robe and slid naked between the sheets.

"That's good," she whispered. She kissed him lightly, then she turned her back to him and pressed her body spoon fashion against his. He put his arm across her waist.

Long after she fell asleep, he lay staring into the cold darkness. His face felt strangely naked and unbound.

"There's no question in my mind that the horses are kin." Robin stared gloomily at the magnificent black stallion as Larnaervon swung off his back and turned to help his wife dismount.

"Own brothers," his visitor replied. "Prince is the older by two years."

"What is my horse's name again?"

"Romany Knight. Their sire was Rom Sable; their dam, Devon Maid. Rom was a descendant of the Byerly Turk through Herod."

Robin nodded vaguely. "I appreciate what you're

telling me, but the stud is really not my main interest. Every horse breeder who comes around here makes statements involving the word Arabian. To me, a horse is a horse. But I'm sure my wife will be most impressed."

"The Byerly Turk was the first thoroughbred," Vivian Larne supplied.

"A thoroughbred." At least Robin had heard of them. "Are you saying that our stud is a thoroughbred?"

"Not really. Many horses descend from the Turk. After all, his get's been in England for over two hundred years." Larnaervon cleared his throat. "The lines have been used not just to breed thoroughbreds, but to add speed and agility to cold-blooded horses—"

"Piers." His wife pinched his arm gently. "I think that story's better saved for later."

"Oh." He smiled down at her. "Sorry."

A shawl concealing her shape, Noelle appeared at the door. Blivens shuffled after her muttering unintelligibly. "Please come in. Don't let my husband keep you standing on the front stoop."

"Ah, the redoubtable Lady Whittcombstone." Larnaervon sprang up the steps and took her hand. "Well met under much happier circumstances. Milady, you are looking in blooming health."

She blushed and pulled the shawl together over her front. "I thank you for saying so, Lord Larnaervon."

"Piers please. For I am determined to call you Noelle."

"Piers then. Welcome to our home."

"And so good of you to entertain us." Vivian bent to catch up her riding skirt. Robin, frowning heavily at Piers' attention to his wife, offered her his arm.

"Blivens will show you to your rooms. They are not nearly so grand as your town house, but—"

"Oh, grandeur is the most overrated thing in the world," Piers assured her. "I was reared in a castle myself—by the channel. Horrible place. It's the far side of wonderful that I didn't die of lung fever."

"No worse than a convent," Vivian added.

Noelle looked from one to the other. Their love shone brightly in their faces. She felt a stab of envy. At the same time the baby moved beneath the shawl and the envy was gone. She smiled brilliantly. "Blivens, show our guests to their rooms. When you have refreshed yourselves, please come to the parlor. We'll have tea."

In the early evening the four strolled down to the stables together. The stallions were cutting up a terrible commotion.

"Obviously, they don't remember each other," Piers remarked.

"Or perhaps they do," Robin said drily.

At one end of shedrow, Romany Knight stamped and snorted. His big body bumped loudly against the sides of his box stall. His iron-shod hooves crashed against the boards. From the other Romany Prince neighed shrilly answering the challenge.

"They must never meet." Noelle listened to the noise with alarm. "They'd kill each other for sure."

Larnaervon stood in front of Knight's stall watching the black pace and turn. Lather dripped from the black neck. "He's not at all as I remember. He was spirited, but this is more like rage rather than spirit. He had a sweet temper. I rode him more often than Prince because of his dependability.

Robin stood beside him, arms folded. "He'll never be dependable again," he said repressively. "Somewhere in his travels, he had been shot. Nobody tended the wound for a long time. The bullet was still in it. We had to stretch him out on the ground and tie him down to get it out. Now he tolerates me on his back, but no one else. He'll never trust anyone, nor can anyone trust him."

As if to illustrate the point, the big black backed into the corner. His eyes rolled, showing the white ring. He pawed the hay up over his back, then with a grunt, he charged. His neck snaked over the door. His lips pulled back from his teeth. Both men instinctively flinched back.

Up he went on his hind legs to the limit of the snaffling lines.

"I see what you mean," Piers agreed. "If he weren't tied down, he'd have been over that door."

"Exactly."

"Do you think it's safe for Prince to stay here?" Vivian asked her husband. "If this goes on too much longer, one or both are going to hurt themselves." A splintering crash from Prince's stall almost drowned the last of her sentence.

"I agree." Noelle moved back along the shedrow. "They're upsetting the mares. And we ladies in our delicate conditions can't stand upsets."

"My horse can be moved to the stable at the Rose and Thistle," Robin suggested. "Fod can take him there and look after him. He prefers the inn anyway.

Fod. Not the horse."

While Robin gave the instructions, Larnaervon shook his head. "I had come with the idea of buying Knight back, but now I see that's not practical. Looks as if he's yours, Noelle. I'll sign his papers over to you."

She smiled happily. "That's incredibly generous of you."

Piers tucked his wife's arm through his own. "This rather writes *finis* to an unfortunate and overlong tale."

Vivian nodded. "I'm just as glad that you didn't get him back, sweetheart. Now it's over forever."

Twenty

"The D-duke of Averill," Blivens announced, his wrinkled face twitching.

The four people in the parlor stared at one another. Beneath the Spanish shawl Noelle put her hand protectively over her middle.

Robin rose from his chair, his face darkening. "I'll meet him in my wife's study, Blivens."

"No need to do that, Whittcombstone. What I have to say can be said in mixed company." The Ice King, resplendent in blue-gray superfine coat and pale dove-gray buckskins, posed in the doorway.

Blivens looked from one to the other in confusion.

"That will be all." Averill shooed the old man away with his silver and crystal quizzing glass, then calculating his moves like an actor, he turned his attention to the room. The Larnaervons were greeted with chilly smiles. His son-in-law rated a cold nod. Lifting his glass again, he peered at the gravid mound on Noelle's lap. "You're looking in good health, my lady."

She did not answer him. Her tongue clove to the roof of her mouth. What did Averill want here?

Robin stepped to her side. "She's in perfect health."

"Good. Good. And you, my dear." The Duke strolled forward to bow over Vivian's hand. "Snow Queen among these dark minions, what may I call

358

you?"

Her hair was almost as pale as his own; her eyes were silvery blue. She smiled faintly. "Vivian Larnaervon."

"Ah, the wife, no doubt, of the Earl of Larne." He pressed his lips to the back of her hand.

When he straightened, he looked into Larne's face. He lifted a white eyebrow. "How do the gentlemen fare these days along the coast, milord?"

Piers's eyes narrowed. His hand tightened fractionally around the stem of his sherry. He set the drink down carefully. "I wouldn't know."

"How odd! But, of course, the crown has taken drastic steps to curtail their activities, I believe."

"Again, I wouldn't know." Larnaervon rose. "If you have something else you wish to say to me, perhaps we should continue the conversation elsewhere where the others will not be bored."

"No, no. Not at all. I have no interest in—er—'brandy, 'backy, laces.' My cellars are quite exceptional, but I have the advantage in that they were all laid down in a more liberal time."

"How fortunate."

Without waiting to be asked, the Duke seated himself and crossed one exquisitely garbed leg over the other. He lifted the quizzing glass to survey them all in turn, then redirected his question to Larnaervon. "But what brings you out from the city? The Season has been deadly dull I know. But not so dull as this place. I can imagine no reason for you to be here."

"Actually, we were invited," Vivian answered for her husband. "The four of us became acquainted shortly after Christmas. We promised to come to further our friendship when the weather became pleasant."

"Ah, yes. Shortly after Christmas. That would be about the time you were—uh—otherwise located, wouldn't it, Whittcombstone?" The Duke's lips pulled back from his small white teeth.

"So you knew about that?"

"Me. Oh, heaven's no. Not until after the fact, I assure you. Believe me, I would have rushed to your aid. You should have told me, Noelle, when I visited you. I would have understood."

"Would you?"

He coughed behind his hand. "Indeed, I did not know until I was contacted, through my factor of course, by the authorities. They questioned at some length the use of my name in securing your release. Of course, I was at first surprised. Shocked rather."

"I'm sure your heart took quite a turn." Noelle could feel her nerves vibrating. Her stomach muscles tightened. The baby kicked hard against the unaccustomed constriction.

"Not my heart. My sense of justice. I was quite round with them. Of course, you didn't have permission to use my name. What could I say to that? I had to tell them the truth. On the other hand had I been informed, I would have been there myself, hammering on the gates."

"I was not believed," Robin murmured.

"Well, of course not, my dear man. Felons are never believed. They tell the most horrendous lies. That's why they're felons. Or is it the other way around?" He gestured with the quizzing glass. "They're felons, that's why they tell horrendous lies." He laughed again and ended with a cough.

"They are not the only liars," Noelle remarked to no

360

one in particular.

"No, my dear Countess, they are not." He lifted the glass and directed his gaze to her stomach. "All of us here are terribly human and therefore terribly flawed." He let the glass swing from his hand by its silk riband. "All born of woman."

The baby kicked so hard the shawl moved. Everyone in the room saw it. Noelle blushed fiery red. The baby kicked again, this time upward. She jumped.

"By God," Averill remarked. "Lively little thing."

This time Robin stepped in front of his wife. "I think you've said quite enough, Duke. I must insist that you accompany me to the study so we may discuss what brings you here?"

"Why what do you suppose, my dear fellow?" The Ice King coughed delicately. He drew a fine linen handkerchief from his sleeve and muffled the sound. "Can you not believe that I've come here merely to pay my respects to your wife, whom I see, by the by, blooming?"

Her hand trembling slightly, Noelle arranged the corner of the shawl over her shoulder. She took a deep controlling breath. "You didn't come to see me, Averill. No one will believe that."

"Ah, but I did, my dear." He gestured to Robin with his glass. "Please step out of the way there, my good fellow. I would converse without a barricade."

Reluctantly, Robin moved aside.

"Ah, thank you. Noelle, you told me you'd influence your husband, but don't you think it's time you kept him, so to speak, down on the farm? This stint in Newgate will not make him welcome in society."

Piers Larnaervon had assumed a pose almost as languid as the Duke's. He smiled at his wife, who nodded encouragingly. "Oh, I beg to differ, Duke. Society will probably embrace them both with open arms." His dark eyes filled with mirth. "Bide-a-wee in Newgate. Lead inmates in escape attempt. (Jolly good that.) Daring rescue by loyal wife. Wild ride through the streets. Why they could become the latest rage."

Vivian took up the joke. "And only think. When he takes his seat in the House, he can sponsor bills for prison reform."

Noelle grinned. "Robin, my love, this may well be a significant turning point in your life."

A coughing spasm shook the Ice King. Noelle rose from her chair. "Robin, will you pour some brandy for Averill. I'll just see about some refreshments, perhaps a cheese and some sweets. And coffee. Would everyone like coffee or tea?"

Averill held up a hand, but his coughing kept him from making his wants clear. Robin held out a pony of brandy and the Duke perforce accepted it.

Noelle gathered her shawl around her and hurried down the hall. In sight of the kitchen door she stopped. Blivens shuffled back and forth outside it. At the sight of her, he froze. He shot a guilty look at the door and drew back against it. "W-what — er — is — do y' need — ?"

She walked straight toward him. He fell back before her. She swung the door open.

"Archie Holmesfield. Seeking employment in kitchens. I knew Averill didn't pay well, but surely you could have found something better."

The two people jumped apart. Mrs. Blivens squawked angrily and whipped her fist around under her apron. A hot flush spread over Holmesfield's features.

"Blivens, y' old fool! Why didn't y' stop 'er?" Mrs. Blivens yelled at her husband.

"Er—stop 'er? Stop milady? I—that is—" Blivens whined from the doorway.

"Exactly, Mrs. Blivens. He couldn't very well stop his lady." Noelle advanced into the kitchen.

Holmesfield stiffened then shrugged. "Thank you for the food, Mrs. Blivens. I'm sure the Duke's coachman and outriders will appreciate it."

"They must have eaten very fast," Noelle said sarcastically. "Not even a crumb to be seen. Mrs. Blivens, you should serve the guests of the house first."

"I've got t' build up th' fire before I can fix anything," the woman muttered.

"On second thought, don't bother." Noelle followed her. "I could tolerate your surly behavior and your poorly prepared food, but I will not tolerate your disloyalty. You are dismissed."

The woman whirled. "You can't dismiss me."

"On the contrary. I have done it. Pack your things and get out. Archie, if you have any sense of decency, you'll give this creature a ride into the village while I prepare some refreshments for my guests."

Mrs. Blivens waved her arms. "I've cooked 'ere for twenty years. The Earl won't let y' just throw me out."

"For most of those my husband was not in residence. He won't support you."

"Er—milady," Blivens whined behind her. "We—that is—I—"

"I'm sorry, Blivens, you'll have to go with your wife."

He shook his head like an old dog. "She ain't no wife o' mine, milady. We just said that when we come 'ere.

363

Th' ol' lord wanted a couple, so we said we was one."

"You old idiot." Mrs. Blivens snatched up a poker from the hearth.

"Help!" Blivens fell back, tangling his leg in the table and fell sprawling. "Don't let 'er get me."

"Holmesfield! This is your doing," Noelle called. "Stop her!"

The factor wrested the weapon from her hand. "Perhaps we'd better get out," he suggested as mildly as he could while using considerable strength to restrain the furious woman. Screeching obscenities, she jabbed her elbow into the factoros ribs. He grunted and let her go.

"Stop 'er! Oh, stop 'er," Blivens cried. He rolled over and tried to crawl beneath the table.

Mrs. Blivens snatched up her long-handled spoon and made for the unfortunate butler.

"What in hell is going on?" Robin appeared in the door of the kitchen.

"I say," Piers Larnaervon peered over his shoulder, "this is better than a mill."

"Oh, Lor' Whitby, Lor' Whitby." Mrs. Blevins burst into crocodile tears. "You'll take me part. Me that's cooked fer y' since y' were a wee bit of a lad."

Robin stared at her as if she were a madwoman. "What is she talking about?"

Noelle laughed. "She wants you to take her part in a bit of a domestic crisis. The Blivenses have just declared themselves unmarried. Mrs. Blivens would like to make herself a widow, it seems."

"And is she going to marry Averill's man?" Robin asked.

Mrs. Blivens shot a terrible look over her shoulder at the unfortunate Holmesfield. She clasped her hands

364

together over her spoon handle. "Oh, y'r lordship," she whined. "They're tellin' lies about me. She's goin' t' dismiss me."

"Which she has a perfect right to do." Robin shrugged. "My wife handles the servants."

"But y'r lordship—"

Blivens crawled from under the table. He climbed laboriously to his feet and managed to pull himself erect. They all waited for what he would say. "Shall I make some tea, milady?"

Robin snorted with laughter. "Good, Blivens. The very thing."

"Is the cook leaving?" Vivian asked from the doorway. "Perhaps I can help. I'm a dab hand at cooking."

"She's really quite good," her husband remarked.

"Naw," Mrs. Blivens bawled. "This is my kitchen."

"Archie," Noelle repeated, "get this woman out of here."

Mrs. Blivens's face turned white. Her shoulders sagged. "I ain't leavin' without m' wages."

Noelle shook her head. "I believe you should apply to Holmesfield for that, Mrs. Blivens. Since he has already paid you something, perhaps he will pay you for whatever else you've done."

More great crocodile tears began to trickle down the fat cheeks. "I'm a good woman, I am."

"Out." Noelle said with a shake of her head.

Holmesfield moved to the kitchen door. "Come, Mrs. Blivens. I'll take you wherever you would like to go."

"This ain't fair," she protested.

The Duke of Averill finally entered. He had opened his mouth to speak, but the sight of his factor stopped him. His features chilled.

Noelle caught the look that passed between them. She marched across the kitchen stopping in front of him. "You should leave too, Averill. You've quite worn out your welcome."

He faced her toe to toe. Intense hatred flashed between them. She withstood it, welcomed it, put her hands on her hips and defied him to do his worst.

Then he dropped his eyes to her belly, its weight seeming too heavy for her figure. His ice blue stare would have peeled the layers of clothing and flesh away if it could.

"Get out," she whispered for his ears only. "Don't come back."

With a strange smile, he bowed to her and to the other occupants of the room. "Till we meet again."

The scream of a maddened stallion shattered the crystalline stillness of the dawn.

Robin sat straight up in bed, the hair rising on the back of his neck. Without thinking he threw himself out of the bed and reached for his pants.

In his bedroom, Piers Larnaervon stirred, then rolled over and sat up groggily, not sure what he had heard. His wife lay curled beside him, her hand curled underneath her chin. He looked around him at the dimness of the room. He must have had a bad dream. He eased back down and closed his eyes.

Robin donned his boots and reached for his shirt. Noelle sat up holding the covers to her chin. "What do you think is happening?"

"Probably nothing." He stuffed the ends of the shirt into his pants. "Go back to sleep." He kissed her swiftly and hurried out.

"Dear liar." She slid her feet over the side of the bed.

As Robin flung open the garden door, wood splintered beneath the crash of iron hooves. He could hear the Cap'n bawling curses. He sprinted for the stables.

He flung one arm around the hitching post to skid to a halt as Romany Prince, Larne's horse, smashed his stall door to kindling and climbed out into the shedrow. Shaking his head and neighing his challenge, he bolted through the stables.

Robin saw Tuck leap aside as the stallion thundered by him, saw the Cap'n climbing to his feet.

The white bars of the stable gate rose before the big horse, but he sailed over it in full stride.

Cursing, Robin dashed down the shedrow. The stable gate latch hung, delaying him for a minute. When he dashed out, the scene beyond the paddock in the home meadow made his blood freeze.

The mares were bunched together in a tight knot, herded there by Romany Knight. His ebony coat glistening with sweat in the dawn light, a living coil of movement and excitement, he whirled and curvetted and snaked. Up on his hind legs he reared, mane swirling over his crested neck.

He came down on the charge, galloping around the mares, bunching them even tighter into a circle. His tail rose straight from his croup flying behind him like a battleflag.

The Cap'n dashed up beside Robin. "Our only chance is to catch him before he gets out."

"Too late."

Romany Prince had halted at the paddock fence. Now with a shake of his head, he whirled and galloped back to the middle of the enclosure. Whirling, he bolted for the five foot fence. His hind quarters bunched under him and again he sailed over it with room to spare.

"Oh, damnation." Robin clapped the Cap'n on the shoulder. "Get the men. Roust 'em out. Get poles, pitchforks, anything. We're going to have to beat them apart."

"Yes, sir."

Knight galloped back to the front of his mares. He reared again, front hooves flailing the air, mane and tail swirling around him. From his stretched jaws came his shrill challenge.

"Dear lord."

Robin turned to find Noelle hurrying panting toward him. "Get back to the house! Get back!" He dashed toward her, waving his arms.

"But — "

"There's nothing you can do. Get back to the house. Rouse Larnaervon if you can. We're going to need all the help we can get."

Prince came to a halt some one hundred yards from his brother. He stretched his neck and lifted his nose to the strengthening breeze. His lip curled back as he scented the gravid mares and the other stallion.

"Maybe they won't fight." Noelle's words were a prayer.

Robin shook his head. "They'll fight. God! How did this happen?"

Prince lowered his head and shook his crest menacingly.

"Hurry. Get Larnaervon." Robin patted her shoulder. "But be careful. Don't hurt yourself."

She looked from him to the horses and back again. Suddenly, she stood on tiptoe and kissed his cheek. "You be careful."

Prince and Knight snaked back and forth neighing shrilly. The lather dripped from Knight's neck and Prince's black coat began to glisten. Ears pricked forward, nostrils flaring, the mares watched with interest.

Drawing in a deep shaky breath, Robin climbed the paddock fence and lowered himself into the meadow.

The Cap'n could be heard in the distance bawling orders to Tuck and Fod. Hardwicke came running, his shirttail flapping. "Glory be!"

"Hi there, Boy!" Robin called as he got closer to Prince. He cautiously approached Larne's horse. "Easy."

If either horse was aware of the men, they made no sign. Suddenly, Prince broke from his stance and lunged forward twenty yards. Robin flung himself at the trailing lead line but missed as it was whisked out of his reach.

Flat on his belly, he watched as Knight screamed again then spun and whipped round the knot of mares. As he flashed past, he nipped Kate on the rump. She whinnied and trotted farther down the pasture. The others followed her as if on tether lines.

Once they were boxed, Knight whirled and came galloping back, head shaking, mane and tail flying. He skidded to a halt fifty yards from Prince. Immediately, he snorted and began to paw the ground.

The Cap'n had managed to unbolt one of the shafts from the governess's cart and arm Tuck with it. The big man came clambering over the fence.

Together he, Robin, and Hardwicke advanced.

"Hardwicke, try to grab that rope on Prince's head-stall," Robin ordered softly. "We'll move between them. Tuck, hit Prince if he tries to charge."

"Yessir."

Knight neighed shrilly. He moved forward and stopped, moved forward again. His eyes rolled showing the white ring. Prince shifted his weight forward. His hind legs stretched back like a huge cat. His head stretched out to the length of his neck. He bared his teeth.

The Cap'n came with a bucket, swishing oats in it. The mare's ears pricked toward him, but the stallions made no sign that they had heard. Fod started to mount the fence with the second shaft in his hands. It slid beneath the top bar and stopped him for a minute.

"I can get it, sir." Hardwicke slipped forward and caught the lead line. He hauled back with all his might. He might as well have been pulling at a mountain. The horse remained immobile.

Suddenly, the muscles beneath the black hide bunched. With a shake of his head, he reared and plunged forward.

Robin waved his arms and shouted, then leaped aside at the last minute. Tuck hauled back with the carriage shaft. It never came round. The stallion's chest caught him and threw him back and the hooves drove into his chest.

The man grunted as he fell backward arms outflung.

"Tuck!" Fod abandoned the second shaft and scrambled over the fence. "Tuck!"

The lead line jerked Hardwicke forward a couple of steps before it was ripped out of his hands.

Knight screamed his anger and plunged forward.

They thundered head on then each swerved aside and slashed with bared teeth at the other's back. Knight's teeth tore a strip off Prince's withers.

Blood spurted from the wound and coursed down the belly, but the horse did not seem to feel any pain. They whirled on each other, circling like dervishes, reaching for the broad backs.

Robin caught up the carriage shaft and ran toward them alone. Hardwicke sat up and spat grass and sod out of his teeth.

Fod fell to his knees beside his friend. "Tuck!" he cried. "Goddammit!"

Prince came in low snapping. His teeth closed over the heavy muscle in Knight's left leg just below the chest. Squealing in fury, Knight reared, taking his opponent up with him. He wrapped his right leg around Prince's neck and flailed, raking flesh from the bones.

The stallions staggered like wrestlers, and Prince's grip was broken. Knight whirled away and kicked out with both hind feet. They struck Prince broadside with a thud like a base drum.

Robin swung the shaft at Knight's hindquarters. It connected solidly, but the maddened animal paid no attention.

Blood coursed freely down his left leg and from numerous wounds along his spine. Its smell was sickly sweet on the morning air mingling with the powerful odors of the horses.

Robin brought the shaft back to swing again. The two plunged away, snapping and fighting as they galloped down the pasture.

"Whittcombstone!" Robin heard Larnaervon's voice from somewhere behind him.

"Come on!" he yelled.

Larnaervon tugged the other shaft through the fence and came running. Together the two dashed down the pasture after the animals. The Cap'n and Hardwicke followed them at a cautious distance.

Again the stallions came together. Rearing and staggering forward, they threw their forelegs over each other's shoulders and kicked and pounded each others backs. Their angry shrieks rang scarcely louder than their blows.

The battle seemed joined interminably when Prince staggered back. Swift as a snake, Knight drove in, his jaws closing on the windpipe, teeth grinding for the jugular.

"Hyaaah!" Larnaervon screamed lashing at Knight's head with the shaft. Robin leaped for the rope that dangled from his horse's headstall and dragged himself into range of the front hooves.

Prince half-reared, but Knight's jaws were cutting off his wind. A shudder went through him. Clearly, he was in trouble.

"Other side," Robin yelled. Risking everything, he slapped his right hand over Knight's nose and squeezed the nostrils together. At the same time he twisted the rope around his left hand and brought the knot up into the sensitive chin groove.

For several seconds the tableau stood frozen. Then Knight's jaws relaxed. When he pulled in a great lungful of air, Larnaervon was able to jerk Prince out of his grip. Hardwicke ripped his shirt off and threw it over Knight's head, blinding him.

Prince lashed out with his hind legs, but Larnaervon punched his fist into the horse's muzzle. The Cap'n threw his coat over Prince's head and between the two of them they led him away.

Noelle and Vivian stood together by the fence. Noelle wept tears she could not stem. Vivian's face was white as chalk. When she saw her husband and the Cap'n urging the bleeding horse across the meadow, she rushed to open the gate.

When Noelle attempted to follow her, she found she had to hang onto the fence with every step. She was panting.

"Stay back!" Vivian waved her away angrily. "You can't help."

Noelle wrapped her arm around the top board and sobbed.

As men and horse hurried through, Vivian slammed the gate shut. Nausea rose in her as blood ran in streams over the stallion's body and front legs and spattered her husband's white shirt. "Are you hurt?" she cried.

"No! But Prince may be bad." Together they led the horse into the stable.

Noelle managed to open the gate again and start across the meadow. Robin had tied Hardwicke's shirt firmly across Knight's eyes and led the animal to a tree. He was in the process of making the rope fast when he stopped and stared at it. He cursed vilely.

Noelle hobbled up behind him. "What is it?"

Robin spun around. He looked like murder personified. Spattered with blood and lather, his stubble blackish-blue in the rising sun, his face contorted in a hideous scowl. He thrust the end of the rope toward her.

"It's been cut," he snarled.

Twenty-one

Fod hunched over Tuck, cradling his friend's still body in his arms. "Damme, y' friggin' bastid," he growled. "Talk t' me. Don't y' lie there like a bleedin' stone."

Robin led Noelle to his side. While she waited, he dropped down on his haunches and pressed his fingertips against Tuck's throat. No pulse beat. He slid his hand inside the coat and felt for the heartbeat. The massive chest was still.

Fod's eyes blazed at Robin. " 'E don't 'ave a mark on 'im that I can tell. Why don't 'e wake up?"

Robin pushed his fingers into Tuck's dusty graying hair. Nowhere beneath the tangled locks could he find an indentation where a hoof might have stove in the skull. Nor could he find a break in the skin. At last he sighed. "The horse crashed into him. He was thrown down and stepped on. Here. Let me see."

Reluctantly, Fod laid his friend down and rocked back on his heels. Noelle put her hand on his shoulder. Robin tore open Tuck's shirt. Over the heart was a dark red hoofprint.

Robin lowered his ear to the spot, then raised up and shook his head. "I've seen something like this once before. A cannon exploded. The breech struck a soldier a terrible blow to the chest. He didn't know what hit him. Even though the thing doesn't break the skin or even break bones, it stops the heart."

Fod growled like an animal. He heaved himself to his feet shaking off Noelle's hand. With fists clenched he started for Romany Knight where the horse stood blindfolded and snubbed to the tree.

"No!" Noelle hurried after him and caught his arm. "No. You mustn't."

"I'll kill that damned 'orse!" He shrugged her off again. Shoulders hunched, he lumbered forward.

"No. It wasn't his fault."

" 'Ell it wasn't. I'll kill 'im." He pulled a long knife from his belt.

"Noelle!" Robin lunged to his feet.

"The rope was cut!" she screamed, throwing her arms around his arm and pulling back. "Someone cut the horse loose, maybe even led him here, so the stallions would fight."

Fod's anger seared her skin. "Y're lyin'. Bleedin' gentry cares more about their friggin' 'orses than poor Tuck." He tried to shake her off.

"No! Fod! No! Please. Listen to me. Let's think about this. Tuck was innocent, but so are the horses. Someone else is to blame." She lost her footing, but she would not let go of his arm.

375

"Don't do something you'll be sorry for."

He stared down at her, his beady eyes red with rage and grief. "Yer friggin' father."

"He's not my father."

"He's a friggin' dook."

She shrugged helplessly. "Please listen, Fod. Please listen to me. We are just as upset as you are. Tuck was a good man. I remember how he helped me, how you both helped me get Robin out of Newgate. I valued him. I value you. We won't let this go unpunished. I promise you."

Fod stared at the horse. Suddenly, his face twisted. His jaws clamped together over a tearing, snubbing sound rumbling out of his throat. He snapped his head to one side and wiped a hand across his face.

She put her arm around his shoulders. "Oh, Fod. I'm so sorry."

Robin slowed his steps so as not to intrude upon the man's grief. Piers Larne came loping across the field to him. "Is there anything I can do?"

Robin turned to meet him. "One of my men has been killed," he said in a low voice.

"Oh no!" Larne looked at the dead man. "I'm sorry."

"And Knight's rope was cut."

"My God!" Larnaervon looked aghast at Robin. "Quite a vicious enemy you've got there."

"So it would seem."

"Whom do you suspect?"

"Averill."

"Your wife's father!"

Robin did not bother to explain the particulars.

"He has a peculiar turn of mind. I believe he's mad. And his madness has lighted on me and Noelle. He would have enjoyed knowing that our stallion was killed."

Larnaervon whistled softly. "Will you bring him before the magistrates for your man's death?"

Noelle had succeeded in getting Fod turned around and now she led him back across the meadow. They heard Piers's question.

Robin shrugged. "I can't prove anything. The rope was cut. That much is certain. I have it for all to see. But anyone could have cut it. Poachers. Mischief makers. Horse thieves. Knight was almost stolen once before in London."

"But Averill was here just last night," Noelle cried. "We know he did it. Or sent Holmesfield."

"His being in the vicinity proves nothing. So were dozens of other people. For instance, how do we know that Larnaervon did not try to steal the stallion to get him back?" He looked to Piers. "No offense intended."

"None taken."

"And so far as we know, he left," Robin continued. "Even if he stayed at the inn and went in and out all night long, that still doesn't prove that he was out cutting Knight loose and leading him back to set him on Romany Prince."

"What about Holmesfield?"

"Unless someone actually saw him cut the rope, we can't prove a thing."

Fod growled softly. His rough hands flexed.

Noelle put her hand over one of them. "We'll find a way. I promise."

"Let's go up the house," Vivian suggested. "Nothing more can be done by standing around in various stages of undress."

Robin nodded. "I'll set Hardwicke and the Cap'n to take Tuck up. Then the Cap'n can ride for the magistrate."

"And the veterinarian," Piers interjected. "One of my men can ride with your man to fetch him."

Robin rubbed his forehead. His head all around the scar was beginning to ache. He moved to put his hand on Fod's shoulder. "We'll send for a minister as well," he told the man gently. "We'll bury him in the family plot at Whitby unless his family wants otherwise. They'll have to be notified."

" 'E didn't have no family that I ever 'eard," Fod muttered. "Only me." He started toward his friend's body, but Noelle caught him.

"Fod, come into the kitchen. We're all going to sit in there where we can talk this through. Since Mrs. Blivens has gone, I'll have to fix us breakfast."

His narrow eyes slitted more tightly. "When did th' ol' flat-back run out on y'?"

"Last night. Or at least she was dismissed last night."

He sank his head lower between his shoulder blades, but said nothing more. She put her arm through his as if he were a gentleman and led him across the meadow.

Midway, they met the Cap'n and Hardwicke coming back. The Cap'n took a look at Fod's face and at the still figure lying in the pasture. He patted the hunched shoulder.

* * *

The Larnaervons departed shortly after breakfast. Piers left a purse to pay for Tuck's funeral and to compensate the grieving Fod.

"We'll return under happier circumstances," Vivian promised Noelle. "And you must come to visit us next year at Stone Glenn. It is a beautiful place in the summer, not at all like Larne's drafty castle. Am I right?"

He grinned. "Of course. I only married her for her estate."

Noelle turned her face into her husband's shoulder when they had waved them off. "I'm so tired, I don't think I can climb the porch," she murmured. "Averill has gone too far this time."

Her husband lifted her in his arms. "Don't let's think about Averill."

"I'm too heavy," she protested.

"I can manage to stagger up four steps and down a short hall. Especially since the hall is short."

Once inside her bedroom, he stretched her out on the bed. She did look pale. Dark circles gave her eyes a sunken appearance. She lay limply on the unmade bed. He pulled the covers up and turned to leave.

"Stay with me." She did not open her eyes.

"You need to get some rest. I'd disturb you."

"I can't rest. I'm so furious, my heart is pounding. My stomach is roiling. The baby is kicking and tumbling." To illustrate her statement, her stomach sank on the left and punched up on the right.

He reseated himself and rested his hand on his child's body. It moved again, this time kicking so hard his wife jumped. He chuckled. "I'm sorry. I'd take him if I could."

"Just stay with me. Until I can get myself under control." She opened her eyes. They glistened with tears. "Please, Robin."

"I'm filthy as a field hand," he protested all the while pulling off his boots. With a sigh he slid beneath the covers. She turned herself spoon fashion against him. He crooked one arm under her head and pushed his thighs up under her buttocks. "You'll be warm now," he breathed in her ear. "Try to relax."

She closed her eyes, but Fod's tormented face and Averill's mocking one kept flashing before her eyes. "He's trying to destroy us," she whispered. "And I don't know why."

Her husband did not pretend not to know whom she was talking about. He stroked her hip. "Ssh, don't think about it. He's mad. If the stallions had killed each other, we still wouldn't have been harmed."

"Unless, like poor Tuck, you got in the way."

"That's a long shot. He wouldn't count on two maddened stallions to do his work for him? I could have been killed easily in London rather then thrown in Newgate. No. He doesn't want me dead. Tuck was an accident."

"Not that he cares," Noelle mourned. "What does he want? Is he mad?"

Robin shrugged. "Most certainly and dangerously so. Everything he's done is vicious malice that's hurting innocent people."

"It's just as Fod says. The gentry don't — as a rule — care what happens to a poor man." She rubbed her cheek against his elbow.

He began to stroke her back. Once the baby rested on the mattress instead of her backbone, it calmed. They lay still for long minutes. At last she whispered, "I want you."

His heart skipped, then stepped up its pace. He had left her alone for over a month. His intention was to remain celibate until her physician released her. Her breasts were full, swollen, their nipples stiff. Her belly was a hard mound. His hand slid over it. The baby was still.

"I —" he hesitated. "I don't know."

She stirred under his hand. "I ache for you. I feel like a tight-wound clock. Oh, please. I feel so hot."

He caressed her breast voluptuously, then moved his hand down over her belly. She sighed and twisted as he pulled up her skirt. She had not donned her petticoats nor drawers in her haste to get out to the paddock.

He slid his hand between her legs. She was wet and hot. He swallowed hard as his own manhood throbbed response that was almost painful. He told himself he could bear it, would bear it, to give her release. Closing his mind to the powerful attraction of her, he slid his fingers between her sensitive lips. There he tantalized her.

"Damn you," she groaned and wiggled her hips so in an effort to find his fingers.

He caught her hair with his other hand and pulled it back away from her face. He put his mouth to her ear. His hot breath blew into it making her set her teeth on a keening cry at this new torture. His tongue circled the shell. His teeth set in her lobe.

"Damn you. I'll murder you," she whispered.

"Not if I kill you first." He bit a little harder, but only a little harder. The heel of his hand pressed down on the center of her pleasure at the same time his fingers slid into her.

"You devil." She turned over on her back. Her hands sought his face. "Kiss me."

His rod leaped against her thigh. She was too close, too seductive. He could smell and taste the arousal of her. She was more exciting than she had ever been before. The lushness of her, the heavy breasts, the straining belly, far from being ugly were incredibly exciting.

He had to get away, but how could he when his hands were wrapped in her hair and buried in her body? He had to or he would take her.

He sat up or tried to, but her arms slipped round his neck. She lifted her breasts to his chest. The turgid nipples rubbed against him. He could feel them through the thin material of his shirt. They rasped and pressed and burned him in a fire that curled and leaped.

"Noelle," he gasped. "Madam Wife."

"Please, oh please, Robin."

He fumbled at the fastening of his breeches. Mouth glued to hers, drinking her kisses, he pushed his clothing down around his hips. She spread her legs, digging her heels into the bed, pushing up.

Shaking, he pushed himself out of her arms, and positioned himself between her legs. "I'll be careful," he promised. "I won't lean my weight on you. If I hurt you, just say. And I'll stop instantly."

"Please," she whimpered. "Please."

Shuddering with the intensity of his feelings, he pushed into her. She closed round him. He straddled her legs so her thighs were between his. Her body throbbed. Her muscles rippled up the length of his shaft. She was tight and short.

"Oh," she sobbed. "Oh, oh, oh. I love you, love you, loveyou, loveyou."

The words baptized him in pleasure. He moved slowly and leisurely, his whole body trembling, tormenting himself with the exquisite sensations.

"Loveyou loveyou."

"And I love you," he whispered never ceasing his movements.

"Loveyou love—" She stiffened and gave a cry that tore out of her heart. Her teeth bit it off. Her back arched. She rose half off thc pillow, her eyes fastened on his face. Then her eyes glazed. She sank back. Her eyelids fluttered closed.

His own climax was long and satisfying. It began as a ripple and grew to a flood. It became a series of tiny explosions that grew closer together and gained in intensity. He clutched huge handfuls of the sheet and leaned back away from her lest he collapse on top of her.

Then with a sigh he rolled to the side and lay

panting. Though the sun was strong in the window, he twisted himself around, pulled her into his arms, and covered them both. His last thought was how Averill was responsible for the most wonderful thing in his life.

Six weeks later, when Noelle rose from her chair at the dinner table, hot liquid gushed down her legs. She stared at the pool around her feet. "Robin," she whispered.

"What is it, my dear? My God." He reached for her, but she fended him off.

"I should walk to the bed. In fact, I should walk a lot. That's what I've heard. Perhaps a walk to the stables and back?"

"Walk? Walk to the stables! Are you mad?"

Exasperated, she snapped at him, "No. Help me."

Suddenly, he felt dizzy. He had to catch himself against the table. "I'll send Hardwicke for the doctor," he muttered.

"Are you all right?"

"Yes, perfectly. I just got out of my chair too fast." He straightened and took a step toward her. "Let me help you to your bed. I think you need to lie down."

She waved him away. "I've been talking to several of the women in the village. They say that a woman needs to walk."

"But what about lying down and resting and conserving your strength?"

"It stands to reason if I'm standing, the baby's

going to drop out. Things fall down. That should help."

He turned ghastly pale beneath his dark tan. His alarmed gaze flicked to the floor at her feet. "Fall!? Down!?"

"Go right now." Putting both hands in the small of her back, she straightened herself carefully. "Send for the doctor. I'll meet you at the front door."

He put his hand to his head. He was thirty-nine, almost forty years old, his wife was twenty. He should be telling her what to do.

"The doctor," she reminded him, wincing as she spoke.

He snapped to attention. "Are you hurting?"

"Not yet."

"Good lord." Familiar with pain himself, the thought of her enduring it made him weak.

Still, he stood rooted to the spot uncertain what to do, as she took a couple of steps. She wrinkled her nose and sighed. "Perhaps, after all, you should help me to my room."

"Right away." At last. He managed to smile faintly. She had made the proper request.

She walked down the hall quite normally, her hand wrapped around his arm. He had put her on his right side and he never took his eye off her. To Blivens he yelled, "Send for Hardwicke."

He opened the door. She stepped inside and immediately began to hike up her skirts.

"Oh, God," he whispered. "Is it coming?"

She paused with her skirts up on both sides. "No, Robin. It'll be a long time yet. I'm just taking these drawers off. They're wet."

She could swear his skin flushed. She was sure he blinked.

"Where is your maid?" He looked around wildly. "Where is that girl Lily?"

She gasped as she struggled with the ties. "She's at her mother's. Her older sister is having a baby."

He held out his hands, realized they were shaking and dropped them to his sides. "Oh, God."

She teetered, the distribution of her weight disturbing her balance.

"Can I help?" He whipped a hand out to her stomach. It was hard as stone and still. He trembled as if he were facing cannon. "Hold still." He stepped back and started for the chest.

"No." She stopped him. "I'm not going to put a clean pair back on. They'd just get in the way."

"Noelle," he pleaded. "You're supposed to be lying down. This is going to hurt. I've heard—" He swallowed hard. This experience was turning him into a school boy. "—that women are in terrible pain for hours—sometimes all day and all night."

"Well, of course, it will hurt," she agreed, biting her lower lip. "But several old women in Whitby told me that it's more like work. That's why it's called labor."

He pressed his hand to his forehead. "What did the doctor tell you?"

"He really didn't have much to say. That's why I talked to some women who had had babies. They all agreed that men really don't know much about it after all." She let the drawers drop to the floor and held out her hand to him. He caught it and she stepped out of the pool of crumpled material, careful not to stumble.

"Let me help you to the bed," he begged again. "Or at least sit down in a chair. I'll open the windows. You can look out at the garden."

She shot him a disdainful look. "I'm going to look at the garden up close. I hope you'll come with me."

At that instant a pain hit her. Her fingernails dug into his hand. Her breath whistled in through her teeth. He sprang forward and closed his arms around her waist. "Let me get you to bed."

"No!" She hung on him as the pain eased away. "No. It's over now. Let's walk."

"Oh, God." He took his arms away slowly as if she might topple over at any minute.

"Now," she said in almost her normal voice. "Let's just stroll among the flowers."

"But shouldn't we boil water and — get the bed ready and — " He racked his brain for the bits and pieces of masculine gossip heard round the campfires on the Peninsula. " — and get a leather strap for you to bite?" He stopped. "My God! That sounds awful. For heaven's sake, Noelle."

She opened the door. "Robin, come for a walk."

The Cap'n and Fod met Hardwicke on the stoop. Blivens, who had been watching through the windows, opened the door. The three had the news before the Earl and Countess heard it.

The doctor was away on a call, but his boy

would go fetch him. He would come as soon as possible.

" 'Tain't good," the Cap'n observed worriedly. "The lady's been walkin' up and down for a couple o' hours now. That'll sometime bring th' babe quicklike."

"Want me t' go after th' doc an' bring 'im back right now?" Fod offered. He seldom spoke since Tuck's death. He exercised horses in the mornings, cleaned out stalls in the afternoons, and did whatever Hardwicke or the Cap'n told him to do; but he had the air of a man waiting. Whenever a visitor appeared in the lane, he studied the newcomer with cold intensity.

"M-maybe it'll be all right," Blivens stammered. "When he hears it's milady, he'll probably come immediately."

"An' maybe not," Fod grunted.

Robin exploded at Hardwicke's news. "Good God, man. You should have ridden with the boy to get the doctor."

The groom blinked. "I never thought of that."

"You idiot."

"Shall I go back, milord?"

"What would you do? There'll be no one at the doctor's."

Hardwicke backed away and retreated down the path.

Robin had both his arms around his wife. Another pain wrenched her. She was red in the face, her breath coming short, her footsteps dragging.

When it had passed, he stooped to slip his arm under her knees.

"No. I can walk."

"But I can't. Not anymore." He lifted her in his arms. "I can't stand another minute."

"Robin—"

"My son is not going to be born in the middle of a shell walk." Even as he started with her, she stiffened. Her arms almost strangled him.

"That was a good one," she moaned when he laid her on the bed.

"Or a bad one, depending on point of view." He wiped the sweat from her brow with the edge of the pillowcase and took her hands. "Noelle, we may have to do this ourselves. The doctor may not arrive."

"And it's all my fault." She managed a tight grin.

"We'll lay blame later. For now, what can I do?"

Another contraction shook her. She threw back her head and yelled.

When she looked for him, he was on his knees beside the bed, his expression agonized.

"I think you'd better get my skirts out of the way and get ready to catch."

"God in heaven." He staggered to his feet.

She screamed again.

He looked around him. There was no one else. No time. If she were a mare—Horses were all he knew. He caught the damp skirt and petticoats and lifted them over the enormous mound of his wife's belly.

Her hips were spread wide, wider than he could

have imagined. He pushed her legs up out of the way. She was panting and with every breath her body seemed to stretch more.

His eye focused on the shining redness between her legs and then he had to bow his head on the bed. He was the consummate soldier, who had seen men blown to pieces in battle, who had been covered with blood himself, who had been wounded and stitched back together. He had to fight off weakness.

"Damn you," she screamed. "Don't you faint on me."

His head snapped up. She could not stretch any more.

Suddenly, she cursed. "It hurts. Oh, God, it hurts." With both hands she grabbed the head of the bed. A scream. Her heels dug into the bed.

He could see something dark glistening between her legs. It took him a minute to realize he was looking at the top of the baby's head. "I can see him," he cried. "I can see him."

She screamed again. Her skin stretched impossibly, tore. The head slid through, streaked with his mother's blood.

At first Robin thought something was wrong. His son had no face. Then he laughed at himself. The baby was born facedown. "He's through," he told Noelle unnecessarily. "His head's through."

"Take him," she gritted.

"Take him?"

"Yes, dammit. Take him."

Hands trembling, Robin supported the little slippery head. His fingers found the little button

390

of a nose first and then the mouth and chin. Hot liquid ran out over his hand. He could swear he heard the baby whimper. "Shall I pull?"

"No," she gasped. "No. No. Yes! But not the neck! By the shoulder."

"Shoulder? But I'll have to—I don't—" Swallowing hard, Robin slid his fingers into the cavity of her body and found the little shoulder.

She moaned and grunted and pushed.

The baby slipped free.

Robin closed his eyes. From out of nowhere a prayer whirled round in his brain. He lifted the baby, more liquid ran out. He heard a squeak. The tiny ribs heaved. He turned his son over on his back. His mouth fell open. He blinked, then looked at his wife, a comical expression on his face.

She let her hands drop from the headboard. Her head slumped to one side. She caught a glimpse of Robin's face. "What is it? What's wrong?"

"It's a girl."

Twenty-two

She was named Susannah Claire for no one in particular. And she was a perfect picture of the Turk. From the day of her birth, her head was covered with coal-black hair. Her eyes, when she opened them, were navy blue that darkened within weeks until neither doting parent could remember when they had not been black.

When Lady Susannah was asleep, her black lashes lay softly curling on her creamy cheeks. Her perfectly arched little eyebrows would draw together in a frown when she yawned or when she was hungry.

Swiftly and devotedly, her father and mother set about spoiling her. They refused to leave the baby in the nursery at night although they had hired a nurse. She slept in a cradle in her mother's chamber. Nor would Robin stay in his own room at night.

Love and tenderness and warmth were in the adjoining chamber. They drew him like a magnet.

Lady Susannah could hardly manage a whimper before one of her parents was up and bringing her to their bed. While Noelle lay on her side and the baby nursed from the breast, Robin would play with his daughter's perfect toes and fingers. He was an absolute fool about her fingers. He never tired of thrusting his own finger into them and feeling her grip him.

Other times he would watch Susannah nurse, pulling aside the blanket to watch her little stomach fill up. He would grin at Noelle when the baby would go to sleep and the nipple would slip from her rosebud mouth. He would even change the nappy.

"No fool like an old fool," he whispered to his black-haired daughter, who lay in perfect contentment, her eyes focused on the halo of a candle. He lifted her onto his shoulder and rubbed her back as he walked her to the cradle. When she yawned, her milk-sweet breath brushed his neck.

Lady Susannah was three months old when she was dressed in a hand-tucked and embroidered dress and cap tied with silk satin ribbons. On a matching pillow she was carried into the village church to be christened. On that morning she smiled so sweetly up into her father's face that she completely unmanned him. During the entire service he stood with tears trickling down his cheek.

At the sight Noelle bowed her head. Her own emotion was doubly powerful for it combined her love for her miraculous daughter with the equally miraculous change wrought in her husband.

* * *

Robin drove the phaeton, rented for the occasion of Susannah's christening, past the front door and down to the stables. Noelle looked at him inquiringly.

"I have a surprise." His delighted grin showed his strong white teeth.

Noelle had never noticed his teeth until his daughter's birth. Now he seemed to be smiling all the time. "There's a surprise at the stable?"

He nodded. "Besides I promised the men that I'd bring Susannah down to see them in her new dress."

Her eyebrow rose. "Oh, you promised them that, did you?"

He shrugged. "She's all dressed up. Every little girl should have a chance to show off her beautiful dress."

"And every father should have a chance to show off his beautiful daughter."

He grinned again as he clucked to the horse.

The Cap'n and Hardwicke came forward to meet the phaeton. Scowling ferociously, Fod took the horse's head.

"Black hair," the Cap'n remarked immediately. He flicked a glance at Robin's head. "Lucky she's got her mother's looks."

Robin cuffed him on the shoulder and laughed.

"She's beautiful, ma'am." Hardwicke craned his neck to look into the baby's face. Then he gasped as the baby opened her eyes and smiled at him. "Just beautiful." He stepped back, sniffling, his mouth tight.

Robin took the baby from his wife and the Cap'n helped her down. Together they walked into the stable, followed closely by the men.

At Kate's stall they stopped. "There she is," Robin announced unnecessarily.

"Oh, she's beautiful!" Noelle exclaimed. Eyes shining, she leaned over the stall door to get a good look at the black foal asleep in the hay.

At her words the filly's ear twitched back, one eye opened. She raised her head and stared into space as if contemplating her next move. Kate dropped her head and snuffled at her daughter's body. The filly bleated and began the crazy, shaky process of organizing her legs and getting to her feet.

"She was born last night," the Cap'n said softly. "She's been up and down twice already."

"Well, of course," Noelle chuckled. "Little girls have to eat to grow big. Their little tummies can't hold very much at a time, so they have to keep after it."

The filly took two staggering steps. Kate presented her side and her eager daughter dived under. Noelle laughed again as the bottlebrush tail began to wave ecstatically.

"Well, there's one thing Susannah can't do," she told Robin.

He looked over her shoulder. "You call that talent. Our daughter makes windmills of her legs and arms. She can get them all going at once, can't you, sweetheart?"

The baby cooed her assent. The adults all smiled.

"What shall we name her?"

Noelle looked at him in surprise. "She's your colt. You should be the one to name her."

"Nonsense. This is your dream. You name her."

Noelle looked back in the stall. The foal's tiny hooves pranced in the straw keeping the wobbly legs straight if slightly spraddled. Kate turned her head to bestow "horsy" kisses and nibbles along the bony little hindquarters.

"That mare's going to be a good mother," Hardwicke observed. "Who'd have thought it? She was such a nervous piece."

"A lot of 'nervous pieces' make wonderful mothers," Robin replied.

Noelle's ears grew hot. She stared at the wavy black coat that would be shiny as polished ebony in a few months. The first colt of Black Horse Stud. Not a spot of white marked the foal, not even on the forehead. All four hooves were blue black. Noelle sighed with pleasure. "She has a Knight for a father and a Shrew for a mother. I could make something dramatic out of that, but I want her name to mean more than that." She closed her eyes. "We'll call her Best Shot. Because that's what we took—our best shot. And look how it all came out?"

"Best Shot." He chuckled. "Best Shot. That's good. She is our best shot."

The foal finished her dinner and lifted her head. She tried to turn around, bumped into her mother, and bounced sideways, catching herself on spraddly legs.

Noelle shook her head with a fond smile.

"Can't quite manage all that stuff hanging down underneath you, can you?"

Best Shot blinked. Kate the Shrew licked the top of the foal's neck. The swipe almost overset her baby again. Then suddenly, exhausted with the entire process, the little horse dropped forward on her knees and collapsed in the hay. Before their eyes she curled her head over her hindquarters and went to sleep.

Robin looked down at his daughter. "This one's about to go to sleep too. We'd better get her back to the house."

After a last look at their first filly, the start of their stables, Noelle and Robin walked down the shedrow. Fod lounged in the entrance. His narrow eyes bored holes in the pillow, but he would not move.

Noelle tucked her arm in Robin's and led him close by the stableman. "Look, Fod," she invited. "Isn't she beautiful?"

He stood still as a stone. Unable to say anything, he nevertheless looked into the tiny face.

A crow cawed overhead in passing. The baby started and opened her eyes. She looked up into Fod's unshaven, nut-brown face. She blinked lazily and then smiled. Calm acceptance of anyone her mother and father presented her to glowed from their indigo depths.

Fod swallowed hard. He hunched his shoulders as if to ward off a blow. He tried to speak, closed his mouth, then opened it again. "Nice."

Noelle smiled. Together she and Robin walked back to the house each aware that their daughter had been paid a compliment richer than rubies.

"I have some things that belong to you." Noelle stood in the doorway a box in her hands.

Robin pushed back his chair and came to take it from her. "For me. You shouldn't have."

She followed him and stood beside him as he set it on the table. "Actually, I probably should have given it to you long ago. It may make you angry when you open it."

He raised one black eyebrow. "What could make me angry with you?"

She put her hand on the box to keep him from opening it. "Don't think I'm a saint just because I've had a baby. I'm no saint."

"This sounds serious." He eyed the box curiously. "It certainly looks innocent enough."

"Remember the circumstances under which we married."

"I've tried to put all that out of my mind." Leaving the box, he walked to the window. "I treated you very badly."

"No worse than I treated you."

"I had the weight on you," he reminded her in boxer's parlance. "You were badly outmatched."

"Yes. But you could have hurt me. You could have done all sorts of terrible things to me. I was afraid you would. I wouldn't have been surprised if you had. But you didn't."

He waited.

"Instead you brought me home and gave me the horses."

"And in exchange you gave me Susannah," he reminded her.

She fiddled with the latch on the box. "She belongs to both of us. She's the best parts of both of us. Do you agree?"

"Indubitably."

"So I'm returning something that I've held for a year now." She lifted the lid and stepped back.

He came forward slowly. It was filled with papers. Then he recognized them. Dark color flushed his cheeks. He unfolded the first. "My notes."

She nodded. "I made Averill give them to me. Since it was my money that paid the debts, I wanted them. To my way of thinking it was my only safeguard."

"Would you have used them against me?" He dropped the paper back into the box.

Unflinching, she met his gaze. "Yes."

The silence grew between them.

"Averill had threatened that he would marry me to a man he deemed suitable. I knew that the marriage would be bad, but I didn't have any idea how bad it could be until—"

"Until you saw me."

"Never. Never." She stamped her foot. "I wasn't going to say that. Don't you ever put those words in my mouth. I have never cared what you looked like."

"You didn't care what I looked like?"

She flung up her hands in exasperation. "Robin Whittcombstone, must I have that engraved on my tombstone? I don't care what you look like. I made him give me the notes before I ever saw you. I wanted them because he told me you were a gambler and a drunkard. I hoped to use them to control you."

Robin returned to the table. He sifted through the notes. Some were folded. Others were flat. He could read in them the whole dark period of his life. The years of pain and shame. "Have you read them?" he asked harshly. "Have you toted up your treasure?"

"When have I had time?" she jeered. "What with doing all the work of this place and being pregnant, not to mention being kidnapped and rescuing you from gaol, when have I had time to read anything? I put them in the bottom of my trunk and left them there."

"It has been awful for you," he admitted humbly.

"And wonderful. Don't forget wonderful."

He scooped up the papers, put them back in the box. Firmly, he closed the lid. With a formal bow he presented them to her. "You keep them. They're yours. Your money bought them, I remember."

She put her hands on her hips and lifted her chin. "I don't need them," she declared. "I can control you in other ways."

The black eyebrow rose. "Is that what you do to me?"

"Absolutely. I control you." She laughed. "You can't even sleep alone anymore. You have to come to my bed every night and lie beside me. You wake up three and four times to bring the baby to me." She lifted her hand and studied her finger-nails. "What's more, you haven't said a word about going to London for the little Season."

He tossed the box onto the couch as casually as if it were valueless. Then he dropped into a crouch and moved toward her, arms spread as if she were a horse he was trying to herd back into its stall. "You realize that I'm not going to let a statement like that go unpunished."

"I'm not afraid of you." She took her cue from him and side-stepped. He followed her.

"You'd better be."

She giggled and lunged in the other direction. "No."

He followed her, but she stepped back, ducked, and darted past him. He whirled and caught her round the waist. Her feet shot out from under her as he hauled her back against him.

"No. Don't you dare! This is embarrassing. Ow!"

"Control me!" He set his mouth to the side of her throat. Like a stallion with his mare, he kissed and sucked at the throbbing pulsebeat.

"Ow! Let me go."

He growled menacingly and shook his head. The hint of whisker stubble rasped against her soft skin. "Not on your life. You'll get what's coming to you."

"Whiskery kisses! Over my bleeding body. Help! Hel—"

He twisted her around and stopped her cries with a kiss. In fact, he did not stop kissing her until she had wrapped her arms around his neck.

When he drew back it was to say, "Who's in control?"

"Not me," she whispered. "And surely not you." She twined her leg around his thigh and pressed her body to his. Her hip ground against his belly. Her tongue slid into his gasping mouth.

They swayed locked together in an embrace that set them both trembling. He recognized that she spoke the truth. He was no longer in control of his emotions or his body. He could barely think. Pure desire blazed through him. His growl changed to a groan. "Madam Wife."

She rubbed her hip against his belly. "Lord Husband."

A couple of strides and he set her onto the edge of the table. Kissing her hard, he knelt between her legs and lifted her skirts. His fingers tantalized her as they took their time parting her flesh.

"Robin," she whispered. "Don't."

"Ssssh." The hot breath sliding from between his teeth prepared her most secret flesh for his mouth.

A pain grew in the pit of her belly. His mouth sent lightning shocks to the nerves in her arms, her legs. The very tips of her fingers and toes felt them. She wanted to push him away. She wanted to clamp him to her. The tension set her muscles vibrating, weakness left them hanging loose.

She had slumped back until she lay across the table, her toes unable to touch the floor, her buttocks clamped to the hardwood, her breasts arched to the ceiling. She was skin, no muscles, no bones, only fiery liquid that moved in rhythm to his mouth.

In one tiny corner of her mind, she could distinguish his tongue and his lips and his teeth, his hot breath, the rasping of his chin. But only a tiny corner. The rest was pure ecstasy.

"Robin," she whispered. "Robin." And then as she exploded, "Robin."

She was barely aware when he rose shakily to his feet and stepped between her legs. Her open body closed round him.

He thrust himself into its steaming depths and bent over to kiss her. His mouth was wet with the taste of her. The same corner of her mind remarked that she had tasted herself. The rest of her was unable to do more than lie still, to let her muscles do the work of love.

With his mouth on hers, his hands under her shoulders, he moved once, twice. Then he too surged forward discovering his own ecstasy.

"What do you want to do with these?" Robin asked his wife.

She reclined on the couch, her arms behind her head. She smiled lazily. "Burn them."

He grinned. "It'll heat up the room."

She smiled lazily. "It'll cool down—again."

He carried them to the fireplace and turned the box upside down. "Are you sure you don't need them as insurance."

She laughed. "I have my mother's diamond necklace. I didn't give it to Averill. It's hidden away. In fact, it's only been out of its hiding place once."

He struck a match and thrust it into the center of the pile. "And when was that?" he asked idly.

"I carried it to London when I went to find you. I thought I might need to ransom you."

He came and knelt at her side. "Even though it would gall him to know it, the Duke of Averill is my best friend."

The coach with the ducal crest rumbled up the lane.

From her window, Noelle watched it arrive, recognizing Averill's equipage. A thrill of alarm went through her. What did he want? She had sent him word of her daughter's birth, but six months had passed since then.

Of course, he had not seen fit to denounce Noelle as a bastard. Susannah was legally his granddaughter.

The outriders reined their horses. The tiger hopped down from the box and opened the door.

Archie Holmesfield stepped down.

Noelle's lip curled. She rose from her new rosewood desk. She would send him away with a flea in his ear. The bell rang. She could hear it from the butler's room. She waited. It rang again.

She grinned as she heard Blivens open the door at the back of the hall. She heard him shuffling past. The bell rang again.

Finally, the old man reached the door. As he opened it, she opened her door and waited.

"I've a message for your mistress." Holmesfield

impatiently pushed the old man aside.

"M-mistress?" Blivens quavered. Noelle rather suspected that the old servant had been taking a nap. He was more vague than usual.

"Your lady." Holmesfield demanded rolling his eyes. "The Countess."

"C-Countess?"

She took pity of them both. "Here I am, Archie." She stepped into the hall. "How poorly served Averill has become! A whole troop of outriders, but not one to send ahead to announce your arrival."

The factor faced her down boldly. "We came with all speed, Lady Noelle. Your father is ill."

She turned on her heel and walked back into her office.

Holmesfield frowned, then followed after her. "Lady?"

She put her desk between them. "Careful, Archie. You know he's not my father."

He closed the door hastily, practically in Blivens face. "Now, miss—"

"Milady will do fine, sir."

"Milady, he's an old man."

"Nonsense. He's six years older than my husband. Believe me, Holmesfield, forty is not old."

"If you say so, milady, but the Duke has been in poor health over the past year. His cough, you know."

"He's had that cough since childhood. Everyone in London has heard it for years. I even think he cultivates it. It announces his presence in the room. They hate to see him coming to the opera because of it."

Holmesfield could feel a light sweat breaking out of his forehead. "Milady, he wants to see you and your husband."

"Why?"

"Please, milady, for the reason I have told you. His health has not been good."

She studied him with such a jaundiced eye that he squirmed where he stood. "Archie, you're lying. His health is perfectly fine."

"Milady. I swear—"

"Archie, we'll get no farther until you tell me the truth."

At that moment the door opened behind him. He pivoted to meet the Earl. "Your lordship."

Robin nodded briefly. "What's this all about?" His question was directed to his wife.

"Some of Averill's plotting, I'm guessing," she answered. "But Archie swears that the Duke is sick."

"He is, milord."

"So he wants to make his peace with us?" Noelle continued. "Pull the other one, Archie."

"Milady, I swear—"

She sat down and folded her hands in her lap. Her expression was purely ironic. "You should feel like the boy who cried wolf, Archie. So many lies that no one will believe the truth."

"Milord, the Duke sends his own carriage, his best and most comfortable one, with a half dozen outriders to provide the best protection. Why even the Prince only travels with four."

Robin looked at his wife. "What do you think?"

"I think we should send him away."

"Please, milord." Holmesfield could feel the sweat trickling down his spine. "I really was not privy to the Duke's thoughts. All I know is that he is very ill. He wants all of you together. What could it be but to clear away the misunderstandings and make his peace with you?"

"What indeed?"

"An ambush perhaps." Noelle ticked the possibilities off on her fingers. "An assassination by a gang of highwaymen. A kidnapping. Perhaps we're to be placed on board a prison ship headed for Australia."

Holmesfield gasped. "Milady!"

"Perhaps we're to be sold into slavery in Algiers."

He flashed a sickly smile at Robin. "Milady reads too many romance novels."

She made a face at him. "I read no romance novels at all, Holmesfield. I have too much work to do. So does my husband. Despite Averill's best efforts, the Black Horse Stud is actually prospering."

"I know he'll be gratified to hear that."

"Somehow I doubt that."

Holmesfield's mouth curved slyly. "Then why not tell him yourself, to his face. And hear what he has to say."

The offer was tempting. She could feel the first stirring of a desire to go, to see Averill and fling her success and happiness in his head. Above all, she wanted to show him her beautiful black-haired daughter. She wanted him to know that he could never lay a claim to Susannah and hurt her the way he had hurt Noelle.

Still she hesitated. "The journey is too long."

Holmesfield smiled. "This is the best carriage money can by. It's like riding in a cradle, I swear. Why the babe won't even know she's not in her own room."

"Oh, she'll know," Robin interjected. "She's not stupid." He looked at his wife. "On the other hand, she is a good traveler."

"But she's never traveled so far."

"Every comfort will be provided all along the way."

Robin waved a hand to silence the factor. "Why don't you let Blivens take you into the parlor, sir? Have a seat. He'll bring you refreshments. We'll discuss this."

Holmesfield wanted to object. He did not want to face the Duke's anger should he not be able to convince them to come. He had the sense that Noelle was wavering. Still, he could not very well object to what amounted to a direct order. He bowed stiffly.

When Robin had closed the door, he came to Noelle's side. "What do you think?"

"I don't know what to think."

"Do you honestly believe we're in any danger?"

After a minute she shook her head. "The Duke will bribe a few felons like the Cap'n and Fod to do his dirty work. But his coachmen and outriders are honest men with families. They wouldn't take part in the murder of a man, much less a mother and baby. No. I don't believe there's any danger."

"Then I'll leave the decision to you."

She pressed her hands to her cheeks. "God help me, Robin. I want to go."

He nodded. "I feel the same way."

"You do?"

"Remember the condition I was in when we married. Why I've added nearly a stone since then. I don't drown my pain and sorrows in the bottle every night. I'm actually enjoying working with the horses. And—" He put his arms around her. "—I'm the happiest man in the British Isles."

She kissed his cheek, her tongue caressing the skin along the leather strip.

He stepped back away from her. "Quit that."

"Oh, very well. But I'll get you tonight."

"I'll be waiting." He held out his arm. "Shall we go then, Madam Wife, and tell the honorable Mr. Holmesfield that we will be returning with him." As he opened the door for her, his hand caressed her buttock.

"You stop that," she warned. "Or we'll have *it* out right here and now."

"I live with hope."

She pushed the door. "Let Archie sweat for a while." She put her arms around her husband's neck. "And we won't leave for several days. I want Averill to pace and worry that we're not coming."

With her foot lifted to climb into the carriage, Noelle caught sight of a familiar face above the blue and gold-braided livery that Averill provided for his outriders. Her toe missed the step and she jolted herself.

A familiar grin broke in an unshaven face. "Careful, there, ma'am."

"Cap'n?"

He doffed the black tricorne and carried it around in front of him to admire it. "Fancy rigging. Makes me look like a bleedin' admiral o' th' fleet."

"Why, Cap'n?"

"Fod and me worked it out, ma'am. Decided you might need a friend or two where you're going."

"Fod's here too."

"T'other side. He's kinda hidin' out. The other bloke's rig didn't fit him too well."

"Where are the other men?"

"Now don't you worry. We didn't do anything to them. We made a deal. They stay here and look after the horses."

"This can't be."

"The Earl went along with it. When we told him what we wanted to do, he thought it was a fine idea."

Noelle shook her head. "You two will do anything to get out of work."

The Cap'n laughed outright. "You've got the right of that. And Fod's hoping for a couple of heads to bang."

She climbed into the coach. "Averill is ill, Cap'n."

"So I've heard, ma'am. And that's probably the truth. But we'll be there to support you if you're overcome with grief."

Robin trotted Knight up to the other side of the vehicle. "Everyone comfortable?"

The nurse took a firmer grip on Susannah's basket. Noelle smiled as her daughter's fist waved above the edge. "We're ready."

Robin nodded to the coachman. "Proceed."

Twenty-three

As they drew within sight of the towers and chimneys of the house, Noelle became more and more nervous. Unfortunately, it was just as cold and forbidding as she remembered it. Had she really only been gone a year and some months? The façade had a closed look, the gray stone blending into gray sky, heavy with the promise of snow.

"We should never have come," she whispered.

"Do you want to turn back?"

"No. I want to do this, but I don't admire myself for wanting to."

Her husband put his arm around her and pulled her close to his side. "We can leave any time."

"What if Averill forbids us?"

"He can't forbid me. Maybe he can train his servants to intimidate a young girl, but they won't stand up to an Earl, with a patch over one eye." He laughed. "And a dirk between his teeth."

He had changed immeasurably in the past half year. The man she married would never have referred to his wound, much less made a joke about it.

"And a pair of brigands at your back?"

"Cutthroats," he corrected amiably.

Averill awaited them in the great hall. Ever the actor, he stood poised beside the huge fireplace where the flames leaped five feet high. The butler led the way down the forty-foot room to an arrangement of silk-covered chairs and couches. His pale eyes scanned Noelle. "Welcome."

Her slender figure was brightly attired in a traveling dress of bright red wool that complimented her creamy complexion. A Spanish shawl that picked up the same color was draped around her shoulders.

"You're looking well," he added.

"As are you, Averill," she replied sarcastically. "I had heard you were near death, but then Holmesfield does tend to exaggerate in your behalf."

"The thought of your visit prompted a miraculous recovery." His ice blue gaze flicked to the nurse, then back at Noelle. "How was your journey?"

"Cold and wearisome, thank you." Throwing him a proud smile, she reached her hands into the basket.

Immediately, the cooing started. Little arms reached up. Noelle lifted Susannah out into view. The baby put one arm around her mother's neck and looked around. The huge fire instantly caught her fancy. While her daughter stared hypnotized, Noelle pulled the lacy cap off the black curling locks.

"Ah," Averill sighed. "A perfect little Turk."

"She *is* perfect," her mother agreed.

"Actually, she looks more like Noelle than she does me," Robin suggested.

On hearing her father's voice, the baby snapped her head around. A big grin flashed two tiny white teeth in her lower jaw. "Da," she said, throwing herself off Noelle's shoulder, arms outstretched. "Da!"

Perfect happiness radiating from him, Robin caught her. She laughed delightedly as she put her arms around his neck and kissed him open mouthed. In doing so, she slobbered gleefully on the leather strap that bisected his cheek.

Averill's face contorted. Sucking in a harsh breath, he turned away.

"Why aren't you tired?" Robin teased Susannah. "And fussing?"

The baby gurgled an answer and tugged at his ear.

"Because the minute the carriage starts swaying, she goes to sleep," Noelle translated. "She's up now and ready to play all night long."

He groaned. "While her old father is dead on his feet."

"I must thank you, Averill, for the use of the ducal coach," Noelle said to the stiff back. "The journey was very comfortable."

He turned. A fierce light shone in the ice blue eyes. "My pleasure." He shook himself. "So. You have arrived. The rooms are prepared. Three. Will that be sufficient?"

"More than enough," Robin assured him. He pressed Susannah's hand to his mouth and blew on the tiny palm. His daughter chuckled appreciatively and pulled her hand away. She patted her father's cheek, then returned her stare to the leaping fire.

The Duke stood turned to stone watching the by-play. His voice was hoarse. "My housekeeper will show you to your rooms. Order whatever you need for the baby. Your nurse's requests are to be carried out immediately."

"The baby's name is Susannah, Averill," Noelle reminded him firmly.

"Susannah. Yes. We will dine a little early tonight I think, for you are fatigued and also used to country hours. We shall meet again at eight." He inclined his head and turned back to face the fire.

"What did you think?"

"I don't know what to think?" Robin shook his head. "He was never sick. You were right about that."

"Of course. It was a lie from the beginning. The question is why. Why does he want to see us? He searched long and hard to find someone thoroughly debauched to marry me to. He was excessively pleased to get me out of the house. Why bring me back?"

"Part of the agreement was that you were never to be seen in London society." Robin ran his hand around the back of his neck. "It's too deep for me."

"Did you see his face when Susannah was kissing you? He looked as if he were frozen. And furious. I've never seen him so angry." Noelle wrapped her arms on her waist.

"None of this makes any sense."

"Nothing that he has done since the wedding makes much sense. Why kidnap me to bring you home, then imprison you in Newgate so that no one could find you?"

He kissed her. "You found me."

"Actually, the Cap'n and his men found you. And they might not have if you hadn't tried to escape."

"Can you believe they actually insisted on coming with us? Loyal lads, those two."

"I wouldn't like to be in Holmesfield's shoes tonight," Noelle said drily. "Fod is primed to have a word with the man who brought Romany Knight back to the stables. I wouldn't want to be in Archie's shoes."

"Should I warn him?"

"Him! No. He's tamped down his conscience all these years and done every nasty thing that Averill's told him to do. He deserves whatever Fod might give him."

"Bloodthirsty wench."

She clenched her fists. "I'm soft as warm butter. You know that."

He threw up his hands to protect himself. "Absolutely. Whatever you say."

Grinning, she sat down at the dressing table. As she surveyed the crystal bottles and jars, all with gold stoppers and lids, her expression changed to one of distaste. "This was my mother's room."

He looked around curiously. The furniture was exquisite. French rococco from the time of Louis XV. White with gold leaf, elaborately curlicued. The carpet was silk from Brussels. The draperies and bedspread were handloomed with fanciful medieval scenes of unicorns and ladies. "Very femi-nine."

"Oui, m'sieur, et très cher."

"Obviously."

Viciously, she began to pull the pins out of her hair. "He knows I hate this room above all others. I never went in here after I found out what she'd done." She snatched up the gold-backed brush, then put it back down again and contented herself with combing her hair with her fingers. "Why would he do this to me?"

"Perhaps he doesn't know that I know how you feel. Perhaps he wants me to see the style that you were accustomed to." He opened the mirrored door into the bathroom. The fixtures were solid gold.

"As if I cared."

He shut the door, his smile wide. "As if you cared."

She stared at her husband in the oval mirror. "Why do you suppose she betrayed him?"

He shrugged. "The Ice King with a warm-blooded Frenchwoman. If she were like you—"

She blushed. "Am I very—er—warm-blooded?"

He stretched his length on the bed where he propped himself up on one elbow. "No, Madam Wife, you are hot-blooded."

She dropped her gaze, but he could see the smile curving her lips.

"You'd better get yourself dressed and stop fishing for compliments. Otherwise, I'll be forced to lie back on this bed and let you have your hot-blooded way with me. If that happens, given my advancing years, I don't see how I'll be able to totter down the stairs to dinner."

"Poor you. I was just thinking about warming your old bones."

"The Duke's servants will appreciate us. We won't use the other bedroom tonight."

Noelle had almost forgotten that she had once been accustomed to the sort of service that the Duke of Averill enjoyed as a matter of course.

Since dinner was *en famille,* it was served in the small dining room where the table was only twenty feet long. A dozen candles glowed in each of three silver candelabras. Between them two towering silver and crystal epergnes displayed fruits and flowers from Averill's extensive greenhouses.

The table cover was white linen deeply edged with lace, the place settings, repousse sterling. The delicate bone china plates rested on sterling chargers. The wines and water were poured into handcut crystal stems.

Despite himself, Robin was dazzled. Whitby was a shabby hovel compared to this wealth and consequence. He stared across the table at his wife, who grinned at him and pulled a face.

The first course began. Appetizers of hearts of endive, slender strips of pepper from Spain, tomatoes from South America, other vegetables that he could not name.

"Very impressive, Averill," Noelle remarked. "You must still have Fontevrault?"

The Ice King forked up the heart of a baby artichoke. "There was no need to rid myself of the finest chef on this side of the Channel."

"I quite agree. Cutting off your nose to spite your face has never been your mode."

The butler poured the wine, allowing the Duke to taste it. He wrinkled his patrician nose. "Without bouquet," he pronounced. "It won't do justice to the fish."

With a murmur of apology the butler hurried away.

"Stop it, Averill!"

He gave her a cold, disdainful look. "Stop what?"

"Stop trying to impress us," Noelle snapped. "We are what you have made us. We're simple country people. You are rich and powerful and can send bottles of fine wine back to the kitchen. But we know what you're trying to do, so the whole proceeding rather loses some of its effect."

"My dear, I swear, the wine was not fit. Were I to allow my guests to drink something below my standards, I would be remiss."

"Indeed. Terribly remiss. But we are not your guests. We were summoned here for reasons which I'm sure you will divulge in your own good time. For the sake of sanity, let's just get on with the meal."

The Duke turned to Robin. "I see marriage has not filed her tongue. I would have thought you would have taken the edge off by now."

Robin smiled at his wife. "Why should I take the edge off? She's like Spanish steel. Supple, razor sharp, accurate to the inch. If I had a wine glass to raise, I would raise it to you, Madam Wife."

With a smile she raised her water glass. He raised his and they toasted each other.

"Stop it, both of you!" barked the Duke.

Noelle grinned at her husband. "Why whatever do you mean?"

"Nothing is that good. You hate each other. Don't try to fool me."

The butler returned at that minute. He poured from a second bottle. The Duke accepted it with barely a taste.

The second course was oyster pâté to be spread on hot crackers fresh from the ovens. Noelle's smile grew strained at the sight. "I'm surprised at Fontevrault. I didn't think you ever ate oyster pâté."

"I had it prepared specially for you, my dear."

"How kind. And what a very good choice."

"The late Duchess," Averill informed Robin, "was inordinately fond of oyster pâté."

Robin glanced at his wife's strained face. He could not tell whether she was hurt or angry or both. He knew she was in the grip of torturous emotions. He refused the dish. "I have never cared for oysters."

The meal dragged on, course after course arrived. Noelle took some of each one but ate little. Her mouth had thinned to a rigid line. The spots of color had faded from her cheeks, but beneath her eyes were the beginnings of dark smudges.

He reached his hand across the table. "Are you tired?"

She took it gratefully, but before she could answer, Averill interrupted her. "Nonsense. She's not tired. Not on her first night home. Perk up, my

420

lear. Have some more wine."

"I don't think wine would be good for me now," she murmured.

"What? What's that you say?" He craned his neck toward her, his eyes glittering in the candle-light. His upper lip had peeled back from his teeth in a travesty of a smile.

"I don't think I want any more wine!"

He swayed back, pretending affront. "No need to be upset. You don't have to drink any more wine. I have it." He held up his hand. "We'll forgo the rest of this meal. Of course, Fontevrault will be upset. He so wanted to prepare all of your favorite dishes, but there will be other nights. Let's adjourn to the parlor. We'll have dessert served there. And coffee. You have nothing against coffee, do you, my dear?"

Robin pushed back his chair and came around the table to his wife. "I think we should retire."

"Nonsense." The Duke rose too. While he did not precisely bar their way, he did come to the other side of Noelle's chair, effectively trapping her between them. "I insist. She shall sit by the fire and put her feet up." He dropped a hand to her shoulder. "And I shall tell you a story."

Noelle sat as close to the fire as she dared. Nervous rigors shook her periodically and made her grit her teeth. With both hands she cupped the brandy snifter Averill had thrust at her.

Robin stood tall and stern beside her.

"You won't drink with me? But I insist," Averill

said silkily. "Surely she hasn't put a petticoat on you and made you into a man milliner. Of course, she vowed she would control you. Didn't you, Noelle?"

He poured himself a glass and tossed it off. He coughed as he swallowed the fiery liquor. He choked, then coughed again more violently as the excitement swelled the slight malformation in his throat.

Noelle raised her eyes. "I did indeed, Averill. How well I succeeded should be apparent to you."

His smile disappeared. He poured himself another drink. "I wouldn't have thought you were the type to let yourself be bossed, Turk."

Robin shrugged. "Our lives are our own, Averill. But sometimes something so wonderful comes along that there really is no choice." He glanced at the Limoges porcelain clock on the mantel. "Tell us the story you want to tell us, or let me take my wife to bed. She hasn't traveled since our daughter was born. The journey has been tiring for her even in your 'well-sprung' carriage."

Averill grinned. Glass in hand he strode down the room. The key rattled in the door. He turned round showing it to his observers.

Robin's jaw clenched. "If you think that would stop me from getting out of this room, milord, you are much mistaken."

"Never. Not at all. I never had any such idea. You are free to go at any time. I've locked the door merely to be assured that we are not disturbed." He started to slide the key into his pocket.

"I suggest you leave it in the door," Robin said softly. "Otherwise, I might have to rip that silk waistcoat beyond all mending."

Averill hesitated. Reluctantly, he put the key back in the hole.

"The story," Noelle prompted.

"Are you sure you're both quite comfortable?" Averill looked at them both. His expression was one of a tiger looking at a pair of lambs. "Very well. I'll begin. Once upon a time—"

He waited in vain for them to smile. He shrugged.

"—there was a handsome young viscount. He decided to affiance himself with a beautiful, penniless, excessively well-born French *émigré*."

"I believe we know this part," Robin interrupted.

"No," Averill contradicted. "You don't know it at all. You only think you do. Or perhaps you know one part of it." He dropped into a chair opposite Noelle where he could see every flicker of emotion in her still face.

"She was absolutely perfect. The flawless stone for the setting of his estates. He took her with him everywhere. And every man envied him. Especially the young officers of the army and navy. They surrounded her in droves. He watched calmly while she danced and flirted with them; for, you see, he was her master. She was his."

"If he was her master, why did he allow her to dance and flirt?" Noelle snapped.

"Because, my dear, she said that they might have news of France. And it pleased him to watch them swarm around her. She believed that if they were sent to fight, they might have an opportunity to help her family, perhaps to save them. So I indulged her. There were an endless number dangling after her, but only a select few in her coterie."

Robin bit his lip.

"Ridley, Longacre—"

"Parkhurst." At her husband's voice Noelle snapped her head around.

"And—" the Duke prompted.

"Myself."

"Ah, yes. The very four."

Robin shook his head. "Ally, Horse, and Clare. They're all gone."

"Yes, they are all gone, except you." Averill bent double with a coughing spasm. "I really had very few strings to pull."

Robin's head snapped up. "What are you saying?"

"I did it." The Duke's voice was chilled steel. "Persuasion, influence, position, blackmail. The job took them all. But in the end I was almost completely successful. Only you, Whittcombstone. Only you remain."

Robin shook his head. "They were killed in battle."

"Yes," Averill sneered. "In the very forefront. And in most cases their men were decimated with them. One even took a whole shipload down with him. And within a couple of years." His eyes blazed with a maniacal light.

"Are you saying?"

"I am a very powerful man. My wife might have flirtations but they would not live to boast about them."

"My God, man."

424

"All gone but you?" Averill cursed. "You had more lives than a cat. I could not kill you. You rode through unscathed. And managed to save a goodly number of your men. I followed your career for fifteen years. And then you didn't die."

Robin's fists clenched. His shoulders hunched. "You're insane."

Averill tossed off the brandy and poured himself another. "Perhaps. But allow me my moment."

Noelle rose from her chair. Her hands were so cold that the very bones ached. Her nerves jumped and twitched. Frisson after frisson skittered down her back. She set the untouched glass down on the mantel. "I'm leaving."

Averill gave a bark of laughter. "Without knowing the truth about your scarred, drunken husband, my dear? Without knowing the power of my revenge?"

Head down she hurried to the door. "I can live without knowing."

He sprang to intercept her. "No. No. You won't leave here until I tell you. I want you both to appreciate what I've done."

Robin shouldered him aside. Put his arm around his shivering wife and fumbled for the key.

"Take your hand away from that lock." From the pocket of his coat, Averill pulled a tiny pistol.

Robin laughed. "Put that thing away. It will only make me angry."

"Will it? Yes, I suspect it will. Military know the power of firearms, or at least they should. However, I wouldn't shoot you, Whittcombstone. I'd shoot your wife. I probably wouldn't kill her either."

"Give me that thing, or I'll be forced to take it away from you."

"Do you want to take the chance that you can wrest it from my grasp before I squeeze off a shot? Shame on you, putting your wife at risk."

Robin growled, but Noelle took his arm. "Let's hear the end of it. Then we can leave this house and never return."

"Oh, indeed. Leave and never return. That is exactly what I had in mind."

She guided him back to the fire. Instead of her sitting in the chair, she pushed him gently down into it. Where she had been in the grip of strong emotion, she now had calmed in the face of Robin's pain.

He leaned forward, hands hanging loosely between his knees. "Parkhurst and Ridley. Alistair Ridley." He shook his head. "His father's only son."

Noelle clasped his shoulder tightly. "I'm so sorry." To Averill, she said, "Get on with this. We want to leave at first light."

He smiled whitely. "And so you shall, Noelle. I'll provide you with a carriage. That is, if you want to leave."

"I'm only staying here tonight out of consideration for Susannah. The night is bitter. I don't want her to take a cold."

"Ah, yes, the Turk's daughter. The perfect black-haired, black-eyed—"

Robin growled warningly.

"But enough for now." He slipped the pistol back into his pocket. "It wasn't loaded," he added. "I was bluffing."

426

"Say what you have to say," Noelle grated.

"Very well. To make short work of it. She knew them carnally. All of them. Before she married me. She came to me no virgin. Of course, she claimed she had been raped by the boatman who took her out of France, but I knew better."

Robin shook his head.

"After ten years I began to wonder why she had not given me an heir. After you were born, my dear, she never conceived again. I went to a doctor. He told me that it was highly unlikely that I would ever father another child. That he was surprised that I had fathered even one." Averill's pale eyes glowed. "And then I knew."

"You knew from that?" Robin shook his head. "You knew nothing. You merely assumed. Highly unlikely doesn't mean impossible."

"My God!"

"I confronted her," Averill continued. "Of course, she denied it."

Noelle's voice was harsh. "But you knew she was lying. I was a bastard."

"Indeed. You are a bastard. But who was your father? How could I find out?"

"This is monstrous," Robin declared.

Averill's face worked as fierce emotions roiled beneath the surface. "I began to think about them. All blondes. All blondes as I was except you." He looked directly at Robin. "All blondes and one brunette."

Robin surged to his feet. "This is ridiculous. She denied it. And you have invented a fairy tale. What kind of man are you?"

"The kind against whom no insult will go unpunished. And this was the deadliest insult of all. It required the deadliest revenge. My centuries-old family name was destroyed. My line was destroyed. I determined to destroy you both."

The couple stared at him horrified.

"You have already guessed what I have brought to pass, have you not?" He laughed. "The Turk's daughter looks enough like the Turk to be him reproduced. And why not? He's her father and her grandfather."

Noelle tottered back. Robin caught her. He put his arms around her waist and lifted her in his arms. As if she had been a child, he sat down with her in the chair. He took her face between his palms.

"It's not true," he said. "I swear to you, it's not true. Maybe one of the others, but I swear to you that I am not your father."

"He's lying," Averill warned. "Of course, he's lying. Just as she lied."

Noelle shuddered, but Robin tightened his arms around her. "I swear to you that I never knew your mother in any way but as a friend."

"How can I believe that? How can I believe—?" She could feel nausea rising in her stomach. Blackness filled her mind. Her husband and her mother. Her husband and her mother. And more terrible than that. Her beautiful daughter. Her exquisite, bright, happy Susannah. She dropped her head onto her husband's shoulder and wept.

Robin looked up at the gloating Duke. "I would kill you, but that would alleviate your suffering. You should live a long time and feel your sins on your soul. The deaths of hundreds of men. You used your influence and power to send men into battle so that they would purposefully get killed."

"The battle had to be fought," Averill scoffed. "They would have died anyway."

Robin shook his head. "There is always an alternative." He could feel Noelle's tears soaking into his jacket. He put his finger under her chin and pushed it up. "Listen to me."

"What are we going to do? What are we going to do?"

He kissed her forehead. "Ssh. Listen to me."

"But —"

"I'm your husband and I've never lied to you. I've never. Have I?"

"No."

"I'm not lying now. I haven't a Bible here, but if you'll wait, we can have one brought."

She shook her head wearily.

"Then listen. I swear to you before God and all His angels that I never had carnal knowledge of your mother. I can never prove that I didn't, but your father can never prove that I did. And your mother, by your father's own words, denied it. One of us is telling the truth. Whom are you going to believe?"

She hung her head. The air was pregnant with suspense. She raised her head. "I know you didn't do it."

"You're an idiot," Averill howled.

"She's every bit as smart as her daughter." Robin rose with his wife's body cradled in his arms. He did an about-face and marched down the room to the locked door. Pausing, he lifted his foot and drove it against the door with all the strength of his leg. The facing broke and the door flew open.

Robin turned, his leg tingling unpleasantly. His smile however was broad. "Don't bother to see us off in the morning."

"Idiots!" the Duke screamed. "Both of you! Idiots!"

Twenty-four

"Burn the stables." Holmesfield repeated the words without emotion. He might have been repeating instructions for answering the week's invitations, or for the selling of a horse.

The Duke of Averill studied his factor through narrowed eyes. "I'm pleased to see that you don't object, Holmesfield."

"Perhaps you should reconsider, sir."

"No!" The word exploded on a violent cough. "The authorities—"

"The opinions of a provincial magistrate can be easily bought. If the need should ever arise." The Duke dismissed the objection with a wave of his hand. He coughed again. "They aren't important."

"A stable fire is a terrible thing, sir."

"Yes, isn't it. And so easy to start. Piles of dry straw and bales of hay. And wood. Wood everywhere."

"Fine horses burning to death. It doesn't bear thinking about."

"Bah! Animals. They don't think. They can barely feel."

Holmesfield felt as if he were drowning. He grasped at one last straw. "The Earl of Whitby doesn't employ ordinary grooms."

"Felons! They'll be no help. They'll run away at the first sign of trouble."

"I don't think so, sir."

He was pacing up and down the room rapidly, his coughing persistent. "Nonsense. A shot in the air will send them scattering like grouse."

Holmesfield pressed his hand to his forehead. Sharp pains were shooting behind his eyes. He stifled a moan.

"Do you have a problem, Holmesfield?"

The words formed themselves in his mind. *I must regretfully tender my resignation, milord.* Or *I cannot serve you in this, milord.* Perhaps the horses would be in the paddocks. Perhaps the men would be away. Perhaps the coach would break down. Perhaps the Duke—

"Holmesfield!"

"No, milord."

The moon was a frosty rind emptying itself into the icy star-filled sky. Holmesfield felt the cold in his very bones. He was getting too old for this sort of prowling around at night. He should have been home in his bed, his nightcap on his head, his feet tucked against a warm brick.

The Duke pulled his horses at the foot of the lane. "Not even a watchman," he scoffed. "Almost too easy." He punched his factor in the shoulder. "And you were concerned."

"I'm still concerned, your Grace." He cleared his throat. "Your Grace, don't make me do this. I beg you."

"You are begging, Holmesfield," the Duke sneered. "Showing the white feather like so many of your kind."

Holmesfield did not even flush. He was too cold, too frightened, too appalled at what he was about it do. "If you say so, sir."

"Get down, you craven. Stand at the horses' heads. I'll handle this myself. I don't need your help. Perhaps when we return to Averill, you might consider seeking employment elsewhere. Perhaps you might take lady's lapdogs for a stroll."

Holmesfield climbed down like an old man and went to the front of the team. Averill wrapped the reins around the brake and climbed down as well. Armed with flint, striker, and a brace of primed pistols, he trotted off into the darkness.

Romany Knight lifted his black nose into the air. Snorting and grunting, he paced round in a circle in his box. He lunged to the front again and sniffed the air. The scent of a stranger filled his nostrils. He blew a roller through his nose, then inhaled again. Coming closer. Coming too near his stall.

The big horse stamped and snorted again. He thrust his great head and shoulders over the stall door and shook his mane threateningly.

"Quiet," came the stranger's whisper, followed by a smothered cough. "Quiet, you stupid creature."

But Romany Knight would not be quiet. He tolerated only four creatures of the human kind—the groom who fed him, the man who treated him fairly and allowed no nonsense, the woman whom he allowed on rare occasions to touch his muzzle, but only when she brought him apples, and the baby. He was an adult. Babies were babies to be protected, never attacked.

He neighed a challenge to the encroacher.

"Quiet, damn you." Coughing, the figure hurried past him. All along the shedrow horses stuck through heads over the stall doors. They were all awake. Hooves thudded on the hard-packed earth as the mares moved restlessly. A tall black whinnied nervously. Attuned to their mother's feelings, the colts climbed to their feet whickering in fear.

Averill stopped in the end of the shedrow. Perspiration had turned to ice on his body. The unaccustomed exertion coupled with high excitement had brought on his coughing. His chest and throat ached from his efforts to smother the spasms. Clutching the flint and striker in his hands, he knelt at the back of an empty stall and struck.

The sparks jumped and fell into the dry fuel. Some died in the air, but one, two, three lit on tinder. A tiny tongue sprang up. It ran along the straw that curled to black ash behind it. Where it crossed another, the two diverged. He moved a few inches and then struck again. More flames and tendrils of smoke joined the other.

In his stall the black stallion neighed shrilly.

Averill threw a hasty look over his shoulder and cursed. He edged back to the entrance. Flames of healthy size greedily consumed then straw and licked at the wall.

"What in bloody hell!?"

Averill lunged up. Risking his hands he scooped the burning straw up and flung it in the face of the groom. Fingers and palms stinging, he followed the fire, barreling into the man and knocking him down.

The stallion squealed. His hooves thundered against the back wall of his stall and then he burst through his door.

"Damn!" The Duke skidded to a stop almost under the furious animal.

Romany Knight reared, hooves flashing. Teeth bared, he dropped on all fours. Mane whirling, eyes showing the white ring, he snaked at the intruder. His teeth snapped together in the air as Averill dodged and dashed away.

"Help! Help!" Coughing between each shout, the Cap'n was on his feet. He made no effort to stop the Duke. Instead, he had grabbed a pitchfork and was pulling the straw away from the wall of the stall.

"My Gawd!" Hardwicke clasped his arms around the Duke as he came barreling out of the stable. "Here. What's going on?"

"Let me go, you stupid clot."

"Your Grace." Hardwicke's arms fell away as

he recognized the Duke of Averill.

Averill cursed violently and pushed the man down. He stumbled, then caught his stride, and dashed away into the darkness.

"Help! Get the hell in here! Hardwicke! Fod!" the Cap'n bawled. The flames licked at his flapping coattails. "Damme!"

Hardwicke vaulted to his feet and dashed into the smoke. Even so little smoke was creating bedlam among the horses. The squealing and neighing, the thunder of stamping hooves, and the trumpeting of the stallion were enough to raise the dead.

Romany Knight dashed out of the shedrow into the paddock and then back in again, furiously angry, thoroughly confused.

Hardwicke ran to the door of the stall, then dashed back for a bucket of water. At the first splash, steam hissed and smoke billowed. So well had the Cap'n succeeded in pulling the fire away from the walls and sweeping it into the center of the stall that almost all of the flames were extinguished.

Hardwicke ran back to meet Robin and Fod coming down with buckets also.

"What happened?" Robin yelled.

"His Grace," Hardwicke coughed. "It were His Grace."

"Averill."

"That's the one."

The Cap'n staggered from the stall. "Gimme a hand here. Save your bloody chattin' for later."

Fod froze. A growl came from deep in his

belly. He thrust the bucket into Hardwicke's hand.

"Fod!" Robin yelled.

But Fod was already gone. He dashed into the paddock and cornered his own nag, a roman-nosed hack. Catching its headstall, he flung himself onto its back.

"Fod!"

The seat was dangerous. He had to lean far out and guide it by the cheekstraps. He could only keep his seat by his balance and the strength of his legs. It was enough.

With a wordless cry, he slashed the reins across the horse's shoulders. It bolted down the lane.

Panting, Averill sprang to the seat of the phaeton. Holmesfield almost missed his grasp as the horses bolted. He was jerked off his feet, but managed to climb up beside the Duke. Using the whip liberally, Averill set the team tearing down the road.

Holmesfield glanced behind him. The darkness was impenetrable, but he had heard the noise from the stable. The Duke must have succeeded. The factor felt the bile rise in his throat. He closed his eyes against the sway of the speeding coach and the thoughts of burning horses.

The whip whistled and cracked. The off horse neighed as the tip flicked its ear.

Averill drove with deadly intensity, burning eyes fixed on the road. He had failed. He knew it. The flame had not been sufficient. If the man who discovered him did not put it out, he could arouse the others.

His only hope was to get away. Even if he killed his own team, he would drive straight home. He would deny that he had been here. It would be his word and the word of his servants against only the unimportant groom—a common felon, at that.

"We're being followed, your Grace."

Averill heard Holmesfield's words and cursed again. Disaster, if he were caught. He must not be caught. He redoubled his efforts with the whip. "How many?"

Holmesfield looked behind him. "Only one, but—"

The Duke's horses were tired. They were slowing despite the maddening bite of the whip. He called to them, but they could not maintain the breakneck pace.

The roman-nosed hack stretched himself into the wind and thundered down the highroad. Fod's lips pealed back from his teeth. The wind whistled by his ears and plastered his woolen shirt to his big body. One with his horse, he rode stretched along its neck, its mane whipping in his face.

They galloped up beside the carriage. The hack's nose was on the boot, then the long step, then alongside the dash rail.

The Duke aimed the whip at his pursuer. The lash cut across Fod's back.

Mouth open, a furious roar issuing from the very depths of his throat, Fod spurred his horse.

In three strides, the hack came alongside the near horse. With a swipe of his long arm, Fod caught the cheekpiece and jerked savagely.

The horse screamed as Fod twisted it off the road. The Duke lost the rein. The second horse had no choice but to follow the other. The phaeton bucked wildly as its wheels spun off onto the rough.

"Get away!" the Duke yelled. "Get away!" The whip cracked over Fod's head, knocking his hat off.

Fod threw a malicious look over his shoulder and dug his heels into the hack's sides. The horse lunged forward.

The phaeton careened on, its wheels bouncing off rocks, tilting crazily over the rough ground. Holmesfield clutched the seat, his face drained of color. The Duke wielded the whip furiously, taking a terrible toll. His blows slashed through the fabric of Fod's shirt, opened the scalp above Fod's ear, ripped open Fod's sleeve.

"The pistols!" The Duke screamed to his factor. "The pistols in my belt. Get 'em, man. Shoot him!"

Holmesfield did not react at first. He was hanging on with all his strength. The coach jolted and tipped him, rocked him back violently, and threw him in another direction.

"The pistol!" The whip snapped again.

Holmesfield fumbled at the Duke's waist trying, finding the butt, trying to pull it out. The sight caught on the Duke's belt.

"You fool!"

Finally, the factor pulled it free.

"Shoot him!"

This time the whip tore Fod's ear.

Never stopping his ululating cry, Fod drove his horse into the near horse, sending the phaeton to the right. The off horse stumbled. The near bowled it over. The vehicle tipped. The front wheel cracked and splintered.

Holmesfield saw the lichen-pocked white boulder the second before it smashed into his face.

The Duke's right arm, raised to whip again, took his weight. He could feel his hand snapped back impossibly, then his elbow, then his chin struck a rock.

The right side of the phaeton splintered. Only the left wheels, clear of the ground, spun on and on. The off horse whinnied and tried to rise. Its legs were entangled in the harness. It struggled and kicked. Finally, it made its feet. The team stood shivering.

Fod rode around the wreck to stare down at the two still bodies. A grin spread across his bleeding face. He lifted it to the ice-ringed moon. " 'Ow's about that, Tuck," he howled, triumphantly. "Look at 'em, Tuck."

With a smile on his face, he sat on the hack staring at the still bodies while he waited for the other riders to catch up.

Robin swung down and hurried to the Duke's side. Averill's right arm was broken, his face was bloody, but he was alive.

Holmesfield was not so lucky. His head with its smashed face was tilted at an odd angle on his trunk. Robin could not find the pulse.

The Cap'n too dismounted and gingerly approached his man. He put his hand on Fod's thigh. "You're bleeding."

Fod grinned. "Nothin' that'll matter. M' face is already a mess."

"I don't understand," Noelle said. "Why would he do such a thing? I accepted the fact that he wasn't my father. I even hated my mother because of her betrayal. He believed that you were my father and had exacted his revenge all these years. But why go on with this thing?"

"Because you didn't believe him," Robin said gently. "You believed me when I swore to you that I could not have been your father. His revenge was to be consigning us all to hell."

She shut her eyes against the pain. "He must have loved my mother very much to turn such love into such intense hatred."

"I doubt that he was capable of love. Pride. Pride rules him."

She shook her head.

"We were supposed to be utterly miserable in our marriage," Robin reminded her. "I was supposed to abuse you and spend your inheritance gambling and drinking."

"Why did he bring you back from town when you first left?"

"Because I had to make you pregnant. That's what Mrs. Blivens was spying for."

"And why imprison you?"

"When you were pregnant, he thought to torture me further by having me thrown into Newgate. But you foiled him there. You foiled him at every turn. With all the kindness and generosity in the world, you accepted me for what I was and am. A wreck old enough to be your father. This was to be a marriage without even the hope of passion."

"And instead we found love," she finished.

"And that he could not abide."

She thought of the broken man in the room at the end of the hall. His wrist, elbow, and shoulder were splinted. Cracked ribs made breathing agony. His bruised face was unrecognizable. "Will he try again? What can we do?"

"Take steps to defang the serpent. I'll place letters with Larnaervon and with Castlereagh." He laughed bitterly. "We'll place letters with your solicitor, to the effect that if anything happens again, they will act for me. And when he's well enough to travel, we'll send him back to Averill with that threat hanging over his head for the rest of his life."

His wife shivered. "Let's go look at the horses."

"Yes."

They strolled together down the shedrow. Two by two, the mares and colts, the very first crop of Black Horse Stud, stuck their heads over their stall doors and craned their necks. The hope of the future in sleek black necks, alert ears, liquid dark eyes.

Best Shot whinnied softly and nuzzled for the apple that was her due. She lipped it off Noelle's palm and backed away with a shake of her short mane. Her tiny hooves pranced in the straw. Kate bestowed an affectionate nibble on her daughter's withers, before having her apple too.

Romany Knight eyed them both suspiciously before he too accepted a treat. When Robin raised his hand to straighten the forelock, Knight backed away hastily.

Robin shrugged. "He'll never be any different. He'll never learn to trust."

Noelle turned her husband back toward the house. "It's his loss."

Her husband kissed her. "It is indeed."

Epilogue

Three years later

"Lady Noelle Whittcombstone and Miss Susannah Whittcombstone, your Grace."

The Duke frowned. He closed his book but remained in his chair by the fire. The butler withdrew.

"Averill," Noelle said coldly. "Please don't bother to rise on our account." She seated herself and patted the settee beside her. Her daughter climbed up and busied herself arranging her feet and hands like her mother's.

The Duke sighed as he touched his hand to his face. He no longer allowed himself any expression of any kind. The wreck had destroyed important nerves in his cheek and jaw. Now only his left side moved when he wished to express either displeasure or joy.

As he looked at his visitor, his hatred kindled. She reminded him of his Duchess whom he had not thought of in a long time. Both she and her daughter were dressed in blue. Her dress was a darker, heavier material with a square neckline. He squinted, then glared. "Those are my diamonds."

"My mother's diamonds," she corrected him.

He leaned forward to study them. "What was in the pouch Holmesfield collected?"

"Coral."

"I see." He leaned back with a sigh. "I am extremely

busy, Noelle."

"I'm sure." She looked pointedly at the book on his lap. "But what I have to say won't take long. It deals with your heir."

He allowed himself to lift the good corner of his mouth into a sneer. That, at least, appeared normal when he practiced it in the mirror. "That is none of your concern. I have made a will. Everything that I own is left to my great-uncle's grandson. He does not have the name, but he at least has the blood."

"I'm sure, but it is terribly diluted, is it not?"

"Better than none at all." The Duke stared at Noelle closely. "Pardon me, my dear, but are you not again — er — increasing?"

She smiled. "Yes. In May we will have another child. I am hoping for a boy. Although Robin is so entranced with Susannah that he more than half wants another girl."

The Duke focused on the three year old, who sat primly on the edge of the settee. Her black hair curled in a profusion of ringlets under her bonnet. "A Turk," he sneered again. "A perfect little Turk. And why not?"

"Why not, indeed? He is, after all, her father."

"And more." The memories agitated Averill. He rubbed his throat and swallowed. He could feel the tickling.

"As I said, I have come to discuss your heir. Susannah. Will you please recite the lesson you have learned?"

The little girl looked up at her mother. A bright blush rose in her creamy cheeks. She sighed unhappily and slipped down. Like a little soldier, she marched across the floor to stand in front of the pale white-haired man whose eyes were most unfriendly.

She bit her lip and clasped her hands. "M-my name is Susannah Claire Whittcombstone. I am the daughter of Lord Robin Anthony Whittcombstone, the Earl of Whitby." She looked over her shoulder at her mother.

"Very good, darling. The Duke appreciates this very much. He is most interested in families."

"I am also the daughter of Lady Noelle Amalie Jacinthe Whittcombstone, the Countess of Whitby. My grandmother was Lady Jacinthe Rivers, the Duchess of Averill."

"Enough!" Averill barked. One side of his face worked, the other remained perfectly still, a monstrous and frightening apparition. "That is an abomination. I forbid it!"

At his words, Lady Susannah shrank back. She turned and ran to her mother arms outstretched, coughing as she ran. She coughed and she coughed. Tears started in her big dark eyes and ran down her cheek. She hid her face in her mother's skirt. "I can't say it," she coughed.

Averill's face turned to ice as the spasms racked the little body. The tickling in his own throat increased. He coughed.

Noelle's face was equally stern. "Listen, Susannah. You have only one more sentence to say. He didn't mean to frighten you. Look, he's sorry he frightened you. Look. He's waiting for you to say it."

Lady Susannah looked over her shoulder. The Duke did not look any more friendly, but he held out his hand. It trembled as he coughed. He coughed just like she did.

She wiped her eyes and took a deep breath. The sensation went away. Again she crossed to stand before him, just beyond the tip of his fingers. "My grandfather is Lord Thomas Rivers, the Duke of Averill."

"That's very good, Susannah." Noelle congratulated her. "Letter perfect."

The little one flashed an expectant smile over her shoulder at her mother.

She coughed once more, but instantly clapped both hands over her mouth.

The Duke drew his handkerchief from his sleeve and tried to smother the agonizing spasms.

Timidly, Lady Susannah stepped forward and laid her hand on his knee. "Hot tea with honey is best," she whispered.

Nodding approval, Noelle rose. "You're right, Susannah. Now, say goodbye and we will go and have some chocolates with our tea." She stooped to lay her cheek against her daughter's. The icy diamonds flashed at her throat. Her eyes were diamond-hard as they met those of the Duke. "She developed this cough less than a year ago," she told him evenly. "The doctors say it's a slight malformation of the throat. Nothing to worry about. They guess that it's hereditary."

The Duke sat alone beside the fire for a long time after they had left. His whole body shook. He knew he would never be warm again.

ZEBRA'S GOT WHAT'S HOT!

A FABULOUS MONEY-SAVING REBATE OFFER FEATURING FOUR SCORCHING NEW SUMMER READS!

This summer, Zebra's offering four fantastic love stories from four of our biggest historical romance superstars—Sonya T. Pelton's LOVE'S LOST ANGEL and Thea Devine's BEYOND DESIRE in July and Kathleen Drymon's PIRATE MOON and Deana James' SEEK ONLY PASSION in August.

And the more sizzling stories you buy, the more you can save!

SAVE $3 with the purchase of any two of these titles; $4 with the purchase of any three titles; and $5 with the purchase of all four.

It all boils down to the hottest deal around